SECRET ASSET

By the same author

Open Secret
At Risk

STELLA RIMINGTON

SECRET ASSET

HUTCHINSON
LONDON

First published by Hutchinson in 2006

1 3 5 7 9 10 8 6 4 2

Hutchinson
The Random House Group Limited
20 Vauxhall Bridge Road, London SW1V 2SA

Random House Australia (Pty) Limited
20 Alfred Street, Milsons Point, Sydney
New South Wales 2061, Australia

Random House New Zealand Limited
18 Poland Road, Glenfield
Auckland 10, New Zealand

Random House (Pty) Limited
Isle of Houghton, Corner of Boundary Road & Carse O'Gowrie,
Houghton 2198, South Africa

Random House Publishers India Private Limited
301 World Trade Tower, Hotel Intercontinental Grand Complex,
Barakhamba Lane, New Delhi 110 001, India

The Random House Group Limited Reg. No. 954009

www.randomhouse.co.uk

A CIP catalogue record for this book is available from the British Library

Papers used by Random House are natural, recyclable products made from wood grown in sustainable forests. The manufacturing processes conform to the environmental regulations of the country of origin

Typeset in Fournier Great Britain by Palimpsest Book Production Limited,
Polmont, Stirlingshire

Printed and bound in Australia by
Griffin Press

ISBN 9780091800192 (trade paperback – from Jan 2007)
ISBN 0 09 180019 6 (trade paperback)
ISBN 9780091800246 (hardback – from Jan 2007)
ISBN 0 09 180024 2 (hardback)

To my granddaughter Leila

1

In the upmarket bathroom shop in Regent's Park Road in North London, the slim brown-haired woman was showing a close interest in the display of tiles. 'Do you need some help?' asked the young male assistant, who was keen to close since it was almost seven o'clock in the evening.

Liz Carlyle was killing time. In trainers and designer jeans, she looked like any of the wealthy young married women who drifted in and out of the interior-design shops and boutiques of this part of London. But Liz was neither wealthy nor married and she was certainly not drifting. She was very focused indeed. She was waiting for the device she held tightly in her left hand to vibrate once – the signal that it was safe for her to proceed to the meeting in the coffee shop further down the road. In the mirror on the shop wall facing her, she could see Wally Woods, the leader of the A4 team providing counter-surveillance backup, taking his time buying an *Evening Standard* from the newsvendor on the corner.

He had already sent the two pulses, which signalled that her contact, Marzipan, was inside the cafe waiting for her. Once his team further up the street on either side were satisfied that no one had followed Marzipan, Wally would send the okay.

A young Asian man, dressed in black jeans and a hooded top, came along from the direction of Chalk Farm Underground Station. Wally and his team watched tensely as he paused to look in an estate agent's window. Moving on, he crossed over and left Regent's Park Road, walking off into the distance down a side street. Now the device in Liz's hand vibrated once. 'Thanks very much,' said Liz to the relieved shop assistant. 'I'll bring my husband in tomorrow evening and we'll decide then.' She left the shop, turned right and walked quickly along the street to the coffee shop, which she entered without hesitating, all under the watchful eyes of the A4 team.

Inside, Liz waited at the counter to order a cappuccino. She felt the familiar tension in her stomach, the quickened beating of her heart, which always accompanied work on the front-line. She had missed this excitement. For the last four months or so, she had been on convalescent leave, following a counter-terrorist operation in Norfolk at the end of the previous year.

She'd gone down to her mother's house in Wiltshire almost immediately after the MI5 doctor had ordered her off work. In the ensuing weeks she'd soon been well enough to help her mother in the garden centre she ran. On days off, they'd visited National Trust houses and cooked elaborate dinners for two; occasionally, at the weekend they would socialise with friends from the neighbourhood. It had been pleasant, tranquil, and agonisingly uneventful. Now on this May evening she was happy to be back at the sharp end of operations.

She had returned to work only that week. 'Take your time. Settle in,' Charles Wetherby had told her, and back in her office in the counter-terrorism agent-running section she had started with the mountain of paperwork, which had accumulated in her absence. But then the message had come that afternoon from Marzipan – code name for Sohail Din – urgently requesting a meeting. Strictly speaking, Marzipan was no longer Liz's business. Her colleague Dave Armstrong had taken him over, along with the immense promise of reliable information that he represented, the minute she had left. But for the moment Dave was in Leeds on urgent business and Liz, as Marzipan's original recruiter and runner, had been the obvious choice to stand in.

She took her coffee and walked to the gloomy back of the cafe where Marzipan was sitting at a small corner table, reading a book. 'Hello Sohail,' she said quietly, sitting down.

He closed his book and looked at her in surprise. 'Jane!' he exclaimed, using the name he knew her by. 'I was not expecting you, but I am so happy to see you.'

She had forgotten how young he looked, but then, he *was* young. When Liz had first met Sohail Din, more than a year before, he had already been accepted to read Law at Durham University. He was still less than twenty. He had taken a job in his gap year at a small Islamic bookshop in Haringey. Though it was not well paid, he had hoped it would provide an opportunity for religious discussion with other serious-minded young men like himself. But he had soon found that the bookshop was a focal point for radical Islamist doctrine – not at all the version of Islam that Sohail had learned at home and at his local mosque. He had been shocked by the casual talk of fatwas and jihad, then still more to find that some of his fellow employees openly supported the tactics of suicide bombers, even boasting of taking up arms themselves against the West. And finally he had come to realise that some of the people who came into the shop were actively involved in terrorist activities. That was when he had decided to act himself. He had found a police station some distance away and had told his story to a Special Branch officer. He was moved quickly through a well-tried route to MI5 and his first contact there, Liz Carlyle. She had recruited him and had developed him as a long-term agent, persuading him to put off his university career for a year. In the months that followed, Marzipan had provided invaluable information about the comings and goings of people of interest to MI5 and the police.

'It's very good to see you again, Sohail,' said Liz. 'You look well.'

Marzipan put down his book, saying nothing, but gazing at her gently, solemnly, his eyes large through his spectacles. Liz could see that he was on edge.

'Are you looking forward to university?' she said, wanting to put him more at ease.

'Very much,' he said earnestly.

'Good. You will do very well there, you know. And we are very grateful to you for delaying your studies.' Gently, she made the transition to business. 'Your message said you needed to see us urgently. Has something happened?'

Now the young man – not much more than a boy, thought Liz – said, 'Two weeks ago, a man visited the bookshop. One of the boys in the shop told me he was an important Imam visiting from Pakistan, and I thought I recognised his face from one of the videos we sell in the shop. I told this to Simon. He said that if the man came back to the shop I should contact him immediately.'

Simon Willis was Dave Armstrong's working alias. Liz asked, 'And you've seen this man again?'

Sohail Din nodded. 'This afternoon. He did not come into the shop. He was upstairs, with three other men. Young men, though one was older than the others. They were British Asians.'

'Are you sure?'

'I am certain. I heard them speak. You see, I was sent upstairs to fix the video player. Aswan – he works in the shop – had installed it, but today is his day off. He had not connected it properly to the aerial.'

'What were they watching?'

'A video the Imam had brought – there was a stack of them next to the VCR. They had one of these in the machine.'

The door to the cafe opened and Sohail peered over Liz's shoulder. But it was only two young women, laden with carrier bags, coming in for coffee after their shopping. Sohail continued, 'When I connected the recorder to the aerial I turned on the machine to make sure it was working properly. That's when I saw part of the video they were watching.'

He paused, and Liz suppressed her impatience and waited for him to resume. 'It was a video of this same man, the Imam. He was speaking in Urdu, which I do not understand well – but from hearing it at home I know a little. He was saying that sometimes it was necessary to die for one's belief; he was talking about a holy war.'

She said, 'Did you see any more than that?'

Sohail shook his head. 'Not then. I didn't stay; I didn't want them to think I was paying much attention.'

'Why do you think they were watching it? I mean, if the Imam was there anyway.'

Sohail paused for a moment. 'I have thought carefully about this. It came to my mind that he had come here to tutor the men. Maybe to prepare them.'

'Prepare them?'

Sohail added quietly, 'I think he was preparing them for a mission. Perhaps a suicide mission. They talk about these things in the shop.'

Liz was surprised. This seemed a very dramatic conclusion. The Marzipan she had known had been calm and level-headed;

now he seemed frightened and overexcited. Liz asked calmly, 'Why do you think that?'

Suddenly Sohail reached down and brought a small paper bag out of his knapsack. He slid it across the table. 'Here's why.'

'What's in there?' she asked.

'I brought the video. The Imam left it behind, along with the other tapes. I went upstairs and watched it just before we closed.'

Liz quickly put the video into her bag, pleased that Sohail had brought it, but also appalled by the risk he was taking. 'Well done, Sohail,' she said, 'but won't they notice that it's gone?'

'There were many other videos upstairs. And I am sure no one saw me go up there.'

'It will have to go back quickly,' she said firmly. 'But tell me first, these three men, how old were they?'

'The young ones were about my age. The other one perhaps in his late twenties.'

'You said they were British. Did you notice anything about their accents?'

'It is difficult to say.' He thought for a moment. 'Except the older one. I think he came from the North.'

'Would you recognise them again?'

'I can't be sure. I didn't want to look at them too carefully.'

'Of course,' said Liz soothingly, for she could see that Sohail's eyes kept returning to the door. 'Do you have any idea where these three have gone to?'

'No, but I know they'll be back.'

Liz felt her pulse pick up. 'Why? When?'

'The same time next week. Aswan asked if he should bring the machine down. But the owner said not to bother, as it would be needed again on Thursday. That is why I think they are in training. There is a series of videos for them to watch. It is a sort of course they are doing.'

'How do you know it will be the same men?'

Sohail thought for a moment. 'Because of the way he said it. "Leave it," he said, "they'll need it again next week." The way he said "they'll" could only mean the same men.'

Liz considered this. They had some time, then, though not very much, to put an operation in place before the group reconvened. She thought hard for a moment, trying to decide what to do next. 'Tell me, could you meet me again later this evening? I'd like to go and copy the video, and also collect some photographs for you to look at. Photographs of people. Can you do that?'

Sohail nodded.

'Let me tell you where to go.' She gave him an address in one of the anonymous streets north of Oxford Street and made him repeat it back to her. Then she said, 'Take the Underground to Oxford Circus and walk west. Do you know where John Lewis is?' Sohail nodded. 'So this is what you do to get to the house. We will make sure you aren't being followed, but if we are not happy, someone will stop you on the street and ask you for the time. They'll ask you twice – and if that happens do not go to the safe house. Walk straight on, catch a bus and go home. And just in case you run into anyone you know, have an excuse ready for what you're doing there.'

'That's easy,' said Sohail. 'I'll say I've been looking for CDs at the HMV shop on Oxford Street. They stay open late.'

Liz looked at her watch. 'It's now seven-thirty. I will meet you there at ten o'clock.'

'Will you be my contact again from now on?' he asked.

'We'll see,' she said mildly, for in truth she didn't know herself. 'It doesn't matter, you know. We all work together.'

He nodded but there was a look in his eyes which Liz at first took for simple excitement, then realised was partly fear. She smiled reassuringly at him. 'You are doing a brilliant job. Just go on being very careful, Sohail.'

He smiled back at her a little bleakly, his eyes darkening. She added, 'If you ever feel you are in any danger, you must tell us at once. Use the alert procedure. We do not expect you to put yourself in unnecessary danger.'

She knew these were empty words. Of course he must be in jeopardy; in such operations risk was inevitable. Not for the first time, Liz questioned her participation in the subtle psychological game of agent running: cautioning the agent to be careful, acknowledging the danger he was in, reassuring him that he would be protected, encouraging him to obtain the information that was needed. The only justification was the harm she was trying to prevent, but faced with a Marzipan, it seemed a difficult balance to preserve.

But Sohail said simply, resolutely, 'I will do everything I can.' Liz was moved but his words did nothing to relieve her feelings of guilt. He was so very young, and yet so very brave. If these men in the bookshop were happy to blow themselves up, she hated to think what they would be happy to do to Sohail. Involuntarily almost, she shook her head and turned away.

2

Liz hailed a taxi at the bottom of Primrose Hill, and directed the driver to the Atrium restaurant on Millbank. From there it was a short walk to Thames House, the massive heavy-set building on the north bank of the Thames, which was the headquarters of MI5. It was a good moment to drive through the West End. The rush hour was over. The theatre crowds were all inside. The pubs glowed with light and warmth that in the ordinary way would have attracted her. Within twenty minutes of leaving Marzipan she was back at her desk.

There was much to do before she could get back to Sohail Din. The video had to be copied, the arrangements for the safe house confirmed, a fresh A4 team conjured up to replace Wally Woods's, now going off duty.

Then Liz sat down to think. Was there an immediate threat? If so she would need to contact Charles Wetherby – dining as it happened with his MI6 opposite number, Geoffrey Fane. If Marzipan was right there was a threat, but not an immediate one. She decided to defer the decision until she had seen him again, and then reached for the telephone and dialled Counter-Terrorist Investigations. Judith Spratt, on night duty, answered.

Judith was an old friend. The two had joined the Service on the same day over a decade before, and both had worked in the counter-terrorism branch now for six years. But while Liz's talents had taken her in the direction of agent running, Judith's sharp analytical skills and attention to detail had turned her into an expert investigator. With almost obsessive tenacity, she and her team of colleagues followed up all the pieces of information that came into the counter-terrorism branch in addition to what the agent runners produced. They were constantly in touch with colleagues overseas, sharing leads, producing identifications, making connections. Investigations Section was the sheet anchor of the whole counter-terrorist effort of Thames House, taking unassessed information and making sense of it.

So it was to Judith that Liz now went for the portfolio of British Asians suspected of some kind of involvement in terrorism. Liz gave her a quick précis of what Marzipan had said, but none of it connected with anything Judith and her team were currently working on. Clutching the large leather portfolio Judith gave her, zipped tight and locked, she took the lift down to the basement garage and collected one of the anonymous fleet vehicles housed there. With three-quarters of an hour still to spare she drove back north, up Regent Street through Oxford Circus, eventually turning into the quiet streets of once-grand eighteenth-century houses, now the consulting rooms of doctors, dentists, psychiatrists, and other specialists serving London's wealthier residents and visitors. Finally, she turned under an arch and into a dark, faintly lit mews of small houses, the former stables of the grand houses. A garage door swung up when she pressed the bleeper in the car, and she drove straight into a small, lit garage.

Above the garage was a warm, cheerful sitting room, furnished with a couple of well-used sofas, covered in what the agent runners all referred to as 'Ministry of Works chintz'. A square dining-room table with several chairs of an unidentifiable wood, a battered coffee table and a framed print completed the furnishings. Safe houses were one of civilisation's dead ends. Strictly utilitarian, they were kept in readiness for use, the kitchen stocked with the essentials for making coffee and tea but never any food. A quarter of an hour later, as Liz was still unpacking the portfolio's collection of photographs onto the dining-room table, the phone rang.

'Ninety seconds,' said a voice at the other end. 'All clear.'

She opened the door immediately the bell rang and led Marzipan up the stairs.

'Would you like something to drink – tea, perhaps, or coffee?'

Sohail shook his head, slowly, seriously, saying nothing but taking in his surroundings. 'Did you get something to eat?' she asked, hoping he had.

'I don't need anything now,' he said.

'All right, then let's get started. I want you to take your time looking at these, but don't think too hard about it. Usually your first instinct is accurate.'

The pictures were from a variety of sources. The best were copies of those supplied with applications for passports and driving licences. The rest mostly came from surveillance – taken from a distance with hidden cameras – and were poorer. Sohail took his time, examining each photograph carefully before regretfully shaking his head. By eleven when they were only halfway through, it occurred to Liz that Sohail's parents would start to worry if he were unusually late. 'I think we should call it a day,' she announced. 'Could you look at the rest tomorrow?'

He nodded, and she said, 'Then let's meet up here again. Shall we say seven-thirty? Come just the same way as you did tonight.' She looked at Sohail. He seemed very tired. 'You should take a cab home. I'll call one.'

She went and made the call. When she returned she said,

'Leave here in ten minutes. Walk out of the mews, turn left, and a taxi will come along the street. As it approaches it will put on its light. The driver will drop you off a few streets from home.'

She looked at the young man, and suddenly felt a concern, a tenderness towards him that was almost maternal. It was a pity he had yet to identify any of the three suspects. But she was not downhearted. She had long ago learned that success in her line of business took time and patience and often came suddenly, and unexpectedly.

3

Maddie came back to Belfast when her mother Molly telephoned to tell her the doctor's news. There was nothing to be done except manage the pain. Sean Keaney would die at home.

So she returned to the small brick house where her father and mother had lived for over forty years, just off the Falls Road in Belfast, a house as minimal and drab as any of its neighbours in the row. Only the most careful observer would notice the extraordinary thickness of the front door, or how the painted shutters of the windows were steel-reinforced.

Learning that death was imminent, the family gathered like a wagon train drawing up in a circle for defence. Though it was a sparse circle, thought Maddie. One daughter had died of breast cancer two years before, and the one son – apple of his father's eye – had been shot dead fifteen years before trying to evade a British Army roadblock. Now only she and her older sister, Kate, remained.

Maddie had come only because her mother had asked her to. As a little girl, her dislike for her father had been matched by the intensity of love she'd felt for her mother, though as she grew up even this was corroded by her frustration at her mother's passivity in the face of her husband's domineering ways. Maddie simply couldn't fathom her mother's willingness to subordinate her own striking qualities – the musicality, the love of books, the Galway-bred country sense of humour – to the demand of her husband Sean that the Struggle should always come first.

Maddie had known that her father's dedication to Irish nationalism brought him admiration of a kind. But this had only increased her dislike of him, her anger at his callous treatment of the family. Yet she was never sure which she felt more contemptible – the man or the movement. She had got away from both as soon as she could – leaving at eighteen to study Law at University College Dublin, then staying on to work there.

There was also the violence – Maddie had been fleeing that as well, of course. She had never bothered to count the number of people she'd known who had been injured or killed. Then there were the others, just ordinary people many of them, who happened to be in the wrong place at the wrong time. She came to believe that the counting would never stop. Her father had been obsessively secretive about his 'professional life', yet as the Keaney family listened to the news of each IRA 'operation' – that euphemism for bombings, shootings and death – the hush that settled over them all was knowing, not innocent. No hush could still the impact of the deaths that studded Maddie's childhood like a grotesquely crowded dartboard. Especially that of her brother, born and bred a Republican, killed before he had any idea that life might give him other choices.

Now she sat with her mother and sister for hours on end, drinking countless cups of tea in the small sitting room downstairs, while in his bed on the floor above them her father lay, heavily sedated. Word went out, through the vast network of comrades, associates and friends, that Sean Keaney would be glad to have final visits from those who had served with him since the Troubles flared in the late sixties. There was never any question of a priest being called, for although Keaney had been born a Catholic, the only faith he held was a rock-solid allegiance to the Irish Republican Army.

The visitors were all known to the family. Kieran O'Doyle, Jimmy Garrison, Seamus Ryan, even Martin McGuinness made an appearance late one night, coming under cover of darkness so his visit would not be noticed – the list was a roll call of the Republican movement. To a man they were long-term veterans of the armed struggle.

Many had served prison terms for their part in assassinations or bombings, and were free now only because of the amnesty provisions of the Good Friday Agreement. During his long paramilitary career, Keaney had managed to avoid any criminal conviction, but along with most of his visitors, he had been interned in the seventies for over a year in the cell blocks of the Maze Prison.

The men were shown upstairs by Maddie, since her mother found the constant up and down exhausting. Standing by the bedside, they tried to make small talk with the man they had known as the Commander. But Maddie could see that Keaney's condition shocked them – once a barrel of a man, he had been reduced in his terminal illness to a small shrunken figure. Sensing his fatigue, most of his old associates kept their visits short, ending them with awkward but heartfelt final farewells. Downstairs, they stopped to talk briefly with Molly and Maddie's sister, Kate; sometimes, if they had been especially close to Keaney, they drank a small whiskey.

Maddie could see how much even these brief visits drained her father's dwindling energy, and she was relieved when there was no one left on the visitors' list they had drawn up. Which made her father's subsequent request, uttered after a night of such pain she thought he would not see the dawn break, all the more astonishing.

'He wants to see James Maguire!' she announced as her sister and mother gathered for breakfast in the small kitchen downstairs.

'You can't be serious,' Kate said incredulously. Even under the umbrella of Irish nationalism, James Maguire and Sean Keaney had at best co-existed edgily, their mutual antipathy held in check only by their devotion to the cause.

'I thought it was morphine talk, but he's asked twice now. I didn't know what to say. We can't turn down a request from our dying father, now can we?'

Her sister looked at her grimly. 'I'll go upstairs and have a word. He must be confused.' But when she came down again, her face was sterner still. 'He absolutely insists. I asked why he wanted to see Maguire, and he said, "Never you mind. Just get him here for me."'

And later that day, about an hour before the Keaneys had their tea, there was a knock on the door. A tall, lean man came into the house, and although he was much the same age as the dying man upstairs, there was nothing frail about him. He displayed none of the modesty shown by the other former associates of Sean Keaney, nor did he shake hands with any members of the family. When Kate took him upstairs, she later told Maddie, she found their father asleep – perhaps the bizarre meeting with a long-time enemy would not take place after all. But as she turned back to the visitor, the man said evenly, 'Hello, Keaney.'

'Come in, Maguire,' the weaker voice commanded, and Kate saw that her father's eyes had opened. He raised a bony hand to dismiss her, which he had not done with his other visitors.

Downstairs Maddie waited in the front parlour with her mother and sister, torn between curiosity and disbelief as the clock ticked and they could hear the low bass murmur of the voices upstairs for five, then ten, then fifteen minutes. Finally after half an hour they heard the bedroom door open, footsteps come down the staircase, and, without stopping for even the curtest farewell, Maguire walked out of the house.

Afterwards, Maddie found her father so exhausted that she could not bring herself to ask about the visitor, and left him to sleep. Her sister, less patiently, waited only until after tea to go upstairs, determined to discover the reason for her father's summoning Maguire. Yet she returned downstairs both dissatisfied and distraught. For sometime during tea their father, Sean Keaney, had died in his sleep.

4

Charles Wetherby, Director of Counter-Terrorism, had been in the office since seven-thirty. Liz had briefed him by phone about her meetings with Marzipan the previous evening, as soon as he had got home from his dinner with Geoffrey Fane of MI6. Wetherby had called a nine a.m. emergency meeting of the Counter-Terrorist Committee, the joint committee of MI5, MI6, GCHQ, the Metropolitan Police and the Home Office. It had been set up immediately after the Twin Towers atrocity of 11 September 2001 at the Prime Minister's insistence, to ensure that all government agencies and departments involved in countering the terrorist threat to the UK should cooperate without any inter-service rivalries impeding the national effort. The CTC had accepted that on the information available, there was a possible threat of an extreme kind, which needed urgent follow-up. It had agreed that MI5 should move forward to investigate Marzipan's information, using joint resources as necessary and keeping everyone informed.

Now at eleven o'clock Wetherby was chairing an operations meeting of the MI5 sections involved. The operations briefing room was in the centre of Thames House. It overlooked the internal atrium but had no windows to the outside world. It was spacious with several rows of chairs around a long table and at one end a screen and other technical equipment. Despite its size the room was crowded and Liz found herself squashed between Judith Spratt and Reggie Purvis, the dour Yorkshireman who headed A4, the surveillance section whose teams had been out providing counter-surveillance for Liz and Marzipan the night before.

Also present was a small army of tough-looking characters in shirt sleeves, mostly ex-military. These were members of A2, the section responsible for 'bugging and burgling' – installing covert listening devices and cameras – nowadays done strictly under warrant. Liz knew them to be experts in the skills required for their risky, nerve stretching business. Filling the remaining seats were colleagues of Judith Spratt from Counter-Terrorist Investigations, 'Technical Ted' Poyser, the chief consultant on all computer matters, Patrick Dobson from the Director General's office, responsible for liaison with the Home Office, and Dave Armstrong, just back from Leeds. Even at a distance Liz could see that he needed a shave, a clean shirt and a good night's sleep.

Liz knew and liked most of her colleagues, even Reggie Purvis who, taciturn and stubborn as he might be, was expert at his job. The sole exception arrived late for the meeting and sat down with a thud in the one remaining seat. Michael Binding had returned the year before from a longer than usual posting in Northern Ireland and was now head of A2, the bugger and burglar in chief. Binding treated all his female colleagues with an infuriating mix of gallantry and condescension that Liz could deal with only by the most iron self-control.

For this morning at least, Liz and Marzipan's video were the star turn. Much of the content of the video had been seen at one time or another by most members of her audience, in excerpts on television or on extremist websites on the internet. What shocked, as the video played, was the sheer malevolent concentration on brutal image, the persistence of the message, penetrating all barriers of language and culture, that it is the duty of some to hate and destroy others, for reasons beyond the control of either side.

In all the clutter of blood and violence, the knives drawn across throats, the cries, the fear, the explosions and the dust, nothing in the video was more sinister, more coldly cruel than the image of a man in a white robe with a black beard, seated on a mat, his voice rising and falling like a siren, as he spoke in a language few in the room could understand. His message of hatred, didactic, unwavering, was only too clear. From the fact that his image recurred between the different scenes of violence, it was evident that his message was intended to illustrate different points of doctrine or method – all to the same end, death. Finally, with a prolonged flickering the video stopped.

Wetherby ended the stunned silence. 'The man in the white robe is the Imam whom our agent Marzipan saw yesterday in a bookshop in Haringey. We'll have a full transcription in an hour or so, but the gist of what he was saying seemed clear enough. Judith?'

Judith had been briefed by one of the transcribers who listened in on intercepted conversations in Urdu. She glanced at her notes.

'He was issuing a call to arms – all true followers to take up the sword and so forth – the Satan America – her evil allies – death should be embraced by those who fight and they will be blessed in another world. That was the concluding sentence. But the interesting thing is that it wasn't just the usual diatribe. The way it was arranged was as a kind of lesson, I thought, with the points being illustrated by the different scenes of violence. A sort of argument, almost.'

'A kind of training video, you mean?' asked Dave Armstrong.

'Yes. Something like that. Not just a sermon anyway.'

'That would chime with Marzipan's account,' Liz commented.

'As would the fact that there was an audience of three,' said Judith. 'That's an ideal team number. It's the number for maximum security and where each team member can watch the others simultaneously.'

'What were the video clips?' someone asked.

Wetherby answered: 'The throat-cutting scene was certainly the murder of Daniel Pearl, the American reporter. The others could have been anywhere, most likely in Iraq. The text will probably help, if we need to know.'

He turned to someone at the end of the table whom Liz did not recognise. He was a broad-shouldered man, smartly dressed in a well-cut suit and scarlet tie with a face that was friendly and a little craggy. Just short of outright handsome, she observed to herself.

'Tom,' said Wetherby. 'What about the Imam? Do we know who he is?'

The man called Tom replied in a soft voice – speaking, Liz wryly thought, in what used to be known as received pronunciation, 'proper English' as her mother would have called it. 'His name is Mahmood Abu Sayed. He's the head of a madrasa in Lahore. And yes he is a teacher, as Judith suggested. But his madrasa is known as one of the radical hotbeds. Abu Sayed himself comes from near the Afghan border. His family has strong Taliban connections. Even as radicals go, he's a hardliner.' He paused for a moment. 'We'll check with Immigration but he probably came in under another name. I'm willing to bet he's never been in Britain before. English students have always travelled out to him in

Lahore. If he's come here then I'd guess there's something pretty important in the wind.'

There was silence for a moment, then Michael Binding, red-faced in his heavy tweed jacket, leaned forward in his chair and waved his pencil to catch Wetherby's eye. 'Look Charles, I sense we are running ahead rather fast. Resources are pretty tight in A2 just now. This Imam may be a firebrand but in his world he's presumably a distinguished kind of fellow. Is it really so remarkable that Muslim youngsters want to hear him speak or that he should get a few budding disciples together? They may just want to sit at his feet. In Northern Ireland—'

Liz interrupted, trying not to sound too impatient. 'That was not Marzipan's impression and to date his instincts have proved at least ninety per cent right. That video wasn't exactly theological. Marzipan thought that these people were preparing for a mission, and I'd back his opinion.'

Binding leaned back in his chair, looking cross, scratching his nose with his pencil. Wetherby smiled grimly. 'CTC have accepted that in the light of these events there may well be a specific threat,' he said. 'And I think so too. Our working assumption has to be that these three young men are preparing an atrocity of some sort under guidance and what we have seen is the conditioning, the stiffening up if you like, designed to make sure they stay the course to the end. With no information to the contrary we must assume that what is in preparation is an attack in this country.' He paused. 'Of an extreme kind,' he added.

A small chill seemed to enter the room. A suicide bomber, unless detected before his mission can begin, is virtually impossible to stop. Three suicide bombers could make it three times more difficult. One would be bound to get through. Exactly what was intended was still unclear but, Liz reflected, Marzipan had at least given them a chance.

Wetherby was speaking again. 'The operation will be run by Investigations and led by Tom Dartmouth. The code word is FOXHUNT. Dave, you will continue running Marzipan – you should be the one who sees him this evening.'

Liz's stomach turned suddenly to lead. She felt her face redden with disappointment. Dave Armstrong was looking sympathetically at her but all she could conjure up was a wan smile. Her time off work hadn't been his fault. He had inherited Marzipan on fair terms, before the agent had become a 'star'. It was logical that he should continue with him. Beyond the feeling of disappointment, she found it difficult to analyse her own feelings. It was something about Marzipan – his vulnerability, his helplessness, almost his *principles*. He was in so many respects alien, a member of a different culture to hers, from a totally different background and yet his principles were identical to hers. Did he fully understand the risks he was running? She couldn't say. There was something almost naive about the way – yes, the way he yielded to them. She bit her lip, said nothing. Wetherby was speaking again. She almost hated the matter-of-fact manner, the steady confident tone of his voice.

'The aim for the moment is to find out more,' he was saying. 'There is no obvious advantage to us in moving in just yet. The video proves nothing. We have nothing to hold anyone on. Our first step must be surveillance on the shop. I'd like eavesdropping and covert cameras too as soon as we can get them in. Patrick, can you see to the warrant?'

Patrick Dobson nodded. 'I'll get on to the Home Secretary's office. He's in London, I know, so it should be quick. Hopefully by six. I'll need a written application within the hour.'

Tom nodded. 'Judith, will you take that on please?'

Wetherby turned to Binding. 'Sorry Michael. That's it. If we get the warrant I want your chaps to go in tomorrow night. Can you do that?'

Binding nodded slowly. 'We can probably do it if Marzipan can sketch a plan of the inside of the building. We'll need prior A4 surveillance of course, who the key people are, what time they leave, where they live, who has keys. We don't want to risk being disturbed. I'll talk to Special Branch as well. Tom, I'll need to know from you how much we can tell them.'

Tom nodded, 'We'll talk about it straight after this.'

Reggie Purvis looked at Liz. 'We'll be briefing the A4 teams at four. I hope both you and Dave can come to the meeting. We'll need to know whatever background on the area and the people you've got from Marzipan.'

Liz looked at Dave and nodded. Wetherby gathered up his papers. 'We'll reconvene tomorrow in my room. I'll want situation reports from one representative of each section. And Judith, an action note, please, through Tom and circulated.'

As the meeting began to break up, Wetherby called Liz over. 'Can I see you in my office, say at noon? I need to make a quick call first.'

As Liz left the room Dave Armstrong came up and walked with her to the stairs. 'Thanks for standing in for me last night,' he said.

'Any time,' she said. 'How did it go up north?'

Dave shook his head. 'A lot of fuss about nothing,' he said, rubbing his bristly chin. 'I've come straight down. Haven't even been home yet. But at least this one sounds real.'

They came out of the stairwell onto the fourth floor. 'Tell

me,' said Liz, 'who is that man Tom? I've never seen him before. Is he new?'

'Tom Dartmouth,' said Dave. 'And no, he's not new. He's been in Pakistan – got seconded to MI6 there after 9/11, poor bugger. He's an Arabic speaker. I should have introduced you but I didn't realise you didn't know him. I suppose he came back while you were off sick. You'll like him; he's a nice bloke. Knows his onions.'

He looked at Liz for a moment, then slowly a smile came over his face. He poked her playfully with an elbow. 'Don't get excited now. I'm told there's a Mrs Dartmouth.'

'Don't be ridiculous,' said Liz. 'You've got a one-track mind.'

5

Walking down the corridor to see Wetherby, Liz felt a mix of trepidation and anticipation. She had seen him only briefly since returning to work, when he had come out to greet her on the first morning, then had to rush off for a meeting in Whitehall. She was very disappointed but in her heart of hearts not surprised that he had returned Marzipan to Dave Armstrong's control, but she hoped that he would have something else equally important for her. Goodness knows, there seemed enough to do – one of the old hands in Counter-Terrorism had said the day before that even at the height of the IRA bombings in London, life at Thames House had not been so frantic.

Wetherby was standing at his desk when she came into the room. As he motioned for her to sit down, she thought not for the first time how little she really knew about the man. With his neatly pressed suit and polished Oxfords, he would merge easily with any group of well-dressed men. But a close observer would have noticed his eyes. Set in his unremarkable, slightly uneven features, they had a quiet watchfulness which could turn suddenly to humour or to coldness. Some people misread his apparently mild demeanour, but Liz knew from experience that a penetrating intelligence and determination lay behind the gentle appearance of the man. On her good days Liz knew she was important to him, and not just because of her skill as an investigator. But this professional relationship remained cool, and pervaded by a subtle irony, as if they knew each other better in some other life.

Wetherby said, 'I had an Irish nanny when I was a boy, who used to ask me, after any upset, if I was feeling "well within myself". Funny expression, but apt. How about you?'

He was smiling but watchful, and she looked him in the eye when she replied, 'You honestly don't need to worry about me.'

'I hear you've been down with your mama. She well?'

'Yes, she's fine. Worried about what the lack of rain will do to the young shrubs.' Liz paused, then asked politely. 'And how is Joanne? Any better?' Wetherby's wife suffered from a debilitating blood disease, which had made her a permanent semi-invalid. Liz thought how odd it was that he always enquired about her mother and she after his wife – without either ever having set eyes on the object of their concern.

'Not really,' said Wetherby with a frown and a slight shake of his head, as if to dismiss the unwelcome thought and move on. 'I wanted to see you because I've got an assignment for you.'

'To do with this operation?' she asked hopefully.

'Not exactly,' said Wetherby. 'Though I want you to stay in the section and keep involved while you work on this. It's a supplementary assignment, if you like, though it's important.'

What could be more important than an imminent suicide attack in Britain? Suddenly she wondered if she was being demoted; it seemed the only explanation.

'Does the name Sean Keaney mean anything to you?'

Liz thought for a moment. 'The IRA man? Of course. But isn't he dead?'

'Yes, he died last month. Before he died he asked to see one of his former comrades, a man called James Maguire. That was strange because the two of them had never got on. Keaney was as much in favour of violence as anyone else in the IRA, but he was willing to talk as well – he took part in the secret discussions with Willie Whitelaw in the seventies. But Maguire always said that even talking with the British was tantamount to treason. Apparently he even suggested that Keaney might have been working for us.'

Liz raised an inquisitive eyebrow.

'The answer is no,' said Wetherby. 'Keaney didn't ever work for us.' He paused, and gave a short laugh. 'But Maguire did, though he was overtly so hard line no one ever suspected him. Except Keaney. That's why when Keaney knew he was dying he asked to see Maguire. He wanted to make sure that what he said to him would get back to us. And it has.'

Wetherby paused again and looked pensive. 'In the early nineties the IRA's Provisional Army Council became paranoid about penetration by British informants. Keaney came up with the idea of turning the tables: he decided to try and infiltrate us. And he told Maguire just before he died that he had succeeded in planting a secret asset in the ranks of the British security services.'

'A secret asset? You mean a mole?'

'Yes, that's just what I mean.'

'What did he mean by British security services? Which service was it supposed to be?'

'He didn't specify. Whether he knew or not, I don't know, but if he did, he didn't tell Maguire. The only fact he told Maguire is that this secret asset went to Oxford and it was there that he – or she – was recruited by an IRA sympathiser. Presumably by a don, though possibly not. The point is, according to Keaney, the mole successfully joined the security services. But more or less at the same time, the peace talks began, and the Good Friday Agreement followed. Keaney decided the mole operation wasn't worth the risk. So, according to Keaney, his agent was never activated.'

'Why did Keaney speak up now? It's been almost fifteen years.'

Wetherby pursed his lips. 'When the IRA were caught bugging Stormont, it almost derailed the peace process. Keaney said he was worried that an exposé of IRA infiltration of British Intelligence would set back the process again, this time possibly for good. All the leaks about *our* informers in the IRA were embarrassing for the IRA, but really just confirmed what they and everyone else had long suspected. But if they had managed to infiltrate us, the news would be explosive.'

'Do you believe that?' asked Liz,

'You mean Keaney's reason for talking now? I simply don't know. I'm afraid where he's gone, we can't question him.'

'Is it possible,' Liz asked tentatively, 'that Keaney might have made the whole thing up? You know, as a last blow by a lifetime enemy against Her Majesty's Government.'

'Could be,' said Wetherby. 'But even if there's a chance that what he said might be true, we can't ignore it. If there really is a member of one of the intelligence services who was happy to spy for the IRA . . . who apparently joined on that basis . . .'

'But was never activated.'

'No,' said Wetherby. 'But the fact he could have been is quite bad enough; someone like that might get up to anything. We've got to find out more about this, Liz. We can't just do nothing.'

Liz saw at once that he was right. Now that they had Keaney's confession, it would have to be followed up – she shuddered to think what would happen if it came to the attention of their political masters or the media, that they had taken no action. The prospect of another Burgess and Maclean, or worst of all, Philby or Blunt, exploding all over the tabloids' front pages didn't bear thinking about. And if MI5 were seen to have pooh-poohed the whole thing, it would ruin the reputation of the Service.

'So we need to conduct an investigation into this. And I want you to do it.'

'Me?' said Liz, unable to contain her surprise. She'd already concluded he would want her involved, but to run the inquiry? She had no false modesty about her work, but she still would have expected a more senior officer to handle such a case. But then perhaps it wasn't quite as important as Wetherby was making out.

'Yes, you.'

'But Charles,' said Liz, a little nervously, 'I've no experience in Counter-Espionage and very little of Northern Ireland.'

Wetherby shook his head. 'I've discussed this with DG. For the moment it is to be left in our hands. We certainly don't want a Northern Ireland expert on this. I need a good investigator, someone with your flair, who is not well known in Northern Ireland, but has *some* knowledge of the place. You had a brief posting there – a few months, wasn't it?' Liz nodded. 'Not long enough to get sucked in,' said Wetherby.

Liz suddenly felt rather flattered.

'If we don't know MI5 was the target, what about the other services?'

'I've talked with Geoffrey Fane,' he said, referring to his counterpart at MI6. 'We both agreed that it was most likely that the target service was MI5. Fane has talked to C and they are not at all anxious to have an internal investigation at present. After all, we took over Northern Ireland from MI6 in the eighties; according to Keaney, the mole joined sometime in the early nineties. It would be MI5 they'd be aiming at. So Fane has agreed we begin by focusing here. He wants to second someone to the investigation, just to keep him informed' – he looked expressionlessly at Liz, who knew that though Wetherby respected Fane's professional skills, he did not entirely trust him – 'but it will be someone junior. You're in charge.

'Now, you'll need a cover story for any interviews you conduct once you have a list of . . .' He paused momentarily, searching for the word he wanted, then said, 'candidates. If you're making new enquiries about certain individuals, we have to have a good reason or it will soon get out and the mole will be alerted. I've agreed with DG that the cover story will be this: the Parliamentary Security and Intelligence Committee is concerned that the security vetting of members of the intelligence services is not reviewed frequently enough. They think it should be done more often. So DG has agreed, on an experimental basis, to redo the vetting of a random sample, to see if it produces anything useful. That's what you will say if anyone asks why you are making enquiries about colleagues. You should use the corner conference room for any private meetings – I've reserved it for your use only. Otherwise, use your normal desk. As far as your colleagues are concerned, you are still in Counter-Terrorism. I think that's enough for now; we can sort out any other details later. Do you have any questions?'

'Just one. I'd like to talk to Maguire's controller.'

Wetherby gave a sad smile. 'Not possible, I'm afraid,' he said. 'It was Ricky Perrins.'

'Oh no.' Perrins had been killed in a car accident three weeks earlier – it was one of the first things Liz learned on her return to work. It was especially heartbreaking, as Perrins had two small children, and a young wife expecting a third.

'Obviously you should look at his report. You might want to talk to Maguire – but I don't think you'll get much more out of him. I gather that having said his piece to Ricky he didn't want any more to do with us.'

6

It was the three men on the street that alarmed her. Doris Feldman was used to all sorts of comings and goings in that shop across the road with all those strange young men – how oddly they dressed; she would never get used to that – but they were as regular as clockwork, and it was always quiet by seven-thirty in the evening.

Doris lived in the small flat above the ironmonger's shop she still owned and ran in Haringey. As she was fond of saying, she was London-born and London-bred, though she was happy to acknowledge that her father had been foreign, arriving from Minsk when he was barely in his teens, with a sack of gewgaws over one shoulder. He'd had a market stall at first, selling flowers, before graduating to fruit and veg, then when he'd scrimped and saved enough to lease a property of his own, it was the hardware business he went into. 'There's money in nails,' he'd liked to say, even in the years when nails were literally ten a penny.

Never married, Doris inherited the shop when her parents died, which meant nothing much more than some stock and the long working hours needed to sell it. The growth of DIY stores had almost been the death of her small shop, but in this dense and not very prosperous part of North London, not everyone had a car, and her long opening hours and her encyclopaedic knowledge of the stock she kept in the boxes, drawers and shelves of her shop attracted sufficient custom to keep her afloat. 'Mrs Feldman, you are the Selfridges of Capel Street', one of her customers once told her, and she'd liked that.

But it didn't help her sleep. Why was it as she entered first her seventh and then her eighth decade, she seemed to have more rather than less trouble getting through the night? Come two o'clock she'd tend to find herself waking slowly until her mind felt clear as a bell. She'd toss and turn, put on the light, turn on the radio, turn off the light and toss and turn some more, then give up – and finally get out of bed. She'd put on her dressing gown and heat up the kettle while Esther, her cat (and almost as old as Doris, at least in cat years), slept in her basket by the stove like a baby.

Which was why, this Friday night – Friday? What was she thinking of? It was Saturday already, three o'clock in the morning – Doris Feldman sat in the armchair warming her hands on her mug and looking out of the window at the street. How this neighbourhood had changed, though oddly, perhaps, it was quieter than it used to be. In her childhood there had been her kind, of course, immigrants from Russia and Poland, mixed with the Irish, who sometimes cut up rough, especially on a weekend night after too much time in the pub. Then after the war, the coloureds. Decent people many of them, but goodness they could make a noise, with their music and dancing and life lived on the street.

Then most recently, the Asians moved in, really the strangest of them all. Quiet people, well behaved – closing time for them meant locking up their newsagent shops, not for them a night out in the pubs. They certainly seemed to pray a lot – she had long got used to seeing the men going to their mosques at all sorts of hours. They'd think nothing of closing their shops right in the middle of the day. But not the bookshop across the street – someone always seemed to be there. People in and out all day long, though they didn't seem to buy a lot of books.

Yet at night the shop was closed, and there was never any sign of life in the building. So this Friday night as she sipped her mug of tea she sat bolt upright when she saw three men suddenly appear in the street and gather in a huddle by the front door of the bookshop. They were dressed in dark clothes, jeans and anoraks, and one man wore a leather jacket. You couldn't see their faces. One of them pointed towards the back of the building, another shook his head and then as two of the men stood on either side, looking up and down the street, the third man was right up against the door – what was he doing – fiddling with the lock? Then suddenly Doris saw the door open and the next minute all three men had slipped inside, and the door closed quickly behind them.

Doris sat there, astonished, briefly wondering if she had seen the men or just imagined them. Nonsense, she told herself, my body's getting old but I'm not going cuckoo. She had never spoken to the bookshop owner, didn't even know his name, but someone was breaking into his shop. Or maybe not – maybe they were friends. Didn't look like it. Up to no good, at this time of night she was sure. Plotting, she wouldn't be surprised, like so many of these young men. She shuddered at the thought, and it was from a sense of duty as well as concern that she got up and dialled 999.

Inside the shop the three men worked quickly. Two went upstairs, and, making sure the curtains were tightly drawn, searched with a torch until they found, at the very back, a square trapdoor in the ceiling which gave access to the loft. Standing on a chair, one of the men pushed away the trapdoor and hoisted himself up with a boost from the man below, who then handed up to him a small tool case. Holding his torch low so it wouldn't accidentally send light outside, the man in the attic examined the beams until he found one directly above a corner of the large room below. Within sixty seconds he was drilling, a slow process since the drill was underpowered to keep its decibel level low.

Suddenly his colleague was standing below the open trapdoor, speaking urgently. 'That was Special Branch. The local police have had a call from a neighbour, someone across the street. She saw us entering.'

'Bugger. What are they going to do?'

'They want to know if we're done in here. There's still time to leave before the car gets sent.'

'No. I need at least ten more minutes.'

'Okay, I'll tell them.'

He went away and the man in the attic resumed drilling. He had just come through the beam and was about to put the probe and microscopic camera gently down the hole he'd drilled when his colleague came back. 'The car's on its way, but they know we're here. They're going to go and speak to the neighbour who called. Apparently it's some old lady.'

'Okay. That shouldn't be too much of a problem.'

And ten minutes later, having carefully brushed away the sawdust made by his drill, and carefully closing over the small drilled hole with filler, the man jumped down and, getting up on the chair, replaced the trapdoor. 'I'm done up there. Anything else need doing?'

His colleague shook his head. 'I've got two mikes in – one's in the plug in the corner, and the other's in the back of the VCR.'

'Have you checked them with Thames?'

'Yes, they can hear them loud and clear. Come on.' They went downstairs and collected their other colleague, who had put three listening devices in place, one above the inside of the shop's front door, another in the owner's small office, and a third in the stockroom in the back. Now even the faintest whisper made on either floor would be heard in Thames House.

Across the street, Doris Feldman poured hot water onto a tea bag for the nice young policeman who had rung her bell. He knew all about the strange goings-on across the street, and had even suggested they might want her help. She didn't see the same three figures slip out of the front door of the bookshop and disappear into the night. But by then Doris was no longer worried.

7

Peggy Kinsolving had met Geoffrey Fane only once before, when he had spoken at her induction course when she first joined MI6 a year or so ago. She couldn't recall much of what he'd said that day but she remembered the tall, heron-like figure and the chilly handshake.

The second meeting was briefer but what he said was more memorable. He was seconding Peggy to MI5 for a month or two, he announced, on a very important assignment that was so confidential she would have to sign a special indoctrination form. She would learn more when she got to Thames House. The one thing Fane wanted to stress was that she should not forget where her loyalties lay. 'Don't go native on us,' said Fane sternly. 'We wouldn't look kindly on that.'

This had taken some of the gloss off the excitement of her new posting, though Henry Boswell, her direct boss – a nice, well-meaning man, looking forward to his retirement – had tried his best to cheer her up. 'It's a marvellous opportunity,' he said, about her temporary move to the other side of the river, but she sensed he had no idea what it was all about.

Peggy couldn't help wondering why, if it were such an important job, Fane himself hadn't briefed her on it. And why (Peggy was being honest with herself) they were lending MI5 someone so junior. Part of her wondered whether MI6 had already decided they did not need her particular skills and whether she was just a pawn in some personnel deal between the two services.

But no, there was a real enough job to do. The following day at Thames House, Charles Wetherby had talked to her for over half an hour. He'd been friendly, and had answered all her questions seemingly very frankly. Wetherby had the rare ability to talk to someone as junior as Peggy as if she were his equal. After her session with him, she was no longer in any doubt about the importance in Wetherby's eyes of what she was going to be doing.

He had explained that Peggy would be working with Liz Carlyle, an experienced and extremely talented investigator, he said, who had particular skills in assessing people. Liz would be leading their two-man team and they would be working direct to him. He would be keeping Geoffrey Fane informed of what they were doing. As Wetherby explained the situation, Peggy began to understand why she had been chosen. She would be following the paper trail and supporting Liz as she made her investigations. This made perfect sense to Peggy. She knew and loved the world of print, fact, data, information – pick your own word, thought Peggy – that was what brought out her skills. It was her métier. She could disinter information which might seem meaningless and sterile to others, then, like a primitive fire maker blowing on a spark, bring it to life. Peggy saw drama where others saw dust.

Peggy Kinsolving had been a shy, serious child, with freckles and round spectacles. A cheerful aunt had once called her Bobbity Bookworm and this had stuck in the family, so that from the age of seven, everybody called her Bobby. She had taken her nickname with her to her school, one of the few remaining Midlands grammar schools, and on to Oxford. At the end of three years' hard work she had a good 2:1 in English and vague scholarly ambitions. There was not enough money in the family to support her through a DPhil so she left Oxford with no very clear idea of what to do next. At that stage of her life Peggy was certain of only two things: if you did your best and stuck at it, things would turn out well, and you should not put up with anything you didn't like. Accordingly she had reverted firmly to the name Peggy.

For want of any better idea Peggy had taken a post with a private library in Manchester. The understanding was that she would assist the readers half the time and the rest of the time was hers. But since only an average of five people a day made use of her services, she had been largely free to pursue her own research into the life and writings of a nineteenth-century Lancashire social reformer and novelist. Why had it palled so fast? For one thing, her topic turned out to be rather drier than she had expected, with not enough facts to satisfy her voracious appetite for detail. For another her days were overwhelmingly solitary, and she had found no way of peopling her evenings. The Miss Haversham-like librarian rarely exchanged a word with her and scuttled off home as soon as the library closed. From this solitude came a growing conviction that however vivid a world she found in books and manuscripts, the world she saw when she lifted her head from the pages was tantalisingly more promising if only she could find a way into it.

She knew she had to leave, and the obvious alternative was London, where her manifest skills earned her an interview, and then an offer of a job, as a research assistant in the British

Library. But the clinical, subdued atmosphere of the modern reading rooms struck her as even less acceptable than the tensions of a working day with Miss Haversham and she never knew what she would have done if an old acquaintance from college had not come into the library one day and told her of a specialised government department that was looking for researchers.

Which was how, at the age of twenty-five, still with round spectacles and freckles, Peggy came to be sitting in the conference room in Thames House next to Liz Carlyle, with half-drunk cups of coffee and a plate of biscuits on the table before them, along with several stacks of file folders, which Peggy had already accumulated after only six days in the job.

Though initially Peggy had approached her with some caution, she had liked Liz from the start. Peggy's previous boss in the library, although herself female, had seemed to resent her on grounds both of age and gender. But Liz was younger, Liz was polite; best of all, Liz was straightforward. Peggy felt from the start they were a team, and the division of labour was clear. Liz would focus on interviews, while Peggy would do the research.

She had spent her first days with B Branch, the personnel department, reading files, taking notes, organising a hunt, which her unfamiliarity with the records system made more difficult than she expected. Liz was going to Rotterdam the next day, and had asked Peggy to brief her on her progress before she went. She handed Liz the first of what she knew were going to be many, many documents. This is the beginning, Peggy thought to herself. But what if there is no needle in the haystack?

Liz was surprised. There were only five employees of MI5 who had attended Oxford during the first half of the nineties, and she knew three of them. Perhaps not so remarkable as they were broadly the same age as she was. She looked again at the list Peggy had handed her:

Michael Binding
Patrick Dobson
Judith Spratt
Tom Dartmouth
Stephen Ogasawara

Peggy had done well, thought Liz. She had taken very little time to get used to what must seem a very alien environment.

'I know Michael Binding,' Liz announced. 'And Judith Spratt.' A friend, she almost said, but didn't. 'Tom Dartmouth I've only just met – he's recently come back from Pakistan. He was seconded to MI6 there for a while. Like you in reverse. And Patrick Dobson was at a meeting I went to yesterday.' She handed back the list to Peggy. 'What's Dobson's job exactly?'

Peggy found his file. 'His job is special liaison with the Home Office on operational matters. Degree from Pembroke College in Theology.' Liz groaned and Peggy gave an unexpectedly lively laugh. Thank God she's got a sense of humour, thought Liz. Peggy continued: 'He's married. Two children. Very active in his local church.'

Liz suppressed another groan and tried not to roll her eyes. 'Right. And Stephen Ogasawara. What have you got on him?'

Peggy found another file. 'He read History at Wadham. Then – unusual this – he joined the Army. Six years in the Royal Signals. Served in Northern Ireland,' she said, pausing meaningfully. 'As the name suggests, he's got a Japanese father. But he was born in Bath.'

'What's his job now?'

'He's not here any more.'

'Oh?'

'No, he left three years ago.'

'What did he go into? A private security firm?' With that mix of military and MI5 experience, Ogasawara was probably making a small fortune as a consultant in Iraq, thought Liz. Though he might not live long enough to enjoy it.

'Not quite,' said Peggy. 'It says here that he now manages a dance troupe in King's Lynn.'

'How exotic,' said Liz, suppressing a smile.

Peggy asked, 'Can I take him off the list?'

'Yes,' said Liz, then thought again. 'Actually, better not. But you can certainly put him low down.' She glanced at her watch. 'You should have plenty to do while I'm in Rotterdam.' Liz gestured towards the files.

'I thought I'd double-check their original applications to join MI5. And check the facts in the updates too.'

'Yes, you might as well go through the basics. And read their references.' Liz looked again a little anxiously at her watch. 'I think we should probably see as many of the referees as we can. Look out for anything on the personal front that looks unusual. And obviously, any kind of Irish connection.'

As Liz got up from the table to go, Peggy said, 'Do you mind if I ask who you're seeing in Rotterdam?'

'Not at all,' Liz said. She had already decided that if they were going to work closely together, she would need to be able to tell Peggy everything. 'I'm seeing a man called James Maguire. He was our source for the story that the IRA had put a secret asset into the security services. The officer he gave that information to is dead, so Maguire is the one person in the world, apart from us and the mole himself, who knows about it.'

'Do you think he can help us?'

Liz thought for a moment. 'Possibly. The question is whether he will. He didn't want to meet me.'

'Well good luck then,' said Peggy.

'Thanks,' said Liz, her lips pursed. 'I have a feeling I'll need it.'

8

The water in the Old Harbour of Rotterdam was sea green, and slopped against the sides of the canal boats and small tugs moored at one end. It was twilight in mid-May, the air was mild, and the light rain felt soft on her face. Liz looked out across the small body of water, relic of the age when it had been the city's main port. Levelled by bombing in the War, Rotterdam was almost entirely modern; its inhabitants had decided not to reconstruct the city as it had been before 1939 but instead to start from scratch. The results were architecturally renowned but bleak to look at; this genuinely old sector of the city was a small sanctuary from the relentlessly new.

The cafe across the harbour was on the ground floor of an old building of dark brick, and lit inside by wall lamps which cast a rich orange glow; at the tables on the veranda candles in bowls provided the sole illumination. Although she had only mug shots from which to identify him, Liz was confident he was not among the cafe's few customers. But as the dark now moved in as if by stealth, she suddenly saw him. A tall figure, lean to the point of gauntness, walking slowly along the far edge of the harbour towards the cafe. He wore khaki trousers and a long raincoat that hung loosely from its padded shoulders, and he carried a newspaper rolled up under one arm.

Liz gave him five minutes to settle, then moved quickly around the perimeter of the harbour, and into the cafe. She spotted him at a corner table and, as the man looked up and nodded, Liz sat down across from him, putting her own coat on an empty chair. She said, 'Hello, Mr Maguire. I'm Jane Falconer.'

The man called Maguire didn't say hello, only remarking curtly, 'I hope you were careful coming here.'

She had certainly been careful. Liz had flown to Amsterdam rather than direct to Rotterdam's small airport, then pursued a standard tourist agenda – a taxi straight to the Rijksmuseum, a tour of the Anne Frank house, and lunch outdoors at a canal-side bistro near Dam Square. Then a train to Rotterdam and – Liz had been particularly careful at that point – an unaccompanied walk to the Old Harbour. She sighed inwardly at the time-consuming nature of it all.

Liz felt at some disadvantage, with her limited experience of the Province. Maguire was used to dealing with old Northern Ireland hands – like Ricky Perrins and Michael Binding. All men and all veterans of the insular yet vastly complicated world of that conflict. Liz couldn't even pretend to follow all its ins and outs.

But then I don't have to, she told herself, deciding she could use her comparative ignorance to advantage. She was not operating in the traditional framework of the place, because all had changed. She was going to have to appeal to Maguire on personal grounds. The question was whether he could respond to that, or whether he would regard his involvement as over, now peace of a kind held in Northern Ireland.

'I was careful,' she assured him.

He looked unappeased. 'I thought I'd made it clear I told everything I know to your colleague Rob Petch,' he said, using Ricky Perrins's working alias.

'I'm sure you did,' said Liz, 'but Rob's dead.' You know that, thought Liz. She had told him when she'd rung him, trying to arrange this meeting.

'I'm sure he reported what I'd said,' said Maguire, giving no ground.

Liz nodded in acknowledgement of this, but then said firmly, 'I wanted to hear the story from you direct. Just in case Rob left something out that could help.'

'Help with what? I told him, Keaney's secret asset, whoever they were, was never activated. I really don't see what you want from me.' His voice was starting to rise. Liz looked anxiously around for a waiter, and one came over – a tall, moustachioed man in a white apron.

'*Kaffe*?' asked Liz, trying to recall her ten words of Dutch.

The waiter looked down at her with ill-disguised amusement. 'White or black, madam?' he said in flawless English. They might have been at the Savoy.

'White please,' she said with a smile. She had forgotten the essential bilingualism of the Dutch. They listened to the *Today* programme and watched the ITN news, and read more English-language novels than all the inhabitants of London. One of Liz's friends from university had lived for six months in Amsterdam and never felt the need to learn a word of Dutch, such was the natives' aptitude for English.

Maguire still looked angry. Liz decided to use the waiter's intervention to change the subject. 'Is Rotterdam a favourite place of yours?'

Maguire shrugged to show his indifference, but then grudgingly started to talk. 'It's where I would have wanted to relocate if I ever got blown. Though Rob always said it would have to be further away. Assuming they didn't catch me first, of course.' He looked at Liz; they both knew what he meant. In the pre-peace years, without exception every informer the IRA had unearthed and managed to get hold of had been murdered.

'Why Holland?' asked Liz, keen to keep the man talking.

'I look a bit Dutch, I suppose,' he said. 'I feel I blend in here.' Viewing his features – ruddy cheeks, the thinning sandy hair, blue eyes – Liz saw the truth in this. Maguire could pass for a senior lecturer at the local university. All he needed was a pipe.

'Is that why you wanted to meet here?'

'Only partly.' He stared out at the harbour with a hard look in his eyes. 'I hope they wouldn't kill me now, if they knew we were talking – or knew that for years I talked to your colleagues. But it seemed safer on the whole to meet outside Ireland.'

Liz wanted to keep him away from talk of danger. She needed to engage his curiosity instead of his fear. Make him think, Liz thought, get him interested. 'Tell me,' she said, 'what do you think happened to the person Keaney recruited?'

'What you mean is, do I think they're still there?' said Maguire almost contemptuously.

'Among other things, I suppose,' Liz said with a diffidence she didn't feel. Don't let him take over the interview, she told herself. 'Assuming Keaney's story is true.'

'Why does it matter?' asked Maguire irritably. 'There couldn't have been any damage done, could there? If there really was a mole in place, it's pretty hard to see what good it did Keaney and his pals.'

He stopped when he noticed that Liz was shaking her head. He looked at her, curiosity subduing contempt, and Liz said sharply, 'You're missing the point.' There was no reason to try to appease this man, she decided. 'Keaney probably never expected his plant to help the IRA directly – after all, he couldn't be sure they'd ever do work on Northern Ireland, could he?

'It was subtler than that. Keaney probably found an entry-level person. Someone flagged as a high-flyer, with the potential to rise within the organisation. An Oxford graduate, presumably, who might in the course of time be able to do a lot of damage. I don't suppose the aim was to help the IRA directly; the objective was to screw up the Brits in some way or another.'

Maguire looked intrigued by this, but equally clearly wasn't going to say so. Instead he argued, 'I can't believe Ireland is top of the agenda these days. The war is over. So what does it matter. I'd have thought it was imams you were after, not Irish.'

Liz shrugged. 'That's the worry of course. That it all gets ignored in a post-9/11 age. Then it starts up again. It's done that often enough before.'

'You think this mole might be active? Even today?' Maguire sounded interested now despite himself.

It was Liz's turn to shrug. 'There's no reason to think a person like that would want a ceasefire, is there?'

The waiter brought Liz's coffee over, and as they waited for him to go, Maguire seemed to check himself. 'I don't believe it,' he declared. The look he gave Liz was unfriendly. 'And, in any case, it's your problem. I've passed on Keaney's message as he asked. And that's it, as far as I'm concerned. I don't care what you do with it.'

Liz said quietly, 'I was hoping you might be able to help,' then concentrated on stirring her coffee, which was hot despite the layer of rich cream at the top of the cup.

'What could I possibly do?' demanded Maguire indignantly. 'Even if I wanted to.'

'Help us find out who Keaney recruited.'

'What makes you think I can do that?'

'Maybe you can't,' Liz admitted. 'But you're better placed than we are to find out. You say Keaney said the mole was recruited at Oxford. There must have been some link between Keaney and the University, but it's not exactly an obvious one to us.'

'Keaney hated my guts.'

'Yes, but you *knew* him. We couldn't get close. At least you can try.'

'Why don't you use another of your touts?' he added caustically, 'I'm sure you've got plenty to choose from. Use someone Keaney trusted.'

'We couldn't do that without telling the person about the mole. Too big a risk. You must see that.'

Maguire ignored her. Suddenly he demanded, 'What's in it for me?'

She didn't even bother to reply. He had never asked for money, and she didn't think he wanted to be paid now. It was just a way of deflecting her request.

Maguire went on. 'What would I be helping, can you tell me that? The situation's changed completely. Whoever this person was, there's nothing they could do to hurt you – or help the IRA. The world's moved on. The war's over. So why do you need me? Other than to help you close the file?'

Liz took a deep breath. Instinct told her that her only chance of winning Maguire's support was to level with him.

'You know as well as I do, Mr Maguire,' she said, 'the war's not over. It's just reached a different stage. I don't need to give you a lecture on the history of the IRA. Or on the nature of treachery,' she added. She saw Maguire flinch. 'Everyone has their reasons, and treachery is nearly always also loyalty. But what matters is the nature of the cause we're loyal to. That's why we need to find this person. Their cause, whatever it is now, is not ours. Nor yours either, Mr Maguire. This is unfinished business. And I'm not talking about the file.'

Again the shrug, superficially uninterested, but this time Liz could see Maguire was thinking. Finally he spoke, and for the first time there was pathos instead of anger in his voice, 'But don't you see, *I'm* finished business? I just want to be left alone.'

And before Liz could reply, he stood up. Without saying a word, he threw some euros on the table and walked away. Liz took another sip of her coffee; it was cooler now. She looked with near despair at the money Maguire had left on the table. And to think she had believed she was getting somewhere.

9

Dennis Rudge was sitting at the wheel of a taxi parked at a rank in the middle of Capel Street. He had a cup of coffee in one hand and a copy of the *Sun* propped on the dashboard. His radio, tuned to Magic FM, was quietly playing soft pop, with occasional voice interruptions, which sounded to passers-by like traffic updates. From where he sat he had a clear view of the bookshop and of Doris's shop front across the road. He was in eye contact with Maureen Hayes and Lebert Johnson, sitting at a table outside the Red Lion pub further down the street. Lebert, who had a glass of something brown in front of him, was doing the *Daily Mail* crossword. Maureen was drinking mineral water, knitting and listening through headphones apparently to her iPod. In the other direction Alpha 4 and Alpha 5 were sitting in a dirty Peugeot 307, bickering noisily whenever anyone came past. Further members of A4 were parked up strategically in side roads, and a couple more cars were circling around the area.

In Doris Feldman's sitting room, above her ironmonger's shop, sat Wally Woods, comfortably ensconced in Doris's armchair, with Esther the ancient cat sharing his knee with a powerful pair of binoculars.

Doris's telephone call to the police five days before at three in the morning had turned out to be a blessing in disguise. As always with A2's surreptitious entries, Special Branch had been told in advance about the operation. Hearing from uniform of

Doris's 999 call, they had promptly rung in to discuss the options with A2 control. The priority was clearly to reassure the caller, and one option was simply to explain that the 'burglary' she'd seen was entirely innocent: the fuses had blown and the owner had sent in friends to replace them – something like that. The Special Branch men were adept at making up plausible stories. But if in the normal course of a day she mentioned the events of the weekend to the bookshop owner, it would be disastrous.

So they had decided to take a risk with the old woman, and at half-past three on Saturday morning, the officer from Special Branch sat in Doris Feldman's sitting room drinking tea and explaining, in the vaguest possible terms, that there were strange happenings going on across the street, which he and his colleagues were trying to find out about. A mention of 9/11 here, a reference to Islamic fundamentalism there, and Doris had readily agreed not to say a word. More important, she happily allowed the use of the flat, which was ideally situated as a static surveillance point. That was how Wally Woods came to be sitting in her armchair, with his colleague at her dining-room table manning the communications. He sat like a spider at the centre of her web, liaising with the people on the street, and with a perfect view of the bookshop.

Coordinating the whole operation was Reggie Purvis in Thames House. He and a couple of colleagues were controlling the A4 teams and all the communications from the Operations Room, at the same time ignoring Dave Armstrong, who sat waiting impatiently beside them. Behind him, Tom Dartmouth paced back and forth, and from time to time, Wetherby came into the room to check progress.

In Doris's flat, Wally Woods sat on, patiently waiting. Just before three o'clock a minicab pulled up in front of the bookshop. The driver, a young Middle Eastern man, got out on the street side and walked around to open the passenger door. After a moment, a much older man got out of the car. He was dressed in a white smock and wore on his head a white cap, with lines of gold thread. As he walked slowly towards the bookshop, the young man ran ahead and held the door open for him.

'Fox One has arrived and is now inside,' said Wally and the man at the table immediately spoke into the microphone. 'All teams alert,' said Reggie Purvis in Thames House. 'Fox One is in. Repeat Fox One is in.'

Nothing obvious changed in the immediate vicinity of the shop, though Dennis Rudge drained his coffee and Maureen put away her knitting. A4 were ready for whatever might happen, which only added to the tension since there was nothing to do but wait.

In Thames House, Judith Spratt arrived in the Operations Room. A tall woman, she had fine features and always looked effortlessly elegant whatever the circumstances.

'There's been a phone call,' she announced to Dave and Tom Dartmouth. 'To the bookshop. It didn't last very long.'

'Who was it?' Tom Dartmouth demanded.

'Hard to say. The owner of the bookshop answered, and the caller asked if Rashid was there. He asked in English.'

'Who the hell is Rashid?' asked Dave.

Judith shrugged, as if to say 'you tell me'. 'The owner said there was no one by that name in the shop. Then the caller hung up.'

Tom asked, 'Do we know who made the call? Anything come up on the eavesdropping?'

'Nothing from the mikes. No sound of Fox One at all. Just casual chat and cups of coffee from others in there. But the trace just came through. It's an Amsterdam number. I'll get on to it now. Give me ten minutes.' She picked up the phone.

In the AIVD office in Amsterdam, Pieter Abbink was reaching for the phone when it rang. Picking it up quickly, he said tersely, 'Abbink.'

'Pieter, it's Judith Spratt. From London.'

Abbink laughed out loud. 'I had my hand on the telephone to call you when it rang.'

'Why was that?'

'We have a surveillance on a house here in Amsterdam. Not so good people. We've had a lot of chatter lately coming out of there. Internet, and some telephone. Somebody in the house just called a London number, and I was about to dial and ask if you could find out where it was.'

'It's an Islamic bookshop in North London. And also a meeting place for some people we'd like to locate. They were meant to show up today, but they're late.'

'Do you know who they are?'

'No, and that's the problem. They've been sighted once by one of ours, but we don't have any names. Though your caller asked for Rashid.'

Abbink chuckled. 'That is a very big help – it's like asking for Jan here in Holland.'

'I know. But it looks like there is some connection with Holland.'

'We'll check the database, don't worry. But why don't I send you the photo bank?'

'You read my mind, Pieter. That's why I was calling you.'

By three-thirty, Wally Woods had told Thames House three times that the men hadn't shown, and by four o'clock, Reggie Purvis was focused on keeping his teams alert. He sent Maureen and Lebert Johnson off in Dennis Rudge's taxi and directed the arguing couple to drive round the neighbourhood, keeping close by. When at last the Imam left the bookshop, his departure was greeted with relief by the A4 teams as they slotted in neatly behind him.

But the departure of the Imam meant the three young men were not going to show. Purvis kept his people deployed nonetheless, waiting forlornly until six o'clock when the staff went home and the shop closed. Wally Woods left his armchair to his colleague – a substitute would take over at eight that night – and went back to Thames House. The only lead lay with the Imam. Please God, thought Dave, still in the Operations Room, let him take us to them.

One hour later Charles Wetherby, having joined Tom Dartmouth and Dave Armstrong in the Operations Room, was dismayed (but not entirely surprised) to learn that Abu Sayed had been driven straight to Heathrow Airport, where he had checked in for a flight to Frankfurt on the first leg of his journey to Lahore.

To his seeming indifference, Abu Sayed had been upgraded to club class. At security no apparent attention was paid to his carry-on bag, and he positively sailed through passport control.

His one piece of checked luggage, an ancient but sturdy Samsonite case, received greater scrutiny. Deftly plucked from the conveyor belt in the outgoing luggage shed, it was inspected with a fine-tooth comb by no less than two veteran customs officers and an attending officer from Special Branch, looking for anything that might indicate the identity and whereabouts of the three young men who had failed to show up at the bookshop that afternoon.

They found nothing. Indeed, the only evidence at all that the Imam had even been in England lay in a neat stack at the very bottom of his suitcase. Whatever else Mahmood Abu Sayed had got up to during his stay, he had managed to find time to buy six new pairs of boxer shorts from the Marble Arch branch of Marks & Spencer.

10

The city of dreaming spires looked wide awake to Liz. The sky was a rich enamel blue, and the temperature was moving into an almost summery seventy degrees as she and a half-breathless Peggy Kinsolving mounted the wooden staircase of the Sheldonian. It was hard to believe graduation ceremonies took place in the small area of this strange old building. Built by Christopher Wren, according to Peggy, when he was only thirty-one years old.

Arriving at the top, Liz and Peggy stood in a painted wooden cupola and looked out at a very different view of Oxford from the dense, almost claustrophobic world seen at ground level. Here church spires and college towers jutted like projectiles to form a jagged historical skyline.

Looking down, Liz watched the groups of tourists thronging the pavements of Broad Street – or the Broad as Peggy called it. Cars were parked in a neat line in the wide belly of the street, and a few others moved gingerly along, more in hope than expectation of a space, eventually coming full circle since the street was blocked at the far end by heavy bollards.

She looked across at Blackwell's bookshop, where she and Peggy had browsed for a few minutes. It was nice to have this brief interlude, thought Liz. They had driven down together in Liz's car, after she had collected Peggy from the flat she shared with two old college friends on the less salubrious side of Kilburn. Going against the London-bound traffic they made good time, then fought their way through a maddening one-way system and parked in a vast open car park on the western side of Oxford city centre. They walked up past the old prison, now finding new life as a luxury hotel, and into a shopping street indistinguishable in its frontage of chain stores from any other in England. But then they turned into a dark, narrow street of Dickensian houses, complete with overhanging shadows and protruding beams. A further turn and they were at Pembroke College, their first stop.

It was a seventeenth-century foundation with medieval bits, according to Peggy, who had swotted up diligently the day before. More obscure than its namesake in Cambridge, it nonetheless numbered among its distinguished alumni the writer Thomas Browne, Samuel Johnson, and more recently Michael Heseltine.

They were directed by a porter through an old quad, with a small square of tended lawn. On the far wall, window boxes were filled with early geraniums. They walked on into another quad and there against the wall of the older part of the College sat a small statue of a woman, hands folded in prayer or lament. Not a good omen, thought Liz, thinking of the impending interview. She was not conventionally religious, and wondered a little nervously what role theology was going to play in the conversation.

Chaplain Hickson turned out to be an enormous man, with a vast beer belly and a thick curly beard, more Friar Tuck than the ascetic theologian Liz had expected. A Northerner, he was jolly and startlingly impious, greeting Liz and Peggy effusively before offering them coffee or – 'since the sun is over the yardarm in France' – a glass of sherry.

Both Liz and Peggy opted for coffee, and perching on a pair

of uncomfortable chairs, held stained mugs of Nescafé while the chaplain hunted high and low for some biscuits. Only when he found them, after several minutes' searching, did their interview begin. He sat down with a happy thump on the sofa, putting a plateful of chocolate digestives within easy reach. By this time Liz had formed the distinct impression that for Chaplain Hickson, material sustenance was more important than prayer.

Liz began by explaining their visit was strictly a formality, to update the original vetting. She had worried, back in London, whether a man of the cloth would be willing to speak freely about a former student's personal life, particularly as it was the morally dubious aspects of that life she most needed to know about. But the chaplain was happy to talk about the young Patrick Dobson.

'He took things very seriously and he worked extremely hard. Nothing wrong with that,' he added with a rolling laugh that suggested there was. 'But it did distance him a bit from some of the others. There was something almost middle-aged about the boy.'

'Nothing wild about him then?' said Liz with a faint smile.

'Certainly not. On every count, he was a model citizen.' He grabbed a biscuit from the plate. 'He joined the Young Conservatives, ate all his suppers in Hall, and avoided temptation. There were no women in his life – not, I should add, because of disinclination on his part. It's just that he was hardly irresistible to the fairer sex. Funny how that seems to happen, isn't it?'

'How did you come to know him so well?' Liz asked, a little taken aback by this very personal portrait.

'He came to chapel a lot. Every week, sometimes on

Wednesday.' He grimaced slightly. 'It may sound odd coming from me, but I found him a little *too* religious, if you know what I mean. Pretty uncommon among lads that age, especially at Oxford.'

'Did he confide in you?'

For the first time the chaplain looked startled. '*Me*? Oh no. You see, there was something of a class divide between us.'

'Really?' asked Liz. If she remembered rightly, Dobson's background was anything but patrician. Or was Hickson suggesting his own was? Looking at this biscuit-loving mountain of a man, she found it hard to believe.

'You see, young Patrick came from a working-class family. By dint of his admittedly healthy-sized brain he managed to win a scholarship to an independent school. There, he developed not only his mind, but' – the chaplain waved a finger, and Liz could see he was starting to enjoy himself – 'a precocious sense of social advancement.'

'I see,' said Liz, masking her amusement.

'At Oxford these aspirations continued. He liked to wear a *jumper* most days,' Hickson continued, almost joyfully stressing the word's initial 'j', 'and sometimes even sported his old school tie. On Sundays, you would see him wearing a checked tweed suit which, he once told someone, was of the sort worn by "gentlemen in the country".' Hickson looked at Liz with a twinkle in his eye. 'You can imagine how much his fellow students loved that.'

'Was that the class difference you mentioned?' asked Peggy, who had stayed silent until now. She looked puzzled.

'Oh, there was no difference to begin with. We were both common as muck,' the chaplain said with a generous grin. 'The thing is, I still am. I'm amazed they have me here. I suppose it's a form of political correctness.' And this time he gave such a laugh that it shook the sofa.

Leaving a few minutes later, after declining another offer of sherry, Liz wondered whether the chaplain's mocking portrait of Dobson provided real grounds for concern. Clearly Dobson had been an earnest, slightly geeky undergraduate, so intent on erasing the traces of his humble origins that, paradoxically, it made him stand out rather than fit in. Liz was uneasy about someone who had invented a persona for himself – checked tweed suit indeed – since if they could base their life on a lie, what would keep them from basing it on more than one?

At the same time, Liz found herself almost sorry for someone so obviously unsure of himself, amused as she had been by the chaplain's satirical account. After all, she thought, remembering the unhappiness of her teenage years, if being a social misfit in late adolescence was grounds for suspicion, Liz would be a prime suspect in her own investigation.

They'd moved on to Somerville College, where they found Judith Spratt's old tutor, an elegant bluestocking named Isabella Prideaux, who must have been near retirement age. In her ground-floor room, with French doors overlooking the enormous quad, Isabella gave a brief and laudatory account of Judith's time as an undergraduate. She seemed to know where her ex-pupil had ended up. 'She keeps in touch,' she said, adding proudly, 'but then, most of my students do.'

They had met at twelve-thirty. After half an hour the ground had been covered, and Liz started to make her excuses, thinking that she and Peggy would go and find a sandwich somewhere. So it came as a small embarrassment when it became clear they were expected to stay for lunch. Peggy looked quizzically at Liz, but there seemed no polite way out, and they trooped to a small dining room near the larger hall.

Here conversation about Judith Spratt was not on the menu, since they sat surrounded by Fellows of the College. Most of them seemed to be men – somewhat to Liz's surprise, since her view of Somerville had been formed by Dorothy Sayers's *Gaudy Night*. After a lengthy disquisition from a Physics lecturer seated next to her about the beauty of quarks, Liz was glad to escape with her host and Peggy for coffee to the Fellows' Common Room, where they managed to occupy a quiet corner by themselves. 'I'm sorry about Professor Burrell,' Miss Prideaux said to Liz, who realised she must mean her lunch partner. 'When I listen to him he might as well be speaking in Urdu.'

They chatted on for a while, then, just as Liz and Peggy were about to go, Miss Prideaux suddenly said out of the blue, 'I was awfully sorry to hear about Ravi.'

Liz's ears pricked up now. 'Yes?' she said.

'I know it sounds old-fashioned, but I do think these inter-racial alliances are always more fragile.' When Liz didn't say anything, Miss Prideaux flushed slightly, perhaps worried that she sounded racist or indiscreet, or both. She made a show of looking at her watch. 'Goodness me, here I am gossiping, and I've got a finalist in hysterics about her Anglo-Saxon paper waiting for me.'

Now, as they stood admiring the view from the top of the Sheldonian, Peggy asked Liz, 'What did Miss Prideaux mean when she said she was sorry about Ravi?'

Liz shrugged. 'I'm not sure. Ravi is Judith Spratt's husband. His name is Ravi Singh; Judith uses her maiden name at work.'

'I gathered that,' said Peggy. 'What does he do?'

'He's a businessman, from India originally. They've been married a long time – I think they met at Oxford. He's charming.'

'Oh, so you know him?'

'A bit. I've been to dinner there a few times.'

Peggy nodded. 'It's difficult, isn't it? There's nothing in Judith's file that says her marital status has changed.'

Liz sighed. She supposed this was the inevitable downside of investigating your colleagues. 'We'd better find out for sure then. Hopefully it's nothing.' But mentally she made a note to talk to B Branch the following day.

Their last interview was in Merton College, which they approached down a narrow alleyway running off the High. The change in tempo from the bustle of a main street to a backwater of almost medieval calm was sudden. As they turned onto the wobbly cobblestones of Merton Street, Liz saw a small churchyard, with a path lined by several magnificent cherry trees. She imagined that this view would not have changed for five hundred years.

His name was Hilary Watts. *Professor* Watts to me, thought Liz, since he seemed to expect that kind of deference. He was an old-school Arabist with, inevitably, strong Foreign Office connections – he had taught summer school at MECAS, the famous Centre for Arabic Studies in the hills above Beirut, and tutored the more obscure relatives of Jordan's King Hussein when they came for a final polishing stint to Oxford.

And he had played a long-time role, in the age before open recruitment, as a talent spotter for MI6. He had taught Tom Dartmouth for his postgraduate degree, and been asked for a reference by MI5 when his ex-pupil had applied. The reference, reeking of a past era of old boys' network and public-school prose, had been three lines long, written on the back of a postcard from the Accademia in Venice: *Sound chap. Good languages. More than clever enough for the domestic service.*

'Domestic service' – once the prevalent Six view of MI5. Small surprise that Watts had not risen when she and Peggy had knocked on his door, but merely called out a peremptory 'Come in'.

Entering, the two women found themselves in a dark room with high ceilings and one vast mullioned window at the far wall, which let very little light in since the curtains – thick velvet but badly in need of cleaning – were half drawn across. The Professor sat in an ancient wing chair, its covers faded to a dull sage. He faced the small slit of undraped window, through which he gazed out at the lush grass of a playing field in Christ Church Meadow.

'Do sit down,' he said, pointing to a long settee that ran at right angles to his chair. Obeying him, they positioned themselves carefully, and Liz examined the man, who continued to look out at the meadow. It was an aged but distinguished face, with a long aquiline nose that was sprinkled with veins, high concave cheekbones, and small darting eyes of vivid blue. He tilted his head onto one shoulder and took them both in. 'Ladies,' he said shortly. 'How can I be of assistance to you?'

Liz noticed that his hand was holding a pipe, and he lifted it now and made a show of knocking out the bowl. Bits of ash scattered over his thick trousers, and he brushed them away irritably while Liz explained they were there to ask him about Tom Dartmouth.

'Oh Tom,' he said. 'Gifted fellow. Came to me for the lingo, though he was already good at it.'

At this he nodded and puffed leisurely at his pipe. Liz asked gently, 'Had you known him as an undergraduate?'

Watts detached the stem with palpable reluctance from his lips. 'I don't teach undergraduates,' he said with a shake of his head. 'But Mason at Balliol said young Dartmouth took the best First in PPE that year.'

'Was there anything distinctive about Tom? Anything you remember as unusual?'

'All my students are unusual,' he said matter-of-factly.

Peggy looked sideways at Liz. Liz had to admire the self-confidence of this dinosaur; it was so pronounced that it did not even sound boastful.

'I'm sure they are,' acknowledged Liz mildly. 'But I wondered if there was anything in particular you remembered about Tom.'

This time Watts seemed happy to take his pipe out. He said sharply, 'Only that he was a disappointment.'

Surprised, Liz asked, 'Why was that?'

'I thought he had the makings of a very fine Arabist. He could have done a DPhil in no time – these days you've got to have one for a university post.'

Was that it? wondered Liz. Watts was cross with Tom because he'd left the land of academe. 'Was that very disappointing?'

'What?' demanded Watts, sounding annoyed. 'That he didn't want to teach? No no, it wasn't that. God knows the world isn't short of academics.'

He looked slightly miffed, as if recalling some slight, and Liz decided not to press him. Though a large part of her wanted to say to this preposterous relic of an earlier age, 'Come out with it. Tell us just how Tom Dartmouth – *best First in his year*, *gifted chap*, *one of us*, *etc etc* – let you, his mentor, down.'

But she didn't have long to wait. With a show of regret that struck Liz as wholly insincere, Watts said slowly, 'I arranged for him to see my friends in London.' For the first time he looked directly at Liz, his eyes opaque, uninterested. 'Your counterparts.'

Six, thought Liz. Certainly the obvious place for a high-flying Arabist. 'What happened?' she asked, discovering that this veteran of the old school was annoying her as much as she clearly annoyed him. Thank God the shutters have opened, she thought, thinking of the comparatively transparent conduct of the intelligence world these days.

Now Watts took his time responding, as if to teach Liz that she was not really in charge of the interview. Eventually he said, 'The boy wasn't interested. I thought at first that meant he wanted to join the Foreign Office, have a proper diplomatic career. But no, not at all. "What is it then?" I asked him. "Money?" I could understand that – he would earn a fortune helping some bank trying to get established in the Middle East. But no it wasn't that either.' Watts paused, as if revolted by the memory. When he spoke again it was with his pipe stem half in his mouth, so he was quite literally biting his words. 'He told me he wanted to work for you people. On the home front is how he put it to me. Said he wanted to tackle the security threats direct. I asked him if he'd really worked so hard and done so well in order to become some kind of bloody policeman.'

Out of nowhere, Peggy piped up for only the second time that day. 'What did Tom say?'

Watts turned and gave Peggy a contemptuous look for her

impertinence. Patronising old buffer, thought Liz, he'd have an absolute heart attack if he knew Peggy was from Six.

He spoke now with an angry current to his voice, 'He laughed, and said I didn't understand.' From Watts's expression, it was clear this was the ultimate sin.

11

Back in London early that evening, Liz dropped Peggy off and drove straight home. She took an unenthusiastic look at the sparse contents of her fridge and decided she wasn't feeling hungry. The light on her answering machine was blinking, and reluctantly she went across to play back the messages, hoping that it wasn't someone from the office. She was tired: what she wanted more than anything else was a deep bath, a large vodka tonic, and bed.

The voice on the phone was faint and slightly hesitant. It took Liz, still contemplating her various meetings in the day, several seconds to realise it was her mother. She was talking about the nursery – how it was suddenly busy after the long flat winter.

Then her voice changed gear, sounding almost artificially light, as if keen to deal quickly with a less pleasant subject. 'Barlow rang,' her mother said, and Liz's ears pricked up. He was her mother's GP. 'Those tests have come back and he wants me to come in. Such a bore.' There was a pause. 'Anyway, give me a ring, darling, when you can. Though I'm just off now, but I'll be in tomorrow night.'

This was not good news. Her mother was a reluctant patient, who saw her GP only when all else – stiff upper lip, hot toddies, simple stoicism – had failed. Barlow must be insisting she come in to see him, which was worrying.

Liz poured herself a stiffish vodka. She was turning on the bath taps when the phone rang.

It was Dave Armstrong. 'Hi Liz, where have you been?' he asked. 'I've been looking for you all day.'

'I've been doing something for Charles,' she said. Feeling unwilling to explain further, she changed the subject. 'Any luck with the photos?'

'Not yet, but there are more coming.'

'How's our friend?'

'Okay so far.' The odds of their conversation being intercepted by the wrong people were virtually nil, but like everyone in their profession they had an inbuilt wariness of the telephone.

'I was trying to find you,' said Dave, 'to say I had to see a contact in Islington. I was going to offer to buy you the world's best Indian meal. The offer's still open.'

'Oh that's nice of you,' she said, 'but I can barely keep my eyes open. I'd be terrible company. Let's make it another time.'

'No problem,' Dave said, habitually cheerful. 'See you back at the farm.'

Liz went to check her bath. It was true she was tired, yet most times she would have joined Dave anyway, since she always liked his company. Tonight, however, with the worry about her mother, she wouldn't have enjoyed herself.

Getting into the bath, she thought, I have to do something about this room. Unwisely, when she'd bought the flat she had decided to wallpaper the walls in the bathroom in a lively lemon yellow that was now looking distinctly bleached out. Worse than that, the combination of a daily dose of hot steam from the bath and the small enclosed space of the room meant the wallpaper was starting to peel. She noted that one patched square right above the tap was just hanging on.

Her thoughts turned back to Dave. He was a close friend in

many ways, though there had never been anything more than friendship between them – and never would be. Funny that: on the surface Dave would look like an ideal candidate for a relationship. He was bright if not exactly intellectual, amusing – and yes, he was good-looking. He wasn't moody, and he didn't complain, and he seemed to have a life subscription to the Power of Positive Thinking. If Liz occasionally thought he was a little too convinced the world was his oyster, at least he always seemed happy to make room for Liz in his shell.

She sat up and turned on the hot-water tap until a small cloud of steam rose from the water's surface, then she turned off the tap and lay back again, relaxing. If not Dave, who could she confide in? No one, she realised, for there was no special man in her life at the moment, something she noted dispassionately, without dismay or regret.

Of course, it would be nice to have someone intimate enough to share things with – especially the bad things, the difficult things like her mother's test results. But you didn't want to do that with just any friend, she thought. In her experience, imparting confidences always caused a strain, creating a kind of artificial intimacy that went beyond friendship. Some women seemed to get away with it – in fact they did it all the time – but it didn't suit her personality. Whereas a 'partner' (horrible word, thought Liz, but she could think of no better) was there precisely to share.

Plop. Water splashed by her toes. She saw that the wallpaper patch had given up the struggle and decided to keep her company in the bath.

12

I hate these early morning starts, thought Liz. It was still only nine-fifteen and she was already halfway across the Irish Sea. The journey so far had been the usual nightmare – a packed Tube train and then the frustrating waiting around at Heathrow as the flight in from Belfast was delayed. You never know what to wear when you start so early, reflected Liz. She had chosen her new linen jacket – a risky option for this time of year and for a journey in a packed plane. Linen always looked so good on the hanger, but after half an hour's wear it could assume the contours of a crushed rag. Luckily she'd been able to hang it on a hook in front of her seat on the plane, and she had every hope it would arrive in a reasonable state.

As she gazed out of the window and saw the shelf of cloud sticking out from Wales give way to blue sky, her mood lightened. Perhaps this trip was going to be more productive and enjoyable than she expected.

She was glad she had only brought hand luggage when she saw the crowds round the baggage carousel, and she was first at the Avis counter where, using her driving licence in the alias of Falconer, she rented a Renault 5.

She drove around the outskirts of the city to avoid the tail end of rush-hour traffic. She enjoyed driving, though she found the Renault underpowered compared to her own Audi, and she pushed it on, not wanting to be late for her appointment. Dr

Liam O'Phelan, Lecturer in Irish Studies, Queen's University Belfast.

It felt strange returning to Belfast after ten years. Thank God I no longer have to check whether the car is being followed, or worry whether someone has put a bomb under it, she thought. Both had been standard concerns when she was last here, in the era when security was precarious.

She thought back to her first posting, several months on the Northern Ireland desk. Based in Thames House she had spent three short stints in Belfast. She remembered how nervous she'd been on her first visit with expectations of violence, fostered by the television images of armoured cars and rioting mobs she had grown up with. But she had missed the worst of the Troubles. In her time there in the mid-nineties, Northern Ireland was on the cusp of peace. There was an occasional sectarian killing, but overall the fragile ceasefire held.

Not that there weren't plenty of other opportunities for conflict, mused Liz, though of a non-violent sort, between the Northern Ireland office, the intelligence-gathering factions of MI5, Army Intelligence, and the then Royal Ulster Constabulary and its Special Branch. She'd had a rapid education in the politics of intelligence-gathering in Northern Ireland. I had to grow up fast, she thought now, remembering how when she'd been given a low-level informant to run, she'd discovered an RUC Special Branch officer trying to pinch him. I soon sorted him out, thought Liz with satisfaction.

Driving north on Stranmillis Road, past the lush Botanic Gardens, Liz parked on a quiet, tree-lined side street off University Road. The neighbourhood of the University was an oasis of calm respected by both sides of the sectarian divide. She walked diagonally across the lawn of a quadrangle, ringed by Victorian High Gothic buildings, looking enviously at the students sprawled on the grass with their books, soaking up the sun, an oddly summer-like scene for May. She felt a pang at the sight. So familiar and so carefree.

With a few false starts, she eventually found the Institute of Irish Studies, one of a row of grey Victorian houses. Liam O'Phelan had his office on the second floor.

He had been almost prissily precise about the time he would see her (11:45 a.m.) but when she found his room and knocked on the door there was no reply. Then a voice called out from along the corridor, 'Just coming.'

From the file Peggy had given her, Liz knew that O'Phelan was forty-two, but his thinning hair and worry lines made him look older. He wore a pale green tweed jacket and flannel trousers. She'd seen many versions of that jacket on middle-aged men who frequented her mother's garden centre, but this one was beautifully cut, and didn't look as if it had been within a mile of a potting shed.

'Dr O'Phelan.'

'That's right,' he said extending a dry soft hand. He looked at her with sharp blue-green eyes. 'And you must be Miss Falcon. My favourite bird of prey.'

'Falconer, actually,' she said.

'Better still,' he said as he opened the door.

The lavish, almost voluptuous decoration of the room took her aback. It was not what she expected in this otherwise drab house. At one end there was a false fireplace of white marble, and covering the wooden floor, oriental rugs in reds and blues. The walls were studded with paintings, prints and drawings, and she recognised portraits of Yeats and Joyce.

O'Phelan motioned Liz to one of two old stuffed armchairs in the middle of the room. 'Please sit down,' he said formally, 'and I'll make some coffee.'

While he did, Liz got her papers out and looked at the notes she'd drafted the night before. She never stuck rigidly to any order of questioning, preferring to let an interview develop naturally, but she wanted to make sure she got answers to all her questions.

O'Phelan brought a tray with two china cups and saucers, and placed them on the small table between them. Sitting down, he languidly crossed one leg over a knee, and sipped the hot coffee, while Liz discreetly examined him. He had straight sandy-coloured hair, slightly crooked teeth and a thin straight nose. Like a younger Peter O'Toole, she reflected.

'You're here to talk to me about one of my old students, I gather.' His accent was cultivated, with none of the harsh burr of an Ulsterman.

'That's right. Michael Binding.'

'And you're from the Ministry of Defence.' He was watching her carefully.

'Yes. You wrote a reference for him when he first applied to the MOD. You do remember him?'

'Very well,' announced O'Phelan. He raised his forefinger, as if to make an announcement. 'I was his thesis supervisor but not for very long. He switched supervisors when I left Oxford to come here.'

'Is that normal practice?'

'What? For me to come here?' He laughed lightly at his deliberate misunderstanding. 'Actually, it depends. In his case I think he probably wanted to change. Certainly I did.'

'You didn't get on?'

O'Phelan shrugged. 'Not particularly, but that was neither here nor there. I didn't agree with his whole approach.'

'To his thesis?' O'Phelan nodded, and she asked curiously, 'What was it about?'

'Charles Stewart Parnell.'

'Anything in particular about Parnell?'

He seemed surprised by her interest. 'His political speeches. How they reflected the politics of the age, and vice versa. Usual stuff. It was only an MLitt.'

'But you say you didn't like the line he took.'

'No, I thought it entirely wrong. Of course, I'm of the school of historians which Conor Cruise O'Brien once called "high-brow Fenian". Parnell to me is first and foremost an Irish nationalist.'

He seemed to be savouring his words, as if mentally punctuating the sentences as he spoke. He continued, 'Binding saw him only in the context of British parliamentary democracy. He seemed to believe that if Parnell had been lucky enough to be English, he would have done great things – on the other side of the Irish Sea.'

'Whereas you think Parnell was great as he was?'

Liz waited for his reply.

'Absolutely,' he said, and for the first time there was enthusiasm in his voice. 'But the fundamental problem I had with Binding wasn't that we held different views. I mean, if I taught only people who agreed with me I wouldn't be a very busy man. No, it was rather – how shall I put this politely? - the simple fact that he wasn't very good.'

He elaborated on this for a few minutes, explaining in soft tones that Binding had been poor at research, neither thought nor wrote clearly, and, in short, had possessed none of the basic intellectual skills one expected of a postgraduate student at Oxford University.

It was a masterpiece of denigration, couched in tones of such apparent regret that it took Liz a moment to see it for the poisonous demolition job it was. Even O'Phelan found the front of ostensible charity impossible to sustain, and he concluded witheringly: 'I was astonished to learn that his thesis had been accepted.'

'I see,' said Liz neutrally. She picked up her pencil from the table. 'I also wanted to ask you about his private life.'

'Ask away, but I'm not sure I'll be able to help you. I didn't know him particularly well. I was at St Antony's and he was at another college – Oriel, I think. One of the smaller ones at any rate.'

'Do you know if he had many friends?'

O'Phelan shook his head. 'No I don't.'

'Or girlfriends?'

He paused and smiled slightly. 'He had girlfriends – more than one.'

'Really?'

'Yes. They used to wait for him sometimes when he came to see me. It happened several times, and there were at least two different girls. I remember thinking, "*Such* devotion."'

Liz smiled politely. 'Did he belong to clubs or play a sport?'

O'Phelan opened his hands to express mild bewilderment. 'That's not something I would know, I'm afraid.'

'What about politics? Was he interested?'

O'Phelan looked thoughtful. 'He was, as a matter of fact. More than most of my pupils at any rate. He loved to argue the toss – he liked to quote the *Daily Telegraph* at me, as if that were an impartial source.'

'So he was a Conservative?'

'Yes. But then so in many ways I am too. It was on the subject of Ireland we disagreed. He'd bring in some Anglo-Protestant rubbish and quote it to me, probably just to annoy me. It usually did.'

After a few more questions, Liz made a show of checking her list, but O'Phelan had told her what she wanted to know about Binding.

I wonder, she thought, and, reaching down into her brief-case, she extracted another sheet of paper from a folder. 'If you don't mind, I'd like to read you a list of names – they are people who were at Oxford at about the same time as Binding. I'm just wondering if you knew any of them.'

And she slowly started to read out the names of the others on her list of suspects, while out of the corner of her eye she watched O'Phelan's reaction. But he sat still, his face impassive and his hands in his lap.

Then suddenly, when she was almost through, he leapt up. 'Excuse me a minute,' he said. 'I think there's someone at the door.' He went and opened it and stuck his head out. 'Ryan, I shan't be long now.'

He returned, saying, 'I beg your pardon,' and sat down again.

Liz read out the last name on the list: 'Steven Ogasawara.'

O'Phelan shook his head. He smiled apologetically, 'I'm afraid none of them means a thing to me.' He raised his fore-finger again, this time as if to correct himself. 'That doesn't mean I didn't know them once. As any teacher will tell you, students come and students go – one simply can't remember all their names.'

'That seems entirely understandable,' said Liz. 'Well, thank you very much for your time.'

'Not at all,' said O'Phelan and he stood up when Liz did and walked with her to the door. 'Let me know if I can be of any further help,' he said, then opening the door peered out. 'Young Ryan seems to have disappeared.'

13

It was his turn to close up the shop, and since it was Thursday it was not until seven-thirty that he turned off the lights, took a last tour of the three rooms on the ground floor in case anyone was so immersed in a book that he would lock them in, then firmly shut the front door and turned the key in the double set of Chubb locks.

It had been exactly a week since the Imam had come to the shop. Then Sohail had deliberately stayed in the stockroom, counting inventory, lest his own tense nerves be obvious. To Sohail's surprise, Abu Sayed had not gone upstairs, but stayed in the office off the main room for almost an hour. No one joined him, and when Abu Sayed did emerge he had walked straight out of the shop into a waiting car.

What had gone wrong? Why had the three young men not shown up? Sohail racked his brain to see if he could have got it wrong. But no, he was certain there had been an appointment set up between the Imam and the young men. Yet the uncertainty of why it hadn't happened gnawed at him like an unappeasable hunger, and he felt he had badly let down both Jane and Simon and their unnamed secret service, which he was certain was MI5.

Was it possible, and he felt his adrenalin stir at the thought, that the people watching – he knew they must have been there – had been detected? He himself had looked for any sign of external surveillance, on his way to and from work; at lunchtime too, he would look around as he walked to eat his sandwich in the park. There was nothing that he could see, hard as he looked.

So what reason would the Imam have to suspect something was amiss? Or the bookshop owner for that matter, who had behaved as he always did with Sohail – slightly aloof, but scrupulously polite? In fact, it was Sohail's colleague Aswan who had been the object of the owner's attention most recently – when Aswan had asked if he should now retrieve the video from upstairs, the owner had responded tetchily, saying he should listen more and ask fewer questions.

Yet could it be, and now he began to feel even more jittery, that somehow it was suspected that Sohail was not what he pretended to be? A young man, quiet, devout, serious, working hard to help his family. He tried to be rational: this portrait was not a front; this *was* what Sohail was, and there was no reason for anyone to think he was anything else at all.

He waited for the bus for almost fifteen minutes, then had to stand for half the journey home. Usually, he could find a seat and read. He was in the middle of *English Torts: A Casebook*, for if he had good reason to postpone university for a year, he thought he might as well not let all the time go to waste. He liked the precision and arid tautness of the prose. The book was almost theoretical in its abstraction, but unlike the Islamic literature he was surrounded by during the day, English law seemed incapable of perversion in the hands of fanatics.

He wondered what it would be like to lead a normal life again. Not to have to worry about what he said, or the expression on his face. To study again, in an environment where different opinions could be expressed in argument rather than violence. It was the approval of violence he found most disturbing in the people around him at work; the casual acceptance of, even applause for, the loss of life, as though lives were not real, as though human beings were just symbols.

Not that England was free of violence. The BNP had almost won a council seat in the area where he lived with his parents. He himself had twice been chased by white youths, shouting racist abuse and once, he had been shaken down for money by two drunks not more than a hundred yards from his home. But at least with such people, they clearly broke the law; they could hardly claim the law was somehow on their side.

He got off the bus early, as he usually did, so he could walk a bit before he reached home. There his mother would have held supper for him on this, the late night of the week, and his little sister would be bathed and ready for bed.

The dark was drawing in, and he quickened his pace as he walked along the main road of his neighbourhood, then turned into a side street. At its end there was a long alleyway, which ran between a warehouse on one side and the back of a row of shops on the other. It was poorly lit, and a little spooky – his little sister would not walk through it even in broad daylight – but it knocked five minutes off the way home and he turned down it without hesitation. As he hurried along, he thought momentarily that he heard someone behind him, but turning around saw nothing except the long shadow of the warehouse cast by the distant street light. Don't be so nervous, he told himself, then thought again of how he had let Jane and Simon down. And possibly – he knew it sounded pompous, but it was true – the country as well.

And it was with these feelings of disappointment that he looked up to see a figure approaching. He was instantly wary, until he saw the person was as dark as he was, and then he relaxed. And as the man came closer Sohail thought there seemed something familiar about him. The man was smiling broadly – even in the dusk Sohail could see his teeth – and he called out, 'Sohail!'

Reflexively Sohail began to smile back, assured this was a friend after all. And sure enough the short man's face was familiar. I know, thought Sohail, it's the little chap who didn't turn up at the bookshop the second time. But what is he doing here?

14

This is more like it, thought Liz, as she booked into the Culloden Hotel. With its acres of gardens, spa, pool and rosetted restaurant it was a cut above her normal overnight accommodation, but she had got an excellent deal on the internet and, unusually for her, she had decided to indulge herself.

Though I won't get to enjoy any of it, she thought, as she went upstairs and ordered a room-service sandwich, kicked off her shoes, and opened her laptop. As it booted, she called her voicemail at Thames House but there were no messages.

Liz wondered if Marzipan had made any progress in identifying the photos that had come from Holland, then she forced herself to stop speculating – it's not your business now, she told herself firmly, turning her mind instead to writing up her interview with O'Phelan.

There was something not quite right about that man. What was it? He had given a polished performance, but it was just that – a performance. But why? Was it simply that he resented anything and anyone to do with the security forces? Behind the jokey front and slightly camp demeanour, she could detect there was something else going on – she could sense it. He was clocking the effect he was making. All the time giving out only what he wanted her to know.

Yes, the interview had been a performance. Liz could tell that he was a man of very strong convictions. She recalled the intensity of his voice when he talked about Parnell. On impressionable students, surely he must be a powerful influence. Though not, it seemed clear, on her colleague Michael Binding.

Liz had arranged to have dinner with Jimmy Fergus, an old RUC Special Branch acquaintance, and an expert in the Loyalist paramilitary groups. She had called him from London, to let him know she was coming onto his turf, and the meal had been his idea.

Waiting for him in the lobby, she glanced at a copy of the local evening paper and saw that a prominent Republican had come forward claiming to have been an agent of the security forces. I wonder what's behind that, thought Liz. Ten years earlier no one would have dared to make such a claim publicly for fear of being found dead on the border with a bag over his head.

She saw Fergus across the lobby. He was a big man, with a pockmarked face and a confident grin that Liz had always found infectious. In his private life Fergus was a bit of lad, what was known in Belfast as a 'chaser' – he had been married so many times that, when asked about his current marital status he liked to say he was 'between divorces'. There had never been anything between him and Liz, and never would be, though Fergus always liked to make a ritualistic pass.

He came from Protestant farming stock in Antrim ('Honest bigots to a man' he'd once declared). As she had got to know him a decade before, she discovered that much of his bluster was a defence – part of a hard man's carapace erected around a sharp intelligence. He was also discreet, which meant that within obvious limits, she could level with him tonight, pick his brain and, if it seemed useful, ask for his help.

'You've come up in the world,' he teased as he ambled towards her, indicating the hotel's ornate lobby, a mix of marble columns, panelled walls and chandeliers. 'I thought of giving you dinner at your hotel,' he said, 'but when I heard which one it was, I decided we'd go somewhere with a little more local colour.'

They drove in his old blue Rover to a fashionably revamped pub, with large open rooms, wood floors, and a brick fireplace. The noise of music and raucous voices hit them as they went in. No chance to talk here, thought Liz. From the welcome Fergus received it was obviously one of his regular hang-outs. 'Have faith,' said Fergus, as they were shown through the bar to a quiet table in an alcove at the back.

Over drinks, they spent time catching up. It had been four years since they'd seen each other, during a trip Fergus had made to London. Liz had been working on organised crime then, though shortly afterwards she'd been transferred to the counter-terrorism branch.

Fergus raised an eyebrow. 'It's ironic that just as life has calmed down here, it's heated up for you.'

'So,' said Liz, 'if you're not chasing the UVF these days, what are you working on?'

'Who says I'm not chasing the UVF?' he said with a grin. 'Same people, different crimes. Murdering Catholics out, extortion, prostitution and gambling in. Standard stuff really.'

As the waiter brought their food, Fergus asked what she was doing in Northern Ireland. Liz gave him her cover story about the new vetting procedures. 'I've been sent to interview someone who gave a reference for one of my colleagues fifteen years ago,' she said, hoping her tone suggested a bureaucratic interference she could have done without.

Fergus grinned. 'I'm glad we're not the only ones with intrusive bosses,' he said. 'Who did you see?'

'A lecturer at Queen's. We used him as a referee for one of his pupils. He taught History at Oxford for a while, then came here about ten years ago to teach Irish Studies. He had strong views. If Ireland had only stuck with Parnell, the country would be unified today.'

Fergus gave a hollow laugh as he cut into his sirloin. 'He probably thinks Gerry Adams has sold out. He sounds what my father used to call an "armchair Fenian". What's his name?'

Liz leaned forward before she spoke. 'Liam O'Phelan.'

'I've heard of him,' he said, musing. 'Didn't he originally come from Dublin?'

'I don't know much about him,' Liz admitted. 'But I don't think he was being straight with me.'

'About his ex-pupil?'

'No, that rang true. A few other things didn't though.' She didn't want to go into too much detail about the interview.

Fergus speared a chip and stared at it for a moment as he answered. 'I could check and see if we have a file on him. We may well do. At one point during the height of the violence we were very concerned about Queen's.'

'Would you mind? I'd appreciate it.'

'Sure,' said Fergus easily, 'but use me while you can. I won't be doing this forever.'

Was Fergus going to retire? It seemed inconceivable. Liz said so, sitting back in her chair, looking at him with affectionate scepticism.

'I'm older than you think,' said Fergus. 'I'll have done twenty-five years this autumn.'

'What would you do next?' asked Liz. She couldn't envisage him back in Antrim, bringing in the wheat crop.

Fergus shrugged, a little dolefully, and Liz wished she hadn't asked. He'd already explained, regretfully, that he was single again, and she knew it was a sadness that he had never had children.

Wanting to change the subject, Liz remarked, 'I saw in the paper that another former agent has gone public.'

'I'm sure there will be more,' said Fergus seriously. 'It's hard now for some of those people who worked as secret assets, sources, agents, whatever you like to call them, during the Troubles – for us, you lot, and particularly for the Army. As politics brings old enemies together, they've got difficult decisions to make. Partly, they're afraid they'll get blown anyway as more and more information comes out through enquiries, freedom of information, or whatever. They won't probably, but they're not sure of that. For some of them, I think, there's a sort of crisis of conscience. They have a need for understanding what they did and why – after all, they don't see themselves as traitors. They'll be feeling they made a contribution to peace in their own way and they'd like some recognition for it. Going public is a dangerous route – but some will go on taking it, even though the peace process won't protect them.'

'They weren't all so high-minded,' said Liz. 'Some of them worked for us for much more selfish reasons – like money. I don't suppose anyone will ever hear from them.'

'No, you're right. They'll just take their grievance somewhere else.'

'Anyway,' said Liz, 'it's not as though the intelligence war is over, is it? Infiltration must be easier now, for the paramilitaries. How many Catholics are there in Special Branch?'

'More than before,' said Fergus, adding cynically, 'not that that's saying much. The new recruiting guidelines call for fifty-fifty overall in the Northern Ireland Police Force. You can imagine how popular that is with some of my colleagues. But infiltration was a worry even when there were no Catholics in the Force at all; it's just that it came from the Loyalists.

'Look, like most of Special Branch, I'm a policeman first and a Protestant second. But once in a while someone gets his priorities reversed. Of course there've been leaks to the Loyalist paramilitaries. When it happens it does a lot of damage. But the greatest damage is the distrust it creates. The damage to the reputation of the Force, if you want to put it that way. You're lucky not to have that problem.'

'How do you know we don't?' said Liz. 'We certainly did once. Remember Philby and Anthony Blunt?'

But Fergus had said his say and was busy signalling to the waiter.

After dinner, Fergus drove Liz back to the Culloden. They sat in the bar on a sofa of plush red velvet while Fergus drank a large brandy and explained what had happened to wife number three. After a while, Liz called for the bill, explaining she had an early flight back in the morning.

'I don't suppose you want help packing,' said Fergus, as they walked back out into the lobby.

Liz laughed. 'You never give up.' Then shaking hands she kissed his cheek and said goodnight, adding, 'You won't forget about O'Phelan, will you?'

She gave a great yawn as she walked to the lift, but by the time she reached her room her eyes were sharp and alert.

Two hours later Liz was still wide awake, sitting at the desk in her room. A glass of mineral water from the minibar sat next to her, untouched, as she looked, deep in thought, at the notes she had been writing.

What she had written were speculations rather than facts, but they were troubling ones, set off by Fergus's offhand mention of infiltration in the Northern Ireland Special Branch. 'You're lucky not to have that problem,' he'd said.

But what about the mole? She wondered, not for the first time, what the IRA had expected of an infiltrator. Suppose they were posted to Counter-Terrorism, possibly even to the Northern Ireland desk. What exactly were they going to *do*?

What *could* they do, working alone inside MI5? Well, for one thing, they could alert the IRA to the identity of informers in its midst. That's what Philby and Blake had done in the Cold War. They could tip them off if one of their operations was blown, and warn them of impending arrests, and even more, they could reassure them when one of their operations *wasn't* blown.

Yet she could imagine something even more damaging. An infiltrator in the right place might be able to feed targeting information that would help the IRA mount a damaging attack. Even if they were not working on the Northern Irish terrorist target and not able directly to help their masters, they could make up false intelligence that could waste valuable resources and harm the Service's credibility. Think of the Iraq dossier and the damage that did to the reputation of the whole of British Intelligence.

Yet wasn't it all academic? In Sean Keaney's time frame, there hadn't been any IRA terrorist activities for the mole to assist. And MI5 hadn't lost any informers. Its reputation had not been damaged. So did that mean the mole had simply retired from business, having never been activated? Perhaps he had just quietly left the Service.

She tried imagining the situation from the mole's point of view. There he was, all primed and ready to go, when the message came from his masters: we don't need you anymore. Or, perhaps worse, no message came at all.

What would that have felt like? How frustrating would that have been? Did our friend the mole cheerfully accept the order, and spend the next decade loyally doing his best in MI5? Was he just one of us, no different from everyone else?

It didn't seem likely.

Liz swallowed a mouthful of tepid mineral water. Time for bed, she thought. As she brushed her teeth, she thought how nothing in the last ten years indicated the mole had done anything – for the IRA. But what if the mole had done something else?

Arranging the over-stuffed pillows, she undressed and got into bed. Could the mole have been placed in MI6? She didn't think so. Surely the original idea had to have been to place him in MI5, where he could subvert the Service's work against the IRA. The fact remained that the original recruitment of the mole had an Irish lynchpin – Sean Keaney's idea to put a mole in place. But as it turned out, the idea had lost its value, like currency taken out of circulation.

She lay back and thought again, uneasily, of O'Phelan. What was it that bothered her about the interview? It wasn't just a feeling that he hadn't told her the truth. There was something else.

Why hadn't she focused on it before? It was obvious: she'd known it all along. When O'Phelan had got up, gone over to the door and spoken to Ryan, the so-called student waiting in the hallway, no other voice had spoken. Because, of course, *there wasn't anyone there*.

O'Phelan had got up to create a diversion. To disguise his reaction to something she'd said. What had they been discussing that made him do that? They hadn't been discussing anything, she realised – she had been reciting the names on her list. Patrick Dobson, Judith Spratt, Tom Dartmouth, etc. That was clearly what bothered O'Phelan, enough for him to try and distract her.

O'Phelan knew one of the names.

She closed her eyes but her mind went on churning all the images of the day. But she was too tired to focus on any of them. She would start again in the morning.

And only then did she remember. She had forgotten to ring her mother.

15

At 9:18 the next morning, as Liz finished her coffee in the dining room of the Culloden Hotel and got ready to check out and drive to the airport, the watcher in Doris Feldman's flat rang Dave Armstrong. He was at his desk in Thames House, writing up his report on his abortive trip north.

'Marzipan hasn't shown up,' the watcher said.

'Perhaps he's running late,' said Dave, annoyed to be interrupted in mid-sentence – writing reports was for him the worst part of his job.

'He's never been late before. We thought you'd want to know.'

'Okay,' said Dave, suddenly attentive, for he realised that what they said was right. Sohail was *always* punctual. 'Ring me in ten minutes and let me know if he's shown.'

By ten o'clock they had rung three more times. There was still no sign of Marzipan. Very worried now, Dave decided to ring Sohail's mobile – something he would normally have been reluctant to do, in case he was with someone else. He was trying to combat the knot in his stomach, hoping this was all a false alarm.

It wasn't. The number rang and a man said, 'Hello?'

An Englishman, Dave noted, with an Estuary accent. Dave asked quietly, 'Is Sohail there?'

'This is the Metropolitan Police. Please identify yourself.'

Landing at Heathrow, Liz bought a copy of the *Evening Standard* before getting on the Underground. It was forty-five minutes into central London, but she had a seat, something unknown in her morning commute to work.

She had been thinking on and off about O'Phelan. Lying to her, if that's what he had done, didn't mean he was necessarily an IRA recruiter, and she couldn't believe it was Michael Binding he would have wanted to recruit. His contempt for his former pupil had been the one part of her interview she had found absolutely authentic.

Yet what if O'Phelan held truly extremist radical views, semi-disguised in respectable intellectual garb? He was slightly larger than life. He could be assertive to the point of overbearing. Take a nineteen-year-old undergraduate with an undivulged grudge and an itch to be a revolutionary. Combining him with O'Phelan could be potentially explosive.

She picked up her copy of the *Standard* and looked through the news pages. She felt as if she had been away for much more than twenty-four hours, but the stories seemed wearyingly familiar: protests from retailers about the effects of the congestion charge, delays in the construction of the new Wembley Stadium, an MP arrested for driving under the influence of alcohol in an insalubrious part of South London. Then on page five she saw an item that riveted her:

TOTTENHAM RACE KILLING

A man discovered dead in a Tottenham alley this morning was the victim of a brutal attack. The body, said to be that of a young Asian man, was discovered by a passer-by early this morning in an alley off Cresswell Crescent, in an area where racial tension has been high. The British National party (BNP) has been particularly active in the local community. Police said the victim, in his early twenties, was wearing a blue anorak, jeans, and hiking boots. His name has been withheld until relatives have been informed.

According to Omar Singh, a local Labour Party Councillor, 'This killing has all the hallmarks of a racial murder. Assaults against young Asian men have become commonplace in the last two years, and this seems to be the culmination of an increasing trend of racist violence.' The BNP refused to comment.

'You all right, love?' Liz looked up to find an elderly man from across the aisle looking at her with concern. She realised she must have been staring at the same page, glassy-eyed, for several minutes.

When she had last seen Sohail Din, in the safe house at Devonshire Place, he had been wearing a blue anorak, jeans, and a pair of hiking boots.

16

Wetherby was sitting at his desk gazing out of the window at the sun sparkling on the Thames, but his face showed no pleasure in the view. The restless tap-tapping of his pencil on a pile of paper was the only sign of his anger and frustration. He was waiting for Tom Dartmouth, whom he had summoned to his office. Wetherby was a man who managed his staff by consultation and advice rather than by diktat, but when things went wrong he took responsibility. It was then that he gave orders without discussion.

And things had gone very wrong indeed. The death of an agent was the worst nightmare for any intelligence service. Agents were recruited by persuasion, cajolery and sometimes by the promise of payment. Some agents, and Marzipan was one, offered their services out of loyalty to the country. In return they were promised protection. That was the deal. For the Service to break its side of the bargain, particularly with a young man like Marzipan, was a professional failure of the worst possible kind.

'Do we know when it happened?' Wetherby asked immediately Dartmouth came in.

'Apparently it was sometime last night,' Dartmouth replied, sitting down cautiously.

'I see,' said Wetherby, standing up, and walking to the window. The spring sunshine had given way to a sudden heavy shower. River and sky merged, obliterating the barge in mid-river.

He turned back to Dartmouth, who was looking tired and ruffled, all of his usual spruceness gone. 'So how did it happen?' asked Wetherby.

'At first glance, it looks like a racist attack,' said Dartmouth levelly.

'Combat 18?'

'Conceivably. We've got no intelligence at all and nor have the police.' He hesitated. 'Could be a lunatic member of the BNP – they're strong in that area. They almost won a seat in the last local council elections.'

'But?' asked Wetherby, noting Dartmouth's pause.

'Well,' said Dartmouth with a hint of dryness, 'slitting someone's throat is an uncommon method of murder in this country.'

'So?'

Dartmouth paused. 'I think we have to assume that this murder is tied to our investigation.'

'I want maximum effort put on this, Tom. We've got to find out what's happened.' Tom nodded. 'And keep me closely in touch,' said Wetherby. He paused, then asked, 'Has anyone spoken to Liz Carlyle?'

'I gather she's expected in just after lunch.'

Wetherby looked at Dartmouth. He was a clever man, that was obvious, and not just because of his first-class degree. He had come back from Pakistan by his own choice – who could blame him, after four tough post-9/11 years? Geoffrey Fane of MI6 had said his performance there had been outstanding. But he was also hard to read. Wetherby had yet to see him show any feelings.

Wetherby said, 'Someone has to tell her Marzipan is dead. It should be me, but I'm due to see the Home Secretary in half an hour. I need to explain the background to Marzipan's death. Where's Dave Armstrong?'

Dartmouth gave a small sigh. 'He's gone with the police to talk to Marzipan's parents.' He waited for a minute, then said quietly, 'I'll tell Liz, Charles. After all, it's my operation.'

Wetherby nodded. He looked again out of the window, seemingly lost in thought. Then the moment of contemplation passed and he turned to Dartmouth. 'I suppose you'll have to,' he said conclusively.

Dartmouth's eyes narrowed slightly and Wetherby continued, speaking at a rapid clip, dictating orders. 'This is now a police case: a murder has been committed. Get them to pull in the bookshop people. We need to talk to them. You'll have to be careful. Maybe one of them will talk, though I doubt they know very much anyway. If Abu Sayed is driving this from Pakistan, they may have let him use the shop as a courtesy and not have a clue who the three others are. You said that Six were watching Abu Sayed over there. Let them know what's happened. *Any* contact with the UK, however innocuous, should be reported to us. Get on to the Dutch and see if they've got anything from their operation.'

He stopped for a moment, thinking hard, his brow furrowed in concentration. 'I want a meeting with you, Dave, and Judith Spratt before close of play.' He thought for a second, then added, 'I think Liz Carlyle should be there as well.'

Dartmouth seemed surprised. 'I thought she was on a different assignment.'

'She is,' said Wetherby shortly, 'but she was Marzipan's controller before Dave; she may have useful ideas to contribute.'

He sighed, and tugged at both shirt cuffs until each was aligned to an equal half-inch display. He checked the knot of his tie and stood up. 'I'm going to walk around.' After news of Marzipan's death, Wetherby knew the mood among the agent runners would be black. It was important for him to show his support.

'The problem remains,' he added as he walked towards the door, 'that we have lost our link to the bookshop group.'

'I know,' said Dartmouth calmly, standing up to leave. For once, Wetherby found his cool imperturbability not entirely helpful.

17

Liz had phoned Peggy Kinsolving from Belfast shortly after seeing O'Phelan, and by eight-thirty the following morning Peggy was on the coach from Victoria heading towards Oxford.

Today she was happily following a paper trail – her forte, though she was delighted that Liz wanted her present at some of the interviews. Peggy was learning a lot from Liz.

She was impressed by how Liz calibrated her approach to her subjects. Some were pressed like juice oranges, some were coaxed, others positively encouraged. Even those who began by behaving like clams, found thirty or forty minutes later that they had been opened.

But today, Peggy was concentrating on something altogether different. After Liz's phone call, she had made a start on Liam O'Phelan, and had unearthed the bare facts. As the bus passed High Wycombe and moved towards the Chilterns escarpment, she mentally reviewed what she'd discovered.

He was born in 1964 in Liverpool to an Irish mother, and an English father who left the family when Liam was ten years old. Liam and his mother moved back to Ireland, to Sandycove, a suburb of Dublin. He had won a scholarship to University College Dublin, where he did well – a starred First in History and the De Valera Prize (whatever that was, thought Peggy, making a mental note to find out).

His doctoral dissertation, *Parnell and the English Establishment* had been published by Oxford University Press. Awarded a Junior Research Fellowship at St Antony's College, Oxford, he had resigned after two years to take up a permanent position at the Institute of Irish Studies at Queen's University Belfast. He was unmarried.

That was the skeleton; now Peggy hoped Oxford would put meat on the bones. The coach swooshed down Headington Hill, then slowed as traffic backed up by the Plain before crossing Magdalen Bridge and stopping across from Queen's Lane where Peggy got off. It was a hazy day, with a thin filter of cloud, but warm, and after crossing the High Street, Peggy stopped and took off her raincoat. She would have liked a coffee, but she had a huge task to get through and she wanted to get back to London that evening.

Her reader's card was still valid, so she went straight to the New Bodleian, a square monstrosity of yellow stone, built in the thirties on the corner next to Blackwell's bookshop.

By one o'clock she had gone through the five-year tranche of the *Oxford Gazette*, *Oxford Today* and the *Oxford Magazine*, looking for any reference to O'Phelan, but her trained eye had found none.

So much for the official publications. She knew that often it was the nooks and crannies of the ephemeral that held the most interesting finds. So she had requested archive issues of *Cherwell*, the student newspaper, which appeared every two weeks in term time and was about as unofficial as you could get. It didn't take her long. At one-forty she saw, on the penultimate page of the 4 April 1991 issue, a listing headed 'Lectures'. These were extra-curricular talks, from the grand (Antonia Fraser talking about Mary Queen of Scots in the Sheldonian) to the not so grand ('Punk Music and Me: A Personal History' in the New College JCR).

And halfway down was a sub-heading for a weekly series of talks, given in the Old Fire Station, labelled 'Fighting Talk'. Four pounds per head, wine and beer available afterwards, all welcome. Three forthcoming talks were listed: 'The Miners' Struggle' by a Labour MP; 'Sexuality and Sexism' by a former editor of *Spare Rib*; 'To Be Announced' by Liam O'Phelan, lecturer at St Antony's and author.

Great title, thought Peggy sourly, the small elation at finding O'Phelan's name at last evaporating in the face of 'To Be Announced'. It probably wasn't important anyway. Given his CV, he had doubtless talked about Parnell. But it irked her nonetheless; she didn't like gaps, especially in her own research.

She explained her problem to the assistant, a helpful woman in glasses and black T-shirt who looked about Peggy's age. 'You say you've checked *Cherwell*. What about the *Gazette*?'

'There's nothing there.'

'And the *Oxford Magazine*?'

'No luck, either.'

The young woman shrugged her shoulders. 'I'm afraid I don't know what to suggest. You see, if it wasn't an official lecture then I can't think of anywhere else you can look. They might have put up a poster, but we don't collect them.'

Peggy thanked the woman and got up to leave. 'Of course there's always *Daily Doings*,' the woman said as an afterthought. 'But it's not really a publication. I doubt anyone keeps back issues – at least not that far back.'

Peggy remembered it: an enormous single-page broadsheet that appeared every day, listing everything from rooms to let to bicycles for sale. Concerts, gigs, poetry readings – all were given space in the three feet of type. 'Are they still on Warnborough Road?'

'I think so. That weird house.'

It was five minutes to two. Peggy stood outside the library, wondering whether to take a break for lunch in the King's Arms or set out on a long, possibly pointless walk to North Oxford.

Duty, or, to be strictly accurate, Liz won out. She remembered the telephone call from Belfast: 'We must find out more about O'Phelan. Anything will help,' Liz had said. That word 'anything' rang in her ears, and twenty minutes later, perspiring from the spring sunshine and a fast-paced walk up Woodstock Road, Peggy was entering the basement door of a tall Victorian house of yellow and orange brick.

She stepped into a large low-ceilinged room in the middle of which were two pine kitchen tables, covered with a jumble of papers, used coffee cups and odd items of cutlery. A laser printer against a side wall was churning out pages, which splashed onto the floor, unsupervised.

'Hello?' said Peggy tentatively, then when no one replied, she called out again more vigorously.

After a moment, a door opened and a young man appeared, so tall that his head almost brushed the ceiling. Taking one look at Peggy, he said in an American accent, 'Don't worry, you've got lots of time. The deadline's not till five.'

Peggy explained she didn't want to place an ad, then told him what she was looking for.

'Hmm,' he said, 'how far back are you looking? If it was last fall there's a chance I could find a copy somewhere around here.'

Peggy swallowed. 'Actually, it was fifteen years ago.'

The American laughed out loud. 'Sorry,' he said, waving an

arm at the clutter. 'No chance. Space, space everywhere and not a drop to use. We only have two rooms,' he added.

'I see,' said Peggy, regretting her decision not to have lunch. 'I don't suppose you have a digital copy.'

He shook his head reflexively, but suddenly stopped, and his mouth opened, in a pantomime of revelation. 'Hang on a minute. The guy who started this place loved computers. He told me he'd bought his first machine in 1979. It was probably the first word processor at the University.'

'Did he keep the disks from then?'

'That's just it. He did. They're next door. Come and see.'

In the next room, which was smaller and even more crowded, he dug around in the bottom of a cupboard and then brought out a big taped-up cardboard box. He cut it open with a Stanley knife to reveal a jumble of disks and reels of magnetic tape.

Peggy looked at the collection sceptically.

'It's all labelled quite carefully. Wonderful the way they did things then,' said the American as he looked at some of the disks. 'Here,' he said, holding one up. 'This is 1990.' He fumbled some more. 'And '91 and . . . '92.'

'That's brilliant,' said Peggy, astonished by her stroke of luck.

'There's just one problem,' he said, putting the disks back in the cardboard box, and pushing it against the wall.

'What's that?' asked Peggy.

'You wouldn't be able to read any of them. They're all incompatible with today's machines. Sorry.'

Her heart sank, but then she thought of 'Technical Ted' Poyser, the counter-terrorist branch's specialist on all matters electronic back at Thames House. 'Listen,' said Peggy, 'could I borrow one of them anyway? I've got a friend who's a real computer whiz. He's got lots of old machines. He might be able to help me.'

The American had not expected this. 'Well, it's not really my property to lend,' he said hesitantly.

'Please,' pleaded Peggy, wondering what Liz would do in this situation. 'Please,' repeated Peggy. 'You said yourself no one can read them. If they're no good to anyone sitting there, couldn't I just borrow one? I promise I'll bring it back.' She could see he was wavering, so she said, 'I'll leave a deposit if that helps.'

He thought about this for a moment, then made up his mind. 'Nah,' he said, and Peggy could not mask her disappointment. Until he added, 'It's cool. You don't have to leave a deposit.'

By five o'clock Peggy was on the third floor of Thames House, consulting 'Technical Ted' Poyser.

Ted's office was more of a cubbyhole, a windowless space, than an office, though even 'space' was an exaggeration. The walls were piled high with hardware devices, wires draped everywhere, and in the middle of it all was Ted, crouched on a stool like a spider in a very complicated web.

Ted had long black dyed hair and wore a gold earring, and as Peggy peered at him through the flickering light from the screens in front of him, his features came and went disconcertingly. A faint aroma of tobacco hung around the cubbyhole. Ted had smoked until Thames House became a no-smoking zone, and rather than join other addicts in the dreadful airless hole set aside for smoking, he had given up. Now his ashtray overflowed with boiled sweet wrappers. But somehow the nicotine aroma had never entirely left him.

Ted looked at Peggy without enthusiasm until he saw the disk she held in her hand. 'What have we here?' he asked. 'A blast from the past?'

Instinctively she tightened her grip on her find. 'Can you read it?' she asked, as if that were a condition of its release.

'Let me see,' he said, extending an arm.

Peggy handed him the disk. He examined it, admiringly, with full attention. Eventually he murmured, 'Why don't you get yourself a cup of tea from the canteen? I'm going to be a minute.'

When she came back a quarter of an hour later there was no sign of the disk. Ted was seated in front of a terminal which seemed to be attached to half a dozen different CPUs on a table. 'Where on earth did you find this?' he asked. 'You've brought me a virtual history of personal computing.'

'It's a long story. But I'm hoping there's something on it I'm looking for. It should be lots of listings.'

'There may be,' said Ted, 'but I think there are printer codes as well. What you've got here is a disk from a North Star computer, circa 1980. It had 64K of RAM.'

Ted looked at his terminal, which was filled with tight columns of alphanumerics. 'The files on the disk are written in a word-processing program called PeachText, and the disk itself is five-and-a-quarter inch, single-sided, single density. It's 360K, which is the rough equivalent of fifty thousand words. Not bad for the early eighties.'

Spare me the details, thought Peggy, get to the point. Ted seemed to sense her impatience, for he turned in his swivel chair and said with maddening deliberation, 'I doubt there is a single machine in the UK today which can read this disk normally.' He made a face, then said in a high-pitched voice,

'"It's digital so it will last forever." Utter bollocks. Formats change twice a decade, at least. Two decades and you're lost.'

'Really,' she said edgily. She was happy to share Ted's delight with the disk, but she wanted to know what was on it. And fast.

'I suppose you want to know if I can actually read the bloody thing.'

'Yes,' she said emphatically.

He smiled, showing surprisingly healthy-looking teeth. 'The short answer is, no, I can't.' When Peggy's face fell he pointed a commanding finger at her. 'But I will.'

18

Liz could hardly sit still. Tom Dartmouth had been talking on and on about Marzipan, but after the first few minutes she'd stopped listening. He had nothing to tell her. Anyway, why was *he* talking to her? He hadn't known Sohail. Marzipan was her agent – she'd recruited him, she'd run him, and almost as soon as she'd handed him over, they'd got him killed. He'd trusted her. She'd promised to look after him and she hadn't. She needed to talk to Charles. Why wasn't he here? Why had he given Marzipan to Dave? Not that she blamed Dave. He was her friend and he was good at his job. But somehow, somebody hadn't looked after Sohail. And now he was dead.

All these thoughts were going round and round and Tom was still talking, sat behind his desk in an expensive blue suit. He was talking in a calm, reasonable voice that Liz was finding more and more infuriating. 'I can't answer all your questions,' he said. 'Not because I don't want to, but because I don't know the answers myself.' He looked at her directly, almost coolly, though his eyes were not unfriendly.

'But why wasn't there counter-surveillance on him? Especially after the three men didn't show.' She clenched her left hand tightly on her lap.

'We certainly thought of it,' said Dartmouth, 'but there was no reason to think that there was any link between their failure to show and Marzipan. Believe me, Dave went through it with him very carefully the next day.'

Liz conceded the logic of this. Protecting Marzipan with counter-surveillance might have increased rather than reduced the risk, since there was always the danger of it being spotted.

But then what had they missed? Or was he suggesting there was nothing there to miss? She asked, trying not to sound annoyed, 'Are you telling me you believe this was a race murder?'

'No, of course not. And we've made it clear to the Met that we have an interest in this. Special Branch have arranged for all the CCTV within a square mile of the murder site to be collected. The local Underground stations are being checked – all the ticket collectors and the stationmasters are being questioned. Ditto the drivers on the bus routes. If any of those three was in the area, I hope we'll spot them.'

Liz nodded. 'Did Sohail look at the Dutch pictures before he was killed?'

Tom shook his head. 'No. Dave was going to meet him at the safe house tonight.'

'Oh God,' said Liz, not far from tears.

Liz had to get out of the building. The death of Marzipan had affected her more than anything in her working life, but it wouldn't do her or anyone else any good at all to show how upset she was. She walked along Millbank, her mood matched by the sodden pavements and the gutters where water had collected in long oil-streaked puddles which passing cars were spraying everywhere.

Sohail Din's murder was such a personal blow to Liz that it was only as the shock subsided that she saw the extent of the disaster. His death had effectively cut their one link to the bookshop three, and unless they could be found, many more people than Sohail might be destined to die. It was hard to separate her upset about Sohail Din from her worry about the catastrophe which might now ensue. Finding Sohail's killers was essential to help them unravel whatever was being planned.

At the Tate's vast front steps, she turned around to walk back to Thames House. The ice-cream van had reopened after the rain, and the vendor smiled at her. He wore a white shirt and red scarf, and looked transported from a Venetian gondola. 'Just one Cornetto,' he sang out to Liz, in a voice that was Puccini via Stepney, but Liz just scowled at him.

Back in the building she stopped by the corner conference room, hoping it would be empty, and found Peggy working on her laptop. 'Oh Liz,' she said. 'Dave Armstrong is looking for you.'

'Thanks,' said Liz with a sigh. 'I can guess why.' Then trying to pull herself together she asked, 'How are you getting on?'

'I've just come back from Oxford.'

She seemed to hesitate, so Liz asked, 'Did you find anything?'

'I don't know yet – I'm waiting to hear from Technical Ted.'

'Okay,' said Liz. 'I'll go and find Dave.'

Oxford and IRA moles seemed inconsequential.

19

Irwin Patel had never wanted the cameras. As he had explained to his wife Satinda, 'What good is this thing supposed to do then? I know which of those little boys stuffs packets of crisps under his jacket. I don't need a camera to identify them. And I can tell when the drunks try and put the wine bottles in their bags. Suppose I catch them on this wretched thing? Do you really think the police will take the time to look at *movies* of a petty theft? It is not realistic.'

But Satinda was insistent. 'That is not the point, Irwin,' she said sternly, in a tone he had long ago learned was not worth arguing with. She had been a beauty when they met, so presumably she must have thought him a promising prospect. How had she put up with the disappointment of his career? Simple, he thought ruefully; she had taken over and now she called the shots.

He had never appreciated being a stereotype, though being an intelligent man, he knew that is what he was. His parents had been Ugandan Asians, thrown out of their country by Idi Amin when Irwin was just five. In England, they had altered the names of their children. Irwin was an English name and Christian, and they liked it, failing to realise that the retention of 'Patel' would give the game away anyway.

Still, his name would hardly have mattered if Irwin had prospered, like the children of so many of his parents' fellow immigrants, and become a lawyer or doctor. But Irwin had struggled, failing the eleven-plus just twelve months before it was abolished by a Labour government, and suffering accordingly. Nearly thirty years after his parents' arrival, he still ran the same newsagent shop his father had bought and run all those years before. True, it carried a wider range and a better class of magazine, but Irwin was all too aware that his was simply one of thousands of shops throughout Britain owned by men called Patel.

'The purpose of the cameras,' Satinda declared, 'is to deter. Whether it catches the offender, that is not important. It keeps people from thieving in the first place.'

And that was that, the end of the argument. So he had paid Steinman & Son, the local security firm, to come in and install the camera, and at Satinda's insistence, had even paid them to make sure it continued to work. And the result? Hour after hour of footage, all of it easily reviewed in the back room of the shop whenever he wanted. Which, rapidly, he did not care to do, since what was the point of looking at footage of the same three rows of shelves in his shop with the same customers buying the same items – a loaf of sliced white, a packet of tea biscuits, a pint of milk – day after day?

So he was puzzled when a local policeman appeared at the till that morning. Usually they came in once or twice a week for cigarettes or a packet of Polo mints, and would chat sometimes, about Arsenal's latest match or when the road repairs in the High Street would finish. Today, however, this constable was all business, with a clipboard, a pencil, and a ground-down expression on his face. 'Morning,' he said, 'I need a word about your CCTV. It works, doesn't it?'

Irwin nodded, a little warily. He had always thought of the police as allies, if unreliable ones, but he tried to ask very little of them and they had never before asked anything of him.

'We need all your footage for the last ten days,' the policeman said curtly. 'Please,' he added as an afterthought.

'Gladly,' said Irwin, wondering how on earth to provide it. He would have to ask his son, Oscar, when he got home from school. Oscar understood these things; he even had his own computer, in the bedroom he shared with his sister, upstairs above the shop. 'What are you looking for?'

The constable shrugged. 'Ours is just to do or die, PC Plod does not ask why.'

He laughed, rather shortly, and Irwin thought it politic to laugh with him. 'Would this afternoon be all right?' he said.

'Only if you can deliver it to the station. I'm trying to collect it all today.'

20

After Wetherby's meeting, Liz decided to go home once it was clear there was nothing useful she could do by staying. As the lift doors on the fourth floor started to close, a hand intervened and they slid open again. Tom Dartmouth entered, and gave Liz a weary smile. She was tired, too. It seemed incredible that she had started the day in Belfast with her mind focused on Liam O'Phelan and since she had arrived back in London she had thought about nothing but Sohail. She was looking forward to getting back to her flat and trying to get the day's events in some sort of order.

'What a day,' he said, loosening his tie with one hand. 'Especially for you. Fancy a drink?'

It was said casually, but warmly. She was still angry, but no longer with Tom – in fact she felt badly for having been so aggressive with him that afternoon. 'Why not?' she said, and glanced at her watch, though she had no plans at all for the evening.

They went to the bar in a new steel and glass hotel not far from Thames House, a venue far slicker than the pubs which were the usual watering holes for MI5 staff. 'I've nothing against the Compton Arms,' Tom explained, 'but I thought it would be a little quieter here.'

The bar was full of well turned-out business types, not the rather seedy bunch of civil servants and journalists that haunted the pubs round Horseferry Road and Westminster. She was wearing the linen jacket she had taken to Belfast, which she was relieved to see had survived its two-day excursion in good order, so she felt reasonably comfortable there. It was the first time she had seen Tom other than in meetings or in the fraught circumstances of earlier in the day and she noticed now how attractive he was. He was a tall man, one or two inches over six feet, and square shouldered, but rangy not muscle-bound. In his lightweight blue suit, a bright tie that any television newsreader might have envied, and the remains of his tan, he was turning a few female heads.

Liz ordered dry white wine and as she found herself almost obsessively crunching her way through a large bowl of rice crackers on the table in front of them, she realised how hungry she was. The last time she'd eaten was breakfast in the Culloden Hotel. She wasn't sure whether Tom saw this outing as an opportunity for a social chat, or as business.

'I wanted to ask you about Marzipan,' he said as soon as their drinks arrived. 'I know Dave was running him while you were off, but you knew him longer.' He took a rice cracker from the rapidly emptying bowl and munched it thoughtfully. 'If there was anything in Marzipan's history that was worth pursuing, you'd be the one to know.'

'I've been racking my brains.'

'Of course,' he said. 'I was just wondering about his friends – you know, that perhaps he'd said something to one of them he shouldn't have. Even the best agents sometimes feel the need to confide in someone.'

'He was a genuine loner,' said Liz. She took a sip of her wine. 'It's one of the things we established when he was first recruited. He didn't have a best friend, or even any really close pals, though he got on all right with his schoolmates. Most of them are at university now.' She faltered slightly. 'As Marzipan was supposed to be . . .' She looked down for a moment to compose herself. She hated being emotional in front of a colleague.

'I know this has been hard for you,' he said sympathetically.

'It's hard for Dave too,' she said a little curtly, then reminded herself that Tom was trying to be nice and besides, none of it was his fault. She added, 'Did you ever have this sort of thing happen to you in Pakistan?'

'Yes, I did once,' he admitted, 'and it happened to colleagues too. It's always awful. The worst in my experience was a Pakistani named Fahdi. He was extremely westernised – I think he'd been to college in Texas. But he worked in Lahore and had relatives on the Afghan border.'

'Like the Imam,' said Liz.

'Yes, only Fahdi was definitely on our side. He was certain that his rural cousins had been helping Bin Laden. This was after the Yanks missed him in the caves at the end of the Afghan war. I have to say I was sceptical – we were getting about twenty sightings a day, none of which materialised – but he was absolutely positive. So we packed him off, with a GPS transponder sewn into the bottom of his rucksack.'

Tom stopped and took a long swallow of his drink.

'What happened?' asked Liz.

'Two weeks later we got notification of the signal. It was just over the Pakistani border in Afghanistan. We sent in a small group of SAS with American backup from Special Forces. They went in at night expecting a firefight – the area was full of Taliban and Al Qaeda. They'd pinpointed the source of the GPS signal in a valley, and the helicopter landed on the hill-side above it. But when the SAS moved down the hill there was no one there.'

'What about the signal?'

'I should have said there was no one there *alive*. They found the body of Fahdi, pinned by his arms to the ground. In his mouth they found the transponder, popped in like a sweet. Apparently, it was still working when the SAS took it out.'

'How horrible,' said Liz.

'What bothered me most was that I let him talk me round. I thought it was far too dangerous, but he insisted. I shouldn't have let him call the shots – that was my job.' He looked up at Liz. 'So I think I know what you're going through.'

She shrugged. 'I'm all right.'

He signalled for the bill, and when it came insisted on paying, despite Liz's offer to go halves. 'Nonsense,' he said, 'I asked you, remember.'

As they walked out of the hotel Liz stopped and pointed in the opposite direction from Thames House. 'I'm going that way to the Tube. Thanks for the drink.'

'Would you like a lift?' asked Tom. 'I've got my car today.'

'You don't even know where I live,' said Liz firmly. 'I might be taking you miles out of your way.'

'Kentish Town, right? Dave Armstrong mentioned it the other day.'

Why was Dave Armstrong talking about her to Tom Dartmouth? She didn't know whether to feel flattered or annoyed. But drinks had been pleasant, and a lift would save her time – not that she had much to do that evening. Solitary supper, the news on TV, her mandatory five minutes reading before she turned the bedside lamp off and tried to sleep.

'If it's really not inconvenient,' she said, 'that would be great.'

In the car both were quiet at first, as Tom navigated around the evening traffic near Victoria. He said, 'I seem to alternate between loving the independence of driving and thinking cars should be banned from all of central London.'

'Compromise. Ban all of them except yours,' suggested Liz, and Tom laughed as he drove towards Hyde Park Corner.

He's much more relaxed outside work, she thought, without seeming to be someone else – some of her colleagues were like Jekyll and Hyde in their split personas between work and non-work. 'Did you grow up in London?' she asked. She didn't really know a lot about Tom other than a collection of facts from his CV: the schools he'd gone to, the subjects he'd studied at Oxford, the maiden name of his mother.

'Yes. In Kensington.' He glanced over at her. 'Back then the middle class could still live there.'

'Then Oxford,' she said quietly.

He seemed taken unawares, then nodded. 'That's right. I did a BA, then another degree. In Arabic Studies.'

'You must have done well to be able to stay on.'

'I scraped a First. My tutor was as surprised as I was.'

'You could have landed a plum job in the City.'

He mused on this. 'Perhaps. But banking never really appealed.'

'So why did you apply to MI5? I'd have thought that if you studied Arabic you'd have been natural Six material.'

'Oh, I don't know. Five does the real business,' he said, with a small deprecating laugh she found appealing. He seemed so self-confident at work that it was refreshing to find he didn't take himself altogether seriously. 'Anyway, it's your turn,' he said, accelerating through a yellow light in Southampton Row, a manoeuvre Liz approved of, since she hated namby-pamby drivers. 'How long have you been in the Service?'

'Almost fifteen years.'

'Never,' he said. 'You're far too young.'

'Flattery will get you nowhere,' Liz declared.

'Well, it certainly won't get me to Kentish Town,' said Tom as they stopped at a traffic light, and he looked around, puzzled.

And for the next ten minutes Liz concentrated on giving directions, until suddenly she realised they were about to turn into her street and the evening, at least as far as it concerned Tom Dartmouth, was about to end. And to think, she told herself, that before she went to Belfast she had actually cleaned up the flat to visitor standard, a rare feat for Liz when she was so busy at work.

She wondered if she should ask him in – she was still regretting her anger that afternoon, and was actually enjoying his company. She hadn't learned much about him, she reflected, but he seemed congenial as well as attractive.

In front of her house he pulled into an empty parking space, and kept the engine running. Hesitantly, Liz said, 'It's kind of you to drive me home. Your family must be waiting for you.'

He looked puzzled. 'Family?'

'I thought you were married.' Liz saw no point being coy.

'Who told you that?'

'Dave Armstrong, naturally,' she said. 'Who else?'

He shook his head with a degree of wonderment. 'He was right about Kentish Town, but wrong about me. I *was* married, that's true enough. But I'm divorced.'

He said this dispassionately, showing none of the emotional baggage so often carried by divorced men – some bitter, some still in love with their ex-wives, a few jubilant as schoolboys at their liberation from a virago they were all too willing to talk about. What a relief not to hear that in Tom's voice, just cut-and-dried acknowledgement of a fact.

And partly because of this, Liz thought again about asking him in. Why not? It wasn't as if she were throwing herself at him; that wasn't what she had in mind at all. But it would be nice to know him better, see what else lay behind the facade of professional competence. She was on the verge of asking if he'd like to come in for coffee when he looked at his watch pointedly. 'Listen, I'd better go and leave you to your beauty sleep. And actually, I could use some myself. I've been flat out at work for the last two weeks.'

She nodded, feeling slightly disappointed, though part of her knew she too was exhausted and needed an early night. Then he added cheerfully, 'Now that I know how to get here, maybe we could do it again sometime.'

'What?' she asked teasingly. 'Another lift home?'

'Why not?' he said. 'One of my uncles was a chauffeur. I'm sure I've inherited some of his genes.'

Liz was a little surprised, having pegged Tom as middle class through and through. He said, 'Do you ever go up to the Heath?'

'Sometimes in summer,' she said. 'It's nice and fresh up there in the evenings. Why?' she asked curiously.

'I used to go there as a little boy with my father. He was absolutely mad about kites, but hopeless at flying them. We'd spend hours trying to get them off the ground.' He gave a little laugh, as if visualising his father's ineptitude.

'Then one Saturday, my father brought home a new kite he claimed was extra special. It was autumn, and we went to Hampstead Heath right away because the light went so early in the afternoon. The wind was blowing incredibly hard – it seemed like a gale in one of those naval films. The kite was about twice as tall as I was, and I was sure we would never get it up into the air. But somehow we did. And then it flew for *hours.*' For a moment he seemed lost in memory. Then emerging from his reverie, he turned and gave a quick smile at Liz.

'What were you doing in North London?' she asked.

'Oh, we used to live around here. Though it wasn't quite so gentrified then.' He gestured at her road. Liz's neighbours were lawyers, teachers, accountants – the working class in her street had long since moved to cheaper pastures.

'I thought you said you grew up in Kensington.'

He nodded. 'I did, but that was after my father died.' He smiled wistfully. 'He got knocked down by a car on his way to work. Once my mother remarried, we moved to Kensington. I suppose you could say she did rather better for herself second time round.' He said this lightly as well, but Liz sensed genuine hostility underneath his mild mockery.

They said goodnight, and Tom waited to drive off until Liz had unlocked the door to her building and waved. As she entered her flat and turned on the light, she nodded approvingly at its rare state of tidiness. Tom doesn't know what he's missing, Liz thought with amusement, since in three or four days the flat would be back to its normal state of half-controlled chaos.

She kicked her shoes off, poured a glass of Sauvignon from an open bottle in the fridge, then sat down on her one comfortable chair. She realised how much she had liked Tom Dartmouth this evening, though not for the reasons an outside observer might deduce.

Yes, he was good-looking in a kind of rough-hewn way that doubtless made some women swoon; yes, he was excellent at his job, tough-minded yet also sophisticated, highly educated without boring you to death with gratuitous displays of erudition.

None of which cut much ice with Liz. On a personal level what had struck her had nothing to do with credentials. If anything, it was Tom's wry, levelling sense of humour that first appealed – especially the fact that he didn't hesitate to poke gentle fun at himself. And he seemed to go out of his way to show he wasn't as inflated as his CV. She liked the way he said he'd 'scraped' a First, though she knew from Watts, the hide-bound Merton don, that he'd had the best degree in his year. And he wasn't afraid to acknowledge his failures, as with the agent Fahdi he'd lost in Afghanistan, or reveal that he felt them deeply.

But the modesty and the sense of humour weren't really what struck Liz now. Underneath Tom's easy-going manner, she sensed a deep, lurking sadness that he had long ago decided to keep buried. He is carrying a wound, thought Liz, the way a war veteran might carry shrapnel deep inside. Somehow she doubted Tom often talked about his father – she felt flattered that he had with her.

Don't get carried away, she told herself, sensitive to the fact that she had no one intimate in her life just then. Still, she was a little intrigued by Tom Dartmouth, and wondered how long it would be before he offered to chauffeur her again. I hope it's soon, she decided, finishing her wine and deciding to get into bed early. Then she laughed as she had an image of herself, standing outside the fourth-floor lift, with her thumb up, hitch-hiker style, but being very choosy about the driver.

21

Three days later, Rose Love, a junior member of Investigations, came to see Judith Spratt in the Operations Room. Judith liked the first-year recruit, and she tried to encourage her. For although Rose had a First from York University and was also a strikingly pretty young woman, she seemed very unsure of herself. Despite the considerable attention paid to her by male colleagues, she was reluctant to be assertive, even when she should. Now Rose spoke to Judith in little more than a whisper. 'Sorry to bother you, but it's about the CCTV footage.'

'Yes,' said Judith loudly, unable to suppress her impatience. Doubtless there was another hitch – a disk wiped by a shop owner, or undated material supplied by the supermarket security men. She was about to tell Rose just to get on with things as best she could when she forced herself to be patient and hear the girl out.

'It's just I think that possibly – I'm not sure – we may have found something.'

For Rose this was virtually a declaration of certainty, which made Judith focus immediately. 'Let me see,' she said, getting up from her seat.

Ten minutes later Judith called Tom Dartmouth to the room downstairs, and they were both looking at a monitor while Rose moved through the footage screen by screen. 'There!'

called Judith sharply, and the screen froze. It was not a very clear picture, but three figures were clearly discernible at the front of the shop by the till, where they were captured at a range of seven feet by the camera positioned high on the wall above the Lucozade clock. They were male, Asian – a mix of colour and dress combined to give that distinct impression – and seemed to be young. None of them looked at the camera, or for that matter at Irwin Patel, who was serving one of them. The time meter said 20:24.

'Sorry,' said Tom Dartmouth apologetically, 'but you better talk me through it. I've never been any good at this – it all looks like ultrasound scans to me.'

'The man at the till. We think he may be a match with one of the Dutch photos.' Judith passed him a printout, which in contrast to the frozen video frame was high resolution and clear. The face that stared out from it was of a personable-looking youth of Asian appearance, half man and half boy, who was struggling to grow a moustache and had a slight overbite and a broad smile.

'They've identified him as Rashid Khan. He's nineteen years old and comes from Wolverhampton.'

'Okay,' said Tom, weighing this, 'but where's the match?' He gave a self-deprecating laugh. 'I don't mean to sound unPC, but for the life of me I couldn't tell you which of these three he's meant to be.'

'Look again,' said Judith. 'The man at the till. See anything unusual about him?'

Tom peered closely at the screen. 'He's not very tall, is he?'

Judith nodded. 'Five foot one-and-a-half inches, to be precise. At least according to the passport application of Rashid Khan. But that's not all – look closely at the face.' Tom did so obediently. 'Same moustache, or effort at one. Same slight prominence of the upper teeth.'

'Can't say I see that,' said Tom.

Rose Love suddenly spoke up. 'It's very difficult,' she announced, then seemed about to lapse back into shyness until something prompted her and she went on. 'If you watch this sort of thing several hours a day it all seems much clearer. Like the ultrasounds you mentioned – parents think they're clear as mud, but to an obstetrician they're picture-perfect.' And after this she blushed and went quiet, while Judith looked at her, pleasantly astonished by this intervention.

Tom held up his hands in a gesture of mock surrender. 'You're the experts. If you say it's a match then I have to accept that.'

'We *think* it's a match,' said Judith. 'No guarantees.'

'Of course,' said Tom. 'But assuming you're right, who the hell is Rashid Khan?'

'We've got no trace under that name,' said Judith. 'I'm seeing Dave Armstrong right after you,' she added, since identifying a suspect might be her responsibility, but finding them was someone else's.

At first Irwin Patel thought the policeman was back in his shop to return the CCTV footage he had taken away the week before. But this time he was accompanied by a man in a grey parka jacket. 'Could we have a word,' asked the policeman, 'in the back of the shop?'

'Oscar,' called Irwin, and gestured for his son to man the till, then led the two men to the small storeroom which doubled as an office – or more accurately, the place where Irwin and his family took their breaks during open hours.

'Yes gentlemen,' said Irwin politely but a little nervously.

The man in the parka spoke. 'We found pictures on the footage you gave us of someone we are interested in.' He handed an eight-by-eleven still photo captured from the CCTV video footage to Irwin, who studied it carefully.

'Do you remember serving this man?'

Irwin thought hard. He wanted to help, but the fact was that probably fifty per cent of his business was passing trade – one-off visitors to his shop he would never see again. 'No,' he said at last.

'Or the men behind him?'

Irwin peered at the photograph for some time. The beat policeman said impatiently, 'Can't you remember a group of three like this? It was probably last Monday, if that's any help.'

Irwin was tempted to remark that his Asian clientele all looked alike to him, but said instead, 'If I had to guess, I would say I serve over fifty Asian men under the age of thirty every day. Some come in alone, some with a friend, and some,' he looked pointedly at the man he now thought of as PC Plod, 'come with two friends. I do not recognise any of these men.'

The constable groaned, but the man in the parka seemed unperturbed. 'How about this man?' he asked, handing another photograph to Irwin. It was the same photo Judith Spratt had extracted from the five hundred or so sent by her Dutch counterparts only days before.

Whether because of the clarity of this picture or its full-frontal pose, this time Irwin's face lit up. 'I've seen this man!' he exclaimed. 'Here in the shop.'

'Did you speak with him?'

Irwin shrugged. 'I must have. He was a customer. But probably only to say thank you, or here's your change. Nothing more than that. I couldn't remember his voice,' he said, suddenly worried they were expecting that.

'That's all right. But do you by any chance remember what he bought?' asked the plain-clothes man.

'As a matter of fact I do,' said Irwin. 'He bought rolling papers – you know, for cigarettes. I remember that because he was very short. Not much more than five feet tall,' he added, proud of his own five feet seven inches. 'I remember wanting to tell him that smoking stunts your growth.'

And at this even the po-faced PC Plod laughed. He looked towards the man by his side. He wasn't sure if he was Special Branch or some higher kind of spook, but he wasn't a bad bloke – he'd said to call him Dave. And Dave was happy now.

22

Miss Prideaux's remark that she was 'awfully sorry to hear about Ravi' had been nagging at Liz ever since that day in Oxford. She counted Judith Spratt as her friend, but Judith had said nothing to her about any problem with her husband. Liz had always got on well with Ravi Singh, a handsome westernised Sikh who was doing very well and earning a lot of money in a City investment bank. Their marriage always seemed so happy that Liz wondered if perhaps Ravi was ill.

Normally, Liz wouldn't have thought of prying into a colleague's matrimonial affairs, but Judith was on the list of suspects. When she had asked B Branch if Judith had recently mentioned anything about Ravi – any change of circumstances in her private life, as she was required to do – the answer came back that she had not. Liz's heart sank. She would have to say something herself.

She was already feeling low. The previous evening she'd phoned her mother, who had seen Dr Barlow about her test results that afternoon.

The phone in Bowerbridge seemed to ring forever, and Liz was about to give up when her mother answered at last. 'Hello, darling,' she said, 'I was in the garden picking some delphiniums. They're wonderful this year. You should come down before they're over.'

How typical of her mother's priorities, thought Liz, with a

daughter's mixed affection and annoyance. 'What did Barlow say?'

Her mother paused, her normal reaction to her daughter's directness. 'It's nothing too terrible, Liz.'

'Good,' she said, trying to sound cheerful rather than impatient. 'Tell me what he said.'

'Well, it seems there might be a problem. He wants me to go into hospital for a surgical procedure.'

'What kind of surgical procedure, Mother?'

'They've found something growing and I guess they want to see what it is. A biopsy?' She said it hesitantly, as if pronouncing the Latin name for a species of rose.

Only my mother, thought Liz, can make a tumour sound like a horticultural phenomenon. 'When is this?'

'Saturday week. It shouldn't take long.'

She'll be in overnight, thought Liz, and immediately said she would come down that Friday. Her mother's protestations did not last for long, and Liz could tell from her mother's voice that she was relieved, and also that she was scared.

Now, as she sat at her desk, suddenly she felt tears in her eyes. She had woken in the night thinking about Marzipan, the mole hunt which didn't seem to be getting anywhere, and the terrorists on the loose, and finally her mother's tests. Now, to top it all off, Liz knew she would have to talk to Judith, since Judith was on her list. And as luck would have it, she ran into her in the corridor later that morning, as Liz was on her way to check on Peggy's progress. Elegantly dressed as usual, in a fawn skirt and cream cashmere sweater, Judith seemed to be in a hurry. She didn't stop at first when Liz said hello.

'Have you got a second, Judith?' Liz called after her.

Her friend slowed down, though her body language spoke nothing but tension. 'Sorry, Liz, I'm in a bit of a rush.'

'Okay,' said Liz, and was about to ask her when she would have time to talk when Dave Armstrong appeared from nowhere. He gave Liz a playful tap on the shoulder. 'Did Peggy find you? She's seems all keyed up about something.'

'I'm just on my way to see her. Hang on a sec,' she added and turned back to Judith. But she'd moved away, striding down the corridor at speed. Damn, thought Liz, thinking of her own reluctance to beard her friend. She clearly doesn't want to talk to me, either. Damn!

She found Peggy in the conference room. 'Dave said you wanted me?'

'We've cracked it,' Peggy announced excitedly.

'Sorry?' said Liz.

'Technical Ted. He's come through at last. Look.' She pushed over a small stack of laser printouts.

Liz sat down and leafed through the first pages, mystified by what seemed an unvariegated mass of listings and announcements from some bulletin. 'What am I looking at?'

'Sorry,' said Peggy. 'Turn the next page. I've circled the relevant bit.'

As Liz did so, Peggy explained. 'It's the talk Liam O'Phelan was giving in Oxford.'

'From Boston to Belfast: Britain's Dirty War in Northern Ireland and Abroad'. Dr L. O'Phelan, St Antony's College. 7:30p.m.

Liz's pulse was racing, but not because Peggy Kinsolving's excitement was contagious. Her younger colleague, Liz sensed, was keyed up because Technical Ted had managed to decipher the disk – which had assumed such significance just because its contents had remained a mystery. That was so often the problem with the investigative process, thought Liz: the more difficult a secret was to uncover, the greater its importance became.

But she sensed that there was something here worth following up. O'Phelan's topic suggested an interest in contemporary Irish political affairs which his high-flown historical chatter about Charles Stewart Parnell did not. It also indicated a strongly Republican and anti-British position. He might have changed his views or at least moderated them in the years between his talk at Oxford and the present day, but Liz doubted that he had mellowed very much.

'Well done,' Liz said to Peggy, and she meant it, for now, she decided, she would need to speak to O'Phelan again and probe this interest in the 'dirty war'. But it would have to wait. First she'd see what Jimmy Fergus unearthed about the sly, intelligent don at Queen's. And there were some other bigger fish to fry before that. With the exception of Tom Dartmouth, she realised, she had yet to speak directly with any of the suspects on the list.

23

For the second time in a month Dave Armstrong found himself in Wolverhampton. It should have been a two-hour drive – at least the way Dave drove – but the congestion at the M6/M42 junction made it closer to three before Dave found himself sitting with a local Special Branch officer in McDonald's. The night before, Dave, who liked to think of himself as fairly fit, had watched a TV documentary about the effects of a McDonald's diet, and now he watched fascinated as the officer tucked into a Big Mac, large fries and a chocolate shake. Dave stuck to black coffee, so hot it burned his tongue on the first sip.

The Special Branch man suppressed a belch, then said, 'We're still not entirely clear how you want to handle this. I've got armed officers at the ready, but you said something about "softly softly" on the phone.'

'Do we know who's in the house?'

'Not precisely. It's a family residence. People named Khan. Respectable couple – the man is a sales rep for a restaurant supply business. His wife works part-time in a laundry. Three kids – all teenagers. Two boys and a girl. Your guy's the eldest but hasn't – as far as we know – left home yet.'

Dave had already planned his approach. He certainly had no intention of risking his life or the life of any officer entering the house of Rashid Khan. He was also well aware how much ill will a heavy-handed approach might cause. If Rashid's family were in the house, it seemed unlikely that a police presence would provoke an armed response, at least not immediately, or that Rashid would blow himself up as soon as he realised it was the police at the door, but he didn't intend to risk it.

'I wouldn't call it softly, but I'd like to start with just a knock on the door. I want concealed backup that's armed and ready and expecting trouble, but they're not to do anything until they see what the initial response is.'

'And who's going to be the man at the door?'

'I am,' said Dave.

He rang the bell and waited. Unarmed, he could not help but think of how helpless he would be if someone answered the door with a gun. He was surprised when a girl, still in her teens and in school uniform, opened the door.

'Yes?' she ventured timidly. It was teatime, and Dave wondered who else would be in the house.

'I'm from the Benefits Office,' said Dave, 'and I wanted a word with Rashid Khan. It's just a routine check about his claim. Is he in?'

Her astonishment seemed genuine to Dave. 'No, but why? Is he in trouble?'

'Is your mother or father at home?'

Ten minutes later Rashid's father's bewilderment was growing. 'Are you sure it is our son you are looking for?' he asked yet again.

'I'm afraid so,' said Dave patiently.

'It doesn't make sense. It cannot be the son I raised. He shared everything with us.'

'Everything?' asked Dave, who had learned nothing from

either parent that would explain their son's disaffection – they thought Rashid had been in Holland for work experience before he went to university.

'Everything,' repeated the father defiantly.

'Then why don't you know where he is now?'

24

He drove to Wokingham with unusual caution, scrupulously observing speed limits and keeping a sharp eye out for cameras. Parking his car in a pay and display car park in the centre of town, he took a taxi from a nearby rank. The address he gave the driver was on an estate on the fringes of the city. To the driver's cheery conversation he merely grunted at first, then as the driver kept talking anyway, he adopted a broad West Country accent and confided that his team was Taunton Town. As planned, this reduced the driver to silence. When they reached 17 Avon Circle Crescent the passenger got out, tipping the driver an unmemorable ten per cent.

The address was not the passenger's final destination. He waited until the taxi had pulled away, then walked to the end of the Crescent, along the side of the brand new children's playground, and on to Somerset Drive, a line of new small brick houses, each with a patch of grass in front, and a small garden to the rear.

At number 48 he turned in sharply and was about to ring the bell when the door opened. Without a greeting, he slid inside and stood in the hallway.

'Where are the other two?'

'Upstairs, watching television. Do you want to see them?'

'No. Leave them.'

The visitor sat down on the sofa but kept his raincoat on.

He motioned for Bashir Siddiqui to sit down across from him on the room's one chair. 'They've had a breakthrough. They checked the CCTV coverage for the area around the alley where the fellow from the bookshop was disposed of, and they've recognised one of you in a grocery store. Rashid.'

'How did they know who he was?' Bashir asked with astonishment. Rashid had been picked partly because he had no UK record of any kind.

'One of Abu Sayed's associates rang from Holland on the day you were supposed to be at the bookshop. The call was traced, and the Dutch security people sent photographs over. One of them was of Rashid; when they compared the CCTV footage they made a match.'

Bashir groaned. He had not wanted to go into any shop that evening, but Rashid had insisted. Worried that the little man was losing his nerve, Bashir had reluctantly agreed.

'Look,' said the visitor, 'I don't want to go into who's to blame for what. What's important now is that you listen very carefully to me and do what I say.'

He stared at Bashir with hard unblinking eyes until Bashir returned his gaze and nodded in submission. Then he said, 'There is no reason to think they are on to you. They know about Rashid, yes, but they don't have any idea where he is. Provided you don't make any more stupid mistakes, there is no way for them to find out.'

'What do you want me to do?'

'Don't *do* anything. Doing things is what has almost got you caught. Sit tight. From now on, there is to be no external communication – especially not with Abu Sayed or any of his associates. Leave that to me, do you understand? None of you should be in touch with anyone, except if you need to contact me.' He looked up at the ceiling. 'I don't care how safe those boys think they are or how careful they think they're being, don't let them communicate with anyone. No mobile phone, no text messages, not even an internet cafe. Is that clear?'

Bashir nodded again, for he was comfortable following the orders of the Englishman. It was the Englishman, after all, who had initially recruited him. Not Abu Sayed or any other imam. He asked hesitantly, 'Can we leave the house?'

The man thought for a moment. 'Yes. It would seem odd to the neighbours if none of you were seen coming in and out. But not all three of you together. And keep Rashid out of the town centre.'

'Shall I tell him he's been identified?'

'How would he take it?'

Bashir thought of that evening when they had hunted down the boy from the bookshop, how Rashid's agitation had been transparent beforehand, even though Rashid's only job was to act as a decoy. He shook his head. 'I think it would frighten him very much. He might get panicky.'

The Englishman nodded. 'That's your answer then.' He got up, and shook hands with Bashir. 'If you can just keep your cool, all will be well. There isn't that much longer to wait.'

25

Patrick Dobson was spending a few days at home. He had fractured his wrist falling from a ladder in the garden while pruning a wisteria. Liz had decided that she and Peggy would call on him rather than wait for him to return to work. She had found from experience that there was a lot to be picked up about a person from their home, and she was hoping the journey would not be a waste of time.

On their drive down, Peggy and Liz had almost got lost, finding themselves following a seemingly endless maze of avenues and drives, each lined by large suburban houses with big leafy gardens.

At last they came to the Dobson residence, a thirties mock-Tudor house of brown brick, with white plaster gables and beams. Peggy said, 'I hadn't realised MI5 paid so well.' Sometimes with Peggy it was difficult to distinguish innocence from irony, but this time there was no mistaking her tartness.

Liz laughed. 'I think you'll find,' she said, 'that there's been another source of funds into the Dobson household.'

Patrick Dobson was not even forty years old, but his home seemed strangely middle-aged. What Dobson grandly called his drawing room had a formality that seemed completely out of keeping for a still youngish MI5 officer. It was panelled in oak and had a large mock Elizabethan fireplace and leaded windows. The sofa on which Liz and Peggy sat was chintz-covered and pillowy soft, the chairs were mahogany, and the carpet was a dull sage green. On the walls hung a mixture of family portraits and watercolours of nineteenth-century colonial scenes – a procession of elephants in Delhi under the Raj, and an antique hand-coloured map of the Imperial City of Beijing.

'What a beautiful room,' said Peggy Kinsolving admiringly.

If you like that sort of thing, thought Liz caustically.

Now Dobson thanked Peggy for her compliment, adding, 'This was my wife's parents' house. Her father was in the Colonial Service. My wife inherited it after they died.'

That explains it, thought Liz. She knew about his father-in-law from the file. He had been a district officer in Uganda. Thank God, she thought to herself, we're not going to have to try and find out how he comes to live in such affluence. There had been a CIA agent in Washington who claimed that his lifestyle was funded by a wealthy wife, when as it turned out it was funded by the KGB, but she did not think they were into that sort of situation with Patrick Dobson.

Dobson sat, neat and upright in a comfortable armchair across from them. He was a short, pie-faced man, with blond hair combed straight back. Wearing a blue blazer, grey flannels, and what looked to be a college tie, he was a model of politeness. But stiff.

Liz decided she had better kick things off, lest they get bogged down in Dobson's efforts to rewrite his past. 'This shouldn't take long, Patrick,' she said cheerfully, in an effort to make things less formal.

They reviewed the bare facts of his CV – his boyhood in South London, his schooling (a scholarship to Alleyn's School in Dulwich), his time at Oxford, followed straightaway by entry into MI5. Dobson gave only short answers at first, but gradually became more expansive, especially when they arrived at his current job in DG's office. He spoke so animatedly about this, explaining what a wonderful perspective he got on all the Service's operations, that for over five minutes Liz was unable to ask a single question.

She was about to interrupt when a knock at the door did the job for her. A woman came in with a tray – a pot of coffee, cups and saucers, and a plate of biscuits. She was dressed for a smart lunch, wearing heels and a floral frock.

'Ah, Teresa. These are the colleagues I told you about.'

She nodded politely, and came forward with the tray. Dobson made introductions, but it was obvious his wife did not want to linger. 'I won't intrude,' she said with a forced smile, looking only at her husband. 'I'm just off to the church to do the flowers before the Women's Institute lunch.'

'Of course, darling. See you later.'

Liz sat back down with her coffee, discomfited. If she didn't take charge, she felt she would soon be lost in this safe suburban world. 'If I could just go back to your time at Oxford,' she said. 'You were very religious as an undergraduate, I gather.'

For the first time she sensed Dobson's antennae quiver. 'Only by the standards of the other students,' he said defensively. 'I went to chapel every week. I still do – go to church that is. My wife attends as well. I don't think there's anything peculiar about it. Do you?'

Liz said mildly, 'Of course not. My cousin's a deacon and one of his daughters is hoping to be ordained.' Technically, a cousin's *husband* had been a deacon, and their daughter's calling had lasted only until she'd managed to get a boyfriend, but Liz wasn't going to tell Dobson that.

He relaxed slightly. 'I imagine you've seen the chaplain at

Pembroke. When I first applied, he said he'd been asked about me. How is he these days?'

'Fine. At least he seemed that way to me.' However caustic Hickson had been about his ex-pupil, Liz was happy to admit she'd seen him.

'Was he sober?'

Liz looked at Dobson impassively. 'He was when we talked.'

'That makes a change,' Dobson said, regaining his confidence. He hadn't touched his coffee.

Liz gave a diplomatic smile. 'He said you were a Young Conservative at Oxford.'

'I was interested,' said Dobson with a shrug. 'Don't tell me that's unusual, too?' For the first time there was an edge to his voice.

Liz shrugged. 'I don't know. It's probably me who was unusual.' She said, half confidingly, 'I was a bit of a leftie at university. I'm surprised I got through the vetting.' She laughed. 'It wasn't the sixties, I grant you, but it was quite a political time. Everyone was worked up about the Palestinians.' She paused. 'And Ireland, of course.'

But Dobson didn't bite. 'The big issue in my day was rent increases,' he said dryly.

'I see.'

Peggy had been a non-participant in the interview so far, studiously taking notes. Now she looked up for the first time. 'But you've got Irish blood, haven't you?' she asked brightly.

Dobson stared at her coldly. 'I believe one of my grandmothers was Irish,' he said slowly.

'Did she emigrate here?'

'Emigrate? What a grand word – I imagine she'd have said she came here for work. The story was,' he said, distancing himself, 'that she was "in service" in Galway for an Anglo-Irish family. When they moved back to London she came with them. She met my grandfather, and married him.' He added pointedly, 'He was English. Owned a string of garages in South London.' This was said, Liz decided, to disabuse them of any idea that his grandfather had been 'in service' too.

'She must have had quite a story to tell,' gushed Peggy. Liz, who was beginning to admire Peggy's skill at drawing people out, sat back and watched. 'Did you know your grandmother?' Peggy asked.

'A bit,' he said reluctantly. 'She died when I was a boy.'

'She must have missed Ireland,' said Peggy sympathetically. 'Did she ever go back?'

'I imagine she went back sometimes.' He hesitated, almost imperceptibly. Liz imagined he was calculating what they already knew, and what they could find out. He'd be surprised, thought Liz, thinking of the day before, when Peggy had proudly shown her a genealogical chart of the Dobson maternal line. It was of almost byzantine complexity, its branches spread out like the limbs of a monkey puzzle tree. That's when Liz had suggested Peggy ask the questions about the family.

'Actually,' Dobson admitted, 'I went with her once. To Connemara. That's where she was from.'

'Family still there?' asked Liz as casually as she could, trying not to trigger a defensive reaction.

Dobson shrugged. 'I would think so. It was a typically Irish set-up – my grandmother was one of seven children.'

Peggy interjected. 'Your grandmother's maiden name was O'Hare, wasn't it?'

Dobson began to nod, then stopped suddenly. 'How did you know that?'

Peggy ignored him, and looking at her notes continued: 'And her eldest brother was named Sean, yes?' She didn't wait for an answer. 'He moved north to Londonderry, before the War – if I've got things right he was quite a bit older than she was. He had two sons, the eldest named Kieran, and Kieran himself had one son – Patrick. Same name as yours. And he was – is, I should say – your second cousin.'

Dobson stayed completely silent until Peggy finished. Then ignoring her, he stared at Liz. She couldn't tell if it was fear or anger in his eyes. 'Yes?' he asked neutrally.

'Well,' said Liz, sounding matter of fact, 'your second cousin was detained and spent twelve months in the Maze. Applicants to MI5 are asked to declare any relative who has been convicted of a crime, spent any time in one of HM's prisons, or been charged with subversive activity. Yet Patrick O'Hare was not on your form. Can you tell me why?'

Outwardly Dobson stayed impressively calm. 'Is there a point to this?' he asked quietly.

'We have to be thorough,' she said firmly.

Dobson looked irritated. 'I knew nothing about this cousin of mine. How could I? For goodness sake, I was five years old when it happened.'

'Of course,' said Liz, and moved quickly onto another topic, to Peggy's mystification.

'So what do you think?' asked Liz, as they joined the M3. Peggy liked the comfort of the Audi, but was a little unnerved by the zippy way Liz drove it.

'I don't believe he didn't know about his cousin.'

'Why not?'

Peggy pondered this. Dobson hadn't liked any of the questions about his mother's Irish roots. Initially Peggy put this down to snobbery – presumably a pig farm in Galway didn't sit easily for a man now accustomed to a wing chair in Surrey. Yet though it was conceded reluctantly, he had acknowledged his background. Whereas he'd flatly denied any knowledge of his IRA relative.

And Liz had backed off. Why? Peggy said tentatively, 'Weren't you surprised he didn't know his second cousin?'

'It seems a pretty remote connection,' said Liz, staring fixedly at the motorway.

'Does it?' asked Peggy with genuine surprise, for she had a vast extended family she knew well – too well, she often thought, as she trekked towards yet another wedding, or christening, or family reunion. 'I thought everyone knew who their second cousin was.'

'Not necessarily,' argued Liz. 'And anyway, on the application it's immediate family they're most interested in. He didn't have to declare his second cousin even if he knew about him.'

'Doesn't matter,' said Peggy, sticking to her guns. 'I still think he was being economical with the truth.'

Liz smiled, checking the rear-view mirror. 'Actually, so do I,' she said.

'Really?' Peggy was surprised. Perhaps Liz had been playing devil's advocate.

'No, I don't think he told the truth,' said Liz, as she merged onto the M4, cutting over quickly into the fast lane. 'But it's nothing to do with his family tree.'

'What then?'

'Dobson said he was only five when his cousin was interned.' She paused as she changed lanes, and Peggy did a mental calculation. Patrick Dobson had been born in 1968; his namesake cousin had been interned in 1973. 'But Dobson *was* only five,' Peggy said, then held her breath, trying not to gasp as Liz accelerated around an enormous HGV.

'I'm sure he was,' said Liz crisply. 'But Internment lasted four years. So how did Dobson know which year his cousin was put in the Maze? I didn't tell him; you didn't either. And yet think of his exact words. He didn't say "I was just a kid when this man I never knew got put away." He was very specific: "I was five years old when it happened."' She flashed a sideways smile at Peggy. 'So no, I don't believe him either. But what we don't know is whether he lied for a purpose, or just because he's got a hang-up about his forebears.'

26

Rashid knew nothing of the Englishman's warning that his identity had been uncovered, and Bashir had conveyed none of his own alarm, though he had stressed to Rashid and the other conspirator that they were not to be in contact with anyone.

And Rashid would have obeyed this unquestioningly had he not been worried about his sister Yasmina. She was sixteen, and vulnerable; he had tried in the last two years, since his own increasing involvement with Islam, to watch over her, grown concerned as she entered adolescence, grown even more concerned when she began to make friends with boys, especially English boys – Rashid knew, even if his parents had not realised, that Yasmina was a pretty girl.

She adored him, her elder brother by three years, but he found it difficult to influence her. Her nature seemed so outgoing and her interests so different from the religious principles he now adhered to.

He had no scruples about leaving the household so abruptly, for his parents no longer featured in his mental galaxy. He didn't hate them, no, he pitied them, for he saw how they, as first-generation implants in an alien society, had lost all sense of their origins and their faith. They would not ever be truly welcome in this new 'home' either, he concluded with some bitterness.

He thought of the young man from the bookshop Bashir had

killed. What kind of Muslim could he have been, to work for Western masters? Had he no shame? Did he not recognise his betrayal of his faith, of his brothers in Islam?

Rashid had not done the killing himself – it was understood that, small as he was, he might have trouble finishing the job quickly. And inwardly, he knew he might have been too scared. He was not by nature violent. Bashir seemed to sense this, for he had told him often enough that his instinctive aversion to violence meant he was a very strong man, to be willing to undertake violence in the name of Allah.

So he had served as the fatal decoy, distracting the boy with his falsely friendly greeting while Bashir sprung out from an obscured doorway at the back of the warehouse which ran along the alley and, running quickly, stabbed the bookshop boy once, hard, in the lower back. As Rashid stood lookout, Bashir had swung his arm around the neck of the already slumping figure and, propping him up, in one violent motion slit his throat.

Now in the early afternoon, after midday prayers in the sitting room and a lunch of soup and bread, Bashir had said he could go out. 'Don't go far,' he said. 'And stay out of shops.'

'Of course,' said Rashid, but within five minutes he was catching the bus into the heart of Wokingham. He got off as soon as he reached an area dense with shops, and in the next street he found one selling mobile phones. He bought the simplest model, pay as you go, and a ten-pound voucher for it.

Just beside the shop was an alley leading into a small courtyard, and there he tried to dial, but there was no signal, and when he looked at his watch he realised he had already been gone almost an hour. Bashir would soon be worried. Back at the bus stop, he waited impatiently for over ten minutes; he did not want to use his phone there, where several people were standing in the queue.

At last the bus came. He got off one stop early and walked quickly, his concern about being away too long outweighed by his urgent need to phone Yasmina. He broke into a run and when he was within a street of Somerset Drive, stopped by some railings and dialled Yasmina's mobile phone. He was far more worried about Bashir's anger than he was about the police. He felt perfectly safe, since his throwaway phone was untraceable – he knew that. Bashir used them, whenever he called the contact point.

'Yasmina?'

'Rashid, are you all right?'

'I'm fine, Yasmina.'

'But where are you?'

'It doesn't matter – I'm not allowed to tell you. But I am fine. That's why I have rung. To tell you not to worry. I should be home in just a few weeks.'

'Are you sure?' Yasmina sounded surprised, and Rashid wondered why. 'Is it safe to phone?' she added.

'Why wouldn't it be?' asked Rashid.

'It's just—' she began, then stopped.

'Tell me, Yasmina.'

'All right, but you mustn't let Papa know. Not even that we talked. A man came here looking for you. He said he was from the Benefits – but I don't think he was. Papa was very upset afterwards.'

Rashid's pulse began to race, and his right hand, holding the phone, shook so much that he had to steady it with his left. A passing woman looked at him oddly, and he turned around to face the railing away from her gaze. 'Why didn't you tell me this?' he asked angrily.

'But Rashid, I didn't know how to reach you. You left without warning. You didn't even take your phone.'

He knew this was true, and tried to calm his agitation and keep it from turning to rage at Yasmina. She was the only ally he had outside his two comrades in the small house. He knew his parents would never understand; they had probably helped the police as much as they could. And his little brother was just that – little, not even fourteen years old. 'Do you know what this man wanted?'

'Yes, Rashid. He wanted you.'

In Thames House the trace came through to the monitors immediately. The phone on Judith Spratt's desk rang. 'We've got a call to Wolverhampton that we're tracking now. Think you'll want to hear this one,' said Lawrence, a junior transcriber, to Judith.

There had been so many false alarms already – a series of mysterious calls for the Khan father which turned out to be secret arrangements for his wife's birthday – that Judith was reluctant to get excited. 'Is it to the house?' she asked sharply.

'No. It's to the sister's mobile – though A4 say she's in the house. We think it's her brother.'

'Fast as you can then,' said Judith, convinced despite herself.

Five minutes later, Lawrence came back with a transcript of the conversation, which Judith, now joined by Tom Dartmouth, scanned quickly. 'Where was the call made from?' asked Tom.

'We're working on it. It was a mobile phone, probably a throwaway,' explained Lawrence.

Tom looked at Lawrence. 'How close a fix can we get on him?'

Lawrence shrugged. 'Can't say at the moment. Two, maybe three miles?'

'In any direction?'

Lawrence nodded and Tom swore softly. 'That's a hell of a big area. Unless he's in the Highlands or North Wales. In any urban area God knows how many thousands of people there are.'

'Thanks, Lawrence,' said Judith, and the junior withdrew. She would praise his quickness later, but now she and Tom needed to determine exactly what they had – and what to do next. She looked at Tom, whom she was beginning to like in spite of herself – generally speaking, she liked to get on with things on her own, and found section heads got in the way rather than helped. But Tom's style was to stand back. He was almost detached, though he offered advice when asked and was always very calm. That suited Judith. She said to him, 'Dave was hoping the family would keep quiet – apparently the parents were totally bewildered when he explained what their son was up to. They promised to cooperate completely. But the sister was always going to be the weak link. Now thanks to her, this Rashid bloke knows we're looking for him.'

'No bad thing,' said Tom calmly. 'If he can screw up this badly when he thinks he's safe, let's hope he screws up even more now that he feels hunted.'

27

Dave Armstrong was tired. He had volunteered to work with Special Branch checking the letting agencies in Wokingham and he was now regretting it. He could have been back in London, working at his desk, or chatting up Rose Love, the pretty new girl in Investigations who had recently allowed that no, she didn't have a boyfriend, and yes, she would consider having dinner with Dave sometime, though not soon as she was very busy at work. She had always seemed so intense that he'd been surprised by this softening. Rose was a younger, prettier version of Liz Carlyle, and now Dave had hopes that she might prove more susceptible to his charms. He knew that however hard he tried, Liz would never see him as more than a good friend, colleague and sparring partner.

He thought of Liz as he finished his interview with the fourth letting agency. What was she up to? She never seemed to be at her desk, and she'd been absent from the most recent meeting of the FOXHUNT operational group. Why was she working in the fourth floor corner conference room, along with that Peggy woman from MI6? Had she been seconded? And to do what? Someone had mentioned vetting updates but that seemed an unlikely job for Liz. She was up to something, but whatever she was doing, she wasn't telling him about it.

Looking at his list, Dave saw with relief that there was only one more agency to visit, and blessedly it was within walking distance of the fourth. So he left his car and walked through the new streets of this extension of Wokingham – Milton Keynes without the planning or the trees, he thought to himself.

He walked deceptively quickly. He was just under six feet tall but was lanky, with long legs, and hair that was a little shaggy by the standards of Thames House. This made him stand out among the more staid senior personnel of the Service, but he fitted in with the people on the streets where he spent so much of his time. Even when he wasn't outside, he was happier in a parka than a suit, and was largely uninterested in the consequences this preference might have for his future career. Now he cut an anonymous figure, which is how he liked it.

At five-fifteen the small tidy office of Hummingbird Lettings was winding down for the day. The receptionist had left, and Dave found himself alone in a large room with four empty desks. Then someone began whistling, and a middle-aged man came out holding a cup of tea. He was thin and bony-faced, with greying hair and black NHS spectacles. Starting at the sight of Dave, he sloshed tea from his cup. 'We're shut,' he said automatically.

Dave smiled broadly. 'I'm Simon Willis,' he said. 'I rang before.'

'Oh yes,' the man said, 'the gentleman from the . . . police.'

'That's it,' said Dave brightly, 'won't take a minute.'

They sat down at the desk and the man introduced himself as Richard Penbury but did not shake hands. He looked dispirited, as if he had had a long and unprofitable day. 'So how can I help?' Penbury asked, making it obvious that he didn't think he could.

'I am making a *discreet* inquiry,' said Dave, trying his best to sound official, 'into the rental of a property to one, possibly two or even three, young Asian males. It might be a small house, or a medium or largish flat.'

The man was shaking his head even before Dave finished his sentence. Another dead end thought Dave, wondering how soon he could get back to London. Call it an hour – no, an hour and a half at this time of the day. He could ring Rose from the road and maybe she'd meet him at the Compton Arms. Then dinner and then maybe . . .

He brought himself back to earth to find Penbury saying, 'No, nothing like that at all. Most of my rentals this year have been repeaters, or long-term lets for properties people have bought for investment – you know, second houses they let out to cover the cost of the mortgage until the place appreciates and they sell it. That's the theory at any rate, though lately it's not been quite so simple. Lots of people have got burned, and between you and me, it's a tenant's market these days.'

Why between you and me? thought Dave with some irritation, disinclined to give much credence to Mr Penbury's analysis of recent trends in the rental market. Instead of ending the conversation, however, this made him press him on. 'Think for a minute please, Mr Penbury, especially about any new rentals. Are you sure none were to Asians? It doesn't matter if they weren't male.'

Mr Penbury took no time to dismiss this as well. 'No Asians. I'm certain. There are some in the area, and we've rented properties for and to them, but not recently. I'm sure of that,' he added decisively.

'Let me ask you this: think back to all the rentals you've made in the past six months. Was there anything unusual about any of them? Anything that comes to mind – I don't care if it seems trivial.' He saw the by now familiar look on Mr Penbury's face, which indicated the imminence of a dismissive 'No', so Dave quickly added, 'Please, Mr Penbury, this is important or I wouldn't be bothering you. Please think hard.'

And slowly, if unwillingly, Mr Penbury seemed to do this. After a long silent period of thought, he said, 'There was one property which was a bit unusual. A house on Somerset Drive. The owner used to live there but she's moved to Devon and we look after it for her. Someone took it on a short-term let this winter – six months. Normally, we wouldn't do that,' he added, 'but what can I say? Better six months than none at all.'

'Who rented it?'

'A man, but he was white. He paid all six months in advance. That's not unheard of, but I wouldn't say it was normal.'

'And?' asked Dave, since this didn't sound so odd that it would have stuck in Penbury's memory.

'Well, the thing is it hasn't been used. The last time I checked – you know, just to make sure everything was all right – no one had been in the house at all. I even asked the neighbours, and they said they hadn't seen anyone there since the owner moved out.'

'When was that?'

Mr Penbury thought for a moment. 'About three weeks ago.'

'Could I see the information for the tenant please?'

When Mr Penbury hesitated, Dave said gently, 'I can get a warrant if you like. But it would save us both a lot of hassle if you'd just let me know.'

Mr Penbury nodded and got up and went to a filing cabinet in the corner. He came back a minute later with a file. Dave scanned it quickly, but inwardly he didn't expect to learn much: if this turned out to be a link to the bombers, then the name used, Edward Larrabee, would not be real. 'Tell me,' he asked, 'do you know the name of these neighbours you spoke to?'

'I do as a matter of fact,' said Mr Penbury, pleased for the first time. 'The wife plays badminton with my wife. They're called Dawnton; I think he's Trevor.'

'Thanks,' said Dave. 'If you wouldn't mind making a copy for me,' he said, handing over the rental agreement, 'I'd be very grateful.'

Penbury nodded resignedly. 'I'll just warm up the machine,' he said, standing up and heading towards the back of the office.

28

After dropping her daughter at school, Maddie Keaney drove her small Ford into the heart of Dublin and left it in the garage near the Liffey where she and the other law-firm partners had their own parking spaces. She was a slight figure, neatly dressed in a conservative grey skirt and white blouse. Walking quickly up to Connolly Street in bright sunshine, Maddie joined the assortment of office workers, students, shoppers and – now it was late spring – American tourists on the city's most famous thoroughfare.

To those who criticised Dublin – lamenting its new commercialism, or the destruction of yet another Georgian square – Maddie would react with the defensiveness of a native. But she wasn't a native, and it was not the virtues of Dublin she admired but the simple fact that it wasn't Belfast.

She had left that city as soon as she was able, coming south against the wishes of her parents to read Law at University College Dublin. After taking her degree (a good one; she had worked hard) and qualifying, Maddie had been offered what was supposed to be a short-term placement with a Dublin firm of solicitors. This morning, as she entered the Victorian building of grey stone that housed Gallagher & O'Donnell, she realised she had been at the firm for exactly fifteen years.

What had made her flee Belfast at the earliest opportunity? Her father – even Sean Keaney's recent death had failed to dent the unalloyed hostility she still wore like mental armour. It was an antipathy she had felt for as long as she could remember.

Reaching work, Maddie took the creaky old lift to the third floor. She stopped in the outer office where Caitlin O'Hagan, the unhelpful secretary she shared with another partner, sat. 'Good morning,' Maddie said. 'What have I got today?'

Caitlin patted her dyed blonde hair, pursed her lips, and looked reluctantly at the desk diary. 'There's a Mr Murphy coming to see you in a quarter of an hour.'

'What does he want?' Maddie specialised in conveyancing, working mainly with a few large developers. It was rare to have a new client.

'I don't know,' said Caitlin. 'He said you'd been highly recommended.'

'By whom?'

'I didn't think to ask,' said Caitlin, aggrieved that so much should be expected of her.

Maddie occupied the next ten minutes in phone calls – to her ex-husband about his maintenance payments (late again), and another to the owner of a Georgian town house who was seeking planning permission to convert it into flats. Then Maddie's phone purred and Caitlin informed her that her appointment was waiting in reception. When Maddie came out, she found a tall shambling figure of a man, putting down the *Irish Times* and slowly getting up from his chair.

He looked to be in his late sixties, possibly older. In marked contrast to her mainly young and sharply dressed clientele, this man wore a long raincoat over a thick sweater and shirt. It hung like heavy drapes from its padded shoulders.

Maddie found her palm engulfed by a hand the size of a large animal's paw. She looked up into a doughy, weather-beaten face that looked as if it had seen too much of life.

There was something familiar about the man, but she couldn't place it, and the name rang no bell. But then in Dublin, Murphy was not exactly a remarkable surname.

She ushered the man into her office, then closed the door. 'Will you have tea or coffee?'

'I will not,' he said as he sat down. His voice was low and soft.

From behind her desk, Maddie glanced at the man and lined up her notepad and pencil. She clasped her hands and conjured up a professional smile. 'So how can I help you, Mr Murphy?'

'It's Maguire,' the man said slowly. 'James Maguire.'

Then Maddie understood why he seemed familiar. It had only been a glimpse or two – the tall shaggy figure climbing the stairs behind her sister, then later leaving the Belfast house without a word of goodbye. But she remembered the raincoat.

She felt herself begin to tremble, for no reason that she could define. She hadn't shared her father's enemies any more than she had shared his politics, but she had known who they were. Hence her astonishment the day when Maguire had come to see her father, that day her father was dying.

So what was the man doing here now, and under a false name? She felt a chill as she looked at her father's enemy across the desk. Was this to be the moment that had haunted her childhood: a sense of certain visitation, the masked men bursting in, the gun drawn and fired as she and her parents sat in front of the television, sitting there of an evening just like normal people. Only normal people didn't grow up waiting for that summons, that knock at the door.

She wondered what she should do as she watched her visitor, trying all the time to still the sense of panic. Call out to Caitlin in the anteroom? Before the woman had even got up from her desk, this man could be on her. Pick up the phone and ring the Garda? Before Maddie had begun to dial he could have a gun out. She thought of her daughter, and fear began to shake her, almost noisily, like a rattle in an empty box. Sweet Jesus, she thought, this is not the way I want to die.

And then suddenly the man's face creased like worked leather into a gentle smile. 'Don't be alarmed,' he said, for he must have seen the fear in her eyes. 'I wasn't sure you'd agree to see me if I used my real name.'

It took a moment for Maddie to gather herself. 'Well then, Mr Maguire, what do you want with me?'

'It's about your father,' he said simply. 'Maybe you remember my visit on the day he died. He asked me to come.'

She looked at him silently.

'He made certain requests of me. But I'm hampered, you see, by not knowing enough.'

'I doubt I can help you,' she said, her voice still shaky. 'I kept myself well out of my father's affairs.'

For a moment Maguire gazed at her, as though summing her up. 'He wanted me to get in touch with some professor he knew. A sympathiser to the cause, you understand.'

Maddie shrugged. 'As I said, I stayed out of my father's business.'

Maguire ignored this. 'He was Irish, this man, but I believe he spent some time teaching at Oxford.'

Maddie gave a harsh laugh. 'It doesn't sound very likely. My father was not an educated man, Mr Maguire.'

He looked at her, unconvinced. 'He was very clear about it.

It was his dying wish that I get hold of this man. I'd hardly be bothering you otherwise, now would I, Miss Keaney?'

Maddie felt irritation overcome any residual sense of alarm. Why was this man dragging her into whatever mucky errand he'd agreed to carry out for her father? She wanted no vestige of that sordid business in her life. 'Why didn't you ask my father when you saw him?' she demanded.

'My dear,' said Maguire, oblivious to how this made Maddie bristle. 'Your father was barely conscious when I saw him.' He had shaken off his hangdog look and was staring at her intently. 'I'm not sure he remembered the name himself by that stage. The only thing he said to me was "Ask Kirsty Brien." You know her, don't you?'

'She used to be my best friend,' said Maddie dully, her heart sinking. She tried to think of her former best friend with equanimity, but it was difficult.

They'd met at University College Dublin and for a time been inseparable, despite all manner of differences between them. Kirsty was tall where Maddie was short, Kirsty was blonde where Maddie had mouse-coloured hair, Kirsty was strikingly pretty where Maddie – she knew this, no one had to tell her – was at the very best 'not bad'.

And most of all, Kirsty was political where Maddie hated even the word. She'd been left wing had Kirsty, about almost every conceivable issue, from nationalised industry to Palestine, capital punishment to Third World relief, but the bedrock of all her beliefs had been a vision of a united Ireland. She worked tirelessly to achieve it – demonstrating, writing letters, organising boycotts. Kirsty was called the new Bernadette Devlin so often that she seemed to believe it herself.

None of this would have mattered at all to their friendship, if Maddie had not taken her best friend home one spring break to stay with her family.

Sean Keaney took to her at once, and she to him. They shared a commitment to the Struggle, of course, but it was more than that. Sean had admired young Kirsty's fiery spirit, her determination, and what he liked to call her 'gutsiness'. In contrast, Maddie assumed, to the diligence, steadiness and not inconsiderable accomplishments of his own daughter, who didn't give a fig if Ireland was ever united or not.

There was nothing unsavoury about the closeness between her father and her best friend – not even in her sourest moments had Maddie thought so. It was worse than that. Sean Keaney was not merely an avuncular figure for Kirsty – no, thought Maddie bitterly, he was an admired *father* figure. Kirsty had unforgivably occupied the space she did not want herself.

'Please,' Maguire said gruffly, as if it were an alien word in his vocabulary. 'It's important.' The bags under his eyes made him look peculiarly mournful. 'It can't hurt your father now.'

'Why aren't you talking to Kirsty Brien instead of me? She'll tell what you need to know.'

Maguire shook his great moose head again, as if she'd missed the point. 'I've tried, but she won't see me.'

'Did you explain to her that you saw my father before he died? And that he asked you to do something?'

'Of course,' said Maguire simply, as if resenting the question. 'But it cut no ice with her.'

That made sense. Kirsty would be rock solid in her loyalties, just like Sean Keaney had been.

'So what do you want to know?' she asked, dreading already the prospect of ringing her former closest friend. She had seen

Kirsty once in ten years – across the grave at Sean Keaney's funeral.

'I want to know who this academic man is.'

She said nothing.

'Look,' he said, 'you know your father and I didn't see eye to eye. Perhaps you didn't always see eye to eye with him, either.'

'Perhaps I didn't,' she conceded, adding tartly, 'but that doesn't mean I'm likely to see eye to eye with you.'

He smiled a little, almost ruefully. 'That may be. But one thing we'd all be agreed on is that the battle's over now. The fighting's done. Your father knew that; so do I. What he wanted me to do for him is not to harm anyone. It's meant to keep the war shut down for good, not open it up again.'

Maddie looked at him sceptically. 'Even if I could accept that about him, how do I know you're telling me the truth?'

'You can't,' he said simply. 'All you can do is look this old man in the face; then I think you'll be able to tell.'

And she did as he said, and found his gaze unflinching. After a moment he said, 'Will you help me?'

'Give me a minute,' she said, looking down at her desk. She stood up. 'I'll get us some coffee.' She needed time to marshal her thoughts.

That last spring at university in Dublin, she had seen very little of Kirsty. Part of it was her own doing – she was already determined to stay in the Republic, and determined to get a good degree. Her interviews with Dublin law firms had gone well, but a poor degree would put paid to her prospects. She worked day and night studying for her finals.

But Kirsty was busy in her own way, too. She had taken up with a postgraduate student, older, good-looking but flamboyant – Maddie thought it strange, he didn't look the type to be interested in girls. But he and Kirsty became inseparable in a matter of weeks They did everything together.

The man was brilliant, everyone said, though arrogant with it. He had just won a Junior Research Fellowship at Oxford, which he was taking up the following year. Maddie wondered if their relationship would survive the distance, though in truth she wasn't quite sure just what the relationship was.

Then one Saturday night, fed up with studying, Maddie had run into Kirsty by herself at the Students' Union. Spontaneously they had gone out, just like old times, to the new wine bar in the Golden Mile. Maddie had drunk three Tom Collins, and had finally plucked up courage to ask Kirsty about her new friend. 'So are you?'

'Am I what?' Kirsty had demanded, her indignation inflamed by her own consumption of Bailey's on ice.

'Are you sleeping with him or not?'

And Kirsty had laughed so loudly that the neighbouring table of students stopped talking to look at them both, as if expecting some imminent outrage. 'Don't be ridiculous,' Kirsty finally said.

'So he is gay then?' Maddie had said.

Kirsty shook her head. 'If you ask me, he's probably nothing at all. But how would I know anyway?' She finished her drink with a flourish and shook the ice in her glass like lucky dice. 'I'm only seeing him for your father's sake.'

'*What?*' Maddie had been speechless, and wanted an explanation. But Kirsty had seemed immediately to regret her admission, and she had stood up abruptly. 'Come on,' she said. 'There's Danny Mills and his mates. Let's join them. I know you fancy him.'

The memory dissolved as now she handed Maguire his coffee.
'Will you ring her for me then?' he asked, entreatingly.

She shook her head. 'There's no need to, Mr Maguire. I know the man you're looking for.'

29

Thelma Dawnton was just about to leave for the badminton club when a man who said he was from the letting agency phoned to ask about the house next door. She was in a hurry to get to her doubles match so, unusually for her, the conversation was brief.

She played doubles in the mixed competition, alongside Evan Dewhart, unattached but so dull that even Trevor, Thelma's husband, couldn't summon up any jealousy. They lost in the final set, against a young married couple – the wife had played for the county. Afterwards Thelma and Evan bought the drinks, and Thelma stayed longer than usual – pleased to be socialising with someone who had played at county level.

When she got home Trevor was in front of the telly. As his programme ended, she mentioned the call from the letting agency earlier that evening.

'What did they want?' her husband asked grumpily.

'He was asking about the house next door. He said they were trying to get in touch with the person who'd signed the lease. He wanted to know if he might be living there now.'

'Why's he asking you? Why couldn't he ask the lot next door direct?'

'That's just it. When I said there were three Asians next door, he sounded surprised. I explained they had only been there a couple of weeks, but he said they shouldn't have been there at all. He was very serious. Said it might be a police matter, so please could I not mention our conversation to any of them until he'd had time to call the authorities.'

When Trevor looked sceptical, she said defensively, 'That's what he said. Anyway, I said I wasn't likely to let them know, being as we hadn't ever exchanged much more than a nod.' Encouraged by the rare interest on her husband's part, Thelma asked, 'Do you think something funny's going on over there?' She jerked her head in the direction of their neighbours. 'Could we have terrorists living next door to us or something?'

'Not any more,' said Trevor, chewing on the last segment of his nan bread. 'Those three Pakis moved out tonight. I saw them packing up their car when I got home. If you ask me, they've cleared out for good.'

'Oh dear,' said Thelma, 'I'd better ring the letting agent in the morning and tell him they've gone.'

Trevor snorted. 'I should think he'll be pleased to see the back of them. I am.'

But Thelma never rang. At five-thirty in the morning she was wakened by the sound of someone knocking on a door. At first she thought it was her door, but as her head cleared and she listened intently over the mild snores of Trevor beside her, she realised it was coming from the house next door. She got up and looked out of the window, curious about who would come so early to an empty house.

What she saw was astonishing.

There was a group of men at her neighbour's front door. Three of them wore helmets and held rifles of the kind she'd seen policemen carrying at Heathrow. One of them, in a policeman's uniform, was pounding on the door, shouting. 'Open up,' he roared. 'The house is surrounded. At the count of ten, we will force our way in if you do not answer the door. One . . . two . . .'

From her vantage point, Thelma could see into the strip of garden at the back of the house, and she saw three other men, their weapons held at the ready.

'Three . . . four . . . five . . .'

In the street lined up were three police cars, a white police van and two Range Rovers.

'Six . . . seven . . . eight . . .'

The police had placed two lines of tape across the street and Thelma saw that at one of them a man in shorts and T-shirt stood, arguing with two constables. It was Dermot Simpson, who lived three doors down, now on the wrong side of the cordon. He was an inveterate early-morning jogger and wanted to get back to his house.

'Nine . . . ten.' There was a pause, and when she looked down at the front door she saw that two other men had appeared, carrying what looked to be a large metal lipstick. Swinging it between them, they suddenly launched it at the front door, and she heard a splintering noise followed by a thud, and then the men disappeared from view into the house.

'Jesus Christ!' It was Trevor, who came to the window and stood next to her in his pyjamas. 'Didn't you tell them they've all gone?'

'How could I?' she asked plaintively. 'You only told me last night. I was going to call the agency when they opened this morning.'

Trevor snorted and pointed at the congregation of armed policemen on the street in front the neighbouring house. 'Do they look like letting agents to you?' He suddenly opened the window, leaned out and bellowed, 'Officer, they've all gone!'

A man with a megaphone detached himself from the tense group. Pointing it right at Trevor and Thelma, his voice was astonishingly clear in the morning air. 'STAY INSIDE! MOVE BACK FROM THE WINDOWS. I REPEAT: MOVE BACK FROM THE WINDOWS.'

They retreated at once and, grabbing some clothes, went into the spare bedroom on the far side of the house from their invaded neighbours. 'Stay against this wall,' commanded Trevor, and Thelma nodded weakly. 'They may have a bomb.' And they huddled together, sitting with their backs to the wall, for a quarter of an hour, until there was more knocking. This time it was their door.

'I'd better answer it,' said Trevor.

'Do you have to?' said Thelma, frightened at the prospect of being left alone. 'What if it's someone from next door? You know, one of the terrorists.' By now, there was no doubt in her mind about the status of her former neighbours.

'It's not very likely, now is it Thelma?' said her husband, rising and moving towards the spare bedroom. 'Not with half the police force outside.'

'I'm coming with you,' declared Thelma, getting up and moving past her husband so quickly that she got downstairs first and opened up the front door.

There was a man standing there, wearing a parka. Behind him stood a policeman, cradling an automatic weapon. 'Mrs Dawnton?' the man in the parka said. 'We spoke last night.'

'You're the gentleman who rang?' He didn't look like a letting agent, especially with that policeman behind him.

Dave nodded impatiently. He was not in the mood for social

niceties. 'You told me there were three Asian men staying next door.' His tone was mildly accusing.

'That's right,' said Thelma.

'There were, Officer,' said Trevor, insinuating himself between Thelma and the man, in what was either old-fashioned gallantry or bruised pride that he was not the Dawnton being addressed. 'But they left last night.'

'After we spoke,' explained Thelma anxiously. 'You see, I was going to ring the agency this morning—'

Dave cut her off. 'What time did they go?' he asked Trevor.

'Half-seven, quarter to eight.'

'Did they have a car?'

Trevor nodded. 'I think it was a Golf. They didn't have much gear. Couple of bags, that's all I could see.'

A policeman came up to Dave and whispered in his ear. 'Excuse me,' said Dave. 'I'd like to come back. Say in half an hour?'

'I don't know,' said Trevor, 'I've got work to go to.'

'I'd be very grateful if you went in late today,' said Dave. 'I'd be happy to ring your boss if you like, and explain we need to talk to you first.'

Trevor looked slightly miffed by the offer. 'I'll tell him. No need for you to speak to him.'

'Right then,' said Dave. 'See you a little later on.'

It was almost ninety minutes before he came back. In the meantime the Dawntons had watched the dogs go in – an Alsatian and two spaniels, their tails wagging wildly. Out of sight of the watchers, upstairs in the house, all three dogs had become very excited when they sniffed the carpeted floor of the wardrobe in one of the three small bedrooms. When white-suited forensics officers disinterred an almost infinitesimal residue from the worn carpet that had triggered this vociferous reaction, their conclusion was that fertiliser had been stored in the house. Stored recently, in fact.

The euphoria of the forensics team after this discovery was not shared by Dave Armstrong, who drove back to London late that night in an unusual state of alarm. It was not simply that he knew he and his colleagues could now proceed in the certainty that the three young men they sought were bombers. That was bad enough, especially since they had no idea where they'd gone, or what they planned to blow up.

But even more worrying was the fact that they had left in a rush – according to Trevor Dawnton, 'they looked like they were two steps in front of the bailiffs'. It was true Rashid's sister had told Rashid the police were looking for him, but that would not have triggered such a panicked departure, since after all, the sister had no idea of his whereabouts. Dave had spent another hour with the Dawntons, long enough to persuade himself that it was simply inconceivable that either of the couple would have tipped off the three suspects after he had rung from the letting agency to inquire about them.

Covering all the bases, Dave also rang Mr Penbury at home, catching him just after he'd walked the dog. He had confirmed, making noises of outraged denial, that he had made no contact with anyone to do with the rented house on Somerset Drive. So as he drove along the M4 going east past Slough, Dave Armstrong was pretty confident that neither the letting agency nor the neighbours were responsible for tipping off the suspects. So why then had they fled in the nick of time? Was it possibly just a coincidence? Had the trio planned such a move, just one of many, from safe house to safe house, up until the date they struck?

Perhaps, but Dave Armstrong wasn't paid to believe in coincidence, and he was certain he was right to proceed on the assumption that the three men they were looking for had been tipped off. Ruling out Penbury, the Dawntons and Rashid's sister left him with possible sources for the tip-off which did nothing but worry him. It was this worry which led him to ring and leave a message on Charles Wetherby's voicemail, asking to see him first thing in the morning.

30

Dave got up extra early at his small flat in Balham, to give himself plenty of time to get to Thames House by eight for his meeting with Wetherby. He was shattered. Dressing, he had thought of putting on a jacket and tie, but decided that instead of impressing Wetherby with his seriousness, it would simply seem out of character. But he was determined to convey his concern.

Now in Wetherby's office he was on edge. Wetherby wore a light grey summer suit and was standing by the window, watching the antics of a large heron on a mudflat below. He seemed preoccupied. As Dave briefed him on the events in Wokingham, including the discovery of traces of fertiliser, he listened without comment. When Dave finished he stood silent for a moment. 'So we almost had them,' he said suddenly, then sighed morosely. 'What bad luck.'

Dave took a deep breath. 'That's just it, Charles. I'm not convinced luck had anything to do with it.'

Wetherby turned around. 'What are you trying to say?' he asked Dave sharply, looking at him with the fixed gaze Dave called the 'X-ray stare' – Liz never seemed to mind Wetherby's scrutinising look, but Dave found it disconcerting. It made him feel guilty, like a little boy caught out by his father telling a lie.

Dave tried to speak calmly. 'According to the neighbours, the suspects left very suddenly. They seemed to be in a big hurry. As if they'd had advance warning we were coming.'

'You mean they'd been tipped off? Who would have done that?'

'That's the problem. I'm confident it wasn't the agent who let the house, and I very much doubt the neighbours did. The woman next door said she and her husband had barely spoken to the men.'

'Who else?'

'The local Special Branch, which doesn't seem likely.' He paused, hesitant to continue, then reminded himself that's why he was here. 'And Thames House,' he said quietly.

Wetherby's gaze did not shift. 'Someone inside the Service?' he asked. Dave found it impossible to tell how he was reacting to the suggestion.

'I realise it may sound bizarre,' said Dave, trying to make it clear he wasn't happy to broach the idea, 'but the fact is, our suspects seem to have known we were coming – twice. It's too much of a coincidence. After all, there was no good reason for them not to show at the bookshop.'

'That could have been a lot of things,' Wetherby declared. 'They might have been put off by the number of people who would see them visiting again. Or they may not have entirely trusted the Imam. Who knows? I don't really see how that and their departure from Wokingham are related.'

'Because in both cases they didn't do what one would expect,' said Dave. Wetherby waved a dismissive hand, but Dave stuck to his guns. 'If you assume, for argument's sake, that the no-show and their flight from Wokingham *were* connected, then of all the people involved, there's only one group who knew about both. The neighbours weren't the same, the police weren't the same. It's only us – those involved here in Thames House – who knew about both operations.'

'Ah,' said Wetherby, returning to sit behind his desk. He was all business now. 'That's precisely where I don't follow you – your assumption that these two situations are linked. It seems to me far more likely that something inside the bookshop alarmed them. And they may have left Wokingham when they did because that's when they'd always planned to leave.

'If these suspects know what they're doing – and so far they've only made one mistake – then they'll have another safe house to go to. Probably more than one. It would be normal for them to keep on the move, right until the day of their action. I imagine they're travelling light so they can leave quickly. That doesn't mean they think we're onto them.'

What had seemed an airtight argument to Dave, shaving in Balham two hours before, now seemed flimsy, unsubstantial. 'Charles, I'm not trying to make a legal case,' he said, floundering for words. 'I just wanted to say my piece. I thought you should know.'

Know what? Dave's words sounded lame even to himself. 'I don't want to get involved in a wild goose chase,' Wetherby said forcefully. 'It would only distract us from the real task, which is to catch these suspects before they do anything.'

Dave nodded unhappily. Wetherby sat back in his chair, easing off slightly. 'Does the name James Angleton mean anything to you?' he asked.

It rang a bell, but only a faint one, so Dave shook his head.

Wetherby got up and walked slowly back to the window. His voice was calmer now, almost reflective. 'Angleton was an American, a senior CIA officer, head of Counter-Intelligence for many years. A very bright man, much respected. But he believed what a series of defectors told him and became convinced that the KGB had penetrated Western

Intelligence at the highest level. It became his obsession, to the exclusion of everything else. It was the classic "wilderness of mirrors". Everything he saw had something behind it. No action was straightforward, no decision had anything but a hidden, ulterior motive; nothing was what it seemed to be.'

Dave gave a hollow laugh. 'Yes, I know. And we had Peter Wright.'

Wetherby picked up a pencil and thumped its end on the desk. 'Yes, Peter Wright caught the same bug. He and his cronies even investigated the Director General, Roger Hollis, for years. On no hard evidence at all. Sheer pernicious nonsense, and it did a huge amount of damage.'

Dave was mortified that Wetherby seemed to be putting him in the same category as a deluded American spymaster and Peter Wright. 'I don't think *I'm* being paranoid, Charles,' he said, aggrieved.

'Nor do I actually,' replied Wetherby, absent-mindedly running a finger down his tie. 'But without any hard facts, I can't afford to worry about your hunch. I'm glad you shared your concerns with me, but it's evidence we need.' He smiled benevolently, which only made Dave feel worse as their meeting ended.

Yet sitting over a coffee in the cafeteria downstairs, Dave was unconvinced. He understood Wetherby's reluctance to think anyone in the Service could be helping the suspects, but he was troubled by the vehemence of his reaction. It was as if Wetherby had had the same idea himself, then rejected it. He isn't going to follow it up at all, Dave thought sourly, cheering up a bit when he realised that Wetherby had not actually forbidden him from doing so.

31

Liam O'Phelan had an extremely low tolerance of ambiguity. This made him notoriously impatient with students who dithered or didn't know quite what they thought, and now it made him impatient with himself. For in the wake of his visit from 'Miss Falconer' he didn't know what to do.

Part of him was tempted to let sleeping dragons lie, as he sensed that stirring them might be dangerous. If the man in London thought he had put all this behind him, then he might be less than pleased to have O'Phelan re-emerge, like the black sheep of a family suddenly returning to the fold.

Who knows? The man might panic and tell all. O'Phelan wondered fleetingly if he could be prosecuted for recruiting him. Then he reminded himself that they had never called on the fellow actually to *do* anything.

Yet part of him – the greater part, he began to recognise as days turned into a week, a week turned into two – wanted to stir things, if only for the sake of his own curiosity. What would have happened to his recruit after all these years? Would he have changed much? Got married, settled down, done his best to forget he'd ever had another agenda dominating his life? Or would the flame still burn? Would he share O'Phelan's disgust with the state of affairs in Northern Ireland, this wretched phoney peace that was no more than a sell-out?

Curiosity won out, and with an energy he hadn't felt in years he went to work in a half-exhilarated, half-anxious state. It took a dozen phone calls, but finally he had the number he wanted. It was a mobile phone number. The first three times he phoned, it was switched off. Finally, stealing five minutes from marking a stack of first-year exams, he rang yet again. This time the other end answered right away.

A sly smile appeared upon O'Phelan's face. 'Hello there,' he said. 'Do you know who this is?'

He waited, and what he heard seemed to please him. 'No flies on you, even after all these years. Now listen, I'm bothering you for a reason, even though it's really you who owe me a call. Very naughty that. But a woman came to see me, asking questions.

'I thought that might get your attention. What's that? Of course I can. I'd say she was in her thirties, mid-thirties. Light brown hair, shoulder length, green eyes, average height. Dressed smartly – not at all bureaucratic in appearance. Attractive in a brisk kind of way, well spoken. Rather cleverer than I thought at first. She said her name was Falconer, and that she was from the Ministry of Defence. I did my best to look as though I believed her. We know better, now don't we?'

32

'Still sceptical?' asked Charles Wetherby, looking up from the menu. He was wearing his horn-rimmed reading glasses, which Liz thought made him look slightly professorial, though the smart light grey suit and polished shoes would have been out of place in a Common Room.

'About the mole? No,' said Liz crisply, giving a hint of a smile to acknowledge that her views had changed. 'I think we may have a problem after all.'

'Let's order first,' said Wetherby, signalling to a waitress. 'Then we won't be interrupted while you tell me about it.'

Keyed up as she was, it was frustrating to have to wait to tell him her news, but Liz was used to momentous events occurring within a framework of otherwise trivial life. She knew the impact even the most banal detail could have: the missed train, the child's cold, the mobile phone that lost its charge. In her last year at school, taking A level English, she had become addicted to W. H. Auden's poems, and she remembered one of her favourite lines describing how even the most dramatic event 'takes place/While someone else is eating or opening a window or just walking dully along'.

They were lunching well away from Thames House and casual observation, at Cafe Bagatelle, a chic restaurant with a dramatic glass roof in the enclosed sculpture garden of the Wallace Collection in Manchester Square. Liz had asked to see Wetherby that morning, immediately after the phone call from

Ireland. He had suggested lunch, which struck Liz as unusual, since previously they had only ever shared tables in the Thames House canteen, and most recently a sandwich at an RAF airfield in Norfolk.

The waitress came up at last. They ordered from the set menu. 'I'm going to have a glass of wine,' said Wetherby, and Liz followed suit gratefully. He seemed relatively relaxed today. Though he was by natural disposition reserved, his sense of humour kept him from taciturnity, and sometimes quite unexpectedly he could be positively voluble, suddenly enthusiastic in a way Liz still found surprising, though she warmed to it. Overall, though, his attitude was one of benign, mildly ironic detachment. He was a cool customer in the nicest possible way, Liz had concluded, and she often wondered if he thought the same of her.

She looked around the airy dining room. It was Wednesday and the restaurant was comparatively quiet – a few businessmen, two or three tables of 'ladies who lunch', and some American visitors to the galleries. Even if it had been more crowded, the round tables and wicker chairs were spaced far enough apart to talk freely without fear of being overheard. Wetherby had chosen it mainly for its privacy.

When the waitress finally left them, Wetherby unfolded his napkin and turned to Liz. 'So what have you found out?'

'I had a call this morning from James Maguire.'

Wetherby looked surprised. 'I thought he wasn't speaking to us.'

'So did I,' said Liz.

Wetherby looked at her and gave a wry smile. 'You must have got to him after all, Liz. Well done.'

Liz shrugged. She remembered her tense, argumentative

meeting with Maguire in Rotterdam. 'I'm not sure I had anything to do with it. His conscience woke up, that's all.'

'Will he help us?'

'He has already. He went to see Sean Keaney's daughter in Dublin. It turns out that one of her great pals at university was an acolyte of her father's. An IRA sympathiser named Kirsty Brien.' Liz paused, and lowered her voice, though there was no one at the two tables nearest them. 'Kirsty had a male friend who in turn became an academic. First at Oxford, now at Queen's Belfast. What's more, she told Maddie Keaney that she was only seeing the man for Keaney's sake.'

Wetherby's eyebrows raised, the sole sign of his surprise. 'So you've closed the circle,' he said. 'Well done. I was sure you were right to have misgivings about O'Phelan – you don't often get it wrong – but I thought it just possible he knew someone on the list, without it having anything to do with the IRA. It could have been any sort of connection.'

He clasped both hands together and inspected them thoughtfully. 'But now that you've linked him to Keaney, it makes it far more likely he was the recruiter.' Liz noticed his cufflink – gold worked into the shape of a cricket bat. Wetherby said, 'But who is it? And what's your next step?'

'I had been planning to interview O'Phelan again anyway, but I was waiting to see what Peggy Kinsolving came up with. I wanted some ammunition this time.'

'You've got that now,' said Wetherby.

Liz nodded. 'I know. I think I'll go early next week. I don't want to alarm him by making it sound too urgent. We still can't prove anything.'

'No, that sounds right to me.'

Their starters arrived, and Liz cut into her goat's cheese

galette. 'Charles, have you thought about what you're going to do if we do find a mole? I mean, especially if he or she was never activated?'

'I'll do whatever it takes to get him or her out of the Service.' He laid down his fork. 'Anything else I'll happily leave to the Attorney General. That assumes of course that they weren't activated – Keaney may not have told the truth about that.'

Remembering her own musings in her bedroom at the Culloden Hotel, Liz pressed on. 'But just supposing the IRA didn't activate the mole, I wonder how they would have felt about that. Badly let down, I would think.'

Charles paused as the waitress cleared the table for their main courses. 'So you've had that thought too. It's been haunting me. I was thinking about something my father once told me. Yours was too young to be in the War, wasn't he?'

Liz nodded.

'Well, my father was commissioned just before the Normandy landings. His regiment was in the first wave of troops, but two days before they were set to sail, my grandmother died, and my father was allowed home on compassionate leave. When he returned to duty, for some reason he was transferred to the Ministry of Defence in London. He never saw combat.'

The waitress put down their plates. Wetherby went on, 'I once asked him about it. I said, "Weren't you relieved you didn't have to fight?" I'll never forget the look on his face. He told me that it was the worst thing that had ever happened to him.'

He looked speculatively at Liz. 'So think about this mole. They've made a momentous decision to work for the IRA, managed to be recruited to the Service, all set to go. And then somebody back in Belfast pulls the plug and the whole *raison d'être* is gone. Can you imagine how a person would feel about that?'

'Is that what's worrying you?'

'Yes.' Wetherby's usual air of diffidence was now replaced by obvious concern. 'I must admit, that at first I was thinking we've got to find this mole, because they're disloyal, but I was also thinking it's unlikely an IRA plant is going to do us active harm at present, so this may not be top priority. But now I'm not so sure about that.'

He hesitated and for a moment Liz thought he was about to say something else. But the waitress came to fill their water glasses and the moment lapsed. 'I'll be leaving work early on Friday,' Liz said. 'I have to go and see my mother.'

'Is she all right?' asked Wetherby. He managed to make his interest sound genuine without being intrusive. It was the kind of tactful concern for which Liz was grateful just then.

'I'm not sure that she is,' admitted Liz. 'They've found a growth, and she has to go into hospital for a biopsy. I want to go down and take her in.'

'Of course,' said Wetherby. He sighed, looking pensive and fingering the knot in his tie.

'I'm sure it will be fine,' said Liz, putting on a brave front she didn't really feel.

Wetherby must have sensed this, for he looked at Liz with the fixed gaze she had come to know so well. At first, Liz, like Dave, had found the 'X-ray stare' unnerving – she couldn't tell if he were amused by her, or slightly doubtful, even accusatory. But she had grown to understand that this look was a sign of concentration rather than some mind-reading exercise.

'Anyway,' she said before the silence became too prolonged, 'how are those boys of yours?'

He smiled with real pleasure. 'They're fine. Cricket and girls – that's their life, and in that order.'

'And Joanne?' she asked more cautiously.

Wetherby shrugged. 'It's been a difficult few months,' he admitted. 'She had a blood transfusion last week which the consultant was very hopeful about.' His face seemed to sag. 'I'm not sure it's been a success.'

Liz wasn't sure what to say. Wetherby had lived with his wife's chronic illness for as long as Liz had known him. For the most part, Liz tried not to venture too far into the topic she mentally labelled Wetherby's Wife. From his rather embarrassed reactions when she did ask after Joanne, she judged that was how he preferred it.

'I am sorry,' she said with feeling. She added, 'It must be very hard on the boys.'

He grimaced slightly, as the waitress took away their plates. Both he and Liz declined dessert, and Wetherby asked for the bill. He looked pensive, Liz thought, rather sad, as they sat waiting for the return of his credit card. Suddenly he reached across the table, and gave Liz's arm an affectionate squeeze. 'I'm sorry, I don't mean to burden you with my problems. I know how badly the whole Marzipan business hit you. It was terrible for us all, but much worse for you. I thought you behaved superbly – but I knew you would. I do hope your mother's news is good.'

And then, looking stern, after this unusual display of emotion, he pushed back his chair and stood up.

33

In these post-9/11 days identification was needed even on a UK flight. In his combination-locked cupboard in Thames House, there was an operational passport, in an alias identity, but he did not want to risk that name appearing on a flight manifest, getting caught up in the net of a random check which would trigger a request for an explanation. That would be fatal.

But he had another passport. It too was in an alias, but not one countenanced by any British government authority. Procuring it had been complicated – he'd used a Czech forger, now retired, who'd done work on and off for years for Mossad – and very expensive. It was his insurance policy and it was proving its worth now.

Like the professional he was, he assumed his false identity as soon as he left his house. He was Sherwood, a businessman with interests in Northern Ireland. He had scheduled the day tightly, catching the seven o'clock flight from Heathrow, along with an unremarkable bunch of corporate types and civil servants.

With any luck at all, he would be back in London at two o'clock. His absence was covered by a few days off work. He had told his secretary that he had some medical appointments and would work from home. That sort of excuse deterred all but the most tactless questioner.

Sherwood thought about the don, as he had done virtually

non-stop since receiving his phone call. Would he be called a 'don' in Belfast? Almost certainly not. Anyway, he was probably a professor by now. There was no doubting his intellect. His judgement was a different matter. That was why he had to go on this quick visit.

What an impressive man the don had seemed – articulate, passionate, charismatic when they'd first met, especially to a fresh-faced undergraduate. Did the don have a 'personal life', that euphemism for sex? Possibly, though it had never been clear. There was that girl he spoke about so often, the firebrand back in Dublin.

There were other ambiguities. The don spent his days in a cloistered world of history and ideas, but was entranced by the world of action. Just talking about it excited him, like an actor who only comes to life onstage. Yet as Sherwood knew from experience, the don lived vicariously. Like one of those armchair Irish-Americans, happy to send money to his IRA cousins from the safety of a Boston barroom, though he'd be insulted by the comparison.

How strange to think of America now, for it was America that had fuelled his own resentments and brought him into touch with the don in the first place.

He had gone to the States during his gap year before university, travelling with Timothy Waring, his best friend from school. They had started in New York, which was to be the first stage of a grand tour by Greyhound bus, the time-honoured mode of travel for English youth keen to see the vast United States.

He never got on the bus. He gave Timothy the $200 they had agreed as the price of collusion, and a selection of postcards, purchased in a pack at a tourist shop on Fifth Avenue.

Niagara Falls, Lake Superior, the Rockies, Glacier National Park, the Golden Gate Bridge. Each one carrying a pre-composed message for home, and each one dutifully posted by Timothy as he visited, solo, all those famous sites in the following weeks.

During which time – three weeks – Sherwood had remained in New York, trying to find out as much as he could about the father he had last seen ten years before, six months before he had suddenly died.

He had learned more than he'd bargained for, once he unearthed his father's closest friend. Harry Quinn, retired features writer on the *New York Daily News*, now living on Long Island, was happy to meet up with his former pal's son at his old watering hole, Costello's Bar on 44th Street.

They had sat in a booth surrounded by hard-drinking hacks. Quinn made small talk for a while as he drank four steins of beer, then explained, with surprising sobriety, what had really happened to his father. It was not the swift heart attack described by his mother. Instead, his father had jumped off the 59th Street Bridge. A suicide, prompted by disgrace.

Disgrace – there was no other word for his father's downfall, or for the opprobrium that had been heaped upon him. Visiting the New York Public Library's newspaper holdings on East 40th Street, his son had discovered the whole seamy story, recounted in the yellowing pages of the newspapers of the time.

It had begun altogether differently. In a series of three articles for the *New York Daily News*, all trailed in a banner on the front page, his father had recounted the confessions of one Samuel Lightfoot, a former member of the SAS. In a long career in the military, Lightfoot had served four event-filled tours of duty in Northern Ireland.

As retold by his father, Lightfoot described a history of brutality and violence by the SAS in Northern Ireland which surprised even its most vigorous detractors. Put simply, according to Lightfoot, he and his fellow SAS members had operated a policy of shoot to kill that was premeditated and sometimes indiscriminate. He described a mission in which he and two other SAS men had shot dead two IRA men on their way to plant a bomb in a Lisburn restaurant; reported in the press at the time, it was viewed only as a successful British counter-terrorism operation. What had gone *un*reported according to Lightfoot was the fact that the two men, when challenged, had attempted to surrender, but were cut down anyway. Both were unarmed, and contrary to reports, no bomb or trace of a bomb was ever found.

On another occasion, Lightfoot had said, a man crossing a field at night in the countryside of Armagh was assassinated, only to turn out to be a local farmer taking a short cut home from the pub, with no connection to the IRA at all. The killing was never admitted to by the British military authorities, and remained a mystery, though speculation appeared in the Belfast press that it was just another in a long line of unsolved sectarian murders.

Throughout all three articles, a wealth of documentary detail was produced, specifying times, locations and people involved in what one New York columnist dubbed 'BA' – which stood not for British Airways, but British Atrocities. It seemed obvious to readers that only a witness to these SAS operations could describe them so vividly and in such factual detail.

The effect of the exposé had been explosive. In the House of Representatives, the Speaker Tip O'Neill, often attacked by his fellow Irish-Americans for his criticism of the IRA, now lent his name to a resolution demanding an end to all British undercover activity in Northern Ireland. The wire services picked up the Lightfoot story at once, ensuring its appearance in several thousand newspapers throughout the country. Even the august *New York Times*, usually sniffy about its plebeian counterpart the *Daily News*, acknowledged the impact of the articles, and one of its Op-Ed columnists suggested their author would be a shoe-in for a Pulitzer prize.

For at least three days his father would have enjoyed a success most journalists would not even dare to dream about. He would have been endlessly congratulated and feted, and would have basked in the triumph of what was indisputably one of the major stories of the decade.

And then the roof had caved in. Four days after his first article appeared, the *Sunday Times* of London had run its own bombshell on the front page. The Lightfoot articles, it declared unequivocally, were built upon a mountain of sand; their source, Samuel Lightfoot, was a conman of the first order and a notorious liar. Far from serving in Northern Ireland, his military career had consisted of a brief part-time membership of the Territorial Army, where his sole contact with the SAS had been a solitary weekend outing to their training facilities in Herefordshire. To add insult to ignominy, Lightfoot had been convicted of fraud in the sixties and served three years in prison.

The uproar had dwarfed even the initial reaction to the articles themselves, making the national evening television news. In Washington Tip O'Neill said 'No comment' seven times to one importuning reporter, and the House of Representatives' resolution was hastily withdrawn. The British Ambassador declared himself 'satisfied that the truth has at last emerged'.

In New York the *Daily News* ran an unprecedented front-page retraction, published an editorial remarkable for its supine contrition, and summarily fired his father. All of which the *New York Times* gleefully reported, with an exhaustiveness missing from its earlier account of the original articles.

Two months later, his father's death merited a one-inch story in the Metropolitan section of that newspaper. The *Daily News* did not report it at all.

The young man had returned to England, where he said nothing about what he had found to his mother or his odious stepfather. They merely thought him uncommunicative, when he proved reluctant to describe much about his bus tour around America.

Inside he was in turmoil, feeling a mixture of bewilderment and shame. How had his father got it so wrong? How had he been fooled by such an obvious charlatan – whose real name, it had emerged, wasn't even Lightfoot? Was the duped author of these discredited articles really the man of his memory? A gallant, confident, carefree figure – eliciting respect, admiration, and devotion to his memory by his son?

The young man felt only misery now, a state which lasted throughout his first year at Oxford, where he found both its academic and social worlds oddly dispiriting in the face of what he now knew. He did his coursework diligently, but kept himself to himself, brooding about what he now saw as an irredeemably tainted kind of inheritance. He even took to religion, to losing himself in every kind of purely conventional behaviour: to imitating the very kind of person the father he remembered had never been.

It was O'Phelan who saved him, though any gratitude on his own part had long evaporated in the face of the tutor's own ultimate betrayal.

In his second year he'd met a girl at a dance in St Hilda's, an all-women's college clinging singularly to its exclusion of men. She had been very left wing, and had asked him to a political talk, one of a series given at the Old Firehouse. He'd gone and been bored half to death – the lecturer, a veteran of the Paris Riots of 1968, had droned on for almost an hour about the 'battle' for the Sorbonne and the iniquities of the CRS riot police. When the girl had asked him to the next one, he was about to decline, until he saw its title: 'From Boston to Belfast: British Dirty Tricks in Northern Ireland and Abroad'. Something like that. It was being given by a lecturer from one of the colleges.

In the event, his left-wing friend couldn't make it, so he had sat alone, in an audience of only twenty or so Trotskyists and Marxists, while a thin young man spoke in a soft voice (only a hint of Irish there) about what he said the British were really up to.

The thesis was simple stuff, familiar to anyone who had ever listened to an IRA spokesman on TV: far from acting as peacekeepers, the British wanted to retain the status quo of imperialist occupation and would do anything (*anything*, the lecturer had stressed) to keep it that way.

But the effect of his talk on his undergraduate listener soon became absolutely hypnotic, for after these prefatory nationalist pieties, Liam O'Phelan (that was the speaker's name) had begun to talk with articulate passion about an undeclared policy of shoot to kill which he said was being conducted by the SAS in Northern Ireland. To the young man's astonishment, O'Phelan even mentioned the murder of the innocent Armagh farmer that had appeared in his father's articles.

Afterwards he had gone up to the young don, waiting

patiently while some Irish acolyte had chatted with him. When it was his turn, he had asked him whether it wasn't true that many of his accusations had long ago been discredited.

'What do you mean?' O'Phelan had asked sharply. 'Discredited how?'

Well, he had explained, hadn't there been that scandal in New York, where a reporter, making accusations not dissimilar to those made by O'Phelan tonight, had either colluded with or been duped by a conman? The charges he had made had been fabricated from the start.

O'Phelan looked at him witheringly. 'Honestly, you Brits,' he said. 'You'll believe anything your tame press wants you to. The whole thing was a set-up. The man calling himself Lightfoot – he was the source of the story – was a plant of British Intelligence. The poor journalist never stood a chance. Most of what he wrote was completely true, but because Lightfoot set him up no one believed any of it. Bloody clever of the Secret Service,' he said, but without admiration. He added with a shrug, 'Not that you'll believe me.'

So perhaps he was surprised to see the student's face, for he was nodding, with the hint of a smile – his first smile in a long time. 'Oh, I believe you all right. The poor journalist was my father.'

And so began their peculiar relationship. O'Phelan had taken him under his wing, and he had resided there quite willingly, becoming (unofficially of course; he continued with his degree) a sort of pupil of the man. He had even affected an interest in Irish history and Irish nationalism to please the tutor, visiting both the North and the Republic. If O'Phelan ever suspected the sincerity of his attachment to his own cause, he never said so, for by then they had hatched their plot. Anyway, who in the IRA would care about his deepest motives, if they managed to insert him into the very heart of their enemy?

And they shared that enemy. The young man fully accepted O'Phelan's assertion that his father had been the victim of a conspiracy. Who were the conspirators? Probably the British Consulate in New York, its 'cultural attaché' – the usual slot for the MI6 resident – working overtime. Add a few Anglophile American officials, briefing hard to a sympathetic reporter, and presto – one life destroyed. His father summarily fired, left without reputation or livelihood, watching a lifetime's hard graft lost in the front-page smear of a tabloid. He may technically have killed himself, but by any humane standard he had been killed. They might as well have pushed him off the 59th Street Bridge, such was the blood on their hands.

Thanks to O'Phelan he saw his father's killers in the raw – the members of the English Establishment that people claimed no longer existed. What nonsense, thought Sherwood, as the plane climbed to its cruising level. The Establishment not only survived, it prospered. He was part of it himself.

He remembered how O'Phelan had seen this as an advantage from the start, and gradually persuaded him that he should not feel any embarrassment about his manifest Englishness. He should instead use it as a secret weapon in what they both now agreed was a necessary war.

'No one will ever suspect,' the don had told him. 'They'll think you're English through and through. Trust me, they never turn on their own. Look at Philby; they believed him when he said he wasn't a mole. Or Blunt. Even when they knew Blunt was a spy, they let him go on working for the Queen.'

Now as the aeroplane moved over North Wales, Sherwood looked down at Snowdonia. The Welsh managed to be despised by the English, he thought, and yet remained so passive. A few holiday cottages torched, an insistence on bilingual road signs; as far as he could tell, this was the sum of their nationalist efforts.

But were the Irish really any better? His father had hoped so, and for those crucial years at the beginning of his career, so had his son. Yet more than eighty years after Partition, the country was no closer to unification than in 1922. More fools them, he thought bitterly. He'd tried to help (just as his father had, God knows), but they hadn't wanted any of it. They'd given up the fight just as he was preparing to join them.

The seduction of power – O'Phelan had been right about that. He'd always said the greatest danger Ireland would ever face was the day the English wanted to negotiate.

Over the Irish Sea he remembered his student visits to Ireland, how he had braved the crossing from Holyhead to Dun Laoghaire in wooden boats the size of oversized tugs. Most of the passengers were male, boisterous and happy to be going home, drinking in the bar until they went out on deck and threw up over the railings.

His plane landed in Belfast in light drizzle with a hard bump that threw spray up under the wing. Disembarking, he moved through the terminal quickly, not making eye contact with anyone, gripping his thin briefcase tightly and pulling up the collar of his coat while he joined the taxi queue. Like many of his fellow passengers, he was on his way to a day meeting in Northern Ireland.

The taxi dropped him in the city centre, busy with office workers hunched up in their coats against the rain. At this early hour of the day Belfast looked like any other city – no bag checks, no soldiers carrying rifles, no sign of armoured cars. As he set out walking quickly towards Queen's, he inspected the people he passed – well dressed, prosperous – so obviously living for the moment and the moment alone. Don't they understand? he thought bitterly, as he looked at them: an old man in a new cloth cap; a couple under one huge umbrella, trendily dressed and holding hands; a black teenager in a hooded top, moving jerkily to the rhythms of his Walkman.

But then, he had never really felt he was doing it for them. They had moved on.

'How punctual,' said O'Phelan, with a thin-lipped smile. As he turned back into the room, his visitor entered and closed the door behind him.

'Have a seat, and I'll make some tea. Or would you prefer coffee? There's whiskey, if you'd like a drink. No? It is a bit early.'

O'Phelan was excited, finding it hard to stand still, gripping the back of his chair with both hands, then letting go and taking a step back to inspect his visitor. 'You haven't aged much, I have to say.' He ran a hand through his thinning hair. 'Would that time had been so kind to me.' He sounded self-mocking.

'I thought we might go out somewhere for lunch. There's a bistro down the road that's rather good. Would that be safe? But first, I want to hear what you've been up to all these years. Tell me all. Oh, but first the coffee, or will you have tea?'

And in his excitement he darted back to the small alcove in the far corner of the room, where he turned on the kettle and busied himself extracting milk from the small fridge, then sugar from the cupboard and two spoons, and of course the china cups and saucers.

'How do you like it, black or white?' he called back over his shoulder. There was no reply, which puzzled O'Phelan only momentarily. For suddenly he was choking, and something was blocking his windpipe. By the time the kettle boiled O'Phelan was dead.

34

When Liz arrived for work she went straight to her desk in the agent-runners room to check her mail. She found a message from Jimmy Fergus, asking her to ring him urgently. This reminded her that she needed to book her flight to Belfast the following week, but she rang Jimmy first. He sounded uncharacteristically subdued. 'I've got some bad news,' he said.

'What's the matter?'

'This man O'Phelan . . .'

'Yes?' There must be nothing on him in the database, she thought. A pity.

'He's been murdered in his room at Queen's.'

'You're joking,' said Liz. 'I was planning to see him again next week. What happened?'

'He was found last night, but the pathologist says he was killed in the morning. Somebody strangled him. Well, not quite – they garrotted him.'

'*Garrotted?*'

'I know. It's straight out of *The Godfather.*'

'Any idea who or why?'

'Not yet. There are about a million different sets of prints to sort out, but I imagine they all belong to his students.'

Liz thought of the arrogant, slightly epicene figure she'd interviewed. 'I can see him being unpopular with them, but killing him is going it a bit. Any other leads?'

'We're looking into his personal life. He was unmarried, but so far nothing's come up on the sexual front.'

'Why did it take so long to find him? Where were his students?'

'He'd cancelled all his supervisions, and his afternoon class. He told one of his students an old friend was coming to see him. We're trying to locate this old friend.'

'Keep me posted please. We have an interest in this one.'

There was a long pause, and Liz could picture the big man at his desk, sitting with a mug of coffee, wondering what exactly MI5's interest was. 'Of course,' he said at last. 'CID are in charge, but I know the lead officer.'

Liz put the phone down, her mind racing. Another death on her watch. Get a hold of yourself, she said half aloud, then saw Dave Armstrong at his nearby desk staring at her. 'You okay?' he asked.

She nodded, but she knew she wasn't. She stood up and walked down the corridor to the conference room she and Peggy were using. Peggy was out of the room, and Liz closed the door and sat down to think things through.

Was she somehow responsible for this one? She wondered if inadvertently she had made a slip, and put O'Phelan at risk. She had better tell Wetherby right away, she thought, just as the door opened and, as if on cue, Wetherby himself came in. 'I thought you might be here,' he said with a thin smile, but then he saw her face. 'What's wrong, Liz?' He pulled back a chair and sat down at the conference table next to her.

'I've just spoken with Belfast Special Branch. Liam O'Phelan, that lecturer, has been murdered.'

Wetherby looked stunned. 'Had you arranged to see him again?'

'No. I was going to ring him this morning.' Liz shook her head. It seemed unreal. She had to keep telling herself that she no longer needed to book a flight to Belfast.

'Did anyone know you'd been to see him?'

'Only Peggy and Jimmy Fergus – I had dinner with him the same night. I wanted to know if O'Phelan was in the Special Branch database over there. People here knew I was away, but I didn't say where.' She paused and saw that Wetherby was looking reflective, as if he were a million miles away. She said, a little bitterly, 'I feel as if I'm back to square one.'

'Not at all,' said Wetherby. He looked at her sternly but his tone was encouraging. 'You know there was a link between O'Phelan and Keaney. And you were sure there was another connection between O'Phelan and someone on your list. So you're just going to have to find that link some other way. There was never any guarantee O'Phelan was going to help you.'

'That's true,' Liz acknowledged. But she would have much rather had the chance of questioning O'Phelan again. He had been slippery, but she felt confident she would have got more out of him second time round, especially now she knew about his ties to Sean Keaney.

'Can you see any connection between your visit and his death?'

Liz shook her head. 'No. But there was something decidedly creepy about the man. I'm certain he knew I was from the Service. I didn't like him at all – not that it matters any more. At first I thought he was a misogynist, though maybe he just hated the English.'

'Not unknown in the six counties,' said Wetherby wryly. 'If he was a specialist in Irish affairs he may have been strongly nationalist. More to the point, his death could have absolutely nothing to do with your visit.'

She realised Charles was looking at her appraisingly. He said, 'You had a bit of a knock last year. Then Marzipan, and now this.' He stood up, tugging at his tie thoughtfully. 'You're a strong person, Liz, and I'm not worried about you. Provided you don't start worrying about yourself.'

'Okay,' she said quietly, taking his point. There was sometimes self-indulgence in feeling guilty, something which she had tried to avoid when thinking about Marzipan. With Liam O'Phelan it was certainly possible that if she had never gone to see him he would not have been murdered, but with that kind of reasoning, she might as well give up her job. Her real regret was that she hadn't gone back to see him sooner. Too late to worry about that, she told herself.

'I need to talk to Michael Binding urgently. O'Phelan was his referee – that's why I went to see him in the first place.'

'Michael's got a few days' holiday, Liz. Won't be back until next week. Part of me is tempted to call him back – we could think of a pretext – but if there is something to worry about, that would set off all sorts of alarm bells prematurely.'

Liz was shaking her head. 'No, it can wait, I think. For all my reservations about O'Phelan, I don't think he was holding anything back about Michael Binding. He was contemptuous about him, to tell you the truth, and it didn't seem in the least contrived. It was something else he wasn't coming clean about.'

'Perhaps you should focus on O'Phelan's time at Oxford.'

She nodded. 'I'll ask Peggy to have another look. I want to

widen the net a bit with the families of the people on our list, and check for even the remotest Irish connection. We've got Dobson and his cousin in the Maze; I want to see if any of the others has something comparable.'

35

The bookshop owner, when called in for questioning, turned out to be Jamaican, an ex-Rasta with a string of narcotics convictions and a history of dabbling in the murkier fringes of what was left of Britain's Black Power movement.

Now a Muslim, he brought to his new creed the fervour of the converted. And a new name – the Kingston-born Otis Quarrie now went under the exotic soubriquet Jamil Abdul-Hakim. Gone were the dreadlocks, and the floppy Rasta hat; now he wore a white caftan and sandals in all weathers. Intellectually he had travelled far – it was clear to Dave Armstrong, as he sat listening to the man talk, that Abdul-Hakim had read many if not all of the Islamist volumes he sold, and was happy to talk about them to anyone at length. Including Dave and a confused-looking Special Branch officer.

Dave had managed to get in a few questions. He had learned that Sohail Din had been a steady employee about whom Abdul-Hakim professed to know very little. He had been punctual, quiet, diligent. Since this account accorded with Dave's own impressions, there had been nothing more to say. Abdul-Hakim had seemed sincerely sorry about Sohail's death; equally, he seemed authentically to believe it had been a racist murder.

'Excuse me,' said Dave now, breaking in on the latest tangent, a defence of the rights of Muslim schoolgirls to wear the jilbab. 'But if we could just get back to this Imam, Abu Sayed. My understanding is that he was supposed to meet certain followers here but the meeting never came off.'

'There were lots of meetings, mon,' said Abdul-Hakim who for all his new identity had not shed his Rasta accent.

'With these men?' Dave handed over the photographs of Rashid Khan and the other two men.

The Jamaican glanced casually at them, then shrugged.

'Do you know who they are?' asked Dave.

'No.'

'But you recognise them, don't you?'

'They were here mon, sure. So?'

'So,' said Dave, finding his patience tried, 'they met once with the Imam and were supposed to meet with him again. What happened? Why didn't they show?'

'You'd have to ask them di question,' Abdul-Hakim said with a trace of defiance.

'It's your bookshop.'

'But it was the Imam's meetings, mon,' said Abdul-Hakim with a smirk, and would not be drawn further.

In the freshly hoovered living room of her house in Wokingham, Thelma Dawnton was distinctly miffed. Trevor had insisted on being present when Simon came back for another chat. He was good-looking, the young Simon, even if he looked a bit scruffy in his parka. He was friendly too, and he liked badminton – though he didn't get to play very often. Thelma would never have dreamed of being anything but a loyal wife (well, she might have dreamed, but reality was different), but glancing over at Trevor she resented his unnecessary chaperoning.

Still, she had to admit that Trevor knew about some things she didn't. Like cars – which Simon seemed very keen on.

At first, they had talked about the men next door, and Thelma knew she had been helpful there – more than Trevor, for sure, since, as he would be the first to admit, he couldn't tell a Pakistani from a Zulu. She'd searched her memory (ignoring Trevor's 'Don't invent') and surprised even herself at what she'd come up with.

One of the men had been short, almost a dwarf Thelma remembered, and she was pretty sure he had a trace of a limp. Maybe he'd twisted an ankle, she offered, and Simon had written this down in his notebook. As for the other two, she really only had an impression of one of them, for he was always scowling, as if – she had thought about this since her last conversation with Simon – he was depressed about something. After all (though she decided not to say this to Simon) hadn't the *Femail* pages in the newspaper said anger and depression were usually linked? And hadn't it said that one out of four Britons were depressed? Or was it one out of twelve?

It was then that Trevor rolled his eyes, which infuriated Thelma and, as the same newspaper said, lowered her self-esteem, though she was determined not to show it. She was going to have a word with her husband about this habit of his, and she would do it sooner rather than later.

This time Simon didn't write anything down, but changed the subject instead. To cars. She'd said the men next door had had a smart motor, and that was when Trevor snorted and Simon smiled – she knew that meant a man thought you were being daft – and focused his attention solely on her husband. 'You said it was a Golf these men drove. Black – or was it dark blue?'

'Black.' Trevor was adamant.

'Can you remember anything else about it? Any kind of quirk, anything unusual?'

And Trevor had sat there and thought. 'It was a T-reg.'

She wanted to say what did that matter, but then she looked at Simon's excited face and decided not to say anything at all. Men, she thought with disgust. Men and cars.

Doris Feldman wanted to help but didn't see how she could. Insomnia might put her in the chair by the window, early in the morning, but there had never been anything to see across the street – not that is, until the night the policemen had shown up. As she said to the young man in the parka who sat sipping a cuppa with her – he could have been her grandson almost, she thought – there was nothing to say about the visitors to the bookshop that she hadn't said before.

The young man nodded. And he didn't seem surprised. Almost perfunctorily, he passed over a sheet on which there were photocopied photographs of three young men. All three were Asian in appearance, and at first Doris shook her head when the man in the parka asked if she recognised them. Then like a light bulb, memory lit up. 'I know him,' she exclaimed, pointing to the photograph of Rashid. 'And him,' she said, pointing to one of the other photos.

'How is that?' asked the man patiently.

'This one,' she said pointing to the picture of Rashid, 'bought some cord rope. He started to ask how strong it was and the other chap got cross. 'Just pay the lady,' he said, as if I wasn't there. Rude if you ask me. That's why I remember him. The other fellow seemed upset. Poor little thing.'

Why had this man come back? He'd told him what he knew already about the lease on 48 Somerset Drive. Which was next to nothing. And Richard Penbury had so much to do – there were three viewings he was conducting that afternoon alone, and about a million chasing phone calls to make.

But here was the policeman again, Simon something, asking him once more to try and remember the man who had let the house on Somerset Drive. A white man, which as he had tried to explain, was precisely the difficulty – an Asian would have been memorable in this part of town. It made for a kind of racism in reverse.

Penbury said, 'I probably saw ten people that day about properties. Multiply by five for the week, that's fifty, and it's been fifteen weeks or so. Surely you can see the problem.'

'Of course I can, but anything at all you can remember about our Mr Larrabee would help. I mean, was he tall or short? Did he have bad teeth? It's things like that you might remember. Had he rung first, for example?'

'He would have done. He wasn't going to come all the way from London on an off chance we had something to let.'

'London?' said Simon quickly. 'How do you know he came from there?'

'Because of his application form. He gave a London address,' said Penbury, weary in the face of the policeman's interest. 'Not because of anything I remembered.'

But curiously something was coming back to him. What was it? Something visual, but it wasn't a face. Something to do with a hand. 'I know,' he said aloud.

The policeman looked startled. 'What is it?' he asked hopefully.

'He had one arm in a sling.'

'A sling.' Simon sounded doubtful. 'Which arm?'

'Well, I can't remember, but I suppose it was his left. He signed stuff anyway, so unless he was left-handed . . .'

'Keep thinking,' said Simon, 'you're doing well.'

Penbury *was* thinking hard. 'Take your time,' said Simon. And he did, concentrating intently, while images of faces, and gestures, and once even a handbag flashed through his mind. But the phone on the next desk rang twice in the space of a minute, loudly, and then Millie, the new girl, shrieked as she spilled tea on her blouse, and it was no good. No good at all. He'd try again, he reassured Simon, who looked disappointed, but now if he didn't mind, he really had better get on with his work.

Sarah Manpini sat on her own in the control room outside Reading, finding the viewing room a relief after yet another session with the late-night shift patrolmen, who even after two years still seemed to find her surname hilarious.

She was on her third hour of CCTV analysis – only it wasn't exactly analytical, now was it? More like mindless viewing, just like any couch potato, only nothing much was happening on this filmed record of the M4 traffic either side of Reading. To be accurate, nothing much *had* happened, since the footage she was viewing was almost a week old. Twenty-seven VW Golfs had triggered the cameras for one reason or another in the forty-eight hour period she was reviewing, but only three had been black or dark enough to pass as black.

Two of those had been heading east and she duly recorded their number plates. The third had been going west like the clappers – the speed had triggered the camera – but its numbers had not come out on the screen. She replayed the segment of the tape and peered at it closely. Luminescent paint had been applied to the plastic strip of numerals. Clever, she thought – that must be the car. She called in further tapes, now that she knew the time the Golf had triggered the camera west of Reading. And bingo – at the Newbury exit thirty minutes later the Golf had left the M4. From the secondary camera she knew only that it had then headed north.

36

Liz hadn't been in Tom Dartmouth's office since the day of Marzipan's death, and then she had not taken in anything about her surroundings. Today she was attending a meeting Tom was chairing of the Operation FOXHUNT team. The room, a standard group leader's room with a six-chair conference table, was full, and more chairs had been brought in. But in spite of all the people, it managed to look surprisingly bare, almost clinical in fact, thought Liz. Tom's desk had none of the bric-a-brac that most people brought in to make their working space more personal. No family photos, no desk set, no curios brought back from abroad. Not even a favourite mug as far as she could see. The rather bleak prints on the wall were from a government-issue set of famous buildings.

There was an air of anxiety and gloom in the room. They were not making much progress in finding the bookshop group or their target. In fact, Operation FOXHUNT did not seem to be getting anywhere. And time was clearly running out.

Tom was chairing the meeting, the first Liz had attended for two weeks. He did it perfectly competently, but lacked Wetherby's ability to bind people into a team. With Charles, even the most junior felt free to have a say, yet bores got cut off before they, well, bored. With Charles, Liz thought, you felt directed yet enabled at the same time, even when things were going badly. Today she felt only a disheartening impotence.

From A4, Reggie Purvis had given his report: there had been no significant visitors to the bookshop or to Rashid Khan's home in Wolverhampton. Surveillance of his sister had produced nothing of interest.

Michael Binding for A2 was more long-winded but equally downbeat: there had been no more phone calls to the bookshop or to Rashid's home from Amsterdam, no more calls of interest to his sister, and nothing relevant off the mikes in the bookshop.

Now Judith Spratt was finishing up her side of things. She had the only positive news to report. 'I've just heard from Reading Control Room that they've got a possible dark-coloured Golf exiting the M4 at Newbury on the night the men left the Wokingham house. It was heading north. They're working on it now. Dave, have you got anything more about the Golf from the neighbours?'

'I spoke to the man Trevor,' said Dave. 'He's certain it was a T-reg. Black. Any good?'

'Yes, thanks, I think we've got that already,' she said.

'Anything else, Dave?' Tom asked, sounding keen to wind things up.

Dave gave a short account of his interviews with Jamil Abdul-Hakim and Doris Feldman, then described his disappointing conversation with the letting agent in Wokingham. This mysterious white male was clearly important, but everyone agreed the sling wasn't going to help identify him. It had probably been a bogus affectation, designed to distract attention from its owner's face. If so, it had certainly done its job well. As Dave paused for a moment, Liz noticed Michael Binding collecting his papers for a quick exit. Judith was busy looking in her bag.

'Then I had a call this morning,' Dave said. Something in his voice made everyone stop and pay attention.

'When I interviewed Trevor yesterday, all he told me about was the car. But his wife rang me this morning to say she had remembered something else.'

He paused again, and Liz wondered what he was up to. She had seen Dave earlier that morning and he'd said nothing to suggest he'd found out anything important. So why the drama? He was milking this audience like an actor keen to take another bow. That wasn't like Dave at all.

She looked around the room. Binding, Judith Spratt, Rose Love, Reggie Purvis and one of his A4 sidekicks, Tom Dartmouth at the head of the table, and of course Liz herself. Who was Dave trying to impress?

'Mrs Dawnton says she saw someone visiting the terrorists a few weeks ago. He was a white male. He came at night, but she got a good view of him because he triggered the Dawntons' security light. She thinks she could identify him if she saw him again. So I'm going down this afternoon to talk to her.'

Nobody said a word. In the silence Liz noticed the hum from a strip light. 'Good,' said Tom at last. 'Keep us posted.'

37

Why didn't I bring my sun glasses? thought Liz, then realised that two days of non-stop rain had made the prospect of decent weather seem remote. Yet in its shaky, hesitant English way, summer was approaching, and as she left London on the M3, the cloud cleared and the dipping sun shone straight into her eyes.

She was feeling gloomy. Her mother's brave front on the phone had been automatic cause for alarm, since with her mother's generation, Liz knew that the more blithe the denial the more serious the problem must be. And work was providing no compensatory distraction. The murder of O'Phelan had stopped her investigation into the mole dead in its tracks. There was no obvious way ahead.

She stopped for a break in Stockbridge almost two hours later, as the light was finally starting to go. It was a pretty Hampshire town with a long, unusually wide high street, nestled between pillow-like hills in the valley of the Test river. It required a small detour, but it was a favourite stopping place for Liz.

She stretched her legs and window-shopped for a few minutes, then bought a box of chocolate truffles from a grocery shop. She knew that despite her mother's protestations they would eat half of them before bedtime. She stopped to look at the trout, swimming lazily in the deep, small pool where the river emerged from under the High Street. It was next to a branch of Orvis, the upmarket fly-fishing shop which was thronged this time of year with enthusiasts preparing for the famous mayfly hatch.

Her first boyfriend had been an avid fly-fisherman, and she smiled at the memory of the hours she'd spent on riverbank dates – reading her book while Josh delicately cast his fly onto the surface of the gin-clear water, or cursed as he snagged it in the willow trees behind him. Her mother had adored Josh, which had made Liz's own recognition that he bored her half to death a slower process than it would be nowadays.

Why did she always think about men when she went to see her mother? Probably because men – or, not to put it too abstractly, a husband – seemed her mother's main concern for her daughter.

Liz couldn't tell her mother much about her work, yet Liz knew that even if she had worked in a normal job, her mother's interest in it would have been outweighed by what she clearly thought were the important questions: Are you seeing anyone? Are you going to marry them? Don't you want a family?

None of the above right now, thought Liz, knowing that particularly with her mother going into hospital these queries were likely to be raised this weekend. As she set off from Stockbridge she found herself admitting that yes, of course it would be nice to have a husband. And a family. But not at any cost. And not, at least for the time being, if it meant giving up the job she loved.

Half an hour later, Liz arrived at Bowerbridge and the octagonal gatehouse where her mother still lived. It was set back from the road, inside the russet brick wall that ran around the perimeter of what had once been a large estate.

Her father had been the estate manager for over thirty years and Liz had grown up there. After his death, Liz's mother had stayed on, and last year she had bought the freehold – unnecessarily in a sense, since at the former owner's insistence she was allowed to live there rent-free for the rest of her days. But behind this acquisition was her unspoken hope that some day Liz would move there, too. Join her in the garden centre, meet a man, get married, have children, settle down. In her head, Liz heard her mother's important questions all over again.

The rest of the estate had been sold, and the 'big house' – a lovely Georgian pile of cream stone – had been converted into flats and ground-floor offices for the garden centre, which now occupied the old kitchen garden. Liz's mother had taken a part-time job there. Being her, she had taken on more and more responsibility, until now she managed the business, at an age when most people would be thinking of retirement. Emerging from the crushing impact of her husband's death, she had a new kind of life – one she was obviously enjoying. Which made the prospect of serious illness seem to Liz an especially cruelly timed blow.

Parking, Liz got out and stood on the gravel drive as her eyes adjusted to the dusk. There were still lights on in the garden centre, for it stayed open late in spring and summer. She hoped her mother would have left work by now, and was relieved to find her in the kitchen, waiting for the kettle to boil.

'Hello, darling,' her mother said. 'I wasn't expecting you this soon.'

'Traffic wasn't bad at all,' said Liz breezily. She didn't want to tell her mother that with Wetherby's blessing she had knocked off early to make sure she got down at a reasonable hour.

'I was just thinking about our supper,' her mother said, pointing vaguely to the Aga. A tin sat open on the table, but

Liz realised it was for Purdey, the white long-haired cat acquired by her mother the year before, and much fussed over.

'Let me do it,' said Liz. Unusually her mother let her take over, and sat down at the kitchen table while Liz fed Purdey, then made scrambled eggs and toast. As they ate, Liz avoided all talk of the next day's hospital procedure, sensing her mother preferred it that way. Keep it light, Liz told herself. For the first time, her mother seemed frail and vulnerable. And more scared than she would ever let on. When it was time for bed, Liz realised that they hadn't touched the chocolate truffles.

Liz took her mother to the hospital after lunch the next day. The doctors planned to keep her in overnight. 'A precaution,' they'd explained, and Liz wasn't going to argue.

The procedure took place at three, under a local anaesthetic. By four o'clock her mother was back in the ward, though drowsy from the anaesthetic and an injection of painkiller the doctor had administered. Liz stayed for half an hour, then left her mother resting, and returned to the gatehouse to feed Purdey.

She was opening a tin in her mother's kitchen, when she heard a car pull onto the gravel on the far side of the house. Walking through to the sitting room, she saw a man slowly getting out of a low-slung sporty model. He was tall, wide shouldered, and dressed in smart casual clothes – suede shoes, a cashmere sweater and dark blue cords with a sharp crease. Then she realised it was Tom Dartmouth.

She had completely forgotten that she'd told him she'd be at her mother's that weekend, and equally that he was, coincidentally, staying with friends nearby. Why hadn't he rung first? she thought crossly, only too aware that in trainers and a grey

T-shirt she hardly looked her best. Then she realised he probably had phoned, while she was with her mother at the hospital.

She opened the rarely used front door and went out to greet him. 'Tom,' she said, 'I've just got back.'

'Good timing then,' he said, as he crossed the drive. 'What's that noise?' he asked suddenly. *Tee-cher, tee-cher, tee-cher* came from the other side of the house, like the metallic sound of an old typewriter.

'Blue tits,' she said, 'there's usually a crowd of them in our holly tree.' Liz stood listening for a moment, until she sensed Tom's impatience and remembered her manners. 'Come on in,' she said, and once inside she steered him into the sitting room, which was tidier than the kitchen. 'Can I get you something? Cup of tea?'

Tom made a show of consulting his watch. 'After six,' he declared. 'Something stronger wouldn't go amiss.'

Liz looked with alarm at the drinks tray – her mother was hopeless about keeping her supplies replenished. 'There's some whiskey,' she said, pointing to a half-drunk bottle of Famous Grouse. There was some dry sherry too, she noted with relief, though she wasn't certain how long it had been opened, and her mother's favourite tipple – Stone's Ginger Wine.

'Any gin?' asked Tom hopefully.

'I'll just see,' she said without optimism.

In the larder she found an ancient bottle of Gordon's with just enough left in it for a large G&T. She hoped Tom was not planning to stay long. She found some ice, though no lemon, a packet of rather stale cheese straws, and brought it all out on a tray to the sitting room. Tom was standing by the French windows. 'Pretty garden,' he announced. 'Does she get someone in to do it?'

'Perish the thought,' said Liz a little sharply. 'My mother doesn't even let me help her.'

'How is she?' he asked. 'You said she was in for tests. When does she get out?'

'Tomorrow. That's when we'll know.'

Tom seemed to sense, rightly, that she didn't want to talk about it, for he pointed outside, saying, 'It's a lovely spot. Has she been here long?'

'Thirty years,' said Liz, handing over the drink. She poured herself a glass of tonic without gin. She added, 'I grew up here. My father looked after the estate.'

Tom came and sat down in the large easy chair where Liz's mother spent her evenings, knitting, reading or watching the television. 'Cheers,' he said, lifting his glass. He drank, then put the glass down and sat back comfortably in the chair.

'Cheers,' replied Liz from the sofa, beginning to appreciate how tired she was. The combination of focusing on her mother and worrying about her, was proving exhausting.

'Welcome contrast to Thames House,' said Tom.

'It's a nice part of Wiltshire,' agreed Liz. 'Where are you staying?'

'My friends are about ten miles west of here. Off the road to Blandford.'

'What's the name of their village?'

Tom shrugged his shoulders. 'They've got a farm, and I'm afraid I haven't taken much notice of my surroundings. I think they said the village was walkable, but I didn't catch its name.' He chuckled. 'I've just been so glad to be in a place where the telephone doesn't ring all the time.'

'You must have been frantic these last few weeks.'

'You could say that,' said Tom, taking a long pull on his

drink. 'Still am. I've left Judith in charge this weekend. How about you?'

'Busy,' she said.

'You're doing something for Wetherby, aren't you?' When she only nodded in reply, he said, 'Sorry, not meaning to pry.'

She shrugged, not wanting to seem pompous. Then it occurred to her that if they were going to talk about work, she might as well use the opportunity. 'Tell me,' she said, 'you were at Oxford. Did you ever come across a lecturer there named O'Phelan? An Irishman.'

Tom picked up his glass and looked at her with interest. 'You mean the guy who was murdered? Just a few days ago. I saw it in the papers.'

'That's the one – I was supposed to see him about something. But now . . .' She left the conclusion unspoken. She decided not to mention her earlier visit to see O'Phelan – she didn't want to influence Tom's account of the man with her own impressions.

'As a matter of fact, I did,' said Tom. 'Well, I didn't know him; it's more I knew *of* him. He was a fairly notorious character.'

'Really? Why was that?'

Tom smiled a little awkwardly. 'O'Phelan was what the obituarists like to call a confirmed bachelor. Each to his own, of course, but he was sometimes a bit predatory with his students. A great pal of mine was taught by him, which was fine for the first year – O'Phelan acted as if my friend had great academic gifts. Then suddenly one day, right in the middle of a supervision, O'Phelan went and locked the door to his rooms, and pounced. My friend literally had to fight his way out.' At the memory, Tom gave a knowing grin. 'Fortunately, he was the fly-half in the College XV so he didn't have much trouble staying out of his clutches. But he did need to find a new supervisor.'

'What was your friend's name?'

Tom looked surprised by her question. It didn't matter, of course, but she liked having names. It helped her remember people's stories.

'Clapton,' he said slowly, 'Philip Clapton. Why do you ask?'

Liz gave an innocent shrug. 'I don't know. Just curious, I guess.' She smiled winningly. 'Anyway, you've opened up a whole new side to O'Phelan. I'd heard he was a staunch Republican.'

Tom looked blankly at Liz. 'O'Phelan? You surprise me.'

'I thought he had always been strongly nationalist. Even at Oxford.'

'Maybe he was,' said Tom. 'That wasn't something I ever came across. What's this stuff?' he suddenly demanded, brushing at his trousers, which were covered from the knees down in white hair.

'Sorry,' said Liz. 'Purdey must have rubbed against you. She likes men.'

'Wretched cat,' said Tom, still picking the hairs off his blue trousers. He looked up brightly at Liz. 'Listen, I've got an idea. The last thing you need tonight is to have to cook for yourself. Why don't you let me give you supper? There's a hotel in Salisbury that's supposed to have a very good restaurant. It'll be my treat.'

She knew it was thoughtful, but it was the last thing she wanted. Right now, she had no intention of eating anything more complicated or substantial than a plate of soup; the thought of a three-course dinner was too much to bear. 'It's really kind of you,' she said, 'but I'm going to have to pass.'

Tom was unwilling to take no for an answer. 'Oh do come,' he said, 'it would be fun. You need to relax. Take your mind off things.'

She forced a smile but shook her head. 'I wouldn't be good company. Anyway, I need to be near the phone. Just in case.'

'Bring your mobile,' persisted Tom. 'We can call the hospital and give them the number.'

'Perhaps some other time,' said Liz, with just a hint of steel.

Tom seemed to get the message at last. 'I'll hold you to that then,' he said. He looked at his watch. 'It's getting on,' he declared. 'I'd better be going.'

And after he left, Liz mulled over their conversation. I'd better call Jimmy Fergus, she thought, and point him in the right direction. Though if 'rough trade' were the answer to the mystery of O'Phelan's death, then why had he been killed in his college room, rather than at his home? And why in the morning?

She went into the kitchen and put some soup on the stove and a slice of bread in the toaster. That and a glass of wine would do her nicely. She wished Tom had not been so insistent; it made her feel ungrateful, even impolite, though not so much so that she wasn't happy to be alone, with a quiet evening ahead of her. She would be happy to have dinner with him – but in London, she thought, not when I'm worrying about my mother.

She had never gone out with a colleague; mixing business and pleasure seemed to invite trouble. Not that dating men outside the Service had proved any easier. Either they were married, thought Liz, or too inquisitive about her work – or both. The curious ones in particular posed a quandary, since their natural interest in her work could never be satisfied: 'How was your day, darling?' was never going to be a question Liz could answer honestly, not unless her partner was in the same business. Perhaps this explained the Service's view of intra-Service romances. They weren't exactly encouraged, but weren't forbidden, either.

Was the prospect of a date with Tom the solution? At least they could talk freely about their work – if she moaned about someone, he would know right away who she was talking about. Suddenly Liz laughed at herself – she'd let her imagination carry her away, expanding a tentative dinner invitation into a full-blown romance. Yet Tom's intentions seemed pretty clear, now didn't they?

Liz wasn't sure whether the prospect of Tom Dartmouth as a suitor was alluring or mildly alarming. Certainly he hadn't seemed very sensitive to her situation this weekend. Did he really think she'd want to go out tonight, while her mother lay in hospital, awaiting her results? Tom may have got the best First in his year, thought Liz with a certain acerbity, but he had been awfully slow to get the message. And he'd been rude about the cat. Then she laughed as she thought of Purdey, shedding hair like snow on Tom's pristine trousers.

38

'I've spoken to your mother already, so she knows the situation,' announced the consultant, a balding man with NHS spectacles and a brusque manner. 'The growth she has is malignant.'

I hope you were gentler with her, thought Liz, feeling furious, though she knew it was the news rather than his method of imparting it which was most upsetting her. 'What happens next?' she asked, knowing that even if he had the bedside manner of a doctor in ER, her mother would have been in too much shock to take it all in.

And Liz herself had to concentrate with all her might as the consultant began to speak dispassionately about the programme that lay ahead. An operation to remove the growth; chemotherapy if they discovered it had spread; radiation after that; possibly drug treatment as well. All this, thought Liz despairingly, for a woman who resisted taking so much as an aspirin.

When the consultant finished and went off to see a patient, Liz thought she had understood it all, despite a queasy feeling that seemed worse every time she remembered that this was not a dream, or a television drama, but the stark facts of her mother's cancer.

39

Peggy was positively buoyant when Liz met her for coffee in the conference room late on Monday morning.

'You were going to speak to Judith Spratt about her domestic situation.'

'Yes,' said Liz, though she had been dreading talking to Judith, who was, after all, a friend whom she felt reluctant to interrogate about her personal life.

'I think I've found out why he's no longer living there. I had a Google Alert tied to his name, and I got a flash this morning. There's an article in this morning's *Financial Times*.'

Peggy pushed a newspaper clipping towards Liz and kept talking while Liz scanned the piece. 'Apparently Ravi Singh and an associate were being investigated by the OFT for insider share dealing. But that's not all. The Serious Fraud Office has been called in, because they think Ravi and this other chap may have been involved in an identity-fraud scam using other people's credit card numbers.'

Liz pointed to the clipping. 'It says here some of the victims are American, so the FBI is taking an interest. It's possible they'll want to extradite them.'

It would be a lot worse for them over there. She handed the clipping back to Peggy. 'This is terrible,' she declared. And silently she asked herself, what on earth am I going to say to Judith?

It wasn't simply that they were friends. Over the last decade, as both of them moved into their thirties, Judith had seemed to Liz the epitome of a woman who had it all – a successful career, a happy marriage, a much-loved child. Everyone knew that was a tough balancing act, yet Judith seemed to manage it with an elegant grace that Liz admired in spite of herself. She would normally find it hard to like such a paragon of virtue, but Judith did everything impeccably, never took anything for granted, and had an impish sense of humour.

Liz had been to her house in Fulham for dinner several times over the years. They were happy occasions, low-key and relaxed. What always struck Liz was the calm efficiency with which Judith ran the household. Ravi had helped, but he worked long hours in the City, so most of the onus was on Judith. What a juggling act: finishing the dinner, getting her guests a drink and simultaneously comforting her daughter, Daisy, who kept getting out of bed to see the guests. And Judith was always so utterly unflappable. I can't even get the laundry done, Liz thought, as she dialled Judith's extension. A surprise visitor to Liz's flat in Kentish Town would currently find two bed sheets stretched to dry on the dining room chairs along with three pairs of tights and an assortment of underwear – all thanks to Liz's failure to fix a date with the repair man to mend her tumble dryer.

Throughout the morning there was no reply from Judith's extension, but at lunchtime Liz found her sitting alone at a table in the far corner of the Thames House cafeteria. Her expression made it clear that she did not want company. Liz joined her, sliding her tray along the table and sitting down opposite her.

'I see you didn't fancy the bolognese either,' said Liz lightly, pointing to their respective salads. Judith managed a wan smile.

She looks terrible, thought Liz; Judith was usually the epitome of elegance. Unlike Liz, she never looked as though her clothes had spent the night on a chair. Though she dressed conservatively, she was a careful shopper with a keen eye for quality and style. Now she looked drab.

'I've been looking for you,' said Liz.

Judith raised a mild, uninterested eye. She had her hair tied back, which usually complimented her sharp, strong features. Today, despite a lot of make-up, it only highlighted her drawn face.

'I haven't said anything, because there hasn't been a need to. But you know the vetting updates the Security Committee ordered?'

'Yes,' said Judith. Liz thought she sounded slightly wary.

'Well, I've had to do some of them. My turn to draw the short straw. It's why I haven't been around all the time, in case you noticed.'

Judith didn't say anything, but just waited for Liz to continue. 'It's meant to be largely a paper exercise and I don't need to interview people . . .'

'Unless,' said Judith impassively.

'Unless,' said Liz, a little doggedly, wishing her friend would make this easier for them both, 'there is some discrepancy. Something that needs explaining.'

'And you want to know about Ravi?'

Her voice was flat, toneless. It made Liz feel she was persecuting her friend, but she knew she had no choice. 'Well it is in the papers. Is he still living with you?'

'No, he left before Christmas.' And she never said a word, thought Liz. '*I'm* still living there,' said Judith a little defensively. She was poking her salad with her fork.

'I know,' said Liz. 'But we're supposed to inform B Branch if our circumstances change. You know that, Judith,' she said, as gently as she could.

For the first time Judith's voice showed animation. '"Circumstances change"?' she said sarcastically. 'You can say that again. You say you've seen the papers. I mean, your talking to me isn't a coincidence, now is it?'

'No,' admitted Liz, 'it's not. Though I was going to need to talk to you in any case.'

'How many other people are you vetting?'

'A lot,' said Liz, happy to let Judith prevaricate provided they got back to the point eventually. 'I'm doing Oxbridge people first. There were several up with you.' Judith didn't reply, so Liz went on. 'Were you friends with any of them?'

'Like who?' she said.

'Patrick Dobson was there.'

'Was he?'

One down, thought Liz. 'Doesn't matter. Michael Binding was at Oxford, too.'

'As he never ceases telling me,' said Judith sourly. Liz knew she shared her own irritation with Binding's condescending treatment of his female colleagues. 'When he wants to show his intellectual superiority he always says' – and here Judith mimicked Binding's bass tones – '"When I was at Oxford . . ." As if I hadn't gone there myself, and as if it meant that much anyway. If you have to interview him, please do me a favour.'

'What's that?'

'Pretend you think his college was St Hilda's. It's the only all-women's college. He'll be mortified.'

Liz smiled at the thought of Binding's sense of outrage. Then she asked, 'What about Tom Dartmouth? He was there at the same time.'

Judith nodded but didn't say anything. Liz prompted her. 'Did you know him then?'

'No. Though I knew who he was.'

'Why was that?'

Judith gave a small conspiratorial grin. 'Didn't you know the names of the best-looking boys at college?'

Liz laughed. 'By heart,' she said, but came back to her question. 'But you didn't know him?'

'No,' said Judith simply. 'However much I may have wanted to. Not that I'd say I really know him now. He's a bit of an enigma. Funnily enough, I saw his wife a few months ago.'

'Aren't they divorced?'

'Yes.' She sighed, seemingly at the comparison with her own shattered ménage. 'She's Israeli, and absolutely stunning. Her father was an Air Force general in the Seven Day War.'

'I thought she lived in Israel.'

Judith shrugged. 'Maybe she was visiting. I saw her in Harrods Food Hall, of all places. I waved but she didn't wave back. She may not have recognised me. I only met her once or twice, and it was years ago.'

Time to get back to the point, thought Liz. Slightly hesitantly she asked, 'Have you spoken to Ravi?'

Judith shook her head. 'Not for weeks. We are communicating strictly through lawyers now. He hasn't even come to see Daisy. It's been incredibly hurtful, but after today's news, I wonder whether he's just been trying to spare us.'

'So you've only just found out about his problems?' Liz had been half assuming it was precisely his 'problems' that had led Judith to throw him out.

'Yes,' said Judith. She looked at Liz, at first quizzically, then with outright disbelief. 'You don't think I had anything to do with them, do you?'

'No, I don't.' She knew Judith too well to doubt her sincerity. 'But I'm sure they'll want to talk with you about it.'

'Who, B Branch?'

'Well, yes, but I was thinking more the Fraud Squad.'

'Happily,' said Judith. 'I'll tell them everything I know. Which, in fact, is absolutely nothing. Zero. Zilch. Nothing . . .' She suddenly seemed on the verge of an hysterical outburst, so Liz reached over and put her hand on her forearm. 'Steady,' she said calmly.

Judith stopped speaking at once, nodding with her chin down. Liz was afraid Judith was going to cry. It was touch and go for a moment, then Judith pulled herself together. Putting her fork down and looking at Liz, she demanded, 'What happens now? Do I get disciplined?'

'It's not up to me,' Liz said, very grateful that it wasn't. 'I can't see it as a very big deal. After all, it's not as if we couldn't have got hold of you. With any luck, they'll just put a note on your file.'

'A reprimand,' said Judith.

'I shouldn't think so. More like a slap on the wrist.'

Judith smiled faintly. 'The thing is, Liz, I know how it looks. People will think either "Why didn't she stand by her husband when he got in trouble?", or "no wonder she threw him out – the man's a crook."'

'Possibly,' said Liz, not sure what Judith was trying to say.

'But don't you see?' and for the first time there was passion in Judith's voice. 'I didn't throw him out. He left me.' Liz tried not to show her own surprise, as Judith collected her cutlery and laid it neatly on her plate, then folded her napkin. It was as if she were trying to control her emotions by paying attention to the most pedestrian detail. 'Look Liz, I'm married to someone who doesn't love me any more. And today I've discovered he's a crook. But do you know the most terrible thing about it all?'

Her voice faltered and this time Liz thought she really would break down. She felt helpless watching her friend's distress. But again Judith seemed to catch hold of herself. 'It's that I'd have him back tomorrow, crook or not. Isn't that pathetic?'

40

He was going to have to get rid of the car, and part of him wanted to get rid of Rashid as well. Stupid! Bashir had thought furiously, as they had driven out of Wokingham and west along the M4. The road had been almost deserted that late at night, lit by a crescent moon that hung like a brooch from a cloudless sky. Rashid had been stupid beyond belief. Though from the way he had sat slumped half asleep in the passenger seat, he was completely oblivious to the trouble he had caused. In the back Khaled also slept.

The temptation to remove Rashid passed – he was needed after all. But Bashir's anger remained. It was not helped by the need to keep a low profile, and stay inside all day. They were living in a small house on the outskirts of Didcot, part of a new estate of starter homes that skirted a golf course. Like all its neighbours their house enjoyed a close-up view of the nearby power station and its reviled cooling towers.

Yet for all the grimness of its surroundings, the house had the bonus of a garage, in which Bashir had put the Golf, swapping places with the white builder's van, which he had parked on the street.

But the car was going to have to go. They needed to work on the van and they'd have to do that in the garage, safely out of sight.

Bashir stuck closely to Rashid in the following days, since he did not trust him enough now to allow even the shortest solitary walk. But staying inside all day was intensely monotonous for all three of them. There was nothing for them to do. Meals and prayers and the Koran – that was their life.

Bashir had a large-scale Ordnance Survey map of the area and spent one afternoon scrutinising it for remote tracks in the unpopulated countryside lying west of them. Then one evening he went out while it was still light, since he was worried he would not be able to find a suitable place in darkness. He gave Rashid and Khaled strict instructions not to leave the house on any account, though it was only Rashid he was concerned about. The landline was disconnected, and he had destroyed Rashid's incriminating mobile phone before they left Wokingham. As long as he didn't go anywhere, even Rashid should be unable to get into further trouble.

He was surprised how quickly the urban sprawl of Didcot gave way to farmland, and drove past field after field of orchards until he turned off the main Wantage road and moved south towards the Downs, pulling over on the small roads from time to time to consult his map. He drove through a village of brick and beam cottages, where a solitary man emerged from the churchyard with a terrier on a lead. Bashir felt conspicuous, and tried to reassure himself – he told himself there were plenty of Asians in Oxfordshire.

He turned onto a road of potholed asphalt that climbed in a series of sharp zig-zags to the top of the Downs. The Ridgeway crossed here, and he could see hikers in shorts and thick boots walking west towards Bath. The road split, the paved fork continuing south, crossing up and down across the humps of the hills. To the right a sandy track, half overgrown, meandered into a small wood. It was clearly never used.

Bashir drove down it cautiously, hearing the grass brushing

the van's bottom, and gorse bushes scratching its side. At the first small clearing, he pulled over and parked under an enormous beech tree.

He got out, locked the van, and began to walk further along the track. On either side, holm oaks towered above him, blocking out the sunlight and casting spooky shadows. Bashir could see that the track remained just accessible enough by car. After two hundred yards he came to a curve in the road, and almost immediately to a small clearing with a shallow pond where the track ended. The water looked mucky, algae-filled. No one would want to swim there.

Mentally Bashir marked a spot next to the pond where he would put the Golf. It should be days, possibly weeks before it was discovered, he thought, and in the state it was going to be in, it wouldn't tell anyone much. In any case, very soon it wouldn't matter even if it did. All he needed now was a full can of petrol.

41

It was the Young Farmers Dinner Dance, but Charlie Hancock was not so young any more. He was too old for dancing. He'd spent the greater part of the evening, after the meal, drinking pints with the other older farmers at the village hall bar. He'd had the one obligatory bop with his wife, Gemma, then let her dance with her girlfriends, while he discussed the impact of the dry winter on the corn crop with his pals. She now sat half asleep in the passenger seat.

By one o'clock they were both ready to leave, and though he was pretty sure he shouldn't really be driving – even the weakest bitter added up after a while – he took the wheel since Gemma's eyes weren't so good in the dark. He'd stuck to the back roads, through the tucked-in village of East Ginge, and the feudal holdings of the Lockinge estate, then relaxed as he climbed up into the Downs, since here at this hour he was unlikely to encounter anyone at all, much less a panda car with a policeman keen to breathalyse a farmer with a bellyful of brew.

He felt a bit sick and he needed to pee quite badly, so though he knew he was less than ten minutes from their farmhouse, he pulled over at the crest of Causewell Hill, where the dead-end track down to Simter's Pond started. Gemma stirred only slightly when he clambered out, breathing in the cool air and looking up to admire Orion in the clear sky as he went about his business. He saw the deep marks of fresh tyres on the track, and would have thought nothing of it – it had become a bit of a lover's lane, this remote stint of a road – had he not breathed in through his nose and caught the strongest whiff of smoke. He sniffed again, more carefully, and the smell was stronger. Something was burning.

Charlie couldn't leave it, no way. This was no time to be stubble burning – not in June, and not in the middle of the night – and fire was a farmer's nightmare. He wasn't sure whose land he was on, since Simter had sold it recently to an outsider, but he assumed they'd want to know if a field were burning, or, worse, far worse, a shed or outbuilding had somehow caught fire.

He got back into the car and started down the lane. Gemma, jogged awake by the rough track, asked him what he was doing, but before he could answer they had turned the corner and before them, just in front of Simter's Pond, they saw a car on fire. It must have been burning for some time, for only its shell remained. The flames had subsided, though they still lapped now in short, erratic breaths in the cool night air, casting a light caramel glow across the surface of the pond.

He stopped then, and got out to check if anyone was in the vehicle – but the heat was still so intense that he couldn't get close enough to make sure.

'Joyriders,' he said to Gemma as he got back into the driver's seat. 'Bloody kids.'

'Hadn't you better ring the police?' she asked drowsily.

He sighed. Part of him was wary of ringing after a night out. There were so many horror stories of even good Samaritans getting done – like that manager of a golf club who, rung by the police after the place had been broken into, drove over at three in the morning because they asked him to, and then got breathalysed and arrested.

But Charlie knew the right thing to do. After all, what if there were bodies in the car? And, of course, whoever owned this land would want to know that someone had dumped and burned a car, stolen in Wantage or Swindon most likely, in the middle of their lane.

He used Gemma's mobile phone to dial 999, gave his name and said what he had seen. When they asked what make of car it was, he told them to hang on a minute, went and looked, then said he thought it was a Golf – a black Golf, though that might just be the effect of the fire. T-reg, he added, since the plates had not yet been burned away.

And fortunately, after taking his name and address, the dispatcher said he could go home himself, which he did, driving extra carefully. Charlie and Gemma were almost asleep by the time the patrol car made its way to Simter's Pond. Unusually for what seemed just another joyriding wreck, a fire engine was sent from Wantage, after an alert duty officer learned that it was a T-reg Golf that had been dumped.

42

Though Liam O'Phelan had been scornful of his ex-pupil, Liz had never thought Michael Binding was a fool. It was his manner she objected to, not his brain. 'Patronising' and 'unfriendly' were the words which usually came to mind, though this morning as Binding sat angrily across the conference table, she thought 'hostile' was more apt. She was grateful for Peggy Kinsolving's presence, though she couldn't blame her assistant for keeping her head down and concentrating on her notes.

Binding was a tall man, dressed today in a check flannel shirt, dark grey flannel trousers, and clunky brown brogues. He sat uncomfortably on the front edge of his steel-framed chair. Liz had begun with what was by now her standard explanation of what she was doing and why she needed to see him. But Binding wasn't buying any of it. 'News to me,' he'd said. 'When did these new guidelines come down? And why weren't we told?'

Liz tried to seem nonchalant. 'You'd have to ask B Branch for the details.'

'Ah, I see,' said Binding, scratching his wrist with the scrubby, bitten fingernails of his other hand, 'you're only following orders.'

She decided patience with his rudeness was only going to encourage it. 'That's right,' she said snappily, 'like we all do.' Binding's pale blue eyes widened – Liz could tell he didn't like the challenge. She continued, 'And one of those orders was that if anyone was obstructive I should report the fact right away.' She noticed that Peggy was sinking even further down into her chair. 'It's up to you,' Liz declared. She gazed vacantly at the wall behind Binding to indicate how tiresome he was being. 'We can take this higher, or you can answer my questions. Either way we're going to end up back here doing the same thing. So which is it going to be?'

Binding propped his hand under his chin and stared defiantly at Liz while he considered this. Sighing audibly for dramatic effect, he said at last, 'Very well. What do you want to ask me?'

'I want to talk to you about Liam O'Phelan.'

'The late Liam O'Phelan? Why on earth do you want to talk about him?'

'He wrote a reference for you when you initially applied to the Service.'

Binding seemed surprised by this. 'What did it say?'

'I have to say he was not very flattering. Thankfully for you, your other referees were. I went to see him last week, just before he was murdered.'

Binding frowned, his eyes narrowing. 'What did he say about me when you saw him?'

'He said you didn't see eye to eye about your thesis.'

Binding laughed out loud. 'If only.' He shook his head dismissively. 'It wasn't that at all. But what is your point, Liz? I fell out with my supervisor fifteen years ago, so I decided to strangle him?' His tone was scathing now. He made a little show of raising both hands to inspect their murderous capabilities. 'Am I a suspect?' he asked.

'I shouldn't have thought so, though obviously it's a police matter over there. So far their view seems to be that O'Phelan probably picked up somebody who turned nasty.'

'Picked up? As in rough trade?' Binding looked horrified.

'Yes. He was single. The thinking is he was gay.' She added casually, 'Wasn't he?'

'Far from it.' Binding was emphatic.

What? thought Liz. If Binding was saying that O'Phelan had been heterosexual, she'd yet to see any evidence of it. 'So he had lots of girlfriends?'

'I didn't say that,' Binding retorted. 'Listen to what I'm saying.'

Liz gritted her teeth, then said calmly. 'I *am* listening. But I'm not sure I get your drift.'

Binding sighed again, and Liz resolved that he would not make her angry. God, how I pity his wife, she thought. I wonder if she lets him get away with it. Probably not, which is why he's like this at work.

Then Binding said, with exaggerated patience, 'O'Phelan wasn't homosexual.'

'How do you know that?' Liz said challengingly.

'Because for a time I knew him rather well.' And suddenly, as if tired of sparring with her, Binding sat back in his chair and began to talk.

There had been a party that spring, one Saturday afternoon in Trinity term, in the grounds of St Antony's College in North Oxford. He'd been invited by his supervisor O'Phelan, who was a Fellow there, though Binding's own college was Oriel.

Binding had spent the earlier part of the afternoon on the river – the Eights Week races were only a month off, and he was already in serious training. He'd hesitated before going all the way to St Antony's, which was at the other end of town, for what promised to be a free glass of plonk and some cheese titbits. But he decided it would be prudent to go – his supervisor had made a point of inviting him.

O'Phelan was young, not much older than Binding himself. He was an Irishman who'd only been in Oxford for a couple of years. He had a Junior Research Fellowship, which normally would have kept him from supervising a postgraduate student, but he'd already got his DPhil, and besides he was considered brilliant. Which Binding wouldn't have disputed – for the first two terms he thought Liam O'Phelan was the most stimulating teacher he'd ever had.

Not that he always agreed with him, especially not about Ireland, where even in the changed atmosphere of the early 1990s O'Phelan continued to see the British presence in the North as a colonial occupation. But there was humour to their exchanges, and O'Phelan didn't take offence, in fact he seemed positively to relish their jousting.

Binding was confident he'd earned O'Phelan's respect for his work, which was on his tutor's own particular passion: Charles Parnell. O'Phelan had been especially encouraging about the draft of a chapter of his thesis, and had begun urging him to do a DPhil, instead of the more modest MLitt he was embarked upon. For the first time, Binding thought he might have a chance of an academic career.

'You have to realise,' he said to Liz, 'I didn't come from that sort of background. Neither of my parents went to university. Becoming a don was a dream I'd never seriously thought possible.' Liz understood. She'd reread his file that morning. He'd had to win scholarships every step of the way until reaching the pinnacle of Oxford, where a don had actually said that the unthinkable might be within his grasp.

Anyway, continued Binding, that afternoon he'd hurried up the Banbury Road, freshly changed from his sweaty crew clothes, wearing his rowing blazer, little realising that the next hour was going to change his life completely.

The party was quite a large affair – all the postgrads and all the Fellows had been invited – and because it was warm for late April, it was held in the College grounds, on the lawn down from the main building. Nothing fancy – no marquee – just a few trestle tables holding bottles of wine, cans of beer and plastic cups. He didn't know many people, but he spotted O'Phelan in the crowd and, taking a cup of wine, started working his way over to him to say hello.

Then he'd noticed a girl he'd never seen before. She was tall, with blonde hair and a strikingly pixie-pretty face. She wore a short pink skirt that was just within the bounds of decorum, and looked very sure of herself – and of her appeal. Running into a postgrad he knew named Fergusson, Binding asked him about the girl, and learned that she was visiting O'Phelan from Dublin. 'Rather lively,' Fergusson added, and watching her Binding saw at once what he meant. For the girl was talking to another student Binding knew, a handsome sporty guy, and she was flirting with him, pretty obviously – stroking his arm, making the kind of eye and body contact that looked destined to head past mere flirtation and into the realm of serious intent.

It was then he noticed O'Phelan's reaction. He was standing slightly further up the slope of lawn, stuck with the Warden and his chatty wife. But every few seconds O'Phelan's gaze moved round to the girl, as if a magnet drew him there. He looked half possessed, watching her seductive performance with the postgraduate student. Fergusson also noticed

O'Phelan's reaction, for he noted dryly, 'Liam doesn't look too happy.'

There was only one conclusion: O'Phelan was besotted with this girl. And embarrassed by his tutor's obvious jealousy, Binding decided to try and do him a favour.

'All right,' he admitted to Liz, 'I suppose I was sucking up. But I was young then, and keen to get on.'

So he had gone up to the girl and introduced himself, ignoring the obvious irritation of the sporty student at this interruption. Possibly because she was a couple of sheets to the wind, the girl seemed equally happy to turn her attentions onto Binding, and within seconds she was flirting with him. She had lively green eyes and a saucy smile, and if she had been anybody's guest but O'Phelan's, Binding would have reciprocated.

She made no bones about being Irish: she seemed to find the very Englishness of the party amusing, and she teased him about it.

'Do you remember the girl's name?' Liz interrupted.

Binding shook his head. 'You'd think I would, given what happened. But it must have gone straight out of my head immediately she told me.' He added plaintively, 'It was just a drinks party.'

And standing there with his own second glass of wine, as the girl became increasingly familiar – at one point she'd asked if his room was nearby – he was anxiously wondering how best to transfer her apparent interest in him onto O'Phelan when he made his mistake.

He began to tease her back, assuming that since she had been teasing him she would take it in good part. She might mouth the platitudes of the need for a united Ireland, he told the girl, but surely the last thing she and her countrymen wanted was to regain the burden of the six counties of Ulster. Wasn't it ironic, he continued, feeling the wine himself and warming to his theme, that so many IRA members, sworn enemies of the British state, actually lived off that state? They couldn't bite off their nose to spite their face, he added, because their nose was stuck, feeding in a British trough.

'Maybe it wasn't as pointed as that,' Binding said now, looking at Peggy Kinsolving as if noticing her for the first time, 'but it wasn't far off.'

And the effect had been of a match striking touchpaper.

Tight as she was, the girl had listened to him with a disbelief he noticed too late – for by the time he had, it had turned to fury. Her voice rising, she'd launched into a tirade, her tone no longer light, her great green eyes suddenly narrowed into mean little slits. Her target was the English: their elitism, their racism, even the way their youth were educated, typified by the awful man she was talking to. This meant him.

Binding was completely taken aback by her reaction to what was meant to be a joke, and he tried to calm her down. But she wasn't having any of it, and her abuse continued. He'd started to feel slightly panicky, afraid they were making a scene, and he'd looked wildly around for help, but no one came to his rescue – O'Phelan was still taken up with the Warden and his wife, and the sporty student had fled the minute the girl had turned on Binding.

And then something in Binding had snapped. He'd tried placating, he'd tried apologising, so finally he too lost his temper. Doubtless he said something abusive.

'Doubtless,' said Liz at this stage of his story, having witnessed minutes before something of Binding's choleric side. 'Do you recall what you said?'

Binding stared ruefully at the expanse of table between them. 'I said, "Why don't you go back to your peat bog?" I'm not proud of it,' he admitted. 'But I was provoked.'

Enraged, the girl suddenly lifted her glass and tossed it right at his face. Then she stormed out of the party, followed by a clearly agitated O'Phelan. Binding stood there, mortified, with red wine dripping down the front of his blazer.

The next day Binding had written to the don to apologise, but didn't receive an answer. Then some days later O'Phelan left a message at the Oriel lodge, cancelling their next supervision; ten days later, he cancelled again. With his deadline looming, Binding submitted his thesis chapter to O'Phelan for formal approval. An ominous silence ensued. It was broken by the tersest of notes:

> Dear Binding
> I am writing to inform you that I will be leaving Oxford to take up a position at Queen's University Belfast in Michelmas Term. I am afraid therefore that it will no longer be possible for me to supervise your thesis, though after reading your sample chapter I cannot in any case advise the Faculty to give you leave to continue.
> Yours sincerely
> L. K. O'Phelan

'I never saw or heard from him again,' said Binding with a shake of his head. 'Not that I wanted to. I was too busy at first trying to keep my place. I went to the Faculty and they weren't very sympathetic – O'Phelan had written to them saying I'd failed the first year chapter requirement. At the last minute I found someone in my own college willing to take me on, but he knew far less about my subject than I did.

'That effectively ended any chances I had of an academic career – you need powerful backers to get a university teaching job. So I took my MLitt and started looking for other kinds of work. When I applied here, naturally I didn't list O'Phelan as a referee. But I guess he got dug out of the woodwork. After what he must have said about me, I'm surprised I was accepted.'

'It wasn't *that* bad,' said Liz. Why had O'Phelan encouraged Binding's aspirations, then tried to destroy them? Or had he – what exactly had O'Phelan been up to?

'Anyway,' said Binding, looking relieved to be finishing his story, 'I was sorry to hear he'd been killed, but don't expect a lengthy mourning period from me. As for why he died, all I can say is he wasn't gay. Not in the least.' He shook his head in disbelief. 'To think I was actually trying to help him, by talking to that stupid girl.' He laughed with undisguised bitterness. 'No wonder they say no good deed goes unpunished.'

He'd finished, and he sat there with Liz and Peggy for several moments without anyone speaking, the faint scratching of Peggy's pencil the only sound in the room.

Liz had only one question. 'What was the name of the student this girl was chatting up before you interrupted?'

Binding looked at her with half a smile. Something of his arrogance had come back. 'This has to be the strangest vetting interview in history. You say you're checking up on me, yet all we've talked about is Liam O'Phelan. Honestly Liz, what are you after?' He raised a hand as if to ward off any reply. 'I know, I know. You'll ask the questions around here, thank you very much. The bloke's name was Clapton. I remember because of Eric Clapton – that song "Layla" was one of my favourites.'

'Was he the rugby player?'

'How on earth did you know that?' asked Binding, with unfeigned astonishment. But Liz wasn't listening any more to anything but her own furious thoughts. She was trying to reconcile three completely contradictory stories. If I can do that, she thought, I'll know who the mole is.

43

Judith Spratt was off work ill, so it was Rose Love who came to find Dave. Something had changed in her, he thought, which he couldn't pin down. She looked older, for one thing, in smart trousers and a crimson blouse. She'd tied her hair back, too. He decided he wasn't going to let her forget their dinner date, postponed since the discovery of the safe house in Wokingham.

'We've got a chassis number from the Wantage police,' she announced. 'I've already been on to the manufacturers in Germany and they've promised to get back to me today.'

'They'll tell you which dealer it got shipped to. But that was a long time ago.'

'I know. The rest will be up to DVLA.'

'How long?' he said anxiously.

'Have you got a piece of string?' she asked with a laugh, and he realised what had changed most. She was more confident. Gone was the shy girl of even a month before.

'What happened to our date?' he asked.

'Much too busy,' she said, but there was a playfulness behind the prim front.

'You are?'

She nodded sagely. 'And so are you.' But her smile was sly enough to give him hope.

44

She couldn't exactly say why, but she thought someone was there. In a doorway, or in the shadows, or behind a car – but there.

Peggy felt it first just after she left Thames House, as she walked along the river towards the Tube station. She stopped just short of the Tate, thinking she had dropped something from her bag, and would not have thought twice about the dark figure fifty yards or so behind her had it not stopped abruptly too. It was a man – she was somehow certain it was a man – though when she peered at him in the distance he had disappeared.

Don't get paranoid, Peggy told herself, but she wished she'd been on the counter-surveillance course. The little she knew made it seem virtually a black art – certainly not for amateurs. She'd got to know Dave Armstrong from lunch and the occasional coffee break, and he'd described a surveillance operation where over thirty people had been involved. And not one had been spotted.

She had no confidence in her own ability to spot a tail, but then she wasn't operational – her job was research and analysis. She'd been told when she joined MI6 that after a few years she might well be posted abroad. That had been part of the attraction for her. It was then she would go on the courses, get the operational training. In a small station abroad they said everyone had to get involved. Researchers, secretaries, even wives got drafted in to fill dead letter boxes, service safe houses, and sometimes meet agents. She looked forward to it, but it was several years away.

Meanwhile, working with Liz Carlyle in MI5, Peggy had discovered an urgency which drew everyone in. She liked the involvement, the recognition that everyone in their different ways had a part to play in what was going on. But she felt ill-prepared for sharp-end operational work.

When the sense of being followed wouldn't go away, she decided to put it to the test. Turning right onto Vauxhall Bridge Road she stopped under the generous portico of one of the stucco Regency mansions, long ago divided into offices, and waited there. Shielded by a column, she watched for several minutes, but no one came around the corner.

Stop fantasising, she told herself, relieved she had been wrong, embarrassed that she had thought she had been right. She entered Pimlico Underground Station, virtually deserted in the late morning, and took the escalator down without a single person behind her or on the opposite side, coming up. As she waited for the Victoria Line train to arrive, there were just two other people on the platform – a young black woman sitting on a bench in one of the recesses, and further down, an elderly man leaning on a walking stick.

At Victoria she switched to the Circle Line, heading for her first appointment. This shouldn't take long, thought Peggy; it was her second meeting, the meeting in Kilburn, from which she was anticipating some excitement.

She'd dug further into Patrick Dobson's extended Irish family, and discovered a lateral branch that had moved to London thirty years before. She wanted to find out if these cousins knew Dobson – he had vociferously denied any contact with the Irish side of his family. Peggy was posing as a sociology student at UCL, writing a dissertation on the Irish in London, a topic she found interesting enough that it shouldn't be difficult to play the part. As the train stopped at South Kensington, she opened her briefcase and took out the genealogical chart she'd compiled, but then thought she had better check her notes for her first meeting, even if it wasn't going to last long.

It should be routine. She was going at Liz's prompting: Tom Dartmouth's wife had been seen in London not long before, which was unusual, since the woman was supposed to live in Haifa. 'She was probably just visiting,' Liz said, 'but please check it out all the same.'

Peggy didn't have a lot to go on from the file:

> Margarita Levy, b. 1967 Tel Aviv, d. of Major-General Ariel Levy and Jessica Finegold. Educated at the Tel Aviv Conservatory and the Juilliard School (NY). Member of the Tel Aviv Symphony Orchestra 1991-5. M. Thomas Dartmouth 1995, div. 2001. No children.

And Margarita had not been easy to locate. At the Haifa address, now inhabited by rehoused settlers from Gaza whose English on the phone she had found difficult to understand, no one knew or cared who had lived there before them. The Tel Aviv Symphony Orchestra initially denied that Margarita had ever played for them, then after conceding she had, could unearth no forwarding address.

Eventually, a painstaking trawl through online music sites proved more productive. A casual reference in a music student's blog, a check in the telephone directory, and Peggy found

Margarita Levy at last, giving private violin lessons. Though not in Haifa, or anywhere in Israel for that matter.

The flat was in a Victorian mansion block off Kensington High Street. Opening the door, Margarita Levy smiled shyly at Peggy and shook hands. She was a tall, striking woman, with lush black hair neatly swept back. 'Come in,' she said and pointed to the sitting room. 'Make yourself comfortable. I will be right with you.' And she disappeared into another room from which came the sound of voices.

Peggy went in and stood in the middle of the room, close to a fragile-looking Empire chair covered in worn silk. The room was comfortably furnished, with curtains tied back from the casement windows, a well-worn sofa with pale yellow covers and cushions, and chairs covered in faded chintz. Two antique side tables held an array of bibelots and marble eggs, and the walls were hung with small oil paintings, mainly landscapes, and a large portrait over the mantlepiece that looked to be of Margarita as a teenage girl. All in all, Peggy decided, it was the sitting room of a genteel, cultured woman, from a comfortable background, but now with more taste than cash.

The door to the other room opened and a sulky pigtailed girl of about twelve came out, carrying a violin case. She ignored Peggy, and headed straight for the front door, which she slammed behind her. Margarita came into the sitting room, turned to Peggy and raised her eyebrows. 'I don't know why some of them bother. If you hate the violin that much, it is not possible to play it well.' She had the faintest trace of accent. 'I blame the parents. If you force a child, what does it do? It rebels.'

She was dressed simply but elegantly in a sleeveless black dress and a single-strand necklace of unadorned gold. Peggy noticed that she did not wear a wedding ring. 'I'm going to make some tea,' she announced. 'Would you like some?'

'I won't, thank you very much' said Peggy. 'I don't need to keep you very long.'

When Margarita moved into the kitchen next door, Peggy followed her as far as the doorway. The kitchen was tiny; opposite it Peggy could see a small bedroom, next to the room used for giving lessons. That seemed to be the extent of the flat, which went some way to explain to Peggy how a violin teacher could live in Kensington.

While the kettle boiled, Margarita took out a china cup and saucer. 'How long have you been back in England?' asked Peggy.

'Back?' asked Margarita. She was filling the milk jug. 'What do you mean?'

Peggy racked her brains. Had she made a mistake? She'd read Tom's file for the umpteenth time before setting off that morning. No, she was certain of what it said. 'We had you down as living in Israel. Not London. That's why I'm here.'

'I haven't lived in Israel for over ten years. Not since I married Tom. Are you sure you wouldn't like a cup of tea?'

'Actually,' said Peggy, curious about the discrepancy between Tom's file and the facts, 'I'd love one.'

Margarita put tea things on a tray and carried it into the sitting room, where Peggy sat down carefully on the Empire chair. Margarita poured the tea, then sipping from her own cup, she sat back on the sofa and looked at Peggy. She hesitated for a moment. 'Tell me something, is Tom all right?'

'He's fine, I believe.'

She looked only slightly reassured. 'I was worried when you asked to see me about him. Pakistan is so dangerous these days. I thought perhaps something had happened to him.'

Peggy realised the woman didn't know Tom was back in London. It must have been an acrimonious divorce, she thought. 'When did you last speak to Tom?'

Margarita grimaced and shook her head. 'Not since he went to Pakistan.' But then she added, 'I did *see* him, at a concert two or three years ago. I assumed he was back on leave. But we didn't speak. He had someone with him,' she smile ruefully and shrugged her shoulders. 'So I just waved at him during the interval.'

It wasn't acrimonious, Peggy now realised. She had come here expecting anything – anger, bitterness, jubilation, or even complete indifference. But not this sense of sad bewilderment.

'You were married in Israel, were you?' asked Peggy.

'No. We married over here and I've lived here ever since.'

'That must have been quite a change for you. To leave all your family and friends like that.'

'Of course,' Margarita said simply.

'Though at least there was Tom's family over here.'

Margarita shook her head. 'Not really. His mother died before I even knew Tom. And I only met his stepfather once, when we first came to England. He was perfectly friendly, but Tom didn't want anything to do with him.'

'Was Tom close to his natural father?'

Margarita shook her head again. 'He had died too, when Tom was only a boy. His stepfather raised him, and Tom took his name. He resented that, I know – it was at his mother's insistence. And it's true to say Tom idolised his own father, though he never knew him as an adult at all.'

'That's often the case, isn't it?' asked Peggy, trying to sound sympathetic. 'If a parent dies before a child grows up, they don't have any objectivity about them.'

'You mean, they don't get to see the feet of clay?' Margarita said, looking amused by the English expression.

'Yes. Though I'm sure Tom's real father was entirely admirable.'

'I'm not,' said Margarita dryly, with a hint of acerbity.

'Oh?' said Peggy neutrally, willing the woman to go on.

Margarita stirred her tea with her spoon aimlessly. 'You must know he killed himself.'

'Well, yes,' lied Peggy, trying to stifle her astonishment. 'How old was Tom then?'

'He couldn't have been more than seven or eight. Poor thing,' she added. 'He didn't find out until he was almost grown. That much I do know,' she said, as if established facts were thin on the ground when it came to her ex-husband.

'Why did he kill himself? Was he depressed?' ventured Peggy.

'He had made a mess of things, so possibly.'

'Was this in London?' Peggy asked, thinking she should be able to track down the details quickly enough. The real father's name would be on Tom's original application form.

'London? No. He'd gone to New York. He was a journalist there. I can't remember exactly; I believe he got into trouble writing about Ireland. Tom didn't talk about it. He only mentioned it once, when we first started seeing each other.'

At the memory, her melancholy seemed to return. She looked at Peggy. 'It is odd, isn't it, ' she said, 'how sometimes people talk less, not more as the years pass.' It struck Peggy that she wasn't expecting an answer. Margarita reached for the teapot. 'Another cup?'

This time, when Peggy said no she didn't change her mind.

As she left the flat, she rang the Dobson relations in Kilburn and postponed her visit. She needed to see Liz Carlyle right away. It was one thing to find Tom had misled the Service about his wife's whereabouts – you could argue Judith Spratt had done the same thing. It was another to find for the first time a possible link between Tom and Liam O'Phelan.

It's the American connection, thought Peggy, thinking of the talk the don had given that night at the Old Fire Station. 'From Boston to Belfast: Britain's Dirty War in Northern Ireland and Abroad'.

She left the mansion block and walked quickly up to Kensington High Street. Turning into the Underground, she was surprised to find the eastbound platform unusually crowded for this hour. A muffled voice over the loudspeaker announced that due to an incident at Paddington Station, Circle Line trains were subject to delay. She saw from the overhead signal board that the next one wasn't expected for another twelve minutes. She waited impatiently as more and more lunchtime passengers gradually filled the platform.

At last, the board signalled one minute before the train arrived, and Peggy moved towards the front of the platform, determined to get onto it, since a time for the next train had not even been posted. Gradually working her way through the crowd, she ended up close to the yellow line. Too close, she decided, and tried to take a step back, but the crowd was simply too dense for her to move.

Thank God the train's coming, she thought, as the board read 'NEXT TRAIN APPROACHING'. She tried again to step back as she saw its yellow headlight in the tunnel, but there seemed to be no free space behind her. She was blocked from moving sideways by a builder holding a toolbox to her left; on her right, a stout woman stood clutching two M&S shopping bags to her chest.

Suddenly as the train broke out of the tunnel Peggy felt a pressure in the small of her back, nudging at first, then more insistent, and pushing. Her feet started to inch towards the track and she instinctively tried to dig her heels in. 'Stop,' she shouted, but the noise of the onrushing carriages drowned the sound. She felt both her feet move again, well over the yellow line, moving irresistibly towards the platform's edge. Panic seized her, and suddenly she screamed, involuntarily, the noise like the drawn-out pitch of a locomotive's whistle. Then all went dark.

The man seemed to be wearing a uniform, and on her face she felt something wet and cold. The blur in her eyes suddenly resolved itself and she saw with snapshot clarity a station attendant in front of her, extending an arm as he dabbed at her cheeks with a wet tissue. She was sitting on a plastic chair in what looked to be a large broom cupboard under the stairs of the Underground station.

'What happened?' she asked, though she had a fair idea she was still alive. If there were an afterlife, she decided, it would not look like this.

'You fainted, Miss.' The man stopped dabbing with his tissue. 'It was a bit of a crush.' He got up and looked down solicitously at Peggy. 'Take some deep breaths.'

'I don't remember,' said Peggy, feeling puzzled. Then she recalled the insistent pressure on her back, the propelling firmness that was carrying her steadily towards . . .

The stationmaster was saying, 'Lucky for you the woman next to you saw you starting to drop. She said she thought you were going to topple over right in front of the train. But she managed to grab you in time – there was a builder bloke who helped her haul you back. The only casualty was a pair of trousers she'd just bought for her husband.'

'I am sorry,' said Peggy, trying to pull herself together. 'Did she leave her name?'

'No, once I arrived on the scene she took the next train. Said she was late as it was.'

And Peggy suddenly remembered her own sense of urgency. She stood up, a little wobbly, but the dizziness soon receded. The man looked at her anxiously, 'Are you sure you're fit to travel?'

'I'm all right now,' she declared, then smiled at the attendant. 'I'm very grateful for your help.'

He stepped out from the room onto the platform and looked at the board. 'You're in luck. The next train's due in two minutes.'

'Thank you,' said Peggy, but she was already moving towards the escalator. She'd decided that in the circumstances, she deserved a taxi, but she would certainly not claim it on her expenses. No one except Liz was going to be told how she'd given in to panic.

45

Westminster Green, a small patch of grass opposite the Houses of Parliament, is a favourite spot for TV journalists to interview MPs. In rainy weather its microphone and camera positions are protected by umbrellas. Today, in the June sunshine, a small crowd was gathered to watch the BBC's political correspondent interviewing a member of the Cabinet.

From where she was sitting on a bench in Victoria Tower Gardens, across the road, Liz could not hear the interview, although she could recognise the two participants, and she guessed that the subject was the counter-terrorist legislation the Government was attempting to get through Parliament, in the face of much opposition. Like most of her colleagues Liz had her own views on the Government's proposals, but for the most part she chose to keep her own counsel, reflecting that they would make very little change to the nature of her work.

Liz was waiting for Charles Wetherby. When she had rung to ask to see him urgently, to her surprise he had insisted that they meet outside Thames House. She had made the ten-minute walk to the little park, and was now enjoying the warm afternoon, trying to catch some sun on her face. If she were right about her conclusion, she wouldn't be seeing much sun or the outside world any time soon.

When Wetherby joined her on the bench a quarter of an hour later, Liz plunged straight in with a description of Peggy's interview with Tom Dartmouth's ex-wife. Then she summarised her recent interviews, setting out their contradictions which she now thought she had resolved. Through a mix of intuition, logic and Peggy's finds that morning, Liz had come to a conclusion. 'Let's go through it all again slowly,' said Wetherby and Liz knew that he was not doubting her analysis, but was trying to assure himself that her conclusion had not emerged from some misperception or misreading which might mislead him too.

'You believe O'Phelan was the recruiter for the mole, at the instigation of Sean Keaney. Just explain again why?'

Liz thought carefully for a moment. 'Because,' she said, trying to speak as clearly as she was thinking, 'O'Phelan was at Oxford; he held strong nationalist views; and he had a connection to Sean Keaney through this woman Kirsty, who by her own admission befriended O'Phelan at Keaney's instigation.'

A man in pinstripes passed by the bench and nodded at Wetherby. Despite the day's bright sun, he was carrying an umbrella, tightly furled. Wetherby nodded back at him, then smiled at Liz. 'The Treasury. One of Her Majesty's more old-fashioned servants. All that's missing is the bowler hat.' He returned to their subject. 'Anyway, let's agree for the moment that O'Phelan was the recruiter. How do we know it wasn't Michael Binding he recruited?'

'We don't for sure, but it seems improbable. There can't be any question that the two of them fell out: O'Phelan's original reference could not have been intended to help Binding get into the Service.'

Wetherby nodded in agreement. 'I saw the file. After a letter like that, Binding was fortunate to be accepted.'

Across the street, the Minister was holding his hand up,

calling for another take. Liz continued: 'It's true that their accounts of why they fell out differ: O'Phelan said it was because Binding's work was second-rate; Binding says it was because he had a row at a party with Kirsty.'

'And who do you believe?'

'Binding,' Liz said without hesitation.

Wetherby gave an ironic smile. He knew Liz's opinion of her patronising colleague. 'Why's that?' he said, not challengingly, but to try and set out the sequence of argument. Liz thought Wetherby would have made an excellent teacher – he was relentlessly searching for clarity.

'I don't believe Binding was a bad student. He had a First from Manchester, and he'd worked too hard to get to Oxford simply to down tools when he was there. In any case Binding's own story may make O'Phelan look vengeful and malicious, but it doesn't cast Binding himself in a very good light.'

'The "go back to your peat bog" remark?' When Liz nodded, Wetherby asked, 'If you ruled out Binding as our mole, why did that lead you to Tom?'

'It didn't, until he added his own ingredient, which was an account of O'Phelan that didn't square with what anybody else had told me. Tom claimed O'Phelan was a sexual predator with his male students, yet none of the evidence from Binding and Maguire, or the police investigation into his murder, backs that up. In fact, the student Tom claimed O'Phelan jumped on was the same rugby heavy who, according to Binding, tried to chat up Kirsty at the party in St Antony's.'

'But if Tom was the mole, why would he invent this story about O'Phelan?'

For the first time Liz felt a slight chill, as their discussion moved from motivation to murder. 'To divert attention from the real reason O'Phelan was killed. Which was to shut him up.' Liz didn't need to wait for the next question. 'And yes, that means in my view Tom murdered O'Phelan. Just as I think Tom is the mole. There's another thing too,' added Liz, almost as an afterthought. 'Tom told me his father was killed in a road accident, but Margarita told Peggy that he committed suicide in New York.'

Wetherby was staring across the street, apparently distracted by the interminable television interview. The lack of attention was unlike him. 'Charles?' she said questioningly.

He didn't answer. Liz said, 'The problem is that we can't prove any of this. If Tom was recruited by O'Phelan for the IRA, he was never activated. He will never admit it. So unless we can tie him to O'Phelan's murder, I don't see what we could charge him with.'

Charles still didn't seem to be listening. What's bothering him? thought Liz. Is Joanne ill again? Or one of the boys? She said, with a trace of impatience, 'We'll have to do *something*, Charles, won't we? I mean I know it may not seem urgent, but—'

Wetherby interrupted her. He said softly, 'It is urgent, Liz. That's what's bothering me.' He sighed and clasped his hands together, leaning forward to sit on the edge of the bench. 'I didn't tell you before, because it wasn't relevant to your investigation. And I didn't want to jump to conclusions that might have affected your own. But after Dave Armstrong missed the terrorists in Wokingham, he came to see me. What is not widely known – because we've kept it secret – is that the terrorists vacated the house only after Dave had requested Special Branch go in. We know exactly when they left because one of the neighbours spotted them, leaving in a hurry.

'Dave decided there must have been a leak: the terrorists' departure was too hasty and too well timed – twelve hours later and we'd have got them. The leak could have come from anywhere – the local police, the estate agent who let the house. Except Dave thinks the same thing happened at Marzipan's bookshop – when the three men didn't show up. Someone tipped them off as well.'

Wetherby sighed, as if he knew he had to finish the argument but dearly didn't want to. 'The only people who knew about both operations were in Thames House. If there was a leak, and I believe there were two of them, we have to think they came from within the Service.'

'You mean there's *another* mole?' asked Liz. No wonder Charles looks preoccupied, she thought. Compared to this immediate threat, an IRA informer who never went to work must seem small beer.

She was about to say this when Wetherby asked, 'Did you ever hear the story about the man who's scared to fly in case there's a bomb on the plane?'

'No,' said Liz, thinking this was unlike Wetherby. He had a fine, dry sense of humour, but didn't go in for jokes, especially in situations as tense as this.

He fingered the knot in his silk tie and sat back on the bench. 'He's sufficiently scared that he won't fly anywhere, so one of his friends tries to help. He tells the man that the odds of there being a bomb on his flight are at least several million to one. But the man isn't satisfied – even these odds seem too short for comfort. So then his friend points out that the odds of there being *two* bombs on the same flight are more than a *billion* to one. Therefore the obvious solution is for the man to take the flight, and bring along a bomb.'

Liz laughed, but Wetherby's expression grew serious. 'I hope you see my point,' he said. 'The odds of there being two moles in MI5 are about the same as the odds of having two bombs on the same flight.'

Liz felt a sudden sense of alarm. 'You mean, that if Tom's the IRA mole, he also tipped off the terrorists?'

'Yes. That's exactly what I mean. I just don't know why. There's something else I should tell you,' said Charles. 'I think you were at the last FOXHUNT operational meeting. You may remember that Dave said that the Dawnton woman, the one who lives next door to the house where the suspects were living, had told him that a white man had called at the house next door. Dave said that she'd seen this man clearly and thought she could identify him. That wasn't true. Dave made it up to see if it flushed anyone out. It did. After the meeting, Tom went to see Dave to find out more. He was clearly worried.'

'I wondered what Dave was doing when he said that.'

Liz's mobile rang, and she looked at the number on the screen. 'Excuse me, Charles, it's Peggy. I'd better take it.' She pressed the green button and said a quiet 'Hi.'

'I can't find him, Liz,' Peggy said at once. 'He's not in the building and he hasn't been seen since this morning. No one knows where he is. Dave Armstrong tried his mobile, but there was no reply.'

'Hold on a minute,' said Liz, and turned to Wetherby. 'I sent Peggy to look for Tom, but he's nowhere to be found. And no one's heard from him.' Which was very odd: it was a cardinal rule, especially for such a senior officer, to be contactable in case of emergency. An hour, two hours out of touch might be excusable – a mobile phone failure, a family emergency. But not eight hours during the middle of a crucial investigation. He's gone AWOL, thought Liz.

'I see,' Wetherby said grimly. 'Please ask Peggy to find Dave

Armstrong and have him meet me in my office in fifteen minutes.'

When she'd rung off, Wetherby stood up. 'I had better get back,' he declared, adding easily, 'Why don't you walk with me? If Tom's done a runner, it doesn't matter if we're seen talking together.'

Liz said, 'When Peggy went to see Tom's ex-wife this morning she was convinced she was being followed. Then afterwards, she thought someone tried to push her off the platform at High Street Ken – just as the train was approaching. It sounds unlikely to me, and Peggy admits she may be wrong about this, but I thought it best to be on the safe side. I sent her to find Tom on a pretext, so he'd realise she'd already briefed me on her meeting. That way, if he had any idea of silencing her, he'd know it was too late.'

'You were right to try and protect her,' Wetherby said, 'though I'm sure you're right to think Peggy was imagining it – she's very young and inexperienced. Still, she shouldn't go home tonight for her own peace of mind. Could you have her to stay with you? I'm going to have Dave start looking for Tom, though I don't want word to spread. If by any chance Tom does come back with an explanation for his absence, I don't want to alarm him until we have all our cards in order. But my hunch is, he's gone.'

She nodded in agreement. Wetherby gave a weary shake to his head, and looked out over towards the politician who was still being interviewed. 'What we have to work out is what Tom's next move will be. I have a terrible feeling we haven't much time. We know the nature of his IRA link, but not what his connection is with the terrorists.'

'Could it have started in Pakistan?'

'Possibly,' said Wetherby pensively. 'I think you should go and talk to Geoffrey Fane. I'll ring him as soon as we get back.'

'I'd better talk to the ex-wife as well. She's the only family connection to Tom we have.'

They crossed the street and passed the small patch of green where, his interview finished at last, the Minister was heading with several minders towards a large parked Jaguar. The television cameraman, still standing on the grass, shook his head at the reporter. 'Six takes,' he shouted, in a loud exasperated voice. 'For about twelve seconds of film. And people say politicians are too *glib*.'

46

Impressive, thought Liz, as she entered Geoffrey Fane's office. It was a large eyrie, beautifully appointed, high up in the postmodern colossus on the South Bank that is the headquarters of MI6. Fane was one floor above the suite of C, the head of the Service.

Fane was on the phone but when he saw Liz in his outer office, he waved her in. She sat down in a padded leather chair in front of his old-fashioned partners desk. He was speaking to South America. Liz's eye was caught by the framed sets of mounted trout flies on the wall and she got up to look at them. She knew Fane was a keen fly-fisherman and she remembered Charles saying that he had been invited to join him for a day's fishing on one of the best beats – the Kennet or the Test.

All the time she was mentally reviewing what she was going to tell him. He'll be surprised, she thought, though I bet he won't show it.

'Forgive me,' said Fane, putting down the phone and standing up to shake hands. 'Our man in Bogota is a little verbose.'

He wore a blue pinstripe suit, which accentuated his height, and an Honourable Artillery Company tie. With his high cheekbones and aquiline nose, he cut a dashing figure, though, as Liz already knew, he was hard to warm to. His manner of talking was articulate and often amusing, and like Wetherby he spoke with an air of appreciative irony, but unlike Wetherby, his irony could suddenly turn to biting wit. For Geoffrey Fane, professional matters were personal. He needed to win and Liz knew that he could suddenly, capriciously turn on people. In their few encounters, Liz had never found him entirely trustworthy.

They sat down again, and Fane looked out of the window. 'Rain's coming, I'm afraid.'

In the distance Liz could see the office blocks in Victoria Street and a tight blanket of scudding cloud fast approaching. The windows at Vauxhall Cross were triple-glazed against mortar attack, and this cast a grey-green filtered tint on the world outside, making it sombre on even the sunniest day. She went straight to the point. 'I wanted to see you about this Irish business.'

'Ah yes, the peculiar legacy of Sean Keaney. Tell me, how is Peggy Kinsolving working out?'

This is not what Liz wanted to talk about. 'She's very good,' she said swiftly. 'She's helped make an important discovery.'

Fane raised an eyebrow. 'Discovery?'

'Yes. We've come to the conclusion that there actually is a mole.'

'Really? In place. Planted by the IRA?' Fane sounded incredulous.

'Originally,' said Liz. 'But we think he's moved on.'

Fane shot both cuffs rather carefully, and Liz suppressed a smile. For all his patrician air, he had a dandy's showman instincts. Wetherby had precisely the same habit, but with him you felt it was done out of a desire for sartorial order; with Fane, she decided, it was designed to show off his cufflinks.

'Left the Service, you mean? Do you know who he was?'

'No. I don't mean left the Service. He's still here. We think it's Tom Dartmouth.'

'*Tom Dartmouth*?' Fane could not disguise his surprise. 'Does Charles share this view?' he said with sharp scepticism.

'He does,' she said coolly. She was not going to be bullied by Fane.

'Are you sure about this?'

'The evidence so far is entirely circumstantial.'

Fane sat up straight. He looked ready to challenge her, so she continued quickly. 'It's likely to remain that way for the moment, too, because Tom has vanished.'

'Vanished?' said Fane, his aggression suddenly deflated.

'Obviously we wanted to let you know right away,' said Liz. 'Particularly because of Tom's secondment to Six. But I'm also here to find out more about his time in Pakistan. We're concerned that he may have moved on from the IRA and that he is helping a small Islamic terrorist group we're trying to find. It's the group you know about from the CTC. The bookshop group. Operation FOXHUNT. We think it's possible he first made contact with them in Pakistan.'

'Yes, of course I know about FOXHUNT, but what has that to do with the IRA?' said Fane. 'I must say, Elizabeth, this seems completely confusing.' By the time Liz had explained her thesis, Fane's expression had turned from scepticism to gravity. 'Well, as it happens, our station chief in Islamabad is with us this week. He's been over at the Foreign Office but he may well be back by now.'

A few telephone calls later, and Miles Pennington, MI6's head of station in Pakistan, walked into Fane's office. Pushing fifty, Miles Pennington had receding hair and a bluff manner. According to Fane he was an 'old Asia hand' – six years in Pakistan, a stint in Afghanistan, another in Bangladesh – and with his deep tan and lightweight khaki suit he certainly looked the part. Extending a firm, dry hand for Liz to shake, he sat down and listened while Fane explained they needed his help. Liz broke in to ask for his signature on the indoctrination list for the mole hunt. 'I already have your signature, Geoffrey,' she said. The indoctrination list, activated for the most secret operations, not only meant that the operation could only be discussed with others on the list, but also produced a complete index of those in the know, in case there should be a leak. As he looked at the sheet which Liz handed him and saw how very few names there were on it – Liz, Peggy, Charles Wetherby and Geoffrey Fane, C of MI6 and DG of MI5, as well as the Home Secretary and a few other names he didn't recognise, Pennington blanched. That sort of list indicated a very serious operation indeed.

'We want to talk about Tom Dartmouth,' said Fane, all languor gone. 'Elizabeth will explain what we're looking for.'

Liz and Fane had agreed that Miles Pennington did not need to know about the IRA angle and so she focused only on the immediate problem. 'We are urgently trying to locate three suspected terrorists here in the UK. They are all British, but of Asian origin – there's one we have identified and he's from a Pakistani family in the Midlands. The other two are unknown to us.'

She paused, aware that Pennington must be wondering what this had to do with Tom Dartmouth, whom he knew only as a junior colleague, seconded from MI5. Taking a deep breath Liz said, 'We have reason to believe that Tom Dartmouth has been in contact with the terrorists, and in fact may be actively helping them.' She ignored Pennington's stunned expression. 'Unfortunately, he's gone to ground. So we're trying to understand what's behind all this.'

Pennington managed a hesitant nod, but was clearly still

trying to take it in. Liz said, 'Could you give me your view of Tom? One of the problems we're having is that he's only been back here in London for four months and before that he'd been with you for four years. What did you make of him?'

Pennington took some time to respond. At last, choosing his words with care, he said, 'Intelligent, fluent Arabic speaker, worked very hard – without getting too intense about it.'

'Intense' – how typical, thought Liz. The cult of the English amateur – legacy of a Victorian public-school ethos – still alive and kicking in the offshore stations of MI6. Work hard but pretend you're not, make the difficult seem easy – all from an era when gentlemen ran the vestiges of an empire.

'What about life outside work?' she asked. 'Did you see much of him then?'

'Yes. We are all pretty close, given the circumstances in Pakistan. Though of course he was in Lahore and I'm mainly in Islamabad. He seemed to fit in pretty well. That doesn't always happen when we get someone from Five.' Pennington suddenly looked embarrassed, remembering where Liz worked. 'He liked a drink, but not to excess. There was the odd girl around, but again nothing improper – he's divorced isn't he?'

'Was there anything strange about him, anything remarkable?'

'Not really,' said Pennington, who spoke with a hint of a drawl. 'He wasn't the most outgoing of colleagues.' Liz could see he was struggling to remember the attributes of a man he had never envisaged occupying centre stage. 'He wasn't mysterious or anything like that. Even with the benefit of hindsight,' he added, glancing at the indoctrination form, 'I'd still say that.'

He gave a low sigh, half regretful, half resigned. 'I suppose the right word to describe him would be "detached". Not so much as to make one notice; as I say, he fitted in well enough. But thinking about it, I'd say he was always keeping something in reserve.'

'Can you tell me about his work?'

Pennington looked relieved to move to less psychological ground. 'Bit of a mixed bag really, but quite straightforward. He kept a sharp eye on the madrasas, to see which were kosher, so to speak, and which were up to no good. In particular, he watched which ones were trying to recruit any of the young British Asians coming out to study. Contrary to what the papers say, many of these students coming from the UK only get radicalised once they're in Pakistan. They go out with perfectly respectable religious motives, then fall under the sway of extremist imams.'

Pennington scratched his cheek lazily, comfortable again. 'He was liaising with Pakistan Intelligence much of the time.'

'How did Tom report to you?'

'Directly,' said Pennington confidently. 'We spoke almost every day, unless one of us was travelling, and once a fortnight he'd come in for our station meeting. He'd always put something in writing – a summary of what he'd been doing.'

'Did you see his reports to MI5?'

Pennington looked startled. 'Not all of them personally, but they would have been duplicates of what he gave us, plus anything else he thought would be of specific interest to your lot. The ones I saw were chiefly about the people he was watching.' He stopped and glanced at Fane, who was studiedly looking out the window throughout this recital. 'And of course his own efforts.'

'Sorry?' said Liz.

Pennington explained. 'Part of his job was to try and turn

anyone we thought either had been or might be recruited – by the extremists. It's always a long shot, but worth a go.'

'And did he have any success?'

'Ultimately no. But for a while he was working on one boy in particular, someone who'd come over for six months.'

'Do you remember his name?'

'No,' said Pennington. 'But it will be in the file.'

In Islamabad, thought Liz, her heart sinking. Pennington turned to Fane, 'You'll have a copy here, won't you?'

'Yes,' said Fane, happy to re-enter the conversation with a solution. 'Give me a moment, Elizabeth? I'll get it dug out for you.'

Liz walked over the bridge and went back to Thames House. You had to hand it to Tom, she thought, with grudging admiration for his act, as she waited for the lift. He had played things perfectly, merging chameleon-like into his environment until even his boss couldn't recall a single distinguishing characteristic.

'Is Judith about?' Liz asked Rose Love, who was halfway through a mug of tea and a chocolate biscuit at her desk.

'She's gone home, Liz. She wasn't feeling very well.'

Damn, thought Liz. She needed help right away. She'd returned from Vauxhall Cross with three names, each the target of an approach from Tom Dartmouth. They included the boy Pennington had mentioned, whose real name – carefully written down by Liz from the copy of Tom's report – was Bashir Siddiqui.

'Can I help?' asked Rose.

Liz looked at her appraisingly. She seemed a nice girl, very pretty, but slightly shy and unselfconfident. Liz was reluctant to use her now. There wasn't any need for Rose to sign the indoctrination form, but Liz didn't want rumours flying around about her pulling the files of a colleague. But she didn't see any alternative; Judith might be out for days.

'Would you do a look-up for me on these names? I think you'll find something about them in reports from Six's Pakistan station. Probably sent by Tom Dartmouth when he was seconded over there. There'll be quite a lot of reports but presumably the names will have been pulled out and indexed. Tom's away at present, so I can't ask him.'

'Okay,' said Rose, cheerfully.

Liz went back to her desk, worried about how long it would take Rose to sift through the reports. She answered some emails and did some paperwork and then went to the conference room she and Peggy were using, intent on looking through Tom's personnel file again. She was surprised to find Rose Love there, chatting to Peggy. 'I was just about to come and find you,' said Rose. 'I've got the answer you wanted.'

'You have? That was quick.'

'I just did a look-up on the names. Two of them are there in the reports, but not the third. I searched for all sorts of spelling variants too. Still no luck.' She handed a piece of paper to Liz. The missing name was Bashir Siddiqui. Protected by Tom, when recruited in Pakistan, by the simple expedient of omitting his name from his reports to MI5.

'Thanks, Rose. Now I just have to figure out how to find him.'

Rose looked puzzled. 'Oh I've done that too.' Seeing Liz's surprise, she turned shy about her show of initiative. 'I thought you'd want that.'

'I do,' said Liz eagerly.

'I cross-checked his name against the list of British Asians travelling to Pakistan for long periods of time.' She added proudly, 'It didn't take long to find him.'

'Do we know where he's from?' pressed Liz. Be patient, she told herself, Rose has saved you days of work.

'Yes. The Midlands.'

'Wolverhampton?'

'How did you know that?' asked Rose.

47

Eddie Morgan didn't want to get fired, but since it would be the fourth time in five years he was at least used to it. 'Anyone can sell,' his boss Jack Symonson liked to declaim. Then with a sarcastic sideways glance at Eddie, 'Well, almost anyone.'

His wife Gloria would be upset, Eddie knew, but she should know by now that there was always another job, another slot in the flexible framework of the used-car business. The pay was tilted so heavily in favour of commission rather than salary that there was little risk in taking someone on – especially if like Eddie they had been around the trade for almost twenty years.

He knew cars – that wasn't the issue. Give him a used Rover with 77,000 miles and he could tell you after no more than a quick sniff how long it would last and what it could be sold for. What he didn't have – there was no use kidding himself – was the ability to close a deal. Customers liked him (even his bosses conceded that) and he could talk fluently about anything on four wheels. But when push came to shove . . . he couldn't close.

Why can't I? he asked himself for the third time that week, as a blonde woman in shorts, recently divorced and looking for something sporty, said 'I'll think about it,' and left the forecourt after forty minutes of his time. Eddie stood, leaning against a five-year-old Rover, soaking up the sun.

Someone whistled, and he looked and saw Gillian, the

receptionist, beckoning him from the showroom door. 'Boss wants to see you, Eddie.'

Here we go, thought Eddie as he went inside, doing up his tie like a man tidying up on his way to the firing squad.

He was surprised, after knocking and entering Symonson's office, to find him with another man. 'Eddie, come in. This is Simon Willis, from DVLA. He wants to ask you about a car.' Willis was young and informally dressed – he wore a parka and chinos. He looked friendly, though, and as Eddie sat down, he grinned.

What was DVLA doing here? wondered Eddie, more curious than nervous. Or was this guy a cop? Whatever his weaknesses, Eddie had always been straight when it came to business, a bit of a rarity in the second-hand car game.

Willis said, 'I'm looking for a Golf, T-reg, that our records say was sold here about two months ago.'

'By me?'

Willis looked at Symonson, who laughed derisively. 'Miracles do happen, Eddie.'

Hilarious, thought Eddie sourly, but gave a fleeting, insincere smile, then looked back at Willis as Symonson continued to chortle at his own joke. Willis said, 'The car was bought by someone named Siddiqui. Here's a picture of him.'

From his lap Willis drew out a photograph and handed it to Eddie. It was an enlarged passport shot of a young Asian man with dark mournful eyes and a wispy attempt at a goatee.

'Do you remember him?' asked Willis.

'I'll say,' said Eddie. How could he forget him? It was his first sale in almost two weeks; Symonson had started making the first of the grumbling dissatisfied noises that had recently approached a crescendo.

Then one morning a young Asian man had come in and started looking around, curtly rejecting the offers of two of the other salesmen for help. Eddie had therefore approached him tentatively, but the man had been receptive enough to let Eddie escort him around the cars in the forecourt, through the Peugeots and Fords and the two used Minis they had in stock, until suddenly the Asian stopped in front of the black Golf. 63,000 miles on the clock. In reasonable nick, though it could do with a respray.

Eddie had begun the spiel, but the Asian – unusually, since as a rule Eddie found those people very polite – had cut him off. 'Spare me the bullshit,' he'd said. 'What'll you take for it?'

Eddie said to Willis now, 'Yes, that's the one. We haggled a bit over price, but in the end he seemed happy enough.' He wanted Symonson to feel he had handled the sale adroitly, but his boss's expression remained indifferent. Eddie asked, 'Why? Is there a problem?'

'Not with the car,' said Willis. Eddie looked at him more closely. Eddie had seen enough policemen over the years to know that, whatever Willis said, this was not your average copper.

Eddie said, 'If he had a problem with the van, that's his lookout. I warned him it was pretty iffy.'

There was silence in the room as Willis seemed to digest this. Finally Willis asked quietly, 'What van?'

'The one he bought two days later. When I saw him come in I reckoned he'd had a problem with the Golf. Or just changed his mind – people often do that right after they buy a car. But no, he wanted a van as well. So I sold him one.'

'What make?'

'I think it was a Ford. It'll be in the books.' He gestured

towards Symonson. 'But it was six years old, I remember that. White, of course. He insisted on climbing into the back to see how big it was. I got three and a half for it. I warned him about the transmission, but he didn't seem to care.'

'Did he say what he wanted it for?'

'No.' The second time the young man called Siddiqui had been even terser than before, so Eddie hadn't bothered trying to pitch.

'Did he say anything about where he might be going?'

Eddie shook his head. 'He didn't say much at all. No small talk. There'll be a name and address in the books but he paid cash – both times.'

Willis nodded but Eddie could tell he wasn't happy. 'If there's anything at all you remember about this man,' said Willis, 'please give me a ring.' He took out his wallet and extracted a card, then handed it to Eddie. 'That's my direct line. Ring me any time.'

'Okay,' said Eddie, looking at the card. I'll be damned, he thought, he is from DVLA after all. 'Is that it?' he said, looking back and forth between Symonson and Willis.

It was Willis who spoke. 'Yes,' he said. 'Thanks for your help.'

As Eddie got up to go, Symonson said, 'Will you be around later, Eddie? I need to talk to you.'

Where else does he think I'll be? thought Eddie sourly. Honolulu? The Seychelles? 'Yes, Jack,' he said, knowing full well what they would be talking about. 'I'll be here.'

48

Liz was surprised to learn that Tom lived in Fulham. She had thought that his flat was in North London, near her own place in Kentish Town. He hadn't actually said as much, that evening when he dropped her off, but he'd certainly led her to believe that she wasn't taking him out of his way.

Liz walked the two or three streets from the Underground station to Tom's address, in a quiet, leafy backwater of uniform, red brick, semi-detached Edwardian houses, mostly divided into flats.

As she approached the front door, two A2 officers emerged as if by magic from a van parked further down the street. Liz recognised the tall broad figure of Bernie, an affable ex-Army sergeant she had worked with before. With him was Dom, his quieter sidekick, a short, wiry man, fit from running marathons. Dom's expertise was locks – he had a vast collection in Thames House. He loved them; he studied them; he brooded over them, like an enthusiast with his stamp collection.

But Dom's skills were not needed at first as the front door to the house was open and a cleaning lady, who had been mopping the tiled floor in the hall, was just leaving. She took no notice as they walked straight past her and up the stairs to the first floor where Tom lived. Bernie rapped sharply on the front door. They were confident from A4, outside watching the flat, that Tom wasn't there, but no one wanted any surprises.

They waited a full minute, then Dom set to work. He picked

the first lock in fifteen seconds, then struggled with the Chubb in the top corner of the door. 'Bugger's had it specially adapted,' he said. It took another three minutes before Dom grunted, pushed, and the door opened.

Liz hadn't known what to expect, and her first impression was of overpowering neatness, an almost Germanic cleanliness. That and the light, which streamed through the front windows of the living room, highlighting the wooden floors, which had been waxed and polished to a sheen. The walls were white, reinforcing the sense of space, and the furniture was modern and looked new: Danish-style chairs and a long pristine white sofa. On the walls hung a few large bland prints in cold metal frames.

'Nice place,' said Bernie approvingly. 'Has he got money of his own?'

Liz shrugged. Presumably Tom's stepfather had left him something in his will. These were comfortable rather than lavish quarters, but it was an expensive part of town. It was hard to see how Tom could live here on his MI5 salary, especially as presumably he gave something to Margarita.

She followed Bernie and Dom into the other rooms: an alcove kitchen and dining area, two bedrooms in the back. Tom slept in the larger one; the spare bedroom was clearly used as a study – there was a small desk in the corner and a filing cabinet.

Bernie asked, 'Do you reckon he was always this tidy, or did he clean up before he did a bunk?'

Liz ran a finger under the desk top and, raising it into the air, found no dust. 'I think it's always like this.'

'It'll take about an hour,' said Bernie. He and Dom left Liz in the sitting room while they went to work, looking for hiding places: from the simple (lifting the cistern cover of the loo) to the complicated – checking the floorboards, and tapping the partition walls and the ceilings for hidden cavities. This was a preliminary search. Later, if necessary, the whole place would be taken to pieces.

Liz focused on what was visible, hoping it would tell her something new about the man she didn't already know. Not that that's a lot, she told herself. The flat had about as much personality as a hotel suite.

She went first to inspect Tom's bedroom. There were a couple of suits and some jackets hanging from a rail in the cupboard. A chest of drawers held boxer shorts and socks, and a dozen crisp, cotton shirts, neatly folded, that had been washed and pressed by a commercial service.

So he dresses well, thought Liz. I already knew that. She looked at the tall oak bookcase set against one wall. Were books the key to a man's mind or his heart? It seemed hard to tell. The reading was a mix of light fiction and heavier stuff – history and politics. Tom obviously liked thrillers, with a soft spot for the works of Frederick Forsyth. It seemed fitting, thought Liz, that Tom the lone wolf should own a copy of *The Day of the Jackal*.

The non-fiction books included three dull-looking tomes on the future of the EU. There were almost two shelves on terrorism, and several recent volumes on Al Qaeda. So what? thought Liz. I've got some of these myself. I've also got a copy of *Mein Kampf*, but that doesn't make me a Nazi sympathiser. These were the tools of his trade.

She noted that there were very few books about Ireland. *The Collected Poems of William Butler Yeats*, and a battered *Shell Guide to Ireland*. Nothing political; no accounts of the recent history of the IRA.

And then she saw it. Tucked into the end of one shelf, a thin blue volume: *Parnell and the English Establishment*. She didn't need to open it to know the author's name. Liam O'Phelan, Queen's University Belfast.

Liz was growing frustrated by the absence, throughout the flat, of anything personal – correspondence, mementoes, photographs. There wasn't even a rug or vase to indicate Tom had just spent four years in Pakistan. Like his office, his flat was overpoweringly impersonal. Deliberately, thought Liz. It seemed likely that Tom had performed his own version of the sweep Bernie and Dom were conducting, scouring the flat and removing anything that might flesh out the bare bones of his past, anything that might indicate what sort of man he was – and what he was planning to do. Though he had forgotten O'Phelan's book.

In the study, Liz was surprised to find the filing cabinet unlocked, but less so when she browsed through what it held – bills in the top drawer, neatly filed by utility and credit card. The second drawer held tax statements, and a protracted correspondence with the Inland Revenue about Tom's marriage-allowance claim in the year he was divorced. Bank statements filled the third drawer, and the bottom one was empty.

As she took out the pile of credit card statements, she noticed that the top one was very recent. It all seemed straightforward until she came to the last entry on the page, the Lucky Pheasant Hotel, Salisbury: £212.83. Looking at it in surprise, she realised its date was the weekend of her mother's biopsy – the weekend Tom had called at Bowerbridge. So he had dinner in Salisbury after all, she thought, remembering his invitation. But £212.83 – for dinner? He must have entertained a large party. No. Much more likely, he'd stayed there.

So much for those friends with the farm off the Blandford road, thought Liz. No wonder Tom had been so vague about the location – the farm probably didn't exist, any more than his friends did. Tom had been staying all along in the Lucky Pheasant. Why? What was he doing there?

Seeing me, thought Liz. Popping by, popping in, then after a long candlelit supper in the restaurant of the Lucky Pheasant, popping the 'How about it?' question. What was she meant to have done? Fall into his arms, and then the feather pillows of his four-poster bed?

That must have been the plan, thought Liz, designed to put her off the path she'd been investigating. He had hoped she would be easily distracted by a new passion for him; that must have been his thinking. The arrogant bastard, thought Liz. Thank God I said no. Now I better go and talk to the woman who didn't.

49

It was all very civilised. The Delft cups and the small Viennese biscuits on a china plate, the strong coffee, poured with a kind of Mittel European courtesy, and in the background classical music softly playing. It was so genteel that Liz wanted to scream.

Time seemed to have stood still, yet a furtive glance at the ormolu clock on the mantlepiece told Liz that she had been there precisely eleven minutes. Sipping her coffee, Margarita cocked an ear. 'Oh dear, I forgot the radio. Do you mind the noise?'

'Not at all. It's Bruckner, isn't it?'

Margarita looked pleased. 'You must like music,' she said. 'Do you play?'

Liz gave a self-deprecating shrug. 'Piano. I wasn't very good.' She had passed Grade Eight and been competent enough, but since then she had lost the habit of playing. There was a piano at Bowerbridge, but even during her recent convalescence there, Liz had hardly touched the keys.

'We could talk all day about music, I suspect,' said Margarita, nursing her cup, 'but that is not why you are here.'

'I'm afraid not.'

Margarita looked at her searchingly. 'It's Tom again, isn't it? The young woman who came to see me before – she said it was just a formality. But it can't be, can it? Not if you've come as well.'

'No, it's not.'

'Is he in trouble?'

'Yes, I think he is. Have you heard from him?'

'No. I told the woman before I haven't spoken to Tom since he went to Lahore. What has he done?'

'Disappeared, for one thing. We can't find him anywhere. We think he may be helping some people. People who want to do harm.'

'What kind of harm?'

'That's what we don't know – and why we need to find him. I've been to his flat, but there weren't many clues.'

'He didn't like possessions. He called them clutter,' said Margarita with a hint of a smile. She pointed to the room around them, full of furniture and paintings and bibelots. 'As you can see, we couldn't have been more different.'

'Was that a problem?'

'No,' said Margarita a touch edgily. 'We worked it out.' She smiled. 'I was allowed certain areas for my things; others were strictly off-limits.'

'A negotiation?' asked Liz.

'Not really,' sighed Margarita. 'More like capitulation on my part. It was usually that way. We got married here, for example, even though my parents were both alive and living in Israel. They wanted the wedding there. But Tom insisted.'

Margarita stood up and walked over to one of the side tables, covered in framed photographs. Most of them were of her family in Israel – one showed an older man in uniform, smiling as he squinted into the sun – but tucked further back was a picture in a silver frame which she handed to Liz. 'I'm afraid this is my wedding album.'

The photograph had been taken in front of the Marylebone

Register Office – which Liz recognised from newspaper photographs of celebrities. Tom and Margarita stood on the steps, arm in arm, facing the camera. What was immediately striking was the difference in their expressions: Margarita, stunning in a pale ivory silk jacket, beamed, her delight quite apparent; Tom, on the other hand, stood in a dark suit with a buttonhole carnation, staring emotionlessly at some point behind the camera. He looks like he's just been sentenced to six months, thought Liz, handing back the photograph. 'You look very happy,' she said diplomatically. 'Who was best man?'

'He didn't have one,' said Margarita, and the words spoke for themselves. She added dryly, 'Our driver that day was the only witness. He took the photograph, too.'

'Weren't your parents there?'

'No. Tom made it clear he didn't want them. Naturally my mother was very upset.'

Margarita remained standing, and moved to the window where she stared out at the rooftops across the street. She wore a grey wool sweater which emphasised her full figure; she was tall, Liz realised, and must have caused quite a stir in the orchestra world. It's not that she is no longer beautiful, thought Liz; it was rather that her beauty was now suffused by a haunting sadness.

'So Tom didn't get on with your parents?'

'He only met them a few times, but it was all right. I'd worried, since he was an Arabist – I thought my father might think he was anti-Semitic. My father lost all his family in Poland, you know, during the War, so he was sensitive about such matters.'

'Was he right about Tom? Is he anti-Semitic?'

Margarita deliberated for a moment. 'I have often thought

about it. It's certainly true that Tom had little time for Israel. He once told me the Balfour Declaration was the root of all modern evil. But I was sympathetic to the Palestinians myself – contrary to what you read, many Israelis are. So we did not really disagree about politics. That wasn't the problem.'

'What was the problem?' Liz asked boldly. This was the tricky bit, the personal probing.

Margarita turned her head and stared at Liz, who suddenly worried she had pushed the woman too hard and too soon. But Margarita answered her question. 'He never loved me,' she said without a trace of self-pity. Liz hated to think how much pain Margarita had suffered before she could speak so dispassionately.

'At the beginning he was charming. Relaxed, funny, irreverent. But I realise now that it was never really about me. Does that make sense?'

She looked so imploringly at Liz that she felt compelled to nod sympathetically. Liz had seen something of that mix of charm and ruthless self-absorption in Tom's aborted overtures to her. Thanks goodness I kept my distance, thought Liz.

Margarita said, struggling for control, 'I thought for a while that he did love me.' She added, ruefully, 'Probably because I so much wanted him to. But he didn't.'

She gestured at the wedding photograph on the table, and paused. Liz felt convinced that Margarita had never talked this way before, even to her most intimate friends, if she had any. She seemed too proud, too demure for self-revelation. Paradoxically, only the promptings of a stranger had unlocked the floodgates.

Margarita shook her head regretfully. 'If you want to know what went wrong with our marriage, I have to say nothing really changed. I had thought, well he is a bit of a cold fish, but he must care or why else would he want to marry me? But then it was as if he had chosen me, then decided to *un*choose me. Like returning a dress that doesn't fit to a shop.' With a strained voice, half raw from emotion, she said, 'Love never entered into it.'

'Was there anyone he did love?'

'His father,' she said without hesitation. 'I mean his real father of course. And that was only because he never really knew him.'

'Did Tom talk about his father?' The background music now was Schubert's 'Death and the Maiden', the cello melancholic and slow.

'Almost never. And when he did, it wasn't about his father so much, as the people who had ruined him. That was the word Tom always used – "ruined".'

'Who were these people?'

Margarita smiled bitterly. 'You may well ask. I did, but he wouldn't answer me.'

Liz said, 'You know, at work Tom was very unemotional, very controlled. Most of us are like that – you have to be in our business. Emotion just gets in the way. But he must have felt strongly about *something*.'

'You mean other than his father?' said Margarita, turning her back to Liz and staring at the photograph on the table.

'I wasn't thinking about what he loved so much as what he didn't love. Did he get angry about anything?'

'He never showed anger,' said Margarita flatly, adding wistfully, 'It would have been better if he had.'

Margarita sat down again. 'He did hate school,' she said, 'but doesn't everybody?' She laughed lightly. 'It seems a peculiarly

English disease, this boarding-school business. And he was made to go to Oundle.'

'Oundle?'

'His stepfather's old school. I know he resented that.'

Somehow Liz doubted Tom was planning to blow up the chapel at Oundle, wherever that might be. 'I wonder—' she started to say but Margarita interrupted.

'The odd thing is that one would expect him to have loved Oxford.'

'Didn't he?' asked Liz.

'Quite the contrary. I kept asking him to show me round. I'd have liked to see his old college with him, all his old haunts. But he refused. I had to go on my own.'

'Did he say why?'

'Not really. He was like that: he decided and that was that. He didn't ever seem to feel the need to explain. I tried teasing him: I said, "What if our children want to go to university there?" This was when I still thought we would have a family.'

'What did Tom say?'

'He said the Empire had been built on power and hypocrisy, and that Oxford still was. I thought he was joking. Then he said he'd sooner not have children than send them to Oxford.'

'Perhaps he was saying it for effect.'

Margarita looked intently at Liz, and Liz sensed she wanted their conversation to end. Perhaps she regretted her candour with Liz, and soon her openness might turn to post-confessional resentment. She spoke less gently now. 'Tom didn't say things for effect. He was very literal-minded – like an American. He could be very icy, even at the beginning. Towards the end he was like a freezer compartment.'

Liz decided she had got as much as she was likely to from

the interview. It was time to go. 'Thank you for the coffee and the chat,' she said, standing up. 'It's been very helpful.' As she moved towards the door, she stopped for a final question. 'Tell me, if you had to guess where Tom had gone, where would it be?'

Margarita thought about this for a moment, then gave a weary shrug. 'Who knows? He had no home of homes, not even in his heart. That's what I've been trying to tell you.'

Had she learned anything about Tom? Liz wondered as she left the mansion block and walked towards the Tube at High Street Ken. The afternoon was turning sultry: a muggy, moist warmth hung in the air, like a stalking horse for thunderstorms.

In Liz's experience, the people she pursued were often fuelled by motives which seemed to an observer almost paltry, even humdrum, compared with the extreme actions they prompted. Money, sex, drugs, a cause, even religion – how could they be justification for the violence to which they drove some people?

But with Tom she was facing something different. He seemed to be a man with no cause. A man who could not – did not – love anything or anyone. How else to explain an IRA recruit who seemed to have lost interest in Ireland? An IRA recruit enlisting British Muslims in Pakistan to commit who knows what atrocity against his own country? Tom seemed to possess a psychology that Liz had never encountered before.

What is this all about? thought Liz. She seemed to be pursuing an ice machine. But Tom must once have felt strong emotions. Why did he accept O'Phelan's approach? Only the most fanatical believer in fighting for a united Ireland would have done so. But did he really feel that strongly? He wasn't Irish.

As she brooded over everything she had learned about Tom, she kept returning to her question to Margarita. 'Was there anyone he did love?' And the answer had been, 'His father. I mean his real father of course.' But how could his love for his father, a disgraced hack who'd killed himself over thirty years before, be a motive *now*?

Suddenly Liz thought, I am only looking at this from one end. What if instead of loving, Tom hated, really hated – could that not be the motive for whatever he was doing?

Who had he blamed for his father's downfall? She remembered the details from Peggy's account. Unsurprisingly, Tom's father had protested his innocence of the charges that he'd faked his story, those many years ago, claiming he'd been the victim of an elaborate sting. According to him, the mythical SAS man – source for his exposé – had been a plant, dangled like bait in front of his nose by . . . by whom?

The British of course, some unspecified cabal of the Army and the Secret Service, with the British Consulate in New York thrown in for good measure. Tom's father had blamed his downfall on 'the British'.

Liz stood stock-still on the pavement outside High Street Kensington Underground Station, as shoppers moved nimbly around her pensive figure. Was that the object of Tom's animus then? The British – his own people? What had he said to Margarita – a country 'built on power and hypocrisy'? And he'd been serious. Deadly serious.

How stupid I've been, thought Liz. She had persisted in trying to discover Tom's attachments – hoping that would lead her to the place he would go to when all else had failed.

Don't try and track him there, thought Liz – that way leads nowhere. There was only one trail to follow, she told herself. Follow the hate.

50

Peggy Kinsolving had enlarged a map of the Home Counties and it sat in front of them on the conference-room table. Wetherby had looked in twice already, and now he came in and sat down. He did not look as though he would be leaving. Liz could tell that he was trying to look upbeat, but she sensed his agitated concern, since she shared it.

She was glad he was there, though, because all afternoon an idea had been brewing in her mind – far-fetched perhaps, but it wouldn't go away. She was counting on Wetherby to decide if she were being foolish or inspired.

Outside a long spiral of black cloud was moving in from the west, and the wind had picked up, whipping at the leaves on the plane trees along the pavement across the street. Liz thought for a moment of the garden centre at Bowerbridge. This was just the sort of weather her mother hated because of the damage it caused the young plants. Then Liz felt guilty for not ringing her the night before. Her mother's surgery was in ten days, and Liz had tried to be in touch every day.

She looked across the table at Dave Armstrong, back from Wolverhampton and reporting on what he'd found there. 'Bashir bought this van a few days after he bought the Golf. The only problem is that there are probably 200,000 of them on the road. It's like a vocational badge: you can't call yourself a builder if you don't own a white van.'

'What about plates?' asked Liz.

'I circulated the licence numbers right away. There are 8,000 number-plate recognition cameras in the UK, so if he's driving with those licence plates they'll get picked up by a camera at some point. But I'm sure he would have changed them – he did on the Golf. Quite cleverly, he kept the T-reg, because it fitted the year of the car, but he changed the number.'

Wetherby spoke up, sounding tired. His voice was low. 'They'll probably keep the van locked up anyway until they need it. That suggests that unless they've got yet another car, they're staying in a town, some place with public transport in case they need to go anywhere.'

Liz looked at the Xs marked on the map in biro. 'London,' she announced, then pointed slightly west, 'then Wokingham.' She moved her hand up, west and north, and jabbed at another spot. 'And most recently, up on the Downs near The Ridgeway.'

'What's near there?' asked Wetherby. 'Wantage?'

Liz shook her head. 'I don't think that could be the target. It's a market town. No military installation. And Peggy's checked for public events.'

'Every Saturday there's a market in the square,' said Peggy, 'but not much else.'

'Doesn't seem likely,' said Wetherby. He pointed at the map. 'What about Newbury?'

'There's a country fair this weekend,' said Peggy, and Wetherby smiled but shook his head.

'Swindon?' asked Dave. 'HQ of W. H. Smith and the National Trust.' This time Wetherby didn't bother to smile.

'How about Didcot?' asked Peggy, who had discussed all these towns with Liz before the two men arrived. She pointed a few miles east from the dumped car's position on the map. 'It's a bigger town than I realised. Its population is 25,000 and growing fast. There are enough Asians for our suspects to blend in. And most important, it's got the power station.'

'Nuclear?' asked Dave.

'No, coal fired, though people often think it is nuclear because it's near Harwell. Those cooling towers would be quite a target.' She looked at her notes. 'Its main chimney is 650 feet high, and the six towers are each 325 feet high. You can see them from miles away. It was voted Britain's Third Worst Eyesore by the readers of *Country Life*.'

'Makes me think better of the place,' scoffed Dave, who was not a *Country Life* reader, being strictly Old Labour.

'Hold on,' said Charles. 'If they're down there, shouldn't we be worrying about Aldermaston? That's where the nuclear bombs are made.'

'But you'd never get near a place like that,' said Dave. 'It must be as well protected as anywhere in Britain. And how would they know what to attack without inside information? There's no reason to think Tom has any.'

'We'd better get on to Protective Security,' said Wetherby without enthusiasm. 'What do you think, Liz?' He seemed to sense her scepticism.

'I can see them *staying* in Didcot – it's such an anonymous place, really just a train junction that's grown. Much better for them than the countryside. As Asians, they'd stick out too much.

'But I can't really see Didcot power station or Aldermaston as the target. Why would Tom think it important to blow up a power station or a nuclear-bomb factory? There's no symbolic value in it. And anyway, you'd need a much bigger operation than he seems to have.'

'That's all very well,' said Wetherby, 'but would symbolism matter to the terrorists? They'd be after maximum impact, surely.'

'But symbolism would be important to Tom, I'm sure. If he's doing this lunatic thing, there's got to be some reason.'

'You're confident then that Tom is leading these men and not just helping them?'

'Yes,' said Liz firmly, thinking of what she'd learned about him in the last two days. 'Tom likes to control things, even if it's behind the scenes. Everything Margarita Levy said confirms that. This is a mission of some sort, and he's leading it. In his mind there's a reason for it.'

'Do you think he's working with Al Qaeda?' Dave asked.

'No. I think he recruited Bashir on his own account in Pakistan. He had plenty of unsupervised access to him – he was meant to be recruiting him for Six.'

Wetherby tapped the end of his pencil on the table. 'All right, if not Didcot or Aldermaston, then where?' There was a hint of impatience in his voice. 'We've got to take some decisions. Which targets are we going to cover? I have a feeling that we haven't got much time,' he added. 'They're panicking – look at the car. Burning it suggests to me that they are on the verge of doing whatever they're planning to do.'

He stared at Liz as if somehow she might hold the answer, and seemed grateful when she spoke up.

'I think it's Oxford,' she said.

'Oxford? Why Oxford? Do you have any particular reason?'

'No single overpowering one,' she admitted. 'But it began with something Margarita said. He hated Oxford, she said, really loathed the place.'

'Well, if it's Oxford, what's the target?' asked Wetherby. 'His college? Or a person or some event?'

'We just don't know. Peggy's been trying to find out if something special's going on there.'

'I'll try again,' Peggy said. 'I haven't alerted the police yet since we're so unsure. I got on to the secretary in the Registrar's office, but she's been out all afternoon.' She got up and left the room in a hurry.

They sat silently for a minute, Wetherby drumming his fingers on the table, lost in thought, while Dave slumped in his chair and stared at the floor.

Suddenly Wetherby looked at Liz. 'I've known people to be unhappy at Oxford,' he said. 'But not hate it with passion.'

'I don't actually think it was the place, so much as what it represented to him. Somehow it's become the Establishment incarnate.'

'Was this the influence of O'Phelan?'

Liz leant back in her chair. 'To an extent perhaps. When I saw him in Belfast O'Phelan certainly didn't sound very positive about his time there. But really I think it has to do with Tom's own feelings. He's carried a deep hatred for England ever since his father killed himself. I'm sure he believes his father was set up, by the intelligence services and the Government and the Establishment – whatever that's supposed to be these days.'

'Was he?' asked Dave.

'No. Some weird things happened in Northern Ireland back then, but I don't believe that story. I think his father was just the victim of a conman trying to make money out of a sensational story that wasn't true. The tragedy in a sense is that his father didn't think he was writing anti-British propaganda; he actually thought he was writing the truth.'

'But then why isn't Tom trying to blow up Thames House? Or Vauxhall Cross?' asked Dave.

'He'd know how difficult that would be. It just wouldn't be worth trying.'

'No, that's not it,' said Wetherby emphatically. He pulled tensely at his tie. 'If he wants to strike *symbolically* at the Establishment – as well as do a lot of damage – we are the wrong target.'

'So he blows up a High Table instead,' said Dave, and Liz could understand his scepticism, but it didn't help. She was working on gut feeling now – getting more and more certain that Oxford would be Tom's target, but terribly anxious that she didn't really know and couldn't be more specific than that. All those colleges, she thought, with libraries, chapels, halls and museums. It could be any of them.

Peggy re-entered the room, looking ashen-faced. 'What's wrong?' demanded Liz.

'I haven't been able to reach the Registrar's secretary because she's been terribly busy with preparations for Encaenia.'

'By God!' exclaimed Wetherby. 'That must be it.'

'What's Encaenia?' asked Dave.

'It's a ceremony at Oxford during the summer term,' Wetherby calmly explained. 'It's held in the Sheldonian. It's a special ceremony where they give out honorary degrees.'

'To students?' asked Dave.

Wetherby was shaking his head. 'No, no. To luminaries. There's usually a foreign dignitary or two – I think last year it was President Chirac. Sometimes a Nobel Prize winner. Famous writers. That sort of thing.'

'It's not just Encaenia,' Peggy said. 'They're installing the new Chancellor as well.'

'Lord Rackton?' asked Wetherby and Peggy nodded.

Dave's mouth made a small moue. Rackton had been a senior Tory minister for many years, often described as the best Prime Minister the country never had.

Peggy was looking at her notes. 'The Chancellor's own ceremony is at eleven-thirty in the Sheldonian. That's followed by Encaenia at half-past twelve. In between, the recipients of honorary degrees and University officials meet in one of the nearby colleges for Lord Crewe's Benefaction.'

'Which is?' asked Liz.

Peggy quoted out loud: '"Peaches, strawberries and champagne." They're refreshments paid for by a legacy of Lord Crewe in the eighteenth century.'

Dave raised an eyebrow at Liz.

Peggy went on: 'After he's installed, Lord Rackton comes and joins them, and they all march off in a procession to the Sheldonian. This year the Benefaction is in Lincoln College, so they only have to go round the corner.'

'It's quite an event,' said Wetherby. 'A sort of showpiece of the University. Very colourful – eminent people, very public, very accessible.' He finished quietly, 'I'm afraid it does make sense.' No one had to ask what 'it' was. The anxiety of not knowing Tom's target was swiftly being replaced by the tension of not knowing if he could be stopped.

'When is this Encaenia?' Dave asked Peggy. Please, prayed Liz, let it be weeks away. She waited with ill-disguised impatience as Peggy consulted her notes. 'The ceremony is always held on the Wednesday of Ninth Week,' she declared at last.

'But which Wednesday is that?' demanded Dave, gritting his teeth. He was sitting upright now.

Peggy looked at him wide-eyed. 'It's tomorrow, of course. That's why the secretary was so busy this afternoon.'

A long low rumbling noise filled the room, as if an aeroplane were passing overhead, and the windows trembled slightly. Standing next to Liz, Peggy visibly started.

'It's all right,' said Dave. 'It's only thunder.'

51

Tom had found a small, shabby genteel hotel near the old green in Witney, a market town west of Oxford. He paid in advance for a week's stay, booking in the name of Sherwood. He used the same name to hire the car and buy the plane ticket.

Living as Sherwood, he found it hard to fabricate a past for the man, so engaged was he with the present. In time, he would be able to fill in the blanks, enough to satisfy the most persistent of questioners, but just now he felt he lived in the perfect existential moment of his life.

He rang Bashir once, after driving carefully to the outskirts of Burford, taking back roads that had no cameras. Tom reckoned it was safe in any case – only Rashid's phone had proved at risk, and that was only through the boy's stupidity. What a mistake it had been to choose him – even though he had brought in Khaled Hassan, who was steady as a rock.

Now he and Bashir reviewed their plans for the hundredth time, and synchronised their watches before Tom rang off. Bashir sounded calm, but then he was of a different calibre – and commitment – from Rashid, who thankfully was destined only for a supporting role. So far, Rashid had been the only mistake. But it was too late in any case to do anything about him.

Part of Tom was relieved about that, for he had got no joy from killing his old tutor O'Phelan, or from ordering the killing of Marzipan. Not that he felt any guilt – they had been necessary murders, and if anything had caused them, it had been the overeagerness of his colleagues in MI5, particularly Liz Carlyle. Tom found it untroubling that Bashir and Khaled were eager to die. He had no interest in their motives or their cause. They would serve *his* purpose. That was the point of them.

And now it was Wednesday morning. D-Day, Tom told himself, as he packed, amused by how English that sounded. Later this day he would drive to Bristol where he had booked another hotel room for the night. An early morning flight to Shannon, and then on to New York courtesy of – fittingly – Aer Lingus. The search for him would by then be intense, so Tom was avoiding Heathrow where he was more likely to be recognised. As Sherwood he should be safe enough at Irish passport control, and certainly safe enough in New York. There he would decide what stage two of his long-term campaign should be. Long term – he had no intention of being anything but a permanent thorn in the side of his father's persecutors.

On his way out, he explained to the lady at the desk that he was off to the West Country and was taking his bag in case he had to stay overnight. He did not want her to think he was leaving abruptly for good. She can be surprised later on, he thought. Just like everybody else. Including Bashir.

52

Liz drove down to Oxford with Wetherby very early in the morning. She had been awake most of the night, thinking of the day ahead. She'd finally fallen asleep, but it was only two days after the summer solstice and she had soon been awakened by the dawn light flooding through her bedroom window.

As they came down through the chalk cut at Stokenchurch, and the Thames Valley opened up ahead of them, Wetherby broke the silence to say, 'Part of me is hoping we're wrong.'

'I know,' said Liz.

'On the other hand, if we are, it may be somewhere else.'

They took the Oxford exit off the M40, then got held up for several minutes queuing at the roundabout on the eastern outskirts of the city. As they sat in the traffic, Wetherby spoke again. 'Where do you think Tom's gone?'

'God knows,' said Liz. 'Even Margarita didn't have any idea.'

'Do you think he would have met up with the terrorists?'

'He might have been in touch, but no, I don't think he'd take the risk of seeing them. Why, do you?'

'No, but I can't see him leaving the country either. Not yet, anyway. He'd want to see the job done. *Job*!' he said with uncharacteristic scorn. He pulled out into the roundabout and overtook a lumbering lorry, then slipped neatly into the road towards Headington. On the pavement children were walking to school, little ones accompanied by their mothers, groups of older children playing tag. It seemed such an ordinary day, thought Liz.

They stopped at the Headington traffic lights. 'Do you feel you understand him now?' Wetherby asked.

Liz watched as a Jack Russell chewed at its lead, while its owner stood and talked to a large woman in a summer dress. She replied, 'Given the resentment he must have felt about his father's death, I suppose I can understand the IRA's appeal, especially when their approach was made by a charismatic figure like O'Phelan. What I don't get is how it could be switched to another set of terrorists and another cause. Especially since I don't think Tom has any particular sympathy for Islam.'

'Does he believe in anything?'

'Not in the sense of a credo. That's why I don't understand what he's trying to do today – assuming we're right. An old Tory is becoming Chancellor; the Peruvian Ambassador is getting a degree. What on earth would be the point of killing them?'

'Don't forget, he murdered O'Phelan,' said Wetherby. They were passing Oxford Brookes University now, new inhabitant of the grey mansion where Robert Maxwell had lived for so many years. 'And caused Marzipan's death, even if he didn't kill him.'

'They threatened to get in his way.'

'Get in the way of what?'

Liz shrugged, thinking of the bombers. 'Presumably whatever he's planning. That must be of critical importance to Tom. Though to want to kill all these people today – I simply can't fathom it.'

'Neither can I,' said Wetherby. 'It doesn't sound right somehow.'

53

At six foot four inches in his stocking feet, Constable Winston was at least an inch taller when he wore the regulation black shoes. He stood out, and he thought of this as an attribute – especially at public gatherings where, like a beacon used by pilots as an aid to navigation, he became a focal point for colleagues lost in the crowd.

Normally he liked working on public occasions. This morning, however, PC Winston was unhappy to be on duty. He usually had Wednesday off, and took the kids to school. He supposed that when the duty sergeant had collared him coming off shift the night before, he could have resisted, but he could tell from the sergeant's tone that it was important, so he had not kicked up. But the shift briefing at 6:45 that morning had not adequately explained the urgency. 'We have been alerted to the possibility of an incident at today's university ceremonies,' the sergeant had proclaimed. 'We will keep you posted as more information becomes available.'

What on earth did that mean? wondered PC Winston, as he moved into the goldfish-shape of Broad Street, entirely peaceful at this early hour. The street was bordered at this end by a line of pastel-coloured shops on one side and by the Victorian gables of Balliol on the other. It funnelled down to a narrow strait by the Sheldonian. Inside, the elaborate Encaenia ceremony would take place, while outside the usual mix of gawking tourists and indifferent locals would fill the street. But now while the sun struggled to emerge after a night of moist cloud cover, the street was virtually empty of pedestrians and cars.

What was supposed to be happening today, PC Winston wondered again, as he approached the corner of the Turl. He stood there for a moment, admiring the still-misty view down the quaint street, with the ice-cream cone spire of Lincoln College Library towering above the College wall. He had been on duty when President Clinton had received an honorary degree, almost a decade before, and remembered the stony brusqueness of the Secret Service men, the way they had insisted that even policemen like himself be vetted for that day. Understandable, in that any president was a potential target for assassination. And that was before 9/11. So was someone that famous going to be here today? He doubted it – he would have heard long before, and not been pressed with so little warning into this extra shift.

He kept walking and passed the 'Roman Emperors', a line of grim-faced busts perched on stone pedestals which punctuated the length of iron railing in front of the Sheldonian. Noticing a van ahead of him, parked on a double-yellow line, he picked up his pace a bit, ready to give them a flea in their ear. Two men, each with a sniffer dog on a lead, suddenly came out of the back of the van.

The dog handler nodded as he approached. 'Is this a problem?' he said with a gesture towards the double yellow.

'Not this early,' said Winston. 'What's up?'

'Beats me,' said the man. 'I've come all the way from Reading for this job. You'd think they'd be better prepared.'

And though PC Winston was himself puzzled by the last-minute alarums, pride in his own force made him declare with a certainty he didn't feel, 'It's the Animal Liberation lot. Very unpredictable.'

It was then that another PC, a young recruit named Jacobs, appeared, moving fast towards them. 'Here you are, Sidney,' he said breezily to PC Winston, who resented the use of his Christian name by someone so young. Smart-arse, he thought, as Jacobs handed him an A4 sheet on which mugshots had been magnified and photocopied. They showed three Asian men, young, entirely innocent-looking. Winston scanned the faces, memorising them, thinking, they don't look like animal lovers to me.

54

At nine-fifteen Liz listened intently as the briefing began. She was sitting on one of a row of uncomfortable plastic chairs in the Operations Room of the Thames Valley Headquarters in St Aldates, facing a projector screen that had been pulled down on the far wall. Along the side of the room, hanging from brackets, was a bank of television monitors.

Next to Liz on one side sat Dave Armstrong, who had come down the night before, and looked tense and exhausted. On her other side were Wetherby and the Chief Constable, a hawk-like man named Ferris. Further down the row sat other senior police officers, including the head of Special Branch, clutching a plastic cup of coffee.

The Deputy Chief Constable, Colin Matheson, in charge of the operation, was addressing them, holding a long wooden pointer the length of a pool cue. He was a trim man in his late thirties with jet black hair and a line in dry wit. His manner was brisk and professional, but there was palpable tension in the room, which nothing he said did anything to allay.

Matheson raised his pointer to signal to someone at the back of the room, and at once a map of the city centre appeared on the screen. 'From what you've told us,' he said, looking at Wetherby, and moving his pointer along Broad Street to the Sheldonian, 'this is the focal point.'

'We think so,' said Wetherby. 'The Installation of the

Chancellor is going to be there, and then Encaenia.'

'Would the Chancellor be a target?'

'It's difficult to predict the target. These are Islamic extremists who want to do as much damage as possible in the most visible way. I think a single assassination would not be their first choice.'

Chief Constable Ferris turned to Wetherby. 'Do we know if they're armed?'

Wetherby shook his head. 'No, we don't. I think it's unlikely they would carry weapons, but we can't rule it out. We do know they possess explosives – we found traces of fertiliser in a safe house they were using in Wokingham. Given that, and their affiliations, and recent history in this country, everything points to their trying to blow something up and kill as many people as they can. Particularly if they're "important" people,' Wetherby added, his tone acknowledging the distinction's absurdity. 'That's even better.'

'So which ceremony are they likely to attack?'

'I'd say Encaenia rather than Installation is the likelier. Don't misunderstand me: these people would be perfectly happy to kill the Chancellor, but it would be better from their point of view if they can kill a lot of other dignitaries as well.'

'Any sense of how they'll do it?' the Chief Constable asked, unable to mask his anxiety.

'I think there are two possibilities,' said Wetherby. 'It could be a suicide bombing on foot, in which case at least one of them will have to get close to the procession, wearing some sort of apparatus. Or they'll use a vehicle, which we think is more likely. We know they have a white Transit van and that the buyer was one of the three main suspects. He was particularly interested in its load capacity, apparently.' He looked at

Matheson, 'Your Special Branch have all the details, including the original plate numbers, though I'm sure they've changed them.'

Matheson nodded and pointed to the blank monitors on the wall. 'We're rigging some temporary video to cover the target area as well as we can. We're using fixed cameras so no one can duck them as they rotate. We expect to have them working in the next half hour.

'Sniffer dogs have come in from Reading and are checking the building for explosives. The handlers are there now. It's going to take a while: I've told them to be extra careful. In addition, there are library stacks from the Bodleian that run underground right next to the Sheldonian. They're serviced by a kind of antique train that runs from the New Bodleian across the street to the Old Library, and then on again to the Radcliffe Camera.' He tracked the train's path with his pointer on the projector screen.

'Do many people know this railway's there?' asked Liz.

Matheson shrugged. 'Most people walking through the courtyard wouldn't have a clue that there's a subterranean world beneath them. On the other hand, every Oxford mystery story from Inspector Morse back to Michael Innes seems to have an underground finale set beneath the Bodleian. If that's what they're planning, we'll stop them.'

'I doubt they are,' said Wetherby, with a shake of his head. 'From what you say, it's too obvious, but I'm glad you're checking anyway.'

The head of Oxford's Special Branch spoke up. 'There was a bit of a hitch with the photographs you sent, but we've got copies now. They're being distributed to all the men in the area.'

He passed copies to Wetherby, who looked at them, then passed them on to Dave and Liz. Rashid looked terribly young, thought Liz. As young as Marzipan.

'Every armed response unit in the Thames Valley has been called in,' said Ferris next to Wetherby. 'And there will be armed officers all along the route.'

'We're also placing four sharpshooters up high as well, with sniper rifles,' Matheson said, putting the pointer directly on the Sheldonian. 'One here in the cupola.'

Liz remembered the stunning view from her tourist's visit to the top with Peggy.

'Another here,' he said pointing to the Bodleian, 'to cover the courtyard between the Clarendon Building and the Sheldonian. And two on Broad Street, one facing east from the top of the Blackwell's music shop. The other facing west from the same position. We'll also have a dozen Special Branch officers in plain clothes mingling with the spectators. All of them will be armed.'

He went on. 'We are looking for any van in the middle of town. We've briefed all the traffic wardens and we've got extra shifts of uniformed officers walking the streets. White vans are not exactly uncommon, and of course they may have painted the van a different colour. But we're doing everything we can.'

After this recital of preventive measures, a silence filled the room. No one seemed eager to break it.

'So,' concluded Matheson at last, his face grim, 'let's all hope that we're fully prepared.'

'And that the levees don't break,' added Dave Armstrong under his breath.

55

Waking early, they ate a simple breakfast, then said prayers. Rashid watched Bashir and Khaled closely. He admired them for what they were about to do, and part of him wished he too was going to become a martyr that day in the struggle against the enemies of Islam.

Mine is the more difficult part, he thought. I will not have my reward yet. But he took comfort from the fact he would still be fighting for Islam. He knew what he had to do and afterwards where he had to go. He would be contacted, he had been told, and taken to Pakistan to join the Imam at his madrasa and then he would truly face death in another operation. He would have liked to be able to go home first, see his parents and look after his sister, Yasmina, but he knew that was not possible. The police were looking for him.

As the three of them squeezed into the front seat of the van, Bashir reluctantly gave Rashid a new pay-as-you-go mobile he had bought in Didcot, walking the mile to the new shopping centre on the main road, up from the station. 'You are to use this once, and only once,' he instructed the small, younger man. 'To ring me as we have planned.'

Bashir had consulted the map carefully and drove to Oxford on smaller roads, eschewing the A34, since it would be an easy route to seal off. He drove through the farmland between

Abingdon and Oxford, then came down Cumnor Hill and into the city from the west. He followed the tortuous one-way system and parked in the quiet central neighbourhood of Jericho, once home to the printers of the University Press, its small brick houses now lived in by well-off young families.

Bashir found himself remembering where it had all begun, many thousands of miles away. He had met the Englishman in the marketplace in Lahore – the man had popped his head out of a shop as Bashir passed and said casually, 'Do you speak Urdu? Can you help translate for me?' Bashir was fluent in Urdu – his parents had spoken it at home in Wolverhampton – and he helped the man negotiate the purchase of one hundred embroidered rugs from Kashmir.

Afterwards they had had coffee together, where the Englishman explained that he worked for an import-export firm in Dubai (which explained the size of the rug order) and was in Lahore on a three-month buying trip. Unfamiliarity with the language was making his task harder; would Bashir by any chance be willing to help? He would be paid of course – a figure was mentioned that made Bashir's eyes blink. Flattered, intrigued (though already a little wary), Bashir had agreed.

On the surface their relationship had been strictly professional, though when the haggling in the market was done each day and they retreated to a cafe for refreshment, their conversation ranged through politics and religion. The Englishman had been friendly, outgoing and outspoken to the point of indiscretion.

Bashir was not naive, and he and his fellow students had been warned from day one at the madrasa to be alert to the presence of intelligence agents from the West. More than once it crossed his mind that the man was not what he said he was.

But in their conversations the Englishman was never probing or intrusive; indeed, he seemed more inclined to explain to Bashir his own views.

These seemed oddly unWestern, for he was very knowledgeable about Islam, especially in the Middle East he seemed to know so well. He was also vehemently anti-American, dismissing 9/11 blithely as a case of 'chickens coming home to roost'.

The Imam had been encouraging Bashir to attend a training camp, to equip him to join his Muslim brethren fighting in Afghanistan or even Iraq. But he had been resistant. Why? He was not sure himself, until at one of their meetings the Englishman had put a new idea in his head. If he were Bashir's age, the Englishman mused, he would want to take up arms against the West. Though not in Afghanistan or Iraq, he added thoughtfully. Why die anonymously in an alien land, when one could instead carry the battle more effectively to one's own homeland? Fighting the Western forces out here, he'd said, was a mug's game. So what if the US and UK armies lost a few soldiers? They had still managed to shift the battle to distant territory which few of their citizens knew anything about. What those powers really dreaded was warfare conducted on their own turf.

The Englishman said all this in a series of random remarks, but for Bashir they crystallised his own thinking – and his own reluctance to volunteer to fight alongside Al Qaeda recruits. Why not go ahead and be trained, he thought, but take the battle home?

But what could he do on his own? At their next meeting, somewhat rashly he said as much to the Englishman. And that was when their fateful bargain had been reached. For the Englishman had offered to help.

It was an offer Bashir was initially suspicious of. He assumed the Englishman was leading him into a trap, setting him up to be captured and imprisoned. Perhaps he made that clear, for the Englishman now made his own confession. He said he understood if Bashir didn't trust him, and Bashir had good reason not to, since the import-export business was not the full extent of his professional activities. Yes, he had ties with intelligence services – better not to be too specific, he declared. But he had agendas of his own, which happened to coincide with Bashir's desire to strike against the West.

Knowing this, could Bashir trust him? asked the Englishman rhetorically. Well, why not? If he had wanted to entrap him, would he really be encouraging him to act on his own? Wouldn't he be trying to get him to join existing cells so the authorities could monitor and then prevent the activities of a wider circle?

The rest was . . . history in the making, thought Bashir now. He had met Rashid and Khaled at a mosque in Wolverhampton and found them eager to wage jihad but just as eager to be led. They were young, and easily swayed. The Englishman had agreed to their enlistment because of these characteristics and also, he had explained to Bashir, because they were both virgins in security terms.

A mistake, perhaps, since Rashid had proved nervy and prone to ill-judgement, but at least he was isolatable – though his Dutch connections were a source of worry rather than the badge of experience they had seemed. Still, on this day Rashid would have little enough to do – just a phone call. So it should be possible to ensure he kept his nerve.

It was eleven-thirty.

Unlike Bashir, Tom had no need of a vehicle in Oxford, and left his rental car with his bag in the boot at the Park and Ride on the northern edge of town. The first step was almost over.

Now he took the commuter bus like any weekday shopper and got off opposite the Radcliffe Infirmary, once the town's hospital. It was an extraordinarily beautiful day now, the sun out in full force, a breeze keeping it from becoming too warm. Tourist buses were parked on St Giles as he walked towards the middle of town. Had they been such a feature when he'd been a student? Probably, but he wouldn't have noticed them then.

And otherwise, it all seemed astonishingly unchanged. But then, why would anything change? It would only do so at outside instigation, since those already powerful enough to force change simply would not do it. Why not? Because they were already on the same side. Oxford, Cambridge, the Foreign Office and the intelligence services, dark heart of the Establishment that had ruined his father. He had infiltrated them in order to hurt them back. At last he was going to begin to do just that. The smugness will soon be gone, he told himself.

Turning into the Broad he walked along to Blackwell's bookshop. There he went to the coffee shop on the first floor, ordered a double espresso, and took it over to a seat by the window. A ringside seat, he thought, looking across the street at the Sheldonian, curved on this side, its yellowed stone topped by the bright white paint of its wooden cupola.

There were no cars parked in the middle of the Broad; it had been cordoned off. He wondered about this, but only momentarily, for it made sense – the cars would mar the beauty of the procession as it moved along the far pavement from the Turl.

He skimmed the copy of the *Guardian* he'd picked up, but kept a regular eye on the street. Students and the occasional don came down the steps of the Clarendon Building opposite, fresh from the Bodleian behind it, carrying briefcases and rucksacks and armfuls of their own books. On the street a final tour bus had been allowed to stop temporarily in front of the Museum of the History of Science, with an open upper deck that was gradually filling up with tourists carrying cameras. At the corner of the Turl, he saw a uniformed policeman, giving directions to an oriental woman. The policeman looked entirely unruffled. Good, thought Tom.

It was exactly noon. He finished his coffee and stood up, then went slowly to the back of the floor, where he glanced at the Literature section, before going downstairs. Had he stayed by the window two minutes longer, he would have seen the policeman joined by four colleagues, two of whom wore bulletproof vests and were carrying Heckler & Koch carbines.

On the ground floor, he stayed away from the front desk, which was manned by two members of staff, and browsed through children's books at the back of the shop, where a mother was trying to keep one eye on her wandering toddler while she bought a copy of *The Wizard of Oz*.

He checked his watch and at exactly five minutes past twelve walked across the floor to the inconspicuous recess of the shop's one lift. He pressed the button, and waited patiently; he had allowed sixty extra seconds in case there was a hitch. If need be, he could go outside.

The lift door slowly opened, and a woman with a walking stick emerged. He smiled pleasantly, then moved in and quickly selected the top floor before anyone could join him in the lift.

As it ascended he keyed the preset number on his mobile; the signal was strong. On the third floor he put his finger firmly on the Doors Close button – he didn't want any interruptions.

Then he spoke: 'Listen carefully. I will not repeat this message . . .'

It was time to move. Bashir started the van and drove up to Walton Street where he passed the imposing facade of Oxford University Press. At the traffic lights he went left and drove carefully for 200 yards, then indicated and pulled over left onto a double-yellow line in front of the Ashmolean Museum. Rashid prepared to climb out. 'There's a traffic warden across the street,' Bashir lied, to avoid long farewells. He reached across Khaled in the middle and extended his hand.

Rashid shook it nervously. 'May Allah be with you,' he offered tentatively. He shook hands with Khaled too and uttered the same blessing.

Bashir gravely repeated his instructions for a final time. 'Take your time walking there. Whatever you do, don't rush or it will draw attention to yourself. I'll expect your call – it should be in twenty minutes. But don't forget: ring only as the procession comes into view.' He looked at Rashid solemnly. 'May Allah be with you,' he intoned, and motioned for Rashid to get out of the van.

There was no time to waste. Bashir turned left onto the wide thoroughfare of St Giles, noting the policeman on the far side of the street. He drove at medium speed towards North Oxford, only to loop back towards the centre of town. About half a mile north of the Sheldonian, he pulled into a quiet side street next to the red brick walls of Keble College, a Gothic triumph of Victorian ambition. There he parked the van, and then he and Khaled sat in silence, waiting for Rashid to call.

Am I nervous? Bashir asked himself. Not really. The Englishman had warned him that he might be, even offered him tablets to help – which he had refused. And in fact he felt a slow wave of calm settle on himself as at last the moment neared.

He turned and reached carefully into the back of the van until his hand found the length of rope. He pulled it gently until the free end was in the front seat with him, where he laid it carefully on Khaled's side of the gearbox. It was almost taut; one sharp tug by Khaled in ten minutes, a half-second delay, and he and Bashir would be in their future.

56

Liz stared intently at the monitors surveying Broad Street. She barely noticed when Dave stuck a plastic cup of white coffee in front of her. 'Six sugars, right?' he teased, noting her preoccupation, and she gave a fleeting smile before resuming her watch. The Chancellor had left the Sheldonian a few minutes before, now 'installed', and had walked to Lincoln College through the Bodleian courtyard, under the watchful eye of a sharpshooter on the library's roof and with the full attention of several plain-clothes policemen on the ground.

Suddenly a young policewoman rushed into the room, her cheeks flushed. Seeing the group clustered in front of the monitors, she stopped short, made suddenly self-conscious by their curious stares. 'Sir,' she said, out of breath, seeming to address both Matheson and the Chief Constable, 'we've just had a warning call. It said there's about to be a major incident on Broad Street.'

'What were the exact words?' demanded Wetherby.

'I can play it back for you,' the policewoman said. She went to a console at the back of the room, hit a switch, and after a hiss and crackle the taped conversation filled the room.

'Special Branch,' a female voice declared.

'Listen carefully,' said an English male voice. 'I will not repeat this message. In fifteen minutes, a bomb will go off in the middle of the procession on Broad Street. Look out for a young Pakistani man. You need to act fast.' The line went dead.

Liz and Wetherby looked at each other tensely.

Ferris the Chief Constable interjected. 'It's not a hoax, is it?'

'No,' said Wetherby. 'It is not a hoax. We recognise the voice.'

'Why did Tom call?' asked Dave, bewildered.

'And what about the other terrorists?' Liz said to Wetherby, worry spreading across her face.

Wetherby was shaking his head. He looked mystified. 'If Tom knows what he's doing, I certainly don't.'

PC Winston's radio had crackled barely two or three minutes before with its urgent message, and he was positioned in front of the double gates of Trinity quad, helping to redirect the flow of foot traffic. The normal robust number of pedestrians was augmented today by visitors wanting to witness the pageantry of the Encaenia procession, and they were slow to clear, despite the urgency of the policemen ordering them away from the direction of the Sheldonian. There was a television crew from the local ITN station who were being particularly bolshie, since if the comparative boredom of yet another Encaenia was being upstaged by an 'incident', they were determined to be there to film it.

Now PC Winston found himself surrounded by Japanese tourists, who paid little to his instructions and were instead taking pictures of each other in front of Trinity. They wanted PC Winston to feature in their snaps as well, which was making his task even more difficult. He was doing his best to redirect one young girl in particular, who had no English at all but was vigorously tapping him on the elbow, when he saw him.

He was tucked in the back of a small group of Italian teenagers who were also ignoring instructions to move down the street. And the little man might have gone unnoticed if he had not been dressed so unlike a teenaged student, wearing a proper shirt instead of a T-shirt, and holding – somehow awkwardly – a mobile phone. And this sense that he was different was confirmed for PC Winston when the man peeled off from the group, moving back against the College gates, not fifteen feet away, and looked out towards the Turl. He's waiting for something, thought Winston, watching him closely as he fingered his phone.

PC Winston could move fast when he had to. The phone had just got to the little man's ear, when Winston's long arm took hold of his hand. 'Excuse me, sir,' he said urgently, 'could I have a look at your phone please?'

Looking up at him, the Asian seemed absolutely petrified. 'Of course,' he said nervously, smiling weakly as he let go of the phone. Then he suddenly turned and took off down Broad Street towards the commercial centre of the town.

Clutching the phone, PC Winston ran after him, shouting, 'Stop him!'

As Rashid ran towards the corner of the Magdalen Street churchyard, he was suddenly thrown against the outer wall of Balliol, then pinned there by the firm hands of another uniformed policeman. Got him! thought Winston, his sense of relief slightly soured when he saw it was PC Jacobs, the young smart-arse, who had made the arrest.

57

Where was he? Why hadn't Rashid rung? Bashir disobeyed the Englishman's instructions and dialled Rashid's mobile, only to find it was switched off. Damn! He checked his watch – the procession would be reaching Broad Street at any moment. What had the Englishman said? 'If there's any hiccup in communications, just go. Whatever happens, you must not be late. Late means *too* late.'

He would wait another thirty seconds, he decided, staring at his digital watch. Next to him Khaled suddenly stirred, and pointed through the windscreen. Looking out toward the end of the street, where the lush green lawns of University Parks were visible in the background, Bashir saw them.

One was in uniform, two were in plain clothes, walking briskly in and out of the street, checking each parked car, then moving on quickly. They were coming this way.

Please ring, please ring Rashid, Bashir exclaimed, in what was almost a prayer. He saw one of the plain-clothes men point towards his end of the street, and then Bashir realised that he was pointing at him. The uniformed policeman looked up and broke into a sprint, grabbing his helmet with one hand while he shouted into a radio held by the other. The two plain-clothes men were behind him, and all three ran at full speed down the middle of the road.

He couldn't wait any longer. He turned the ignition and the

van coughed into life. Revving the engine, he pulled out sharply, intending to accelerate towards Parks Road, where he would turn onto the half-mile street that would lead them to their target. Seeing him start up the van, the man in uniform veered off onto the pavement, and one of the plain-clothes policemen drew a gun from inside his coat, and crouched behind the rear of a parked car.

Then Bashir saw a large van – the kind used to ferry policemen back and forth from football matches – stop directly across the far end of the side street, blocking his exit. He braked sharply just in time to swerve into a small road that circled behind the back of Keble College. Racing along behind the modern extensions at the back of the College, he negotiated the ninety degree left turn with a small screech of his tyres. But he cursed out loud when he saw *another* police van pulling up to block off this side road as well. There was nothing for it: Bashir floored the accelerator, driving straight towards the police vehicle, then just short of it he threw the steering wheel abruptly right. His front tyre hit the high corner of the pavement and the van shot into the air, missing a passing girl by inches. She screamed, the noise filling the air like a siren, slowly dying away as the van landed with a heavy thump on Parks Road.

Bashir regained control and accelerated down the tree-lined street towards the Encaenia procession. It must have reached the Broad, he told himself. Mustn't be late, mustn't be late. The road was free of traffic but he forced himself to slow down as the speedometer reached sixty-five. He was worried he wouldn't make the turn. He touched the brakes lightly once, then twice, and got ready. Out of the corner of his eye he saw Khaled grip the free end of the rope tightly.

The traffic light ahead was turning amber but he ignored it, praying no one would shoot out from Broad Street. Instead, ahead on his left, a student emerged from Holywell Street, riding a bicycle. As if in a film, a policeman came from nowhere and threw himself at the student, knocking him and his bicycle to the ground.

Before Bashir could fully take this in, he was in the junction, turning sharply right. He scraped inside the far pavement, just in front of the lower steps of the Clarendon Building, and struggled to aim the van towards the procession that should be heading straight towards him. He was going to drive along the pavement and then Khaled would pull the rope. The explosion would kill anyone within a hundred yards. That was what the Englishman had said. A hundred yards.

But the Broad was *absolutely empty*. There was no one on the pavement or on the street. No procession, no pedestrians, not even a student on a bicycle. It was like a ghost town.

Bashir began to panic as he felt a heavy thump against his front left tyre. What had he hit? Then almost simultaneously he felt the heavy *whoomph* of another tyre blowing. Suddenly he lost control of the steering.

The van skewed sharply left, in a curving skid propelling him directly towards the wall in front of the Sheldonian. Bashir knew in a flash that Khaled didn't need to pull the rope. The impact alone would trigger the detonators, he thought.

58

Liz crouched with Charles Wetherby behind one of the police cars, taking cover as soon as she saw the first tyre shot out by the marksmen. She waited for an explosion, and covered her ears with her hands. Beside her, Wetherby spontaneously threw a protective arm around her shoulders.

There was a harsh, grating sound of metal hitting an immoveable object, and a muffled thump which seemed half sound, half vibration.

And then there was silence. Liz began to raise her head but Wetherby pushed her down again. 'Wait,' he said. 'Just in case.' But there was no explosion, and as the pressure from his arm eased, Liz peered cautiously over the bonnet of the police car.

The van had hit the retaining wall and been thrown upwards, where it lay against the tall iron railings, pointing towards the sky, its front tyres spinning in the air.

Matheson moved out from the protection of the cars and began shouting orders. A fire engine appeared from Debenhams behind them. Avoiding the forbidding bollards at that end of the Broad, it trundled heavily up along the pavement by the shops, squeezing slowly through the narrow gap before accelerating, siren now blaring, towards the van.

As it arrived, armed policemen emerged from the crannies and doorways where they had sheltered, and moved towards the crashed vehicle. A Special Branch officer in plain clothes got to the van first, reached up and tugged at the driver's door, fruitlessly. He's brave, thought Liz, since there was a petrol tank that could still detonate.

She came out from behind the car and began to walk with Wetherby cautiously towards the van. Dave Armstrong joined them, breathless and looking stunned. 'What was that about?' he asked. Neither Liz nor Wetherby responded.

As they moved down the Broad, firemen were shooting powerful jets of foam over the van.

Liz said, 'I don't understand why Tom made the phone call.'

'Well he didn't warn us about the van,' said Dave sharply.

Wetherby shrugged. 'Perhaps he felt he didn't need to.'

Liz looked at him inquiringly, just as Matheson intercepted them. 'There were two men in the van. They're both dead,' he announced.

'Killed by the crash?' asked Wetherby.

Matheson nodded. 'They had a fertiliser bomb in the back of the van, but it didn't go off. It's too early to say for sure, but it looks as if the detonators didn't work.'

'I'm not sure they were meant to,' said Wetherby slowly.

Liz looked at him again; Wetherby's expression seemed entirely enigmatic. 'You think they knew there wasn't going to be an explosion?' she asked.

'No, but I think Tom did,' said Wetherby. 'You said yourself that you couldn't understand why he'd want to kill so many innocent people. He wanted the van to get through, but he knew it wasn't going to blow up.'

'Why would he do that?' asked Liz. 'What would the point be?'

Wetherby shrugged. 'I suppose to demonstrate it could be done. To show us up as dangerously incompetent.' He pointed up the street, where Liz could see a television crew advancing.

'That may be a local crew,' said Wetherby, 'but you can be confident their footage is going to make the national news this evening. None of us is going to look good after that kind of exposure.'

'So that's what he wanted?' asked Liz. 'To destroy the Service's reputation?'

'Something like that.'

'Hang on,' interrupted Dave. 'He didn't care if the two blokes died, did he?' he asked impatiently, gesturing towards the crashed van.

'Of course he didn't,' said Wetherby. He gave a mirthless laugh. 'I'm not defending Tom. I'm just saying I think his objective was more subtle than we gave him credit for. And thank God.' He looked around the Broad, full of policemen standing by while the firemen continued to cover the van with foam. 'Think how many people could have been killed. If Tom hadn't phoned, this place would have been full of people . . .'

They were standing in the middle of the Broad, only yards from the van. Liz looked around, still amazed that there had been no explosion, and no casualties other than the driver and his passenger. Then along the high railings above the wall which the van had hit, she saw that two stone pedestals were empty – their 'Roman Emperor' heads had gone. It was surreal.

Wetherby pointed at some smashed fragments littering the Broad. He said wryly, 'Somehow I don't think those are the only heads that are going to roll.'

59

The policeman was moving everyone away from the windows, though Tom knew it wasn't necessary. They were led to the vast downstairs room of the bookshop and made to stay there for almost half an hour. He kept a careful eye on his watch, and after eight minutes smiled involuntarily as the countdown finally ended. Three years, he told himself, I planned this for three years – and now at last the moment's come.

He felt absolutely jubilant. He knew that upstairs on the street the police would be reeling with confusion as they discovered the crashed van contained fertiliser that had not exploded: the detonators he had given Bashir were useless – they wouldn't light a cigarette, thought Tom, much less set off a bomb.

The local reaction, as news spread like wildfire about this near-disaster, would be relief, though Tom was certain Oxford would never know another public Encaenia procession. But further away, at Thames House, the reaction would be altogether different. In Thames House, he reckoned, the inhabitants would be having a collective heart attack.

For they would have no idea where he was, and no lead to finding him. They would be worried sick that he would strike again – and they were right to worry. Oxford was just the beginning, and he could see no reason why he could not stay one step ahead of his former colleagues for a long time to come.

He looked at his watch. In three hours he'd be in his hotel room on the outskirts of Bristol. In little more than twenty-four, his plane would be preparing to land at JFK.

In the short term as well, he had given MI5 plenty to cope with. Their embarrassment at this close call would rapidly give way to anxious post-mortems, internal inquiries, a media storm, questions in the House, the blame game, the indisputable damage to the reputation of the intelligence services. 'Why had they failed to stop the bombers?' 'What if the detonators had worked?' And that was before they'd even begun to grapple with the knowledge that for almost fifteen years, they'd had a mole in their midst. A mole they couldn't catch.

Now a policeman let them out at last, and they all trooped up the staircase that led directly out onto the Broad. Tom lagged a little behind, for safety's sake, and was very glad he did. Twenty feet short of the exit, he looked out at the street from the top stair and saw the familiar figure of Liz Carlyle standing in the middle of the road, talking to Charles Wetherby.

At first, he didn't believe his eyes. How had they got on to him here? How had they known his target? It didn't make any sense; he had been so careful.

Could they have turned one of the bombers? No, for only Bashir had known the exact target – Khaled had been content not to know, and Rashid was too weak ever to be trusted either by him or Bashir. Bashir would never betray a cause he was so willing to die for. And if any of them talked now – he assumed they would have been captured minutes before – they would know nothing that would let either the police or Tom's former colleagues find him.

Who then could have given him away? Had O'Phelan talked

before Tom had got to him in Belfast? It seemed inconceivable – why would the lecturer have rung Tom and warned him that Liz had been to see him, asking nosy questions?

There seemed no obvious answer to what had gone wrong, but he had no time to think it through. Turning back, away from the door, he moved back into the building. One of the Blackwell's assistants touched his arm – she had been like a Border collie, herding them up the stairs from behind – and he flashed the charming smile he'd learned to use like a weapon. 'I left something behind,' he explained.

She'd smiled back, and let him go. Patience, he told himself. Don't panic. But you've got to get out of here fast. This was just stage one, after all. He mustn't be stopped now.

60

The marksman in the Sheldonian's cupola was still there. Turning round, Liz noticed another sniper, holding his carbine, on the roof of Blackwell's music shop at the corner.

Something about the scene was bothering her. She looked at Charles, and suddenly a thought came from nowhere. 'I think Tom is here,' she suddenly said. 'He'll want to see all this.'

Wetherby was startled. 'Really?' he said doubtfully. Then he seemed to think about it. 'Maybe you're right. As far as he knows, we're still in London, wondering where the devil he's gone.'

Matheson came back to them again. 'We've got about thirty people still in Blackwell's, downstairs in the Norrington Room. We put them there for their own safety. I'm about to let them out, unless you have any objection.'

'No, that's fine,' said Wetherby, and Matheson was on his way to the bookshop when Liz called after him. 'Excuse me,' she said. 'Could we just check everyone as they leave?'

He looked at her, surprised, then turned to Wetherby, who nodded approval and said, 'If you bring them all out through the same door, we could have a quick look.'

They walked over, and stood at the Trinity College end of the shop front, where at the back of a small ground-floor room a steep staircase led down to the cavernous Norrington Room. Matheson and a tall policeman stood with them outside as the customers – most looking impassive, a few irate – emerged.

There was no one they recognised.

'I need to find out what they've done with the suspect they arrested,' declared Wetherby. He turned as he set off to Dave and Liz. 'Have a final look inside to be extra sure.'

'Can you keep someone here in the front?' Liz asked Matheson.

'All right,' he said reluctantly, clearly thinking he had better uses for his men.

And Dave was shaking his head. 'I know great minds think alike,' he said, gesturing first at the retreating figure of Wetherby, then pointing his finger at Liz. 'But if Tom had been anywhere near here, he'd be long gone by now. And if he was in the bookshop, wouldn't he have just gone out the back door?'

'No.' It was a Northern voice, and belonged to a stocky man in a check jacket. 'I'm from Blackwell's,' he said. 'When the police said they wanted everyone downstairs, I locked the staff exits at the back. It was more to keep anyone from wandering in than to keep anyone from leaving. But it would have done that too.'

'Come on,' said Liz to Dave. 'Nothing to lose by looking.' He shrugged, and they went together through the shop's main entrance. They stood for a moment on the ground floor, looking at the tables stacked with newly published books. 'It's much bigger than it looks from outside,' said Dave without enthusiasm.

'Let's split up,' said Liz. 'You start downstairs. I'll go to the top floor and work down. We can meet in the middle.'

'Okay,' said Dave. 'Watch yourself,' he added, but by then Liz had started up the staircase.

The first floor was eerily empty. The cafe was deserted, though its tables still held coffee cups and half-eaten pastries – clearly people had been moved out at speed. She looked down towards the other book-lined end of the first floor, also deserted. The effect was slightly spooky – Liz felt as if she were in a museum after closing time. Noises filtered through from the street, dimly audible, but here inside there was only a heavy silence – except for the sound of her footsteps, which clattered on the wooden stairs.

She moved on to the second floor and kept climbing – she would cover these lower floors on her way down. Reaching the top floor, she found a swing door on her left and a sign for the toilets. Liz went through cautiously, then opened the door to the ladies' room. Both cubicles had their doors wide open; there was no one in the room.

Slightly hesitantly, she went into the men's room. The single stall was empty, but the window was open at the bottom. Ducking down, she peered out. The vast front quadrangle of Trinity loomed in the distance. Sticking her head out, she saw directly below her a small, inner courtyard. From the window to the paving stones was a straight drop of almost fifty feet. Tom wouldn't have survived that, thought Liz.

As she came out again into the main corridor, Liz heard a noise – a long low gliding sound, as if something were being dragged along. Was it downstairs? She stood still, listening hard, but didn't hear it again.

Suspicious, she walked cautiously around the corner into a long light room full of second-hand books. There was a faint aroma of old leather and dust. At the end of the room a door was marked 'Staff Only', and Liz was walking towards it when she saw the window in the corner. It was wide open.

Moving quickly, she looked out. Immediately below her was the low roofline of a modern annexe of the College which adjoined the shop.

An easy way out, Liz thought. And then she saw him.

Leaning against the slanted line of tiles, holding onto the frame of a wooden skylight cut into the roof.

It was Tom.

He was trying to open the skylight, and Liz realised that if he succeeded, he would jump down and disappear into the building. Yes, Matheson's men might find him, but since Liz imagined warren-like interiors with hundreds of places to hide, she wouldn't want to bet on it.

She had her mobile phone in her bag – she could call and make sure the building was surrounded by police. But by the time she got through – and to whom? Dave was downstairs, Charles at St Aldates checking on the surviving terrorist – Tom might have escaped.

'Tom!' she shouted, leaning out of the window. Her voice rang out, echoing in the tiny courtyard below.

He paused, but only momentarily. He didn't look back, but deciding to give up on the skylight, began to edge his way along the roof.

He was headed towards the line of older buildings. There he could move at greater speed along the gabled roofs stretching to the gardens at the back of the College. Then he'd be off.

'Tom!' she called again. 'There's no point. You might as well come back. They're waiting for you on the ground.'

This time he did react. He hauled himself up onto the roof ridge. Crouching there, he looked almost boyish, like an undergraduate, climbing in after the gates were locked at night. Slowly he turned around, and his eyes swept across until they reached the window where Liz stood.

There was nothing playful in his steady stare. His eyes were steely, and his face looked filled with determination.

'Tom,' Liz said again, mildly this time, trying to keep her voice under control. But before she could say anything else, he shook his head emphatically. And then, swinging nimbly down the far side of the slanted roof, he disappeared out of view.

Liz stood stunned for a fraction of a moment, waiting for Tom to reappear. Then realising he wasn't going to, she acted at once, running towards the staircase. She was halfway down when she ran into Dave Armstrong, coming up. 'Quick,' she said, grabbing his arm and turning him round. 'He's on the roof next door. Hurry!'

As they ran out of the shop onto the Broad, blinking in the bright sunlight, they could see Matheson standing next to an ambulance, talking to two uniformed policemen.

'He's next door,' Dave shouted out to him, and he and Liz kept running fast towards the entrance to Trinity. The small gate by the lodge was open. The porter came out, trying to stop them.

'Police!' Dave shouted. 'Get out of the way!' Liz veered around the man and, ducking under the branches of an enormous cedar tree, headed right across the quad. The lawn and paths were empty and she wondered if the College had been evacuated with the rest of the street. That would make it easier for Tom to escape, she thought, as her eyes scanned the line of gables for any sign of him.

Dave yelled, 'I'll take the far end.' Liz continued towards the courtyard under Blackwell's window. Coming through its archway, she slowed down, her neck craned skyward, examining the roof where she had last seen Tom. The skylight looked undisturbed – he had not come back this way.

She heard a footstep behind her and started. 'It's all right,' a voice said, and she turned around to find Matheson with a young policeman. 'I've got men searching the College,' he said.

'We'll need them on the rooftop too,' said Liz, pointing upwards. She suddenly stopped, listening intently. 'What's that noise?'

'What noise?'

Then she heard it again. Through a second archway, leading back into the recesses of the College on this side. It was a low wailing sound, as if someone were in distress. Its painful keening was almost animal.

She moved quickly through the archway and found herself in a long, outside gallery, bounded on three sides by College buildings. At the open far end Liz could see the flowering shrubs of a large garden. There was no one in sight. So what had she heard?

And then to her left she saw a girl – she looked barely out of her teens. She was standing by the entrance to a stairwell, crying uncontrollably. Behind her, almost in the corner, there was a man on the ground, lying flat on his back, motionless.

Liz walked quickly over to the girl. 'It's all right,' she said gently, as Matheson went over and knelt down by the man.

The girl stopped crying and looked up at Liz, with a face that was young and fearful. From the far end of the gallery, Liz heard a shout and looking up, saw Dave running towards them.

'What happened?' Dave demanded, looking first at the girl, and then at the body in the corner. Matheson was holding the prone man's wrist, checking for a pulse. He stood up, looked at Liz and shook his head.

'He must have fallen,' said Liz quietly. And she raised her eyes to indicate the roof above them.

'Unless he jumped,' said Dave.

Stifling her sobs, the girl spoke for the first time. 'No,' she said, wiping her eyes. 'He didn't jump.'

'Did you see it?' asked Liz.

The girl nodded her head. 'I was asleep,' she explained. 'I woke up and realised I was late for my tutorial. When I came out I saw' – she hesitated – 'this man walking across the roof. I thought that's odd because he seemed too old to be up there.' She gave a nervous laugh, and Liz put her arm around her – the last thing they needed now was hysterics.

'Then suddenly he seemed to slip and started sliding down the roof. He tried to grab on to the tiles, but he couldn't. He just kept sliding until . . . he fell off.' And she began to cry again.

Liz looked past her at the figure lying on the ground. Letting go of the girl she went and stood next to Matheson, then looked down at the man. She'd known it was Tom from the moment she'd seen the body.

In many ways he looked as he always did, smart and handsome in his blue suit, looking as if in a minute he would bounce up and be his old self again. Which self is that? thought Liz bitterly. The man she'd thought she'd begun to know? The big man, tall and rangy, confident but easy-going, soft-spoken but knowledgeable, charming – at least when he wanted to be.

Or the different, secret self of someone she'd never really known at all? A man possessed by internal demons she had never remotely imagined.

Torn between tears of sadness and tears of rage, Liz shut her eyes and shed neither. Turning sharply on her heels, she walked back towards the crying girl. She could comfort her. There was nothing she could do for Tom.

61

In contrast to the morning, the drive back to London seemed to take forever. As they left Oxford, low scudding banks of cloud moved in from the south, dispelling the sun and turning the sky a dull hazy grey. Rain began to fall, first in fierce short-lived downbursts, then in a steady monotonous drizzle. The M40 soon clogged up in an unending line of slow-moving lorries and cautious cars.

Numbed by what had happened, not quite certain whether to be pleased that they had prevented an atrocity or dismayed that they had almost allowed it to happen, Liz and Charles barely spoke to each other at first. Then as if by mutual consent, they talked almost compulsively about anything and everything. Except the events of the day. Favourite holidays, favourite restaurants, favourite parts of the country, even *The Da Vinci Code*, which neither she nor Wetherby had read. Personal talk, but not intimate: Wetherby's wife Joanne wasn't mentioned, and Liz didn't say who had accompanied her on any of those favourite holidays. It was an almost manic defence against the sheer unbelievability of what they had just witnessed. And a defence, too, against the questions, the accountability certain to come.

Yet both being realists, the avoidance strategy couldn't last. As they swept down into the large bowl at High Wycombe, Wetherby sighed, cutting short his account of a particularly happy holiday spent sailing around The Needles. 'How did you know Tom would be there?' he asked.

'I can't say I knew,' said Liz. 'It was just a hunch.'

Wetherby gave a small snort. 'I have to say your hunches are better than most of the rational analysis I receive.'

It was a compliment, but Liz couldn't help feeling that luck had played as large a role as prescience. And what if Tom hadn't slipped? She felt in her bones that he would have got away.

Wetherby seemed to read her thoughts. 'Where do you think Tom was going to go?'

Liz gazed at a golf course carved out of the side of a hill, and thought about this. Presumably Tom would have left the country, and gone on the run abroad. But where? It was not as if Tom had had some cause or place to defect to – he wouldn't have gone unnoticed for forty-eight hours in Northern Ireland and, in any case, the IRA wouldn't want him anywhere near their newly peaceful selves.

'Tom spoke fluent Arabic,' she said at last, 'so conceivably he would have tried to slip into one of the Middle Eastern countries, and carve out some sort of new career for himself with a new identity.'

'He'd have run the risk of being spotted. It's a small world – Westerners in the Arab world.'

'Perhaps he'd have gone to New York,' said Liz. 'You know, following his father's footsteps. I think there was certainly more he wanted to do.'

'More of the same?' asked Wetherby mildly.

'Who knows? But revenge on some other institution, I think. The newspaper who fired his father. MI6, I would imagine. Then he'd probably have had another go at us.'

'He'd have had to keep moving, whatever new identity he tried to assume.'

'That's true,' said Liz. 'But maybe that would have suited him.'

They were nearing the junction with the M25, and the road signs listed Heathrow, which somehow seemed appropriate for this talk of Tom's plans. 'But why did he run in the first place?' she asked rhetorically. 'I mean, if he had stayed put, what exactly would have happened to him? Or more precisely, what would we have been able to pin on him? O'Phelan's death wasn't solved – no witness, no fingerprints, no trace of Tom in Belfast. The same with Marzipan. The forensic investigation found absolutely nothing to point towards his killer.'

Wetherby smiled wistfully. 'I see your reasoning, but I think you are missing the point. Tom fled because Tom wanted us to know.'

'But why? What difference would that make?'

'To Tom,' said Wetherby patiently, 'all the difference in the world. For Tom, the point was to humiliate us. He wanted us to be in his control. He wanted us to feel powerless and small. Helpless actually.'

'Like his father must have felt,' murmured Liz.

'I suppose,' said Wetherby. 'But my point is, Tom's motives weren't political. If they had been, the detonators would have worked.'

'And he wouldn't have made the phone call.'

'Quite. He didn't want to kill dozens of people. He just wanted us to know he could have. And he would have wanted to show us that again and again, each time probably killing one or two people who got in his way – like Marzipan. The irony is, he probably would have ended up killing as many people as he would have today with a bomb.' Wetherby shook his head in dismayed wonder.

'So was he simply mad?' asked Liz.

'We'll never know now,' said Wetherby. 'What we do know is that he wasn't who we thought he was.'

62

The meeting was ending, but the long grim process had only just begun.

The press coverage of the aborted bomb attempt in Oxford had been sensational. 'TEN SECONDS FROM DEATH' announced the *Daily Mail*, with a split front page showing the crashed van on one side and a picture of the new Chancellor on the other, looking shocked in his academic gown. 'IT'S A DUD!' proclaimed the *Sun*, which managed to get a picture of Rashid Khan, his head shrouded in a blanket, being led out to a prison van at the St Aldates police station. The *Express* featured a photograph of the Chancellor's procession, beadles, stewards, vespers and all, which Liz realised had to have been taken years before – it showed the trail of dignitaries on the Broad, which they had never reached, and had at its head the old Chancellor rather than his new successor. The broadsheets were more circumspect. *The Times* account – 'BOMBERS' PLOT FOILED IN OXFORD' – was followed by its other upmarket colleagues in emphasising the fact that the conspiracy had been detected rather than how close it had come to success. The *Guardian* had much the same coverage together with an article by an architect on the damage to the historic railings in the Broad.

All of course mentioned the deaths of the van driver and his passenger, and also the death of a Security Service officer – though readers eager to learn more about that fatality would not find their curiosity assuaged. A D notice had landed within hours on the desk of every newspaper editor in the UK, so other than reporting the fact of Tom's death, described invariably as a 'tragic accident', nothing else appeared about him.

However events were described, the facts were undeniable: two terrorists had been within a whisker of blowing up a symbol of one of Britain's oldest institutions along with a host of dignitaries. If some of the newspapers credited the security services with foiling the plot, others directly criticised them for letting it get so close to fruition. None suggested it had been anything but a very narrow squeak.

Fortunately for Liz and her colleagues, the media's shrill attention proved short-lived – displaced by a particularly horrific attack in Baghdad and by another spat between the Prime Minister and the Chancellor of the Exchequer. Coverage of the Oxford Plot (as it was already coming to be known) moved after two days to the inside pages and the occasional comment column, and though the debacle would be cited endlessly in future as an example of the formidable threats the country was now facing, its news value was reduced with each day's passing.

Within MI5 and MI6, however, the impact of the Oxford Plot was anything but temporary. Analysis of what happened and why was just beginning. This initial meeting was going to be the first of many. Already the various sections were starting their own damage assessments, and would be meeting regularly to share them.

As people gathered their papers and started to leave the room, Dave Armstrong caught Liz's eye. 'Got time for a coffee?' he asked.

'Maybe later,' she said, for something was making her feel she wanted to stay behind.

As the room emptied she found herself alone at the table with Wetherby, who was looking tired and subdued even by his undemonstrative standards. He managed a rueful smile at Liz. 'I've chaired happier meetings in my time.'

'At least everyone knows what they've got to do.'

'Yes. It's obviously important to track right back through all this. Everything. Right back to Tom's recruitment,' said Wetherby, lifting a hand in acknowledgement of the detail they had all just waded through. 'We need to understand why we didn't pick up that there was something wrong about him. Why we didn't notice anything. There'll be an inquiry,' he said, with a tone of resignation. 'Not a public inquiry, I don't think, though there'll be pressure for one, but a big internal one. The Home Secretary's talking about getting a judge to conduct it. He actually had the nerve to say "*Quis custodiet ipsos custodes?*" You'd think he'd have thought of something more original.' Wetherby shook his head in disbelief. Liz had forgotten the little Latin she had learned at school but she knew that phrase very well: 'Who is to watch over the guardians themselves?' 'I have to say DG was very good in the meeting,' Wetherby added.

'What about Six?' asked Liz. 'What's Geoffrey Fane saying?'

'I talked to him. He expressed suitable outrage about Tom's treachery. Though there was just a faint suggestion that we'd been a little careless, seconding a traitor to MI6. But on the other hand if Tom made contact with the bomber in Pakistan, that's when he was under their control. I intimated that perhaps they need to look at their own supervision.'

Liz nodded, remembering Fane's initial disbelief when she had named Tom as the mole.

'Is Peggy going straight back to Vauxhall Cross?' she asked.

'Not yet. I've asked Fane to let her stay on for a bit to help with the damage assessment.'

'I need to speak to you about her, actually. She's making noises about trying to stay here. It seems she likes MI5.'

Wetherby raised his eyebrows. 'That will really help things with Fane.' He paused and glanced tensely at his watch, then relaxed. He had time to talk, and Liz sensed he wanted to. 'About halfway through the meeting I began to have the oddest feeling. As if something were missing. You know that sensation when you've left your watch at home or forgotten your wallet? You don't know what you've lost; you just know something should be there that isn't.' Wetherby looked at Liz. Then, all vagueness gone, his expression hardened. 'And then I realised it wasn't any *thing* that was missing. It was a person.'

'Tom.'

'Exactly,' he said, his eyes now focused on her.

It was true, Liz realised. Around the table minutes before had sat Michael Binding, looking dour, with a couple of his men from A2; Patrick Dobson, flushed and uncomfortable; Reggie Purvis and his deputy from A4; Judith Spratt, still looking shaky but at least present; Liz, Dave, Charles . . . all the usual attendees. Except one.

Wetherby said, 'He hadn't been back very long, but he did feel very much like one of us.'

'That's why he was so hard to catch. He fitted in perfectly.'

'That was part of the plan,' said Wetherby, propping his hand on his chin and looking thoughtful. 'And yet,' he said sadly, 'part of me still thinks that some of his act was actually sincere. He was good at his job; I think he genuinely enjoyed it. But as it turns out, it was a different job he was doing. He was never with us right from the beginning. But his hatred, it seems to me, was for the Service, not for its officers. Somehow I find it hard to take that personally. Don't you?'

Liz thought of the weekend Tom had 'dropped by' her mother's house. She hadn't told Wetherby about Tom's overtures, but then, had she been right about them? Could she have imagined more than there was to his invitation? It was only supper, after all. Was some personal vanity she wasn't aware of skewing her judgement? But then she remembered the hotel receipt, and Tom's lies about his friends on a farm. No, she wasn't imagining things. He had been trying to use her for his own twisted reasons.

'No Charles,' she said, 'I do take it personally. He was never loyal to the Service or to any of us. He was using us as a means to an end. He was loyal only to his own warped sense of mission to destroy everything we work for. In the wilderness of mirrors he was the wrong way round.'

'Of course you're right,' conceded Charles with an easy smile. 'It's meaningless to make a distinction between the Service and its officers. What was it E. M. Forster said? "If I had to choose between betraying my country and betraying my friend, I hope I should have the guts to betray my country." I've always felt our duty was precisely the opposite.'

'Me too,' said Liz simply.

They sat in silence for a moment. Wetherby asked quietly, 'How's your mother?'

He is a nice man, thought Liz. Here he is, with – let's face it – his career in the balance after such a near disaster, and he manages to remember my mother. 'Okay, I think,' she said gratefully. 'She's had the operation and it seems to have gone well.'

'Good,' said Wetherby encouragingly.

'Yes, they think they've got it all,' said Liz. And for some reason she thought of Tom and the damage he had caused. 'At least it seems that way,' she said, adding carefully, 'though you can never be sure.'